LANTERN CITY

Published by
ARCHAIA™

ROSS RICHIE CEO & Founder
MATT GAGNON Editor-in-Chief
FILIP SABLIK President of Publishing & Marketing
STEPHEN CHRISTY President of Development
LANCE KREITER VP of Licensing & Merchandising
PHIL BARBARO VP of Finance
BRYCE CARLSON Managing Editor
MEL CAYLO Marketing Manager
SCOTT NEWMAN Production Design Manager
IRENE BRADISH Operations Manager
CHRISTINE DINH Brand Communications Manager
SIERRA HAHN Senior Editor
DAFNA PLEBAN Editor
SHANNON WATTERS Editor
ERIC HARBURN Editor
WHITNEY LEOPARD Associate Editor
JASMINE AMIRI Associate Editor
CHRIS ROSA Associate Editor
ALEX GALER Assistant Editor
CAMERON CHITTOCK Assistant Editor
MARY GUMPORT Assistant Editor
KELSEY DIETERICH Production Designer
JILLIAN CRAB Production Designer
MICHELLE ANKLEY Production Design Assistant
AARON FERRARA Operations Coordinator
ELIZABETH LOUGHRIDGE Accounting Coordinator
JOSÉ MEZA Sales Assistant
JAMES ARRIOLA Mailroom Assistant
STEPHANIE HOCUTT Marketing Assistant
SAM KUSEK Direct Market Representative

 Macrocosm Entertainment, Inc.

TREVOR CRAFTS CEO & Founder
ELLEN SCHERER CRAFTS COO
MATTHEW DALEY VP of Development

LANTERN CITY Volume Two, July 2016. Published by Archaia, a division of Boom Entertainment, Inc., 5670 Wilshire Boulevard, Suite 450, Los Angeles, CA 90036-5679. Lantern City is ™ & © 2016 Macrocosm Entertainment, Inc. All Rights Reserved. Originally published in single magazine form as LANTERN CITY No. 5-8. ™ & © 2015 Macrocosm Entertainment, Inc. All Rights Reserved. Archaia™ and the Archaia logo are trademarks of Boom Entertainment, Inc., registered in various countries and categories. All characters, events, and institutions depicted herein are fictional. Any similarity between any of the names, characters, persons, events, and/or institutions in this publication to actual names, characters, and persons, whether living or dead, events, and/or institutions is unintended and purely coincidental.

BOOM! Studios, 5670 Wilshire Boulevard, Suite 450, Los Angeles, CA 90036-5679. Printed in China. First Printing.

ISBN: 978-1-60886-848-3, eISBN: 978-1-61398-519-9

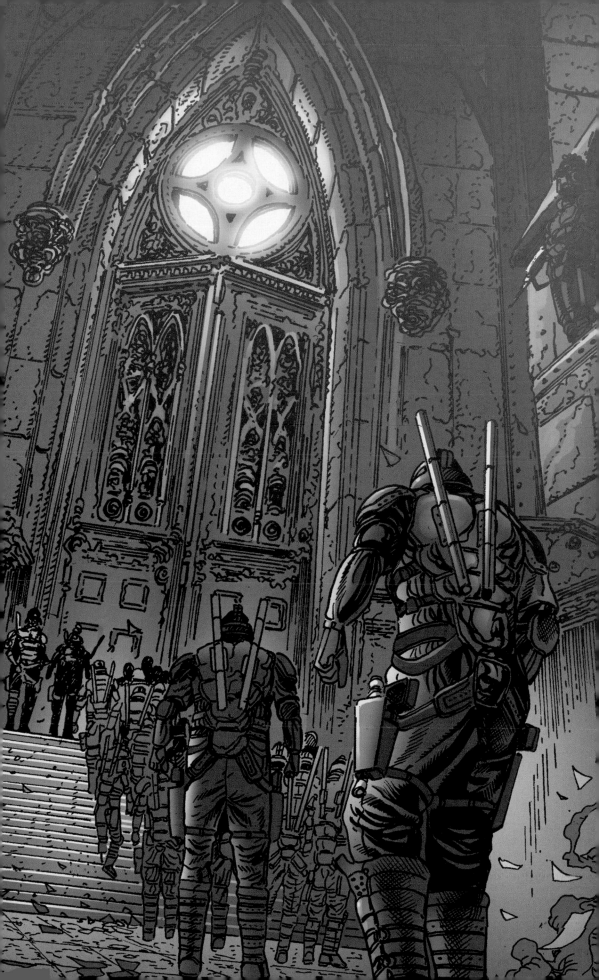

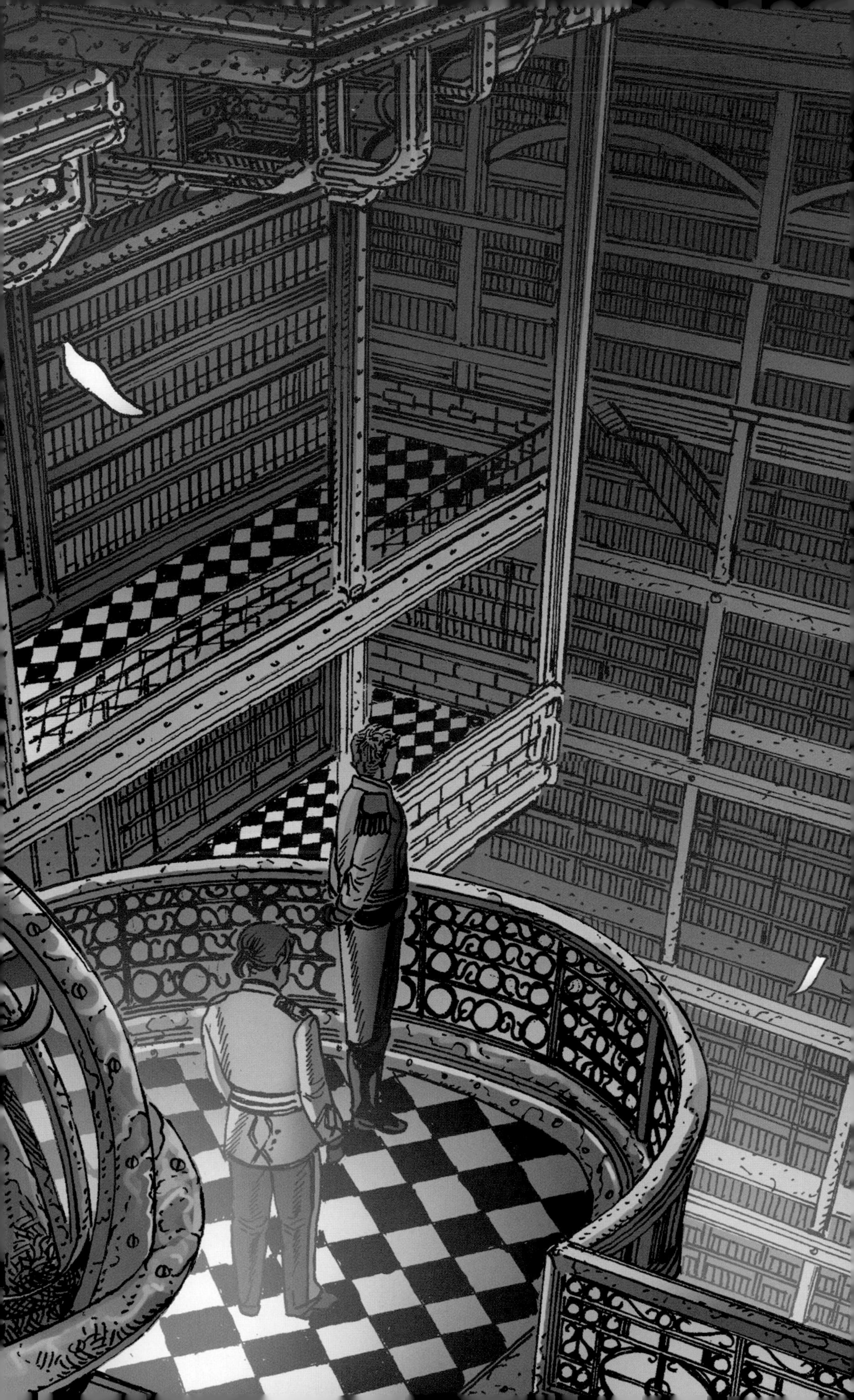

CREATED BY
TREVOR CRAFTS

CO-CREATORS
MATTHEW DALEY
BRUCE BOXLEITNER

WRITTEN BY
MATTHEW DALEY
& MAIRGHREAD SCOTT

ILLUSTRATED BY
CARLOS MAGNO

COLORS BY
CHRIS BLYTHE

LETTERS BY
DERON BENNETT

COVER BY
BENJAMIN CARRÉ

DESIGNER KELSEY DIETERICH
ASSISTANT EDITOR MARY GUMPORT
EDITOR DAFNA PLEBAN

CHAPTER FIVE

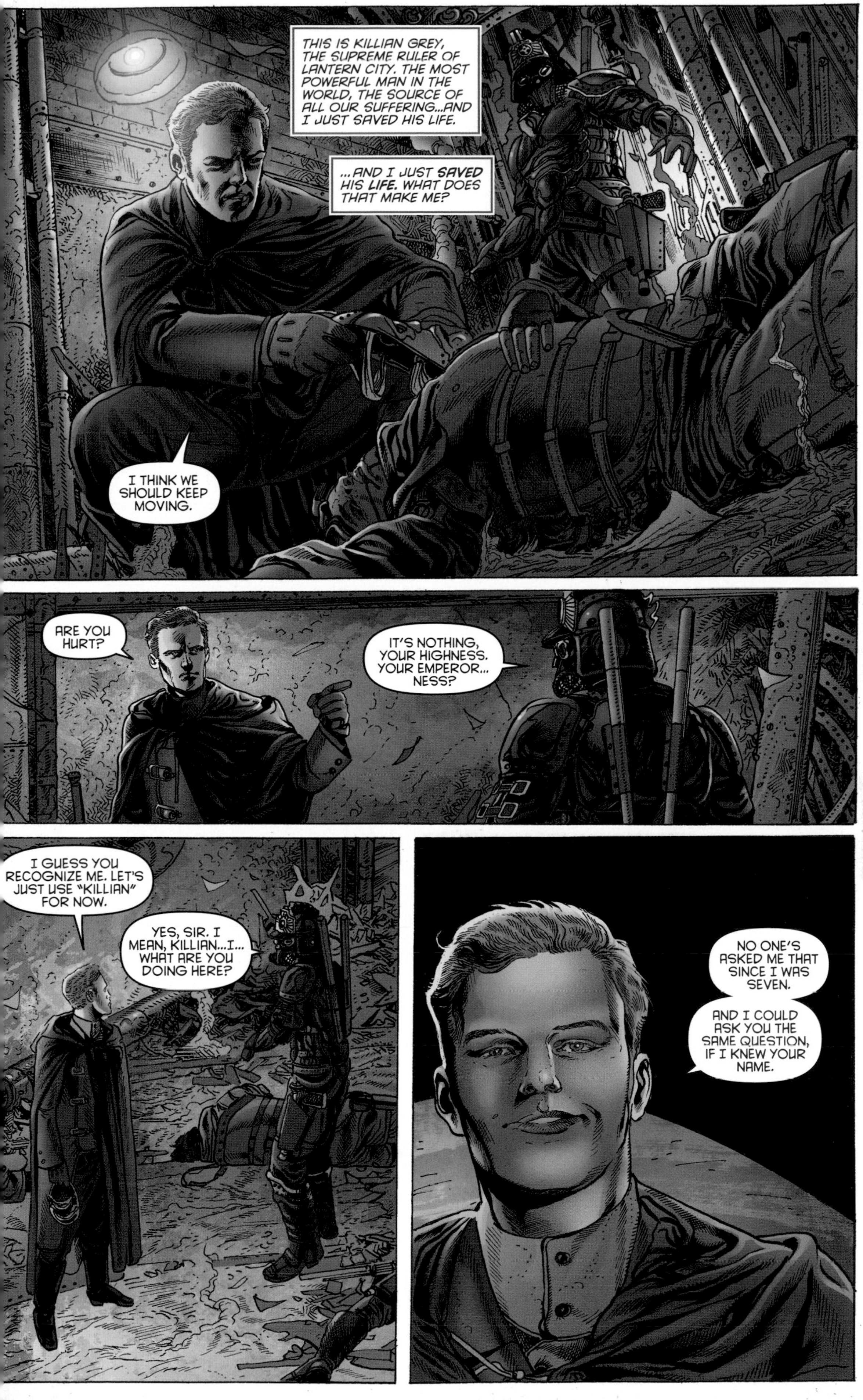
THIS IS KILLIAN GREY, THE SUPREME RULER OF LANTERN CITY. THE MOST POWERFUL MAN IN THE WORLD, THE SOURCE OF ALL OUR SUFFERING...AND I JUST SAVED HIS LIFE.
...AND I JUST **SAVED** HIS **LIFE.** WHAT DOES THAT MAKE ME?
I THINK WE SHOULD KEEP MOVING.
ARE YOU HURT?
IT'S NOTHING, YOUR HIGHNESS. YOUR EMPEROR... NESS?
I GUESS YOU RECOGNIZE ME. LET'S JUST USE "KILLIAN" FOR NOW.
YES, SIR. I MEAN, KILLIAN...I... WHAT ARE YOU DOING HERE?
NO ONE'S ASKED ME THAT SINCE I WAS SEVEN.
AND I COULD ASK YOU THE SAME QUESTION, IF I KNEW YOUR NAME.

NOT THAT I EXPECT IT. THE ONLY REASON GUARDS COME TO THE UNDERGROUND IS TO BUY ILLEGAL GOODS.

THERE ARE OTHER REASONS...

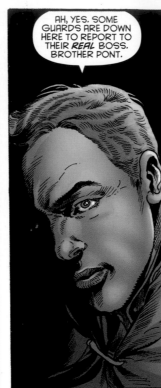

AH, YES. SOME GUARDS ARE DOWN HERE TO REPORT TO THEIR *REAL* BOSS. BROTHER PONT.

BUT IF THAT WERE TRUE FOR YOU, I WOULDN'T BE ALIVE. SO WHY ARE YOU HERE?

I SUSPECTED SOME OF MY MEN OF WORKING FOR PONT. I WAS RIGHT.

YOUR MEN? AREN'T YOU A LITTLE YOUNG TO BE A CAPTAIN?

AREN'T YOU A LITTLE YOUNG TO BE SUPREME RULER?

STUPID! WHY DID I SAY THAT?!

I'M SORRY, I--

YOU HAVE NO IDEA.

WHAT'S YOUR NAME, CAPTAIN?

ORLIN. IT'S ORLIN, SIR.

WELL, CAPTAIN ORLIN, I OWE YOU--

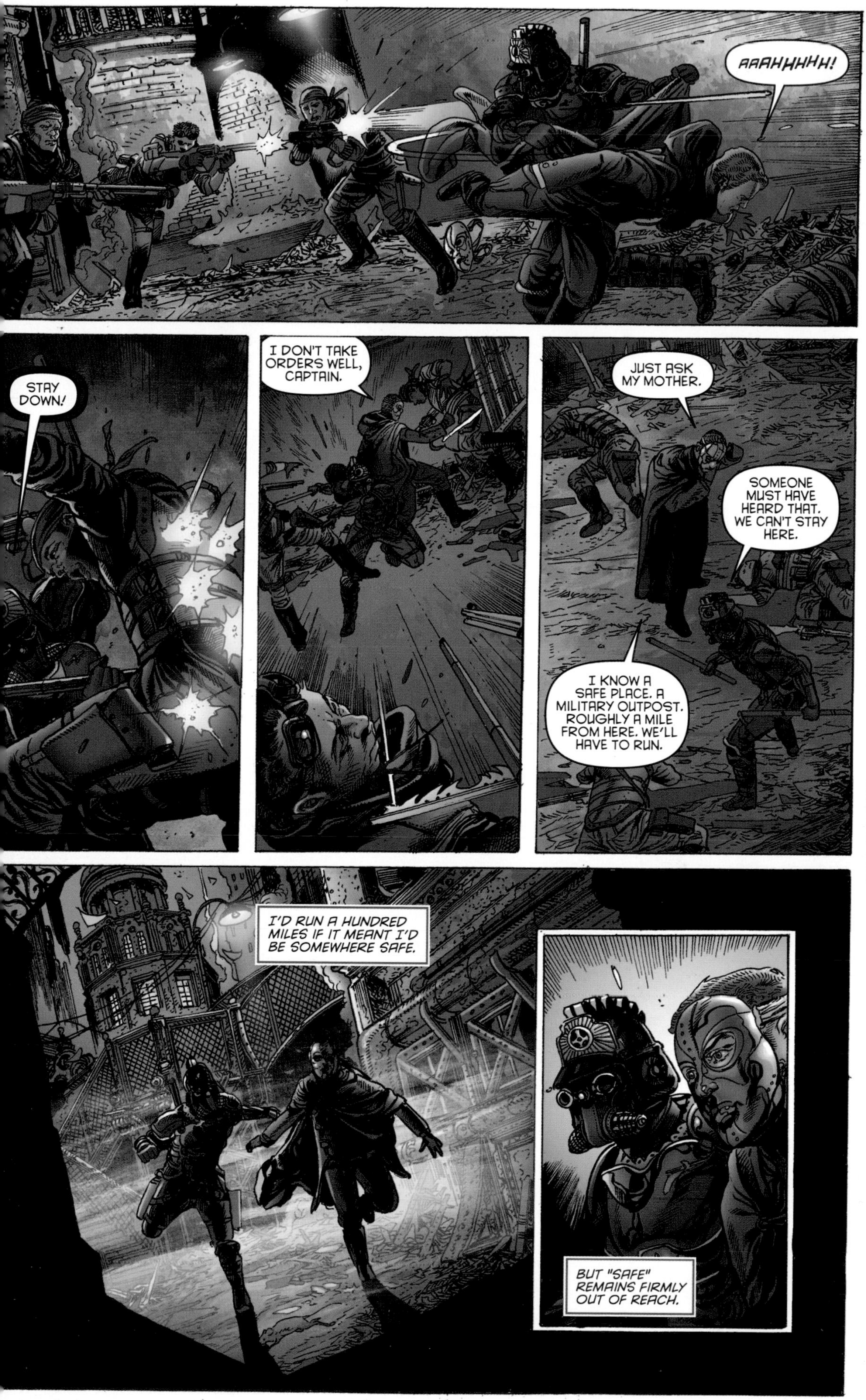
AAAHHHHH!
STAY DOWN!
I DON'T TAKE ORDERS WELL, CAPTAIN.
JUST ASK MY MOTHER.
SOMEONE MUST HAVE HEARD THAT. WE CAN'T STAY HERE.
I KNOW A SAFE PLACE. A MILITARY OUTPOST. ROUGHLY A MILE FROM HERE. WE'LL HAVE TO RUN.
I'D RUN A HUNDRED MILES IF IT MEANT I'D BE SOMEWHERE SAFE.
BUT "SAFE" REMAINS FIRMLY OUT OF REACH.

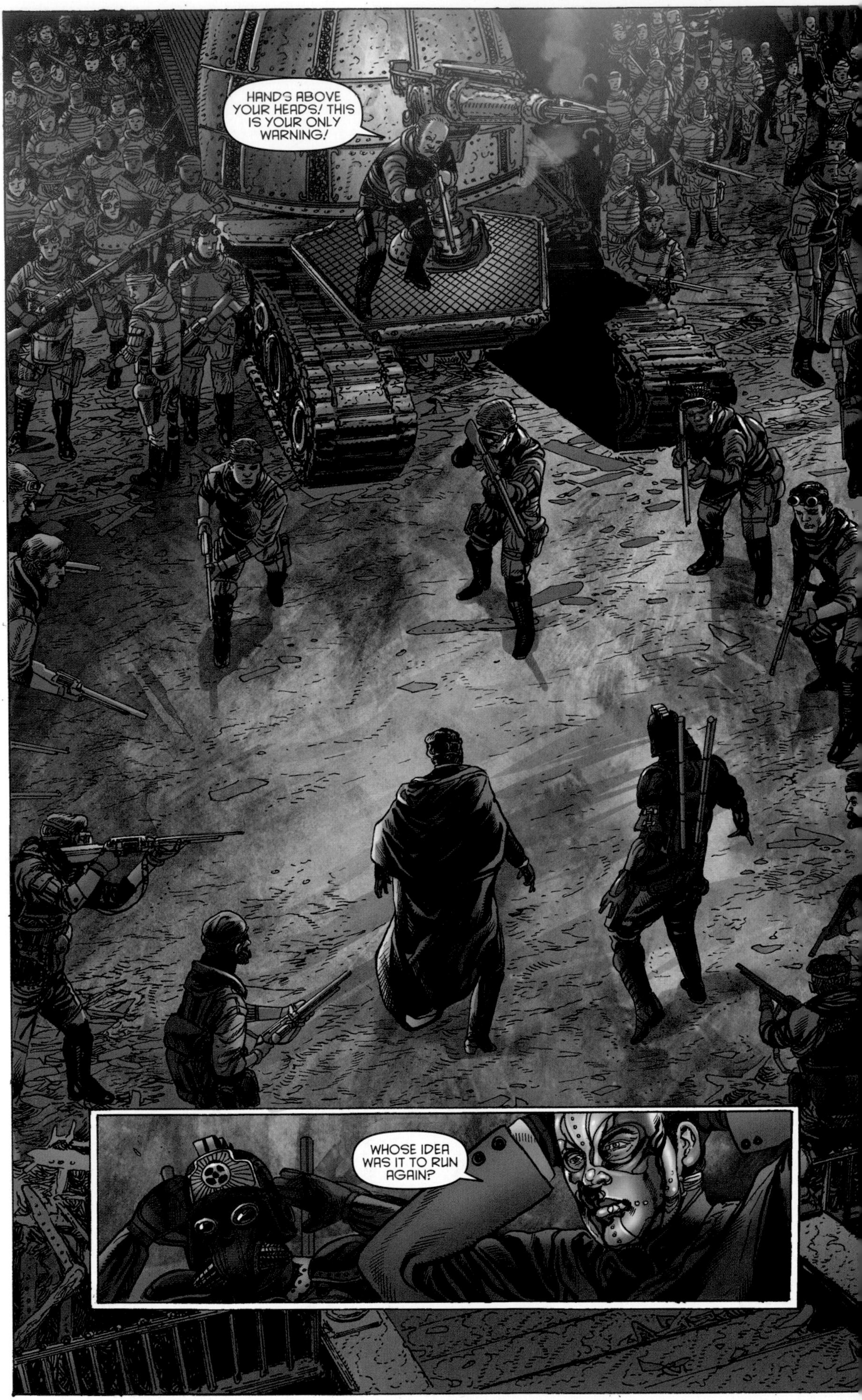
HAND'S ABOVE YOUR HEADS! THIS IS YOUR ONLY WARNING!
WHOSE IDEA WAS IT TO RUN AGAIN?

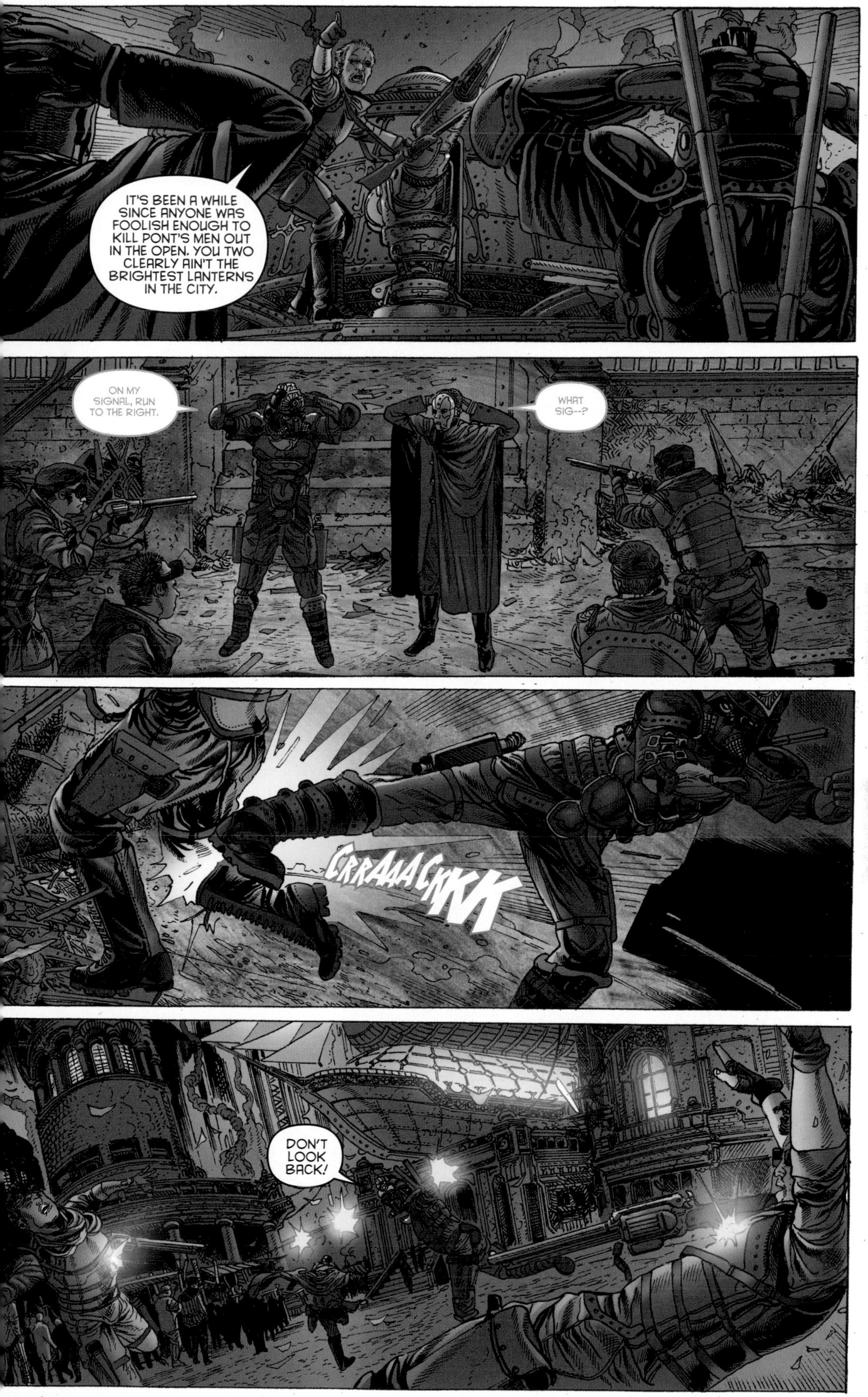
IT'S BEEN A WHILE SINCE ANYONE WAS FOOLISH ENOUGH TO KILL PONT'S MEN OUT IN THE OPEN. YOU TWO CLEARLY AIN'T THE BRIGHTEST LANTERNS IN THE CITY.
ON MY SIGNAL, RUN TO THE RIGHT.
WHAT SIG--?
CRRAAACKKK
DON'T LOOK BACK!

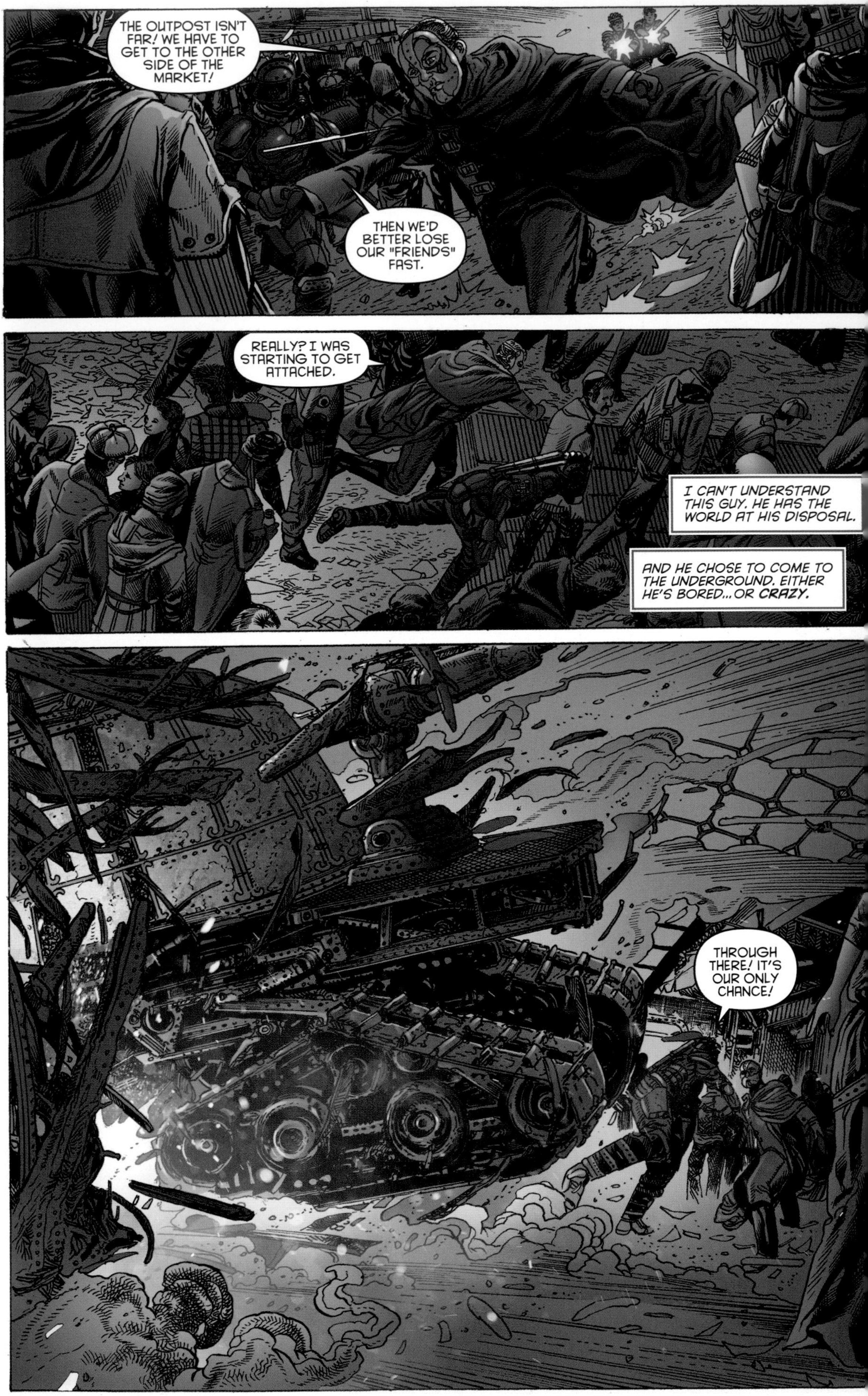
THE OUTPOST ISN'T FAR! WE HAVE TO GET TO THE OTHER SIDE OF THE MARKET!
THEN WE'D BETTER LOSE OUR "FRIENDS" FAST.
REALLY? I WAS STARTING TO GET ATTACHED.
I CAN'T UNDERSTAND THIS GUY. HE HAS THE WORLD AT HIS DISPOSAL.
AND HE CHOSE TO COME TO THE UNDERGROUND. EITHER HE'S BORED...OR CRAZY.
THROUGH THERE! IT'S OUR ONLY CHANCE!

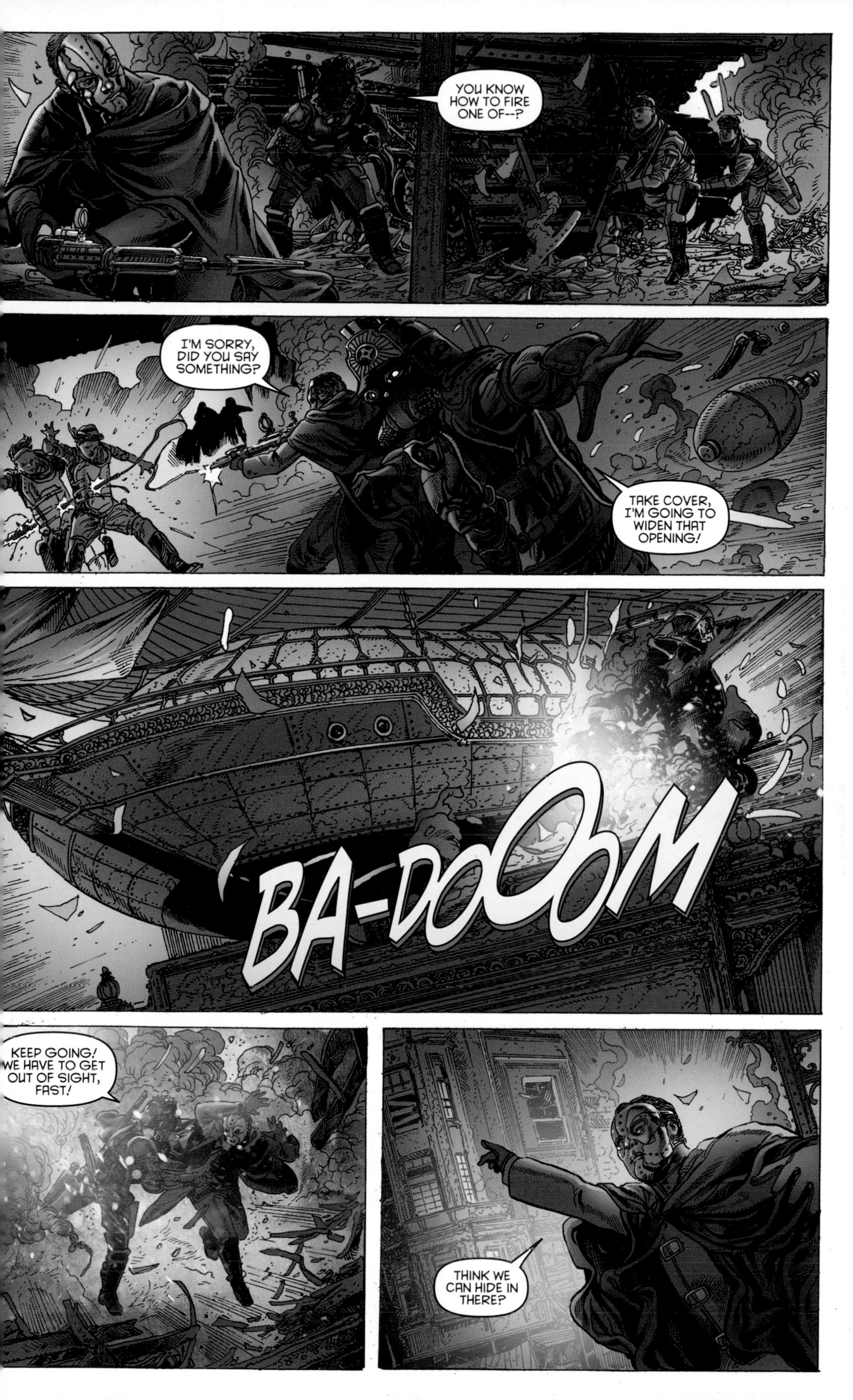
YOU KNOW HOW TO FIRE ONE OF--?
I'M SORRY, DID YOU SAY SOMETHING?
TAKE COVER, I'M GOING TO WIDEN THAT OPENING!
BA-DOOOM
KEEP GOING! WE HAVE TO GET OUT OF SIGHT, FAST!
THINK WE CAN HIDE IN THERE?

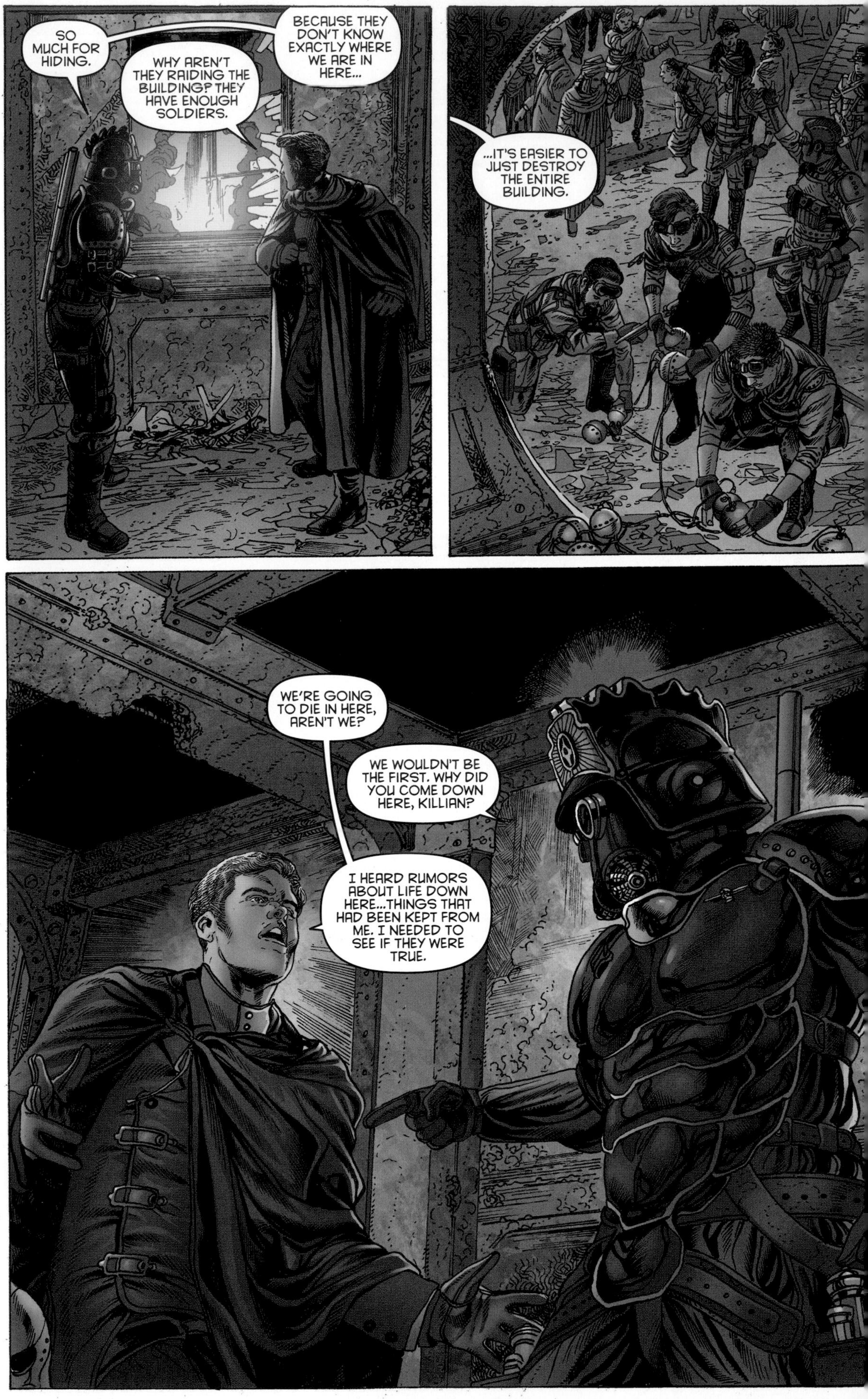
SO MUCH FOR HIDING.
WHY AREN'T THEY RAIDING THE BUILDING? THEY HAVE ENOUGH SOLDIERS.
BECAUSE THEY DON'T KNOW EXACTLY WHERE WE ARE IN HERE...
...IT'S EASIER TO JUST DESTROY THE ENTIRE BUILDING.
WE'RE GOING TO DIE IN HERE, AREN'T WE?
WE WOULDN'T BE THE FIRST. WHY DID YOU COME DOWN HERE, KILLIAN?
I HEARD RUMORS ABOUT LIFE DOWN HERE...THINGS THAT HAD BEEN KEPT FROM ME. I NEEDED TO SEE IF THEY WERE TRUE.

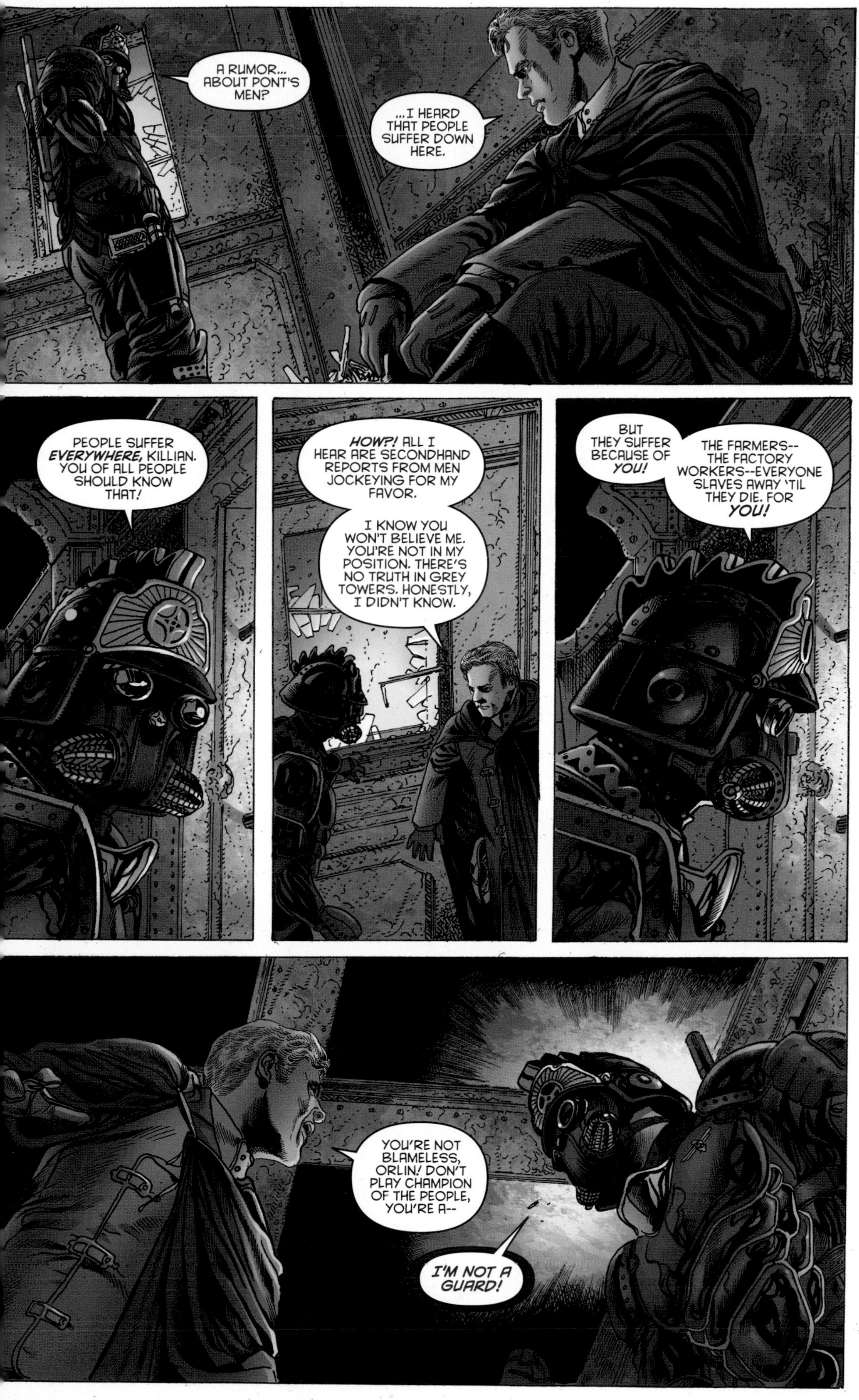

A RUMOR... ABOUT PONT'S MEN?
...I HEARD THAT PEOPLE SUFFER DOWN HERE.
PEOPLE SUFFER *EVERYWHERE,* KILLIAN. YOU OF ALL PEOPLE SHOULD KNOW THAT!
HOW?! ALL I HEAR ARE SECONDHAND REPORTS FROM MEN JOCKEYING FOR MY FAVOR.
I KNOW YOU WON'T BELIEVE ME. YOU'RE NOT IN MY POSITION. THERE'S NO TRUTH IN GREY TOWERS. HONESTLY, I DIDN'T KNOW.
BUT THEY SUFFER BECAUSE OF *YOU!*
THE FARMERS-- THE FACTORY WORKERS--EVERYONE SLAVES AWAY 'TIL THEY DIE. FOR *YOU!*
YOU'RE NOT BLAMELESS, ORLIN! DON'T PLAY CHAMPION OF THE PEOPLE, YOU'RE A--
I'M NOT A GUARD!

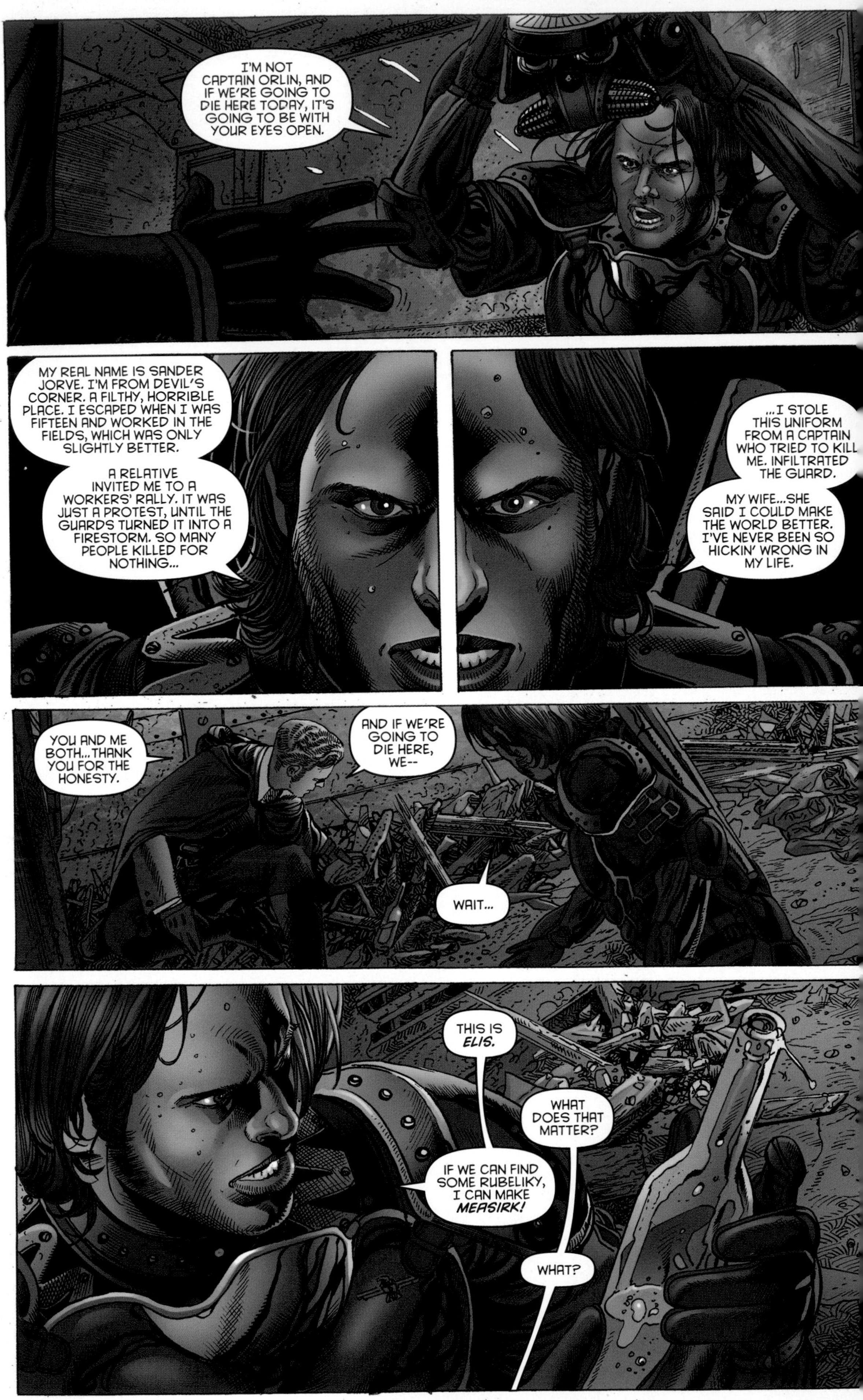
I'M NOT CAPTAIN ORLIN, AND IF WE'RE GOING TO DIE HERE TODAY, IT'S GOING TO BE WITH YOUR EYES OPEN.
MY REAL NAME IS SANDER JORVE. I'M FROM DEVIL'S CORNER. A FILTHY, HORRIBLE PLACE. I ESCAPED WHEN I WAS FIFTEEN AND WORKED IN THE FIELDS, WHICH WAS ONLY SLIGHTLY BETTER.
A RELATIVE INVITED ME TO A WORKERS' RALLY. IT WAS JUST A PROTEST, UNTIL THE GUARDS TURNED IT INTO A FIRESTORM. SO MANY PEOPLE KILLED FOR NOTHING...
...I STOLE THIS UNIFORM FROM A CAPTAIN WHO TRIED TO KILL ME. INFILTRATED THE GUARD.
MY WIFE...SHE SAID I COULD MAKE THE WORLD BETTER. I'VE NEVER BEEN SO HICKIN' WRONG IN MY LIFE.
YOU AND ME BOTH...THANK YOU FOR THE HONESTY.
AND IF WE'RE GOING TO DIE HERE, WE--
WAIT...
THIS IS *ELIS.*
WHAT DOES THAT MATTER?
IF WE CAN FIND SOME RUBELIKY, I CAN MAKE ***MEASIRK!***
WHAT?

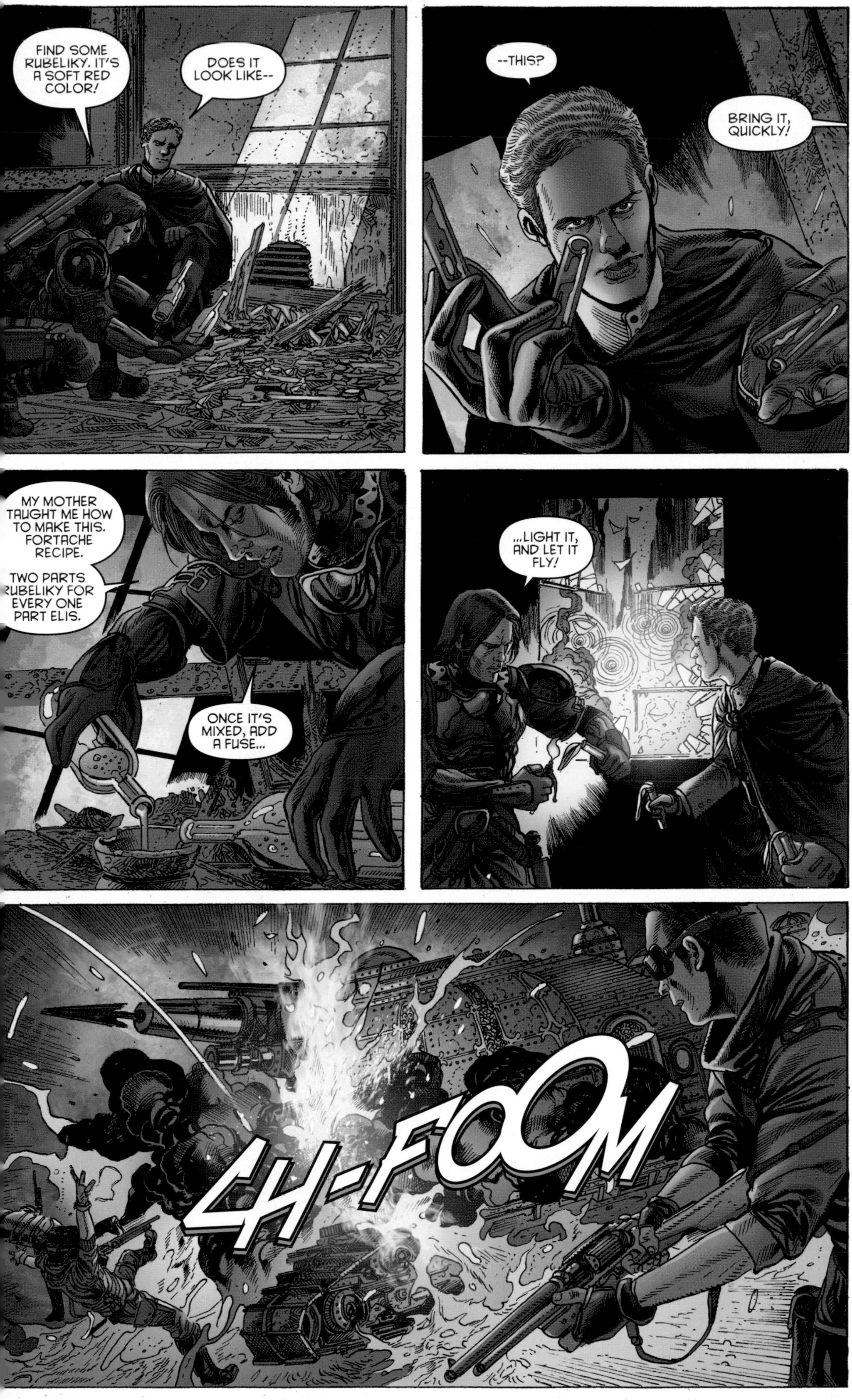
FIND SOME RUBELIKY. IT'S A SOFT RED COLOR!
DOES IT LOOK LIKE--
--THIS?
BRING IT, QUICKLY!
MY MOTHER TAUGHT ME HOW TO MAKE THIS. FORTACHE RECIPE.
TWO PARTS RUBELIKY FOR EVERY ONE PART ELIS.
ONCE IT'S MIXED, ADD A FUSE...
...LIGHT IT, AND LET IT FLY!
CH-FOOM

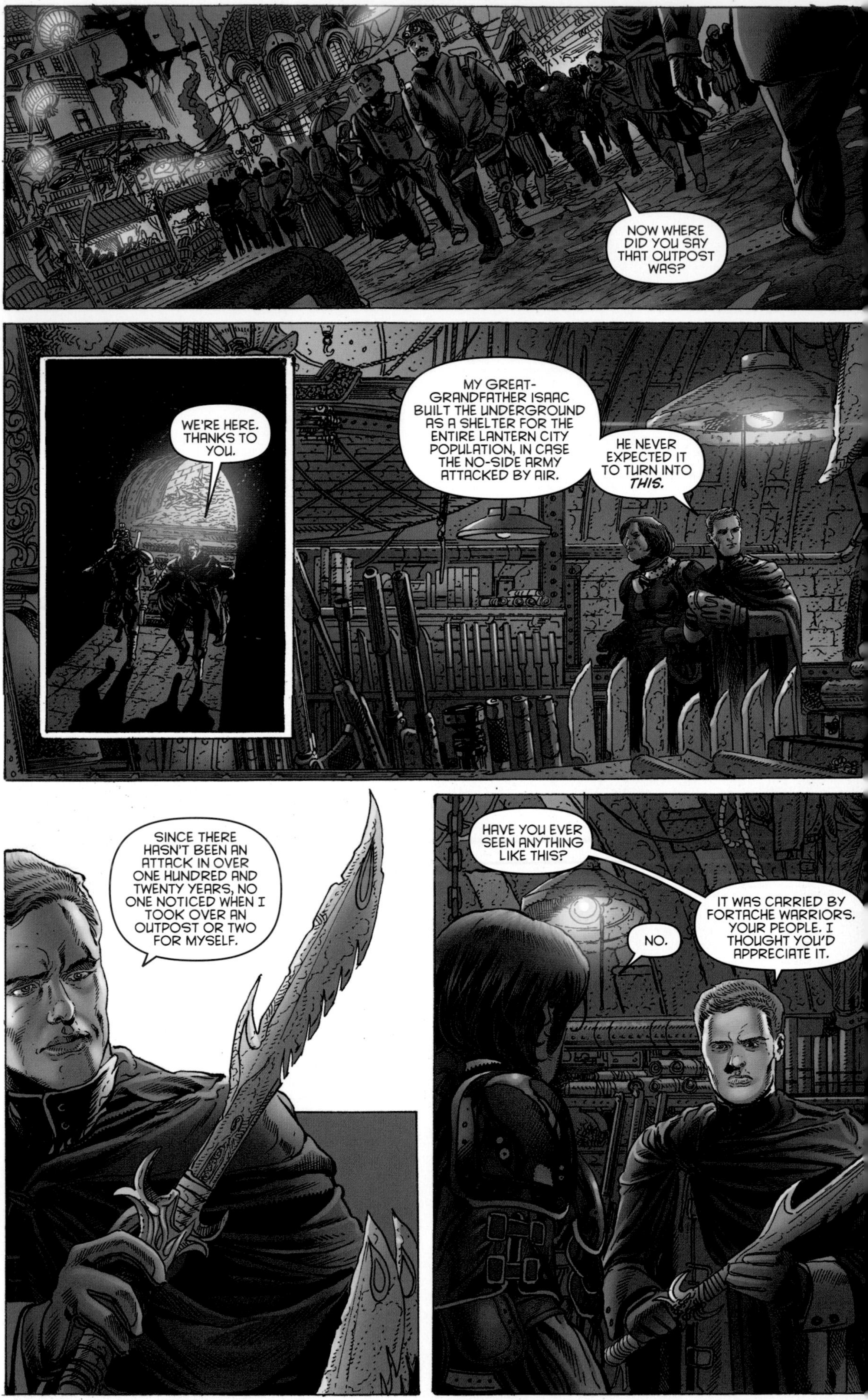
NOW WHERE DID YOU SAY THAT OUTPOST WAS?
WE'RE HERE. THANKS TO YOU.
MY GREAT-GRANDFATHER ISAAC BUILT THE UNDERGROUND AS A SHELTER FOR THE ENTIRE LANTERN CITY POPULATION, IN CASE THE NO-SIDE ARMY ATTACKED BY AIR.
HE NEVER EXPECTED IT TO TURN INTO *THIS.*
SINCE THERE HASN'T BEEN AN ATTACK IN OVER ONE HUNDRED AND TWENTY YEARS, NO ONE NOTICED WHEN I TOOK OVER AN OUTPOST OR TWO FOR MYSELF.
HAVE YOU EVER SEEN ANYTHING LIKE THIS?
NO.
IT WAS CARRIED BY FORTACHE WARRIORS. YOUR PEOPLE. I THOUGHT YOU'D APPRECIATE IT.

THE FORTACHE WERE ALWAYS GREAT FIGHTERS.

IT LOOKS ALMOST NEW...

TIMELESS CRAFTSMANSHIP. THAT'S A FORTACHE TRAIT. ANOTHER I ADMIRE.

DO YOU REALLY WANT TO HAND ME THIS?

WHY, BECAUSE YOU MIGHT *KILL* ME?

I DON'T THINK YOU'LL HAVE THE TIME. AFTER ALL, YOU HAVE TO REPORT BACK TO DUTY, DON'T YOU...CAPTAIN ORLIN?

AS I'M SURE YOU DO TOO, YOUR HIGHNESS.

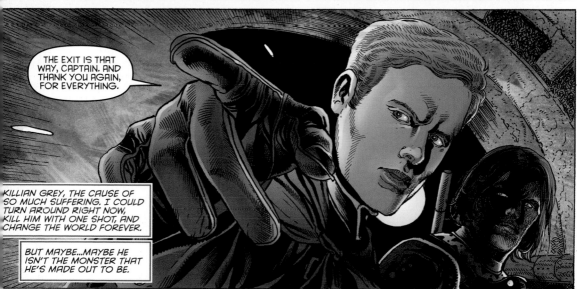

THE EXIT IS THAT WAY, CAPTAIN. AND THANK YOU AGAIN, FOR EVERYTHING.

KILLIAN GREY, THE CAUSE OF SO MUCH SUFFERING. I COULD TURN AROUND RIGHT NOW, KILL HIM WITH ONE SHOT, AND CHANGE THE WORLD FOREVER.

BUT MAYBE...MAYBE HE ISN'T THE MONSTER THAT HE'S MADE OUT TO BE.

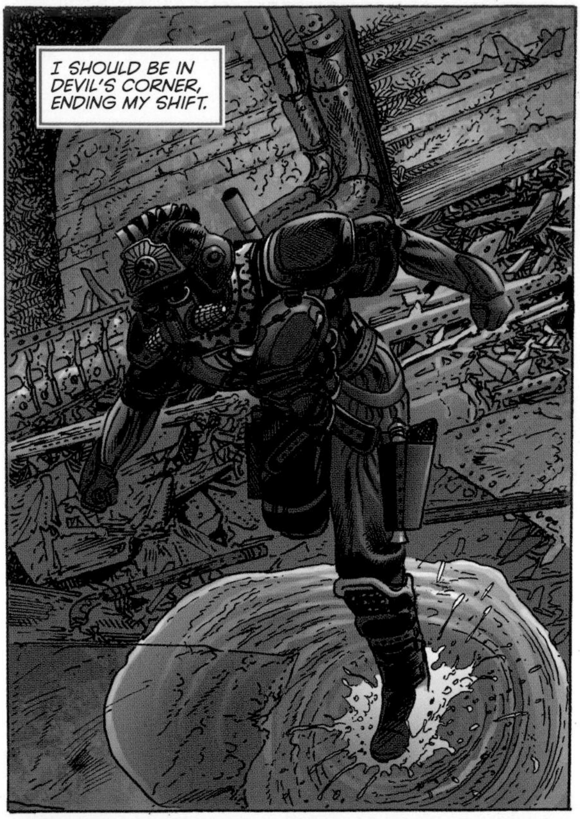
I SHOULD BE IN DEVIL'S CORNER, ENDING MY SHIFT.

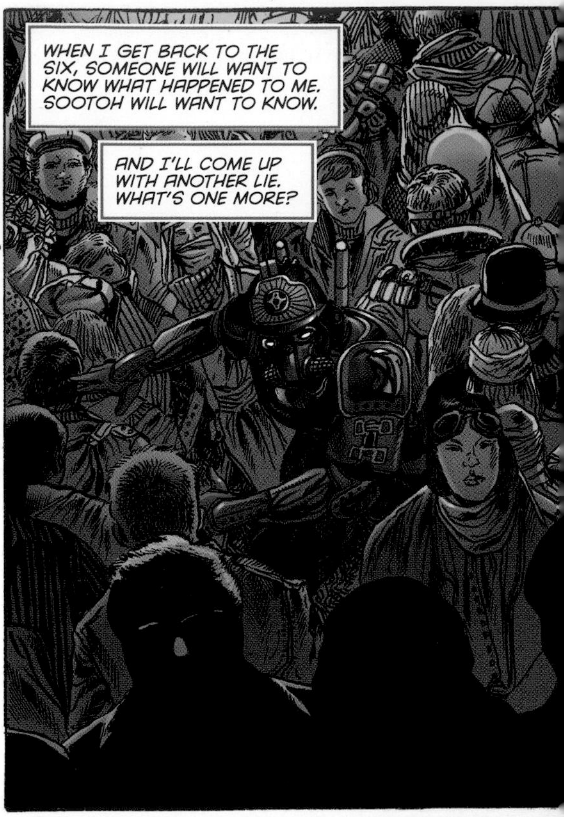
WHEN I GET BACK TO THE SIX, SOMEONE WILL WANT TO KNOW WHAT HAPPENED TO ME. SOOTOH WILL WANT TO KNOW.
AND I'LL COME UP WITH ANOTHER LIE. WHAT'S ONE MORE?

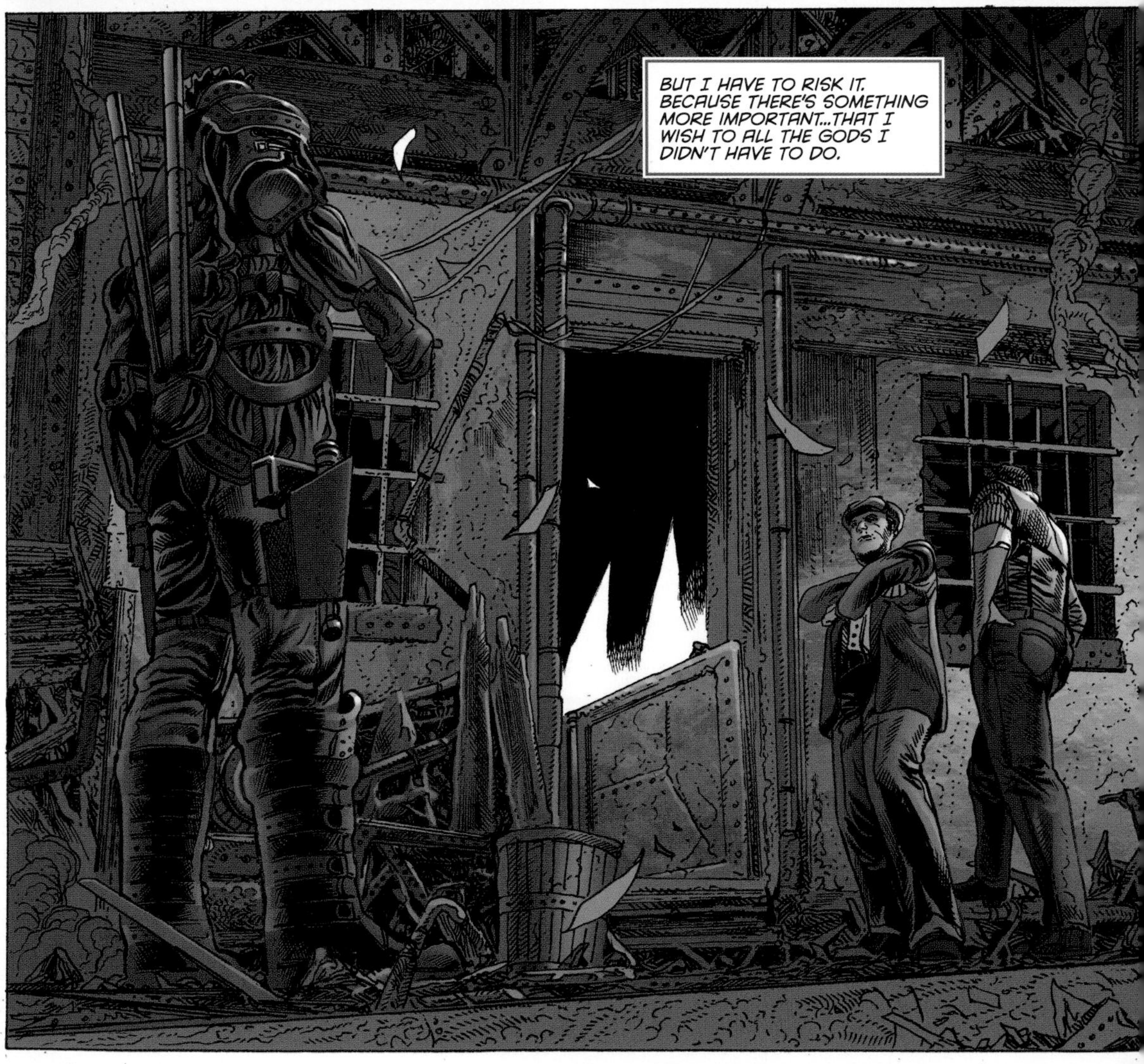
BUT I HAVE TO RISK IT. BECAUSE THERE'S SOMETHING MORE IMPORTANT...THAT I WISH TO ALL THE GODS I DIDN'T HAVE TO DO.

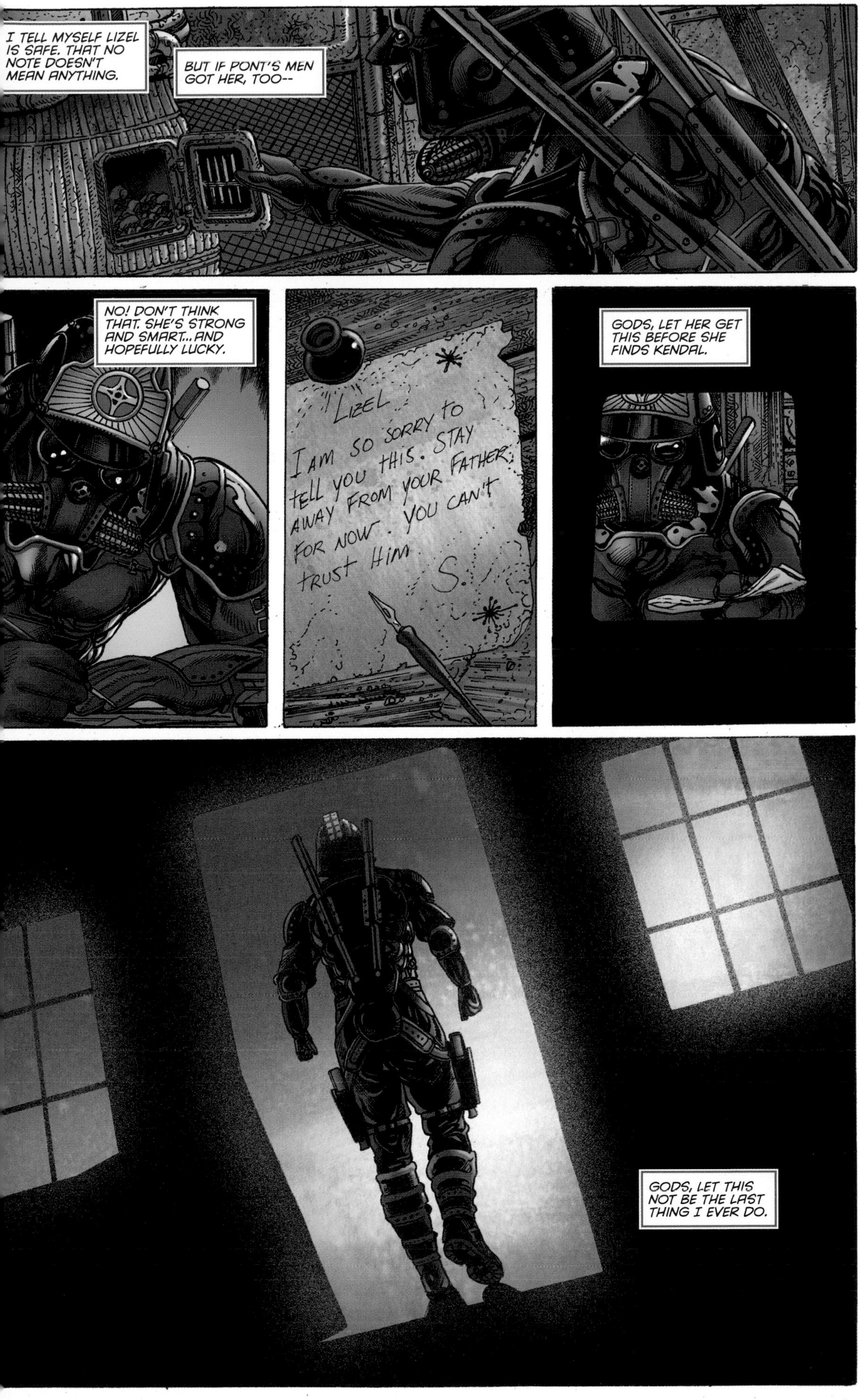
I TELL MYSELF LIZEL IS SAFE. THAT NO NOTE DOESN'T MEAN ANYTHING.
BUT IF PONT'S MEN GOT HER, TOO--
NO! DON'T THINK THAT. SHE'S STRONG AND SMART...AND HOPEFULLY LUCKY.
LIZEL
I AM SO SORRY TO TELL YOU THIS. STAY AWAY FROM YOUR FATHER FOR NOW. YOU CAN'T TRUST HIM
S.
GODS, LET HER GET THIS BEFORE SHE FINDS KENDAL.
GODS, LET THIS NOT BE THE LAST THING I EVER DO.

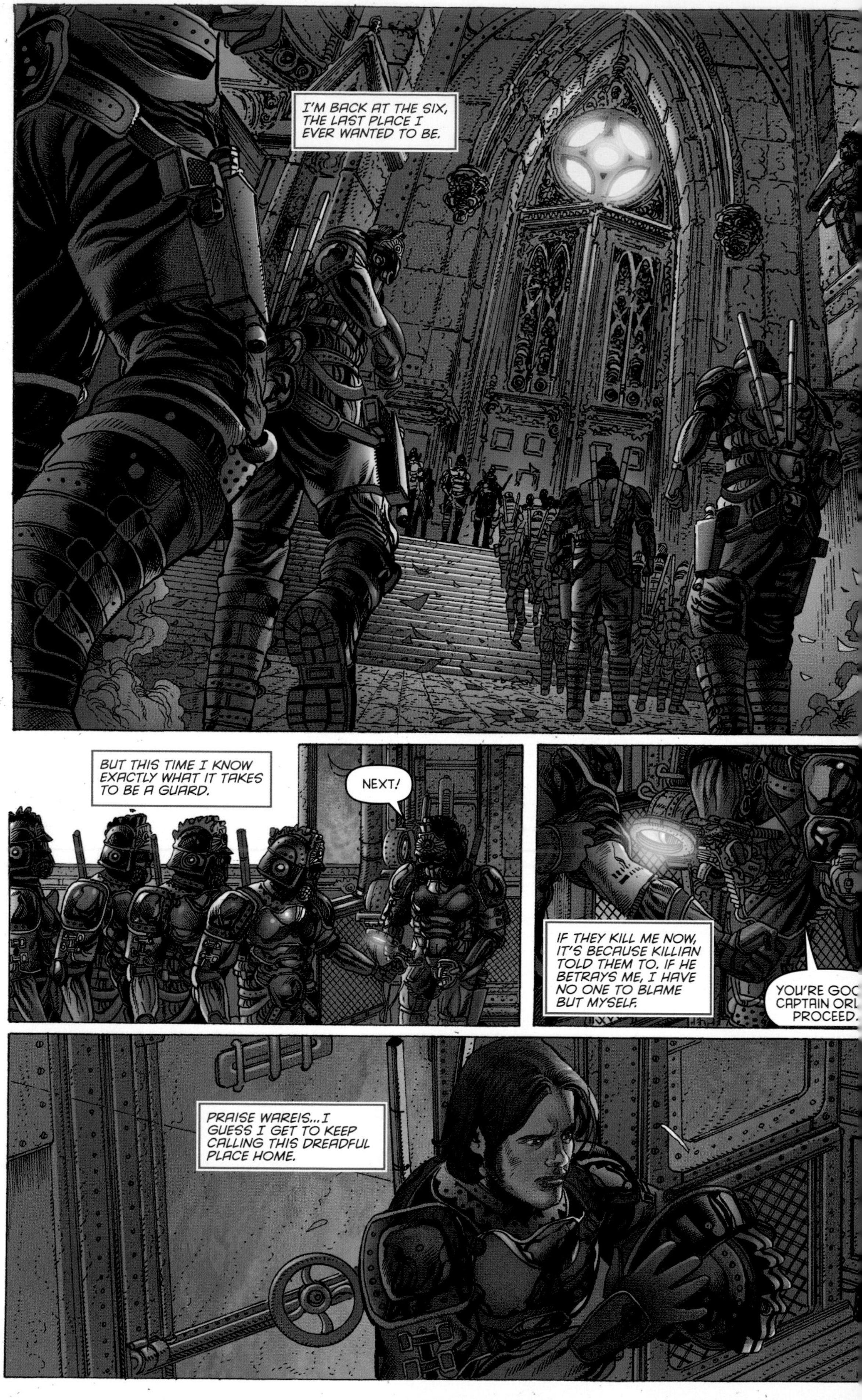
I'M BACK AT THE SIX, THE LAST PLACE I EVER WANTED TO BE.
BUT THIS TIME I KNOW EXACTLY WHAT IT TAKES TO BE A GUARD.
NEXT!
IF THEY KILL ME NOW, IT'S BECAUSE KILLIAN TOLD THEM TO. IF HE BETRAYS ME, I HAVE NO ONE TO BLAME BUT MYSELF.
YOU'RE GOO
CAPTAIN ORL
PROCEED.
PRAISE WAREIS... I GUESS I GET TO KEEP CALLING THIS DREADFUL PLACE HOME.

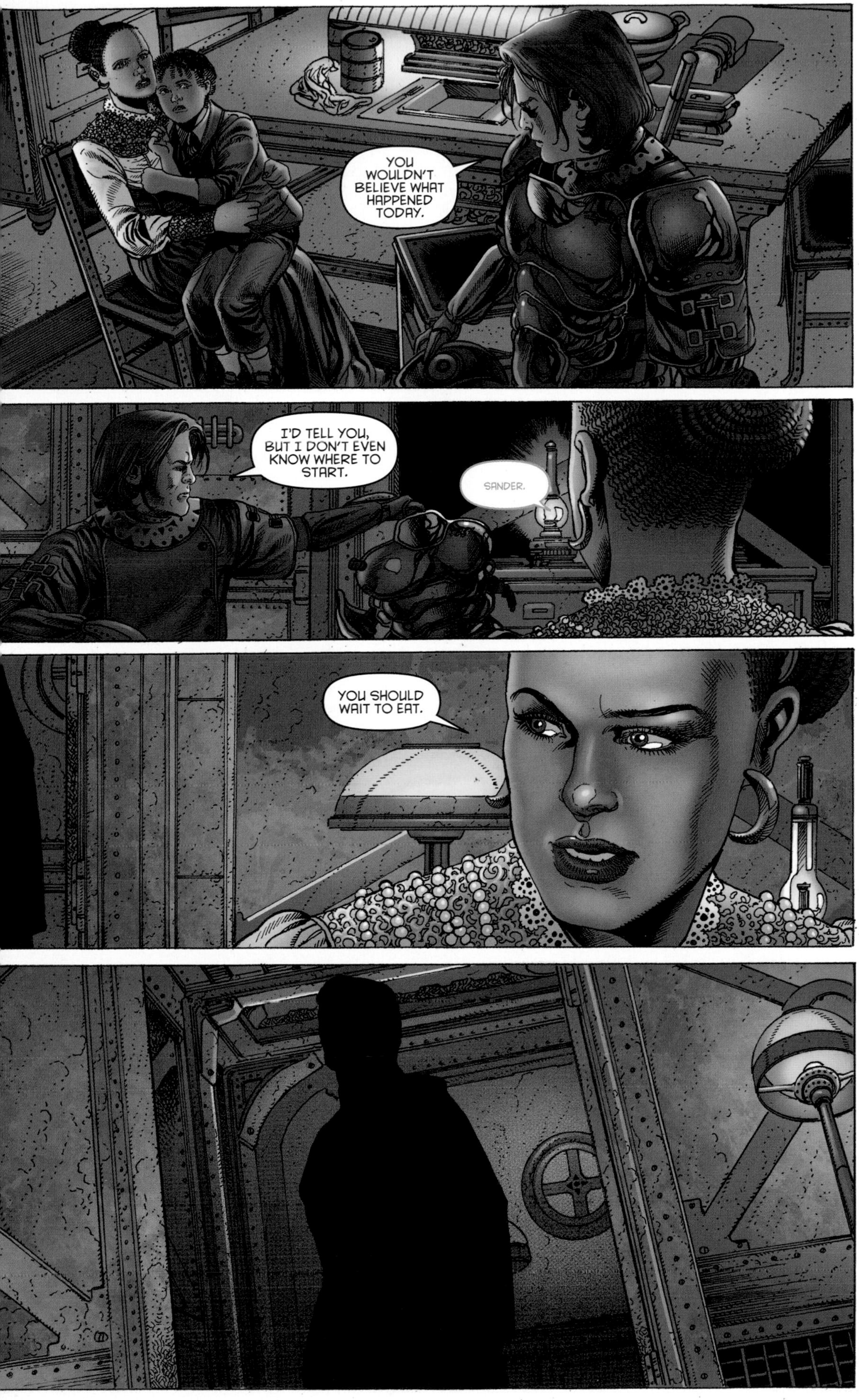
YOU WOULDN'T BELIEVE WHAT HAPPENED TODAY.
I'D TELL YOU, BUT I DON'T EVEN KNOW WHERE TO START.
SANDER.
YOU SHOULD WAIT TO EAT.

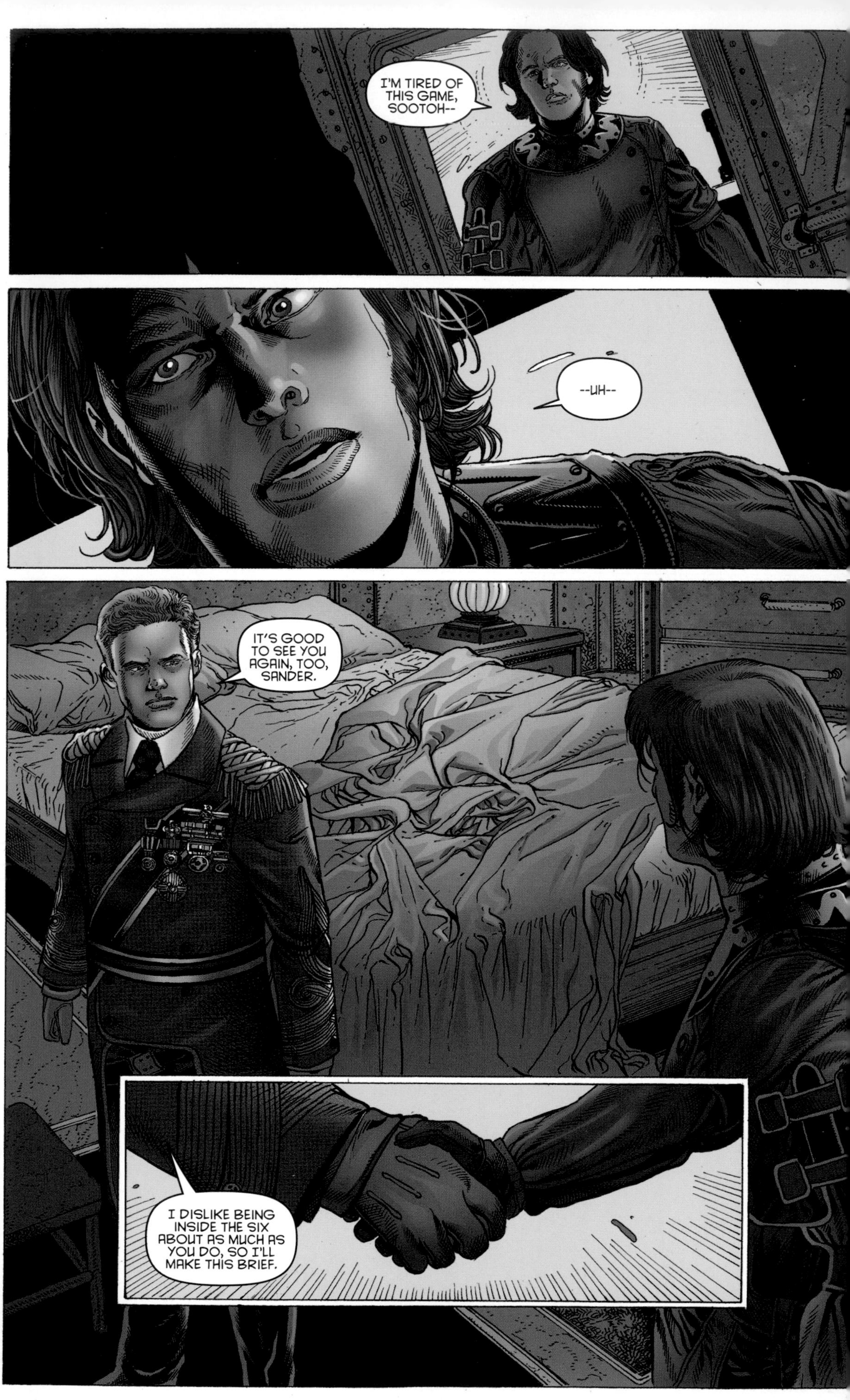
I'M TIRED OF THIS GAME, SOOTOH--
--UH--
IT'S GOOD TO SEE YOU AGAIN, TOO, SANDER.
I DISLIKE BEING INSIDE THE SIX ABOUT AS MUCH AS YOU DO, SO I'LL MAKE THIS BRIEF.

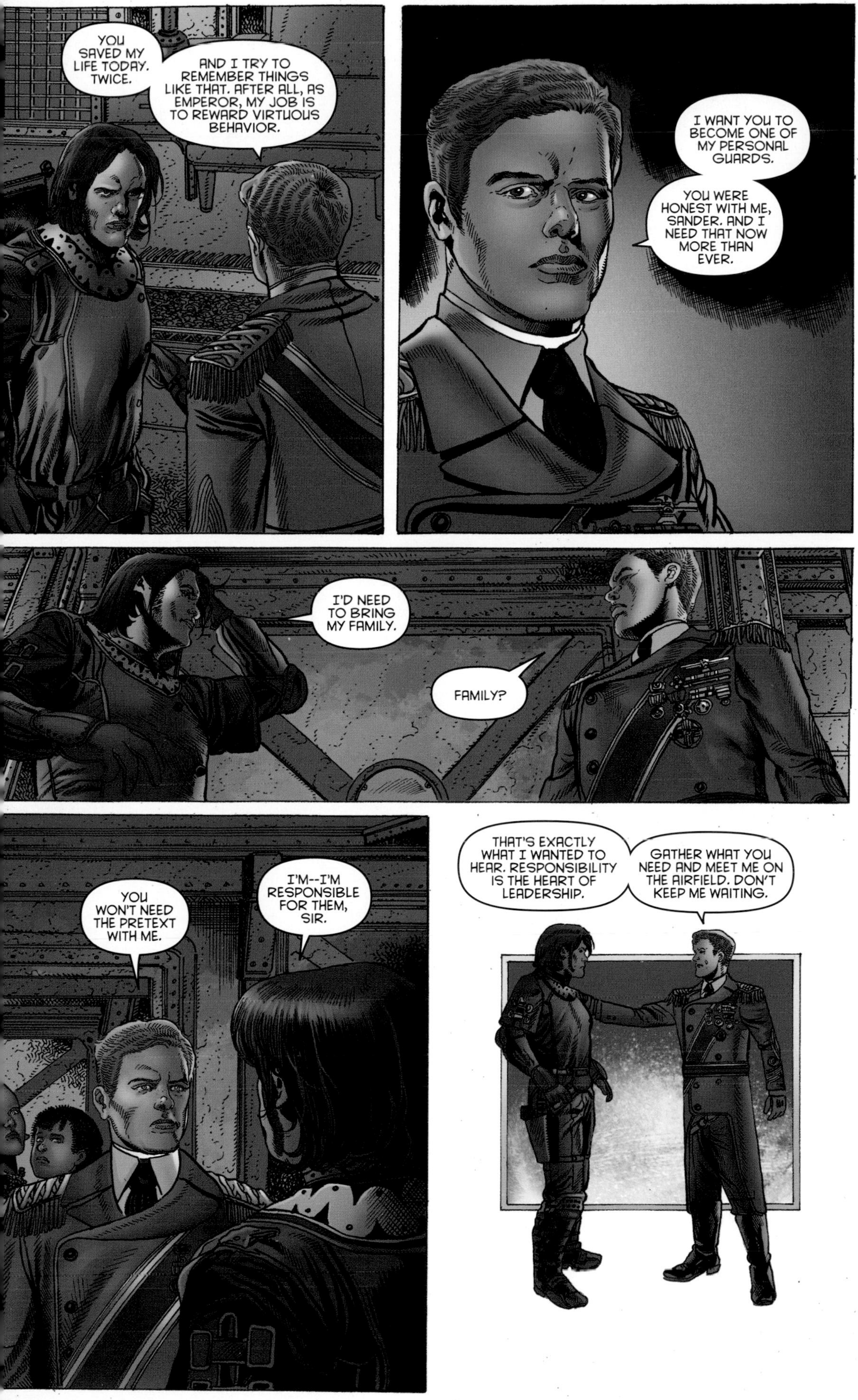

YOU SAVED MY LIFE TODAY. TWICE.
AND I TRY TO REMEMBER THINGS LIKE THAT. AFTER ALL, AS EMPEROR, MY JOB IS TO REWARD VIRTUOUS BEHAVIOR.
I WANT YOU TO BECOME ONE OF MY PERSONAL GUARDS.
YOU WERE HONEST WITH ME, SANDER. AND I NEED THAT NOW MORE THAN EVER.
I'D NEED TO BRING MY FAMILY.
FAMILY?
I'M--I'M RESPONSIBLE FOR THEM, SIR.
YOU WON'T NEED THE PRETEXT WITH ME.
THAT'S EXACTLY WHAT I WANTED TO HEAR. RESPONSIBILITY IS THE HEART OF LEADERSHIP.
GATHER WHAT YOU NEED AND MEET ME ON THE AIRFIELD. DON'T KEEP ME WAITING.

TERNA, I KNOW THIS IS A LOT OF CHANGE, BUT THINGS ARE GOING TO GET *BETTER* FOR YOU AND JOM. MAYBE FOR *EVERYONE*, IF I HANDLE IT RIGHT.

IT WILL, SANDER. EMPEROR GREY TOLD ME THAT YOU SAVED HIM, AND NOW YOU'VE SAVED US TOO. YOU CAN BE PROUD OF THAT.

BUT YOU CAN'T TRUST *ANYONE* IN GREY TOWERS.

IT WAS MY *JOB* TO KNOW THEM, SANDER. ALL OF THEM WANT WHAT GREY HAS: POWER. THEY'LL DO ANYTHING THEY CAN TO GET IT.

HE PICKED ME, TERNA. HE WANTS TO HELP.

MAYBE HE DOES. BUT YOU HAVE TO REMEMBER, IF YOU *DIDN'T* WANT TO GO...DO YOU REALLY THINK YOU COULD HAVE REFUSED?

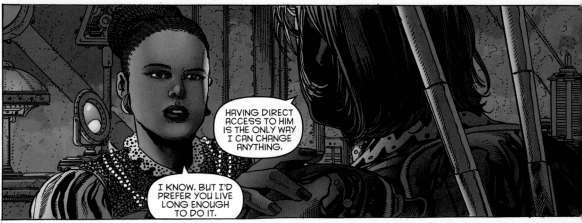

HAVING DIRECT ACCESS TO HIM IS THE ONLY WAY I CAN CHANGE ANYTHING.

I KNOW. BUT I'D PREFER YOU LIVE LONG ENOUGH TO DO IT.

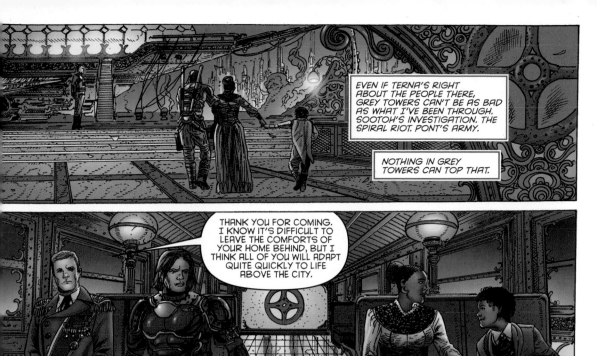

EVEN IF TERNA'S RIGHT ABOUT THE PEOPLE THERE, GREY TOWERS CAN'T BE AS BAD AS WHAT I'VE BEEN THROUGH. SOOTOH'S INVESTIGATION. THE SPIRAL RIOT. PONT'S ARMY.

NOTHING IN GREY TOWERS CAN TOP THAT.

THANK YOU FOR COMING. I KNOW IT'S DIFFICULT TO LEAVE THE COMFORTS OF YOUR HOME BEHIND, BUT I THINK ALL OF YOU WILL ADAPT QUITE QUICKLY TO LIFE ABOVE THE CITY.

NO DOUBT IT WILL BE AN ADJUSTMENT. DIFFERENT FOOD. DIFFERENT WAYS OF DRESS. DIFFERENT... PRIORITIES.

BUT IF THERE IS ANYTHING YOU NEED, I CAN ARRANGE FOR YOU TO GET IT.

I OWE SANDER MY LIFE. THE LEAST THAT I CAN DO IS ACCOMMODATE YOU.

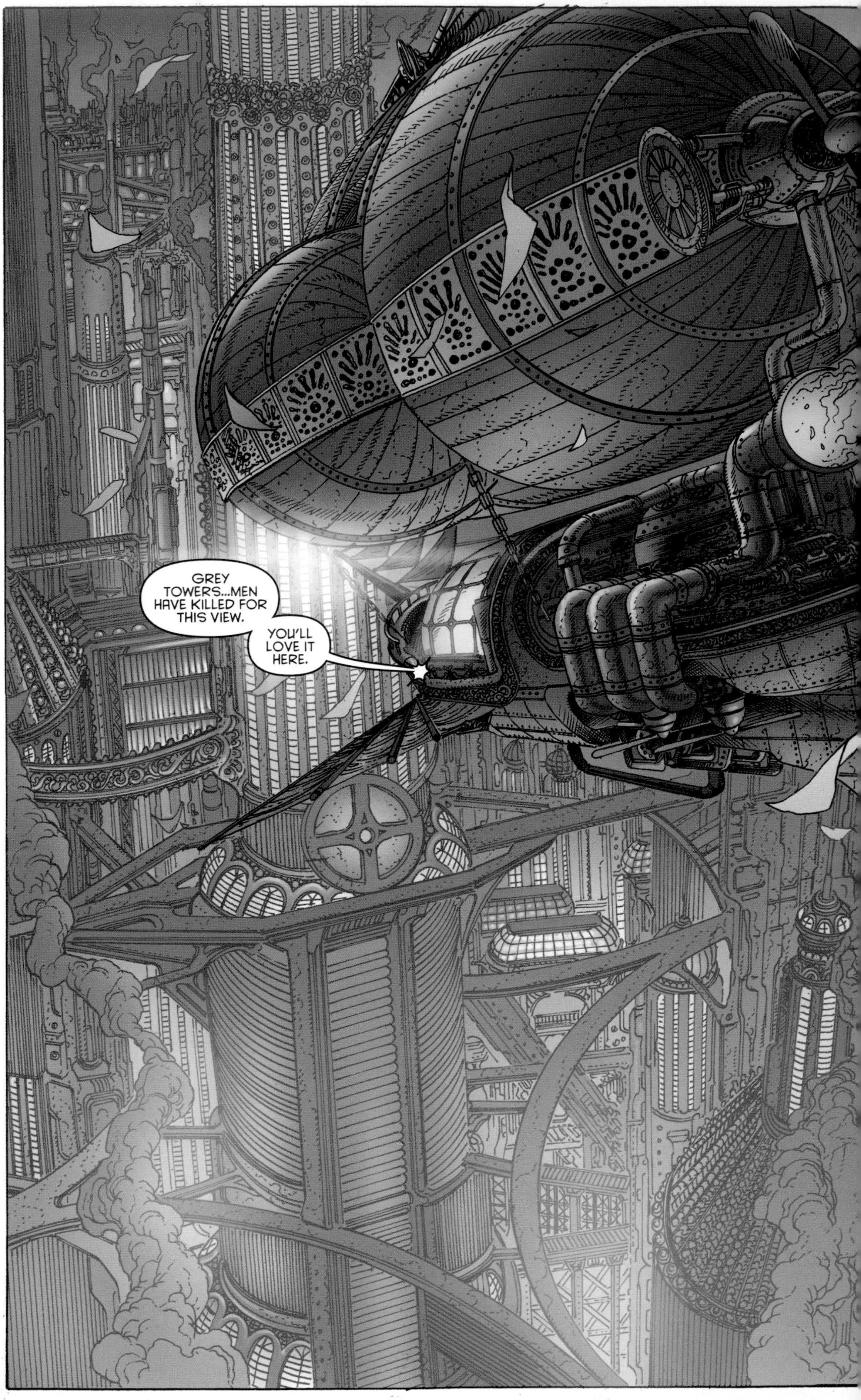
GREY TOWERS...MEN HAVE KILLED FOR THIS VIEW.
YOU'LL LOVE IT HERE.

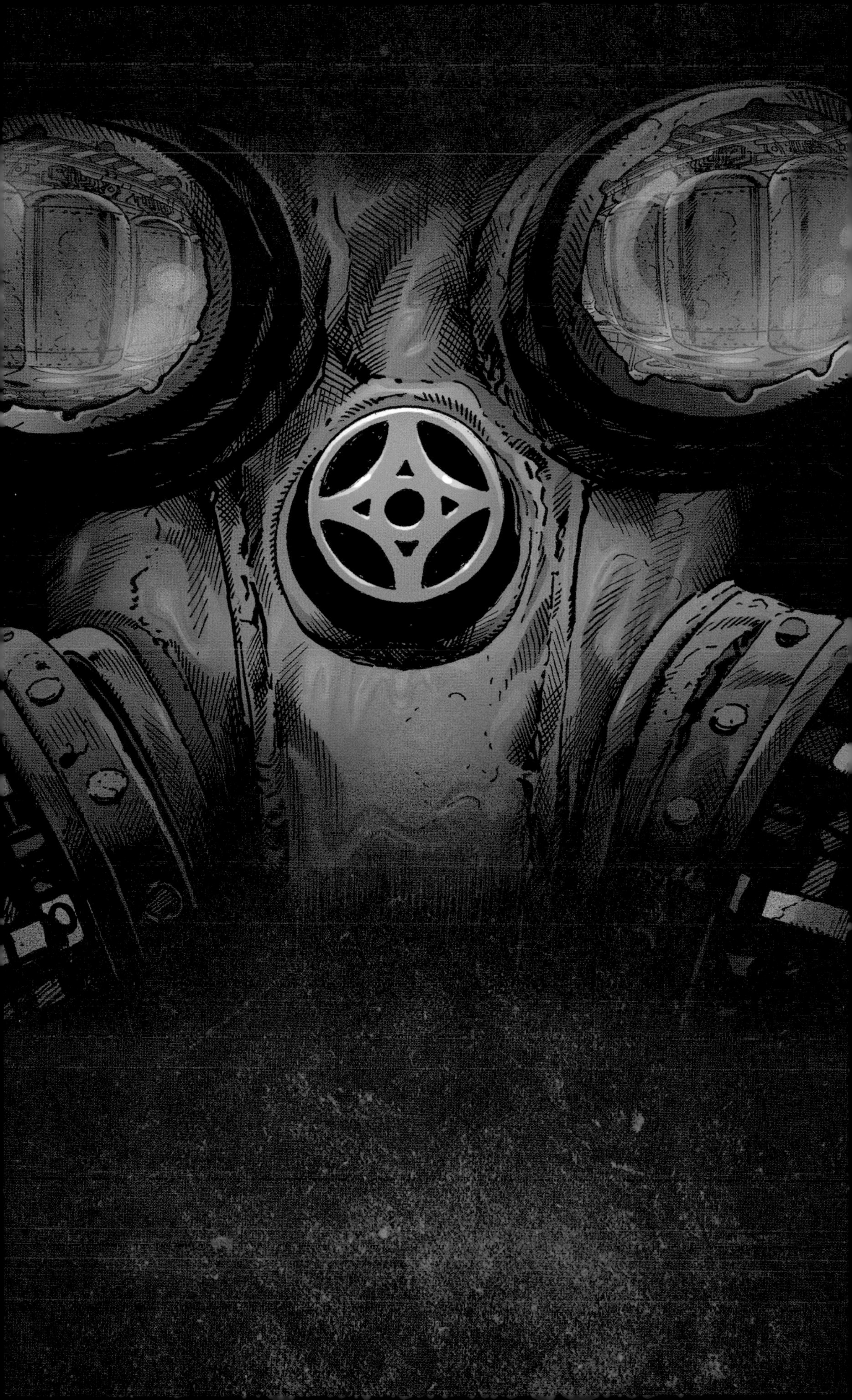

CHAPTER SIX

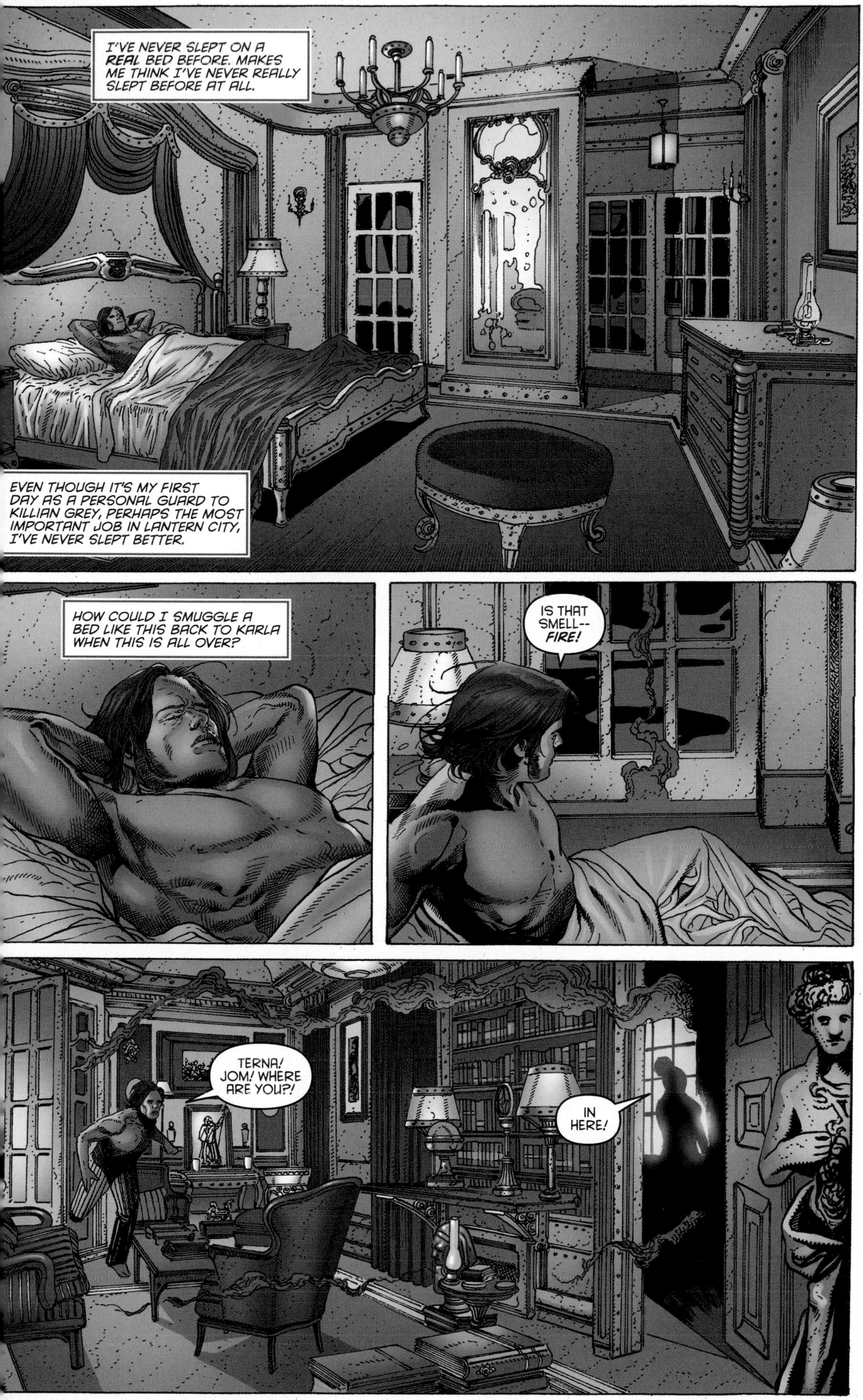

I'VE NEVER SLEPT ON A REAL BED BEFORE. MAKES ME THINK I'VE NEVER REALLY SLEPT BEFORE AT ALL.
EVEN THOUGH IT'S MY FIRST DAY AS A PERSONAL GUARD TO KILLIAN GREY, PERHAPS THE MOST IMPORTANT JOB IN LANTERN CITY, I'VE NEVER SLEPT BETTER.
HOW COULD I SMUGGLE A BED LIKE THIS BACK TO KARLA WHEN THIS IS ALL OVER?
IS THAT SMELL-- FIRE!
TERNA! JOM! WHERE ARE YOU?!
IN HERE!

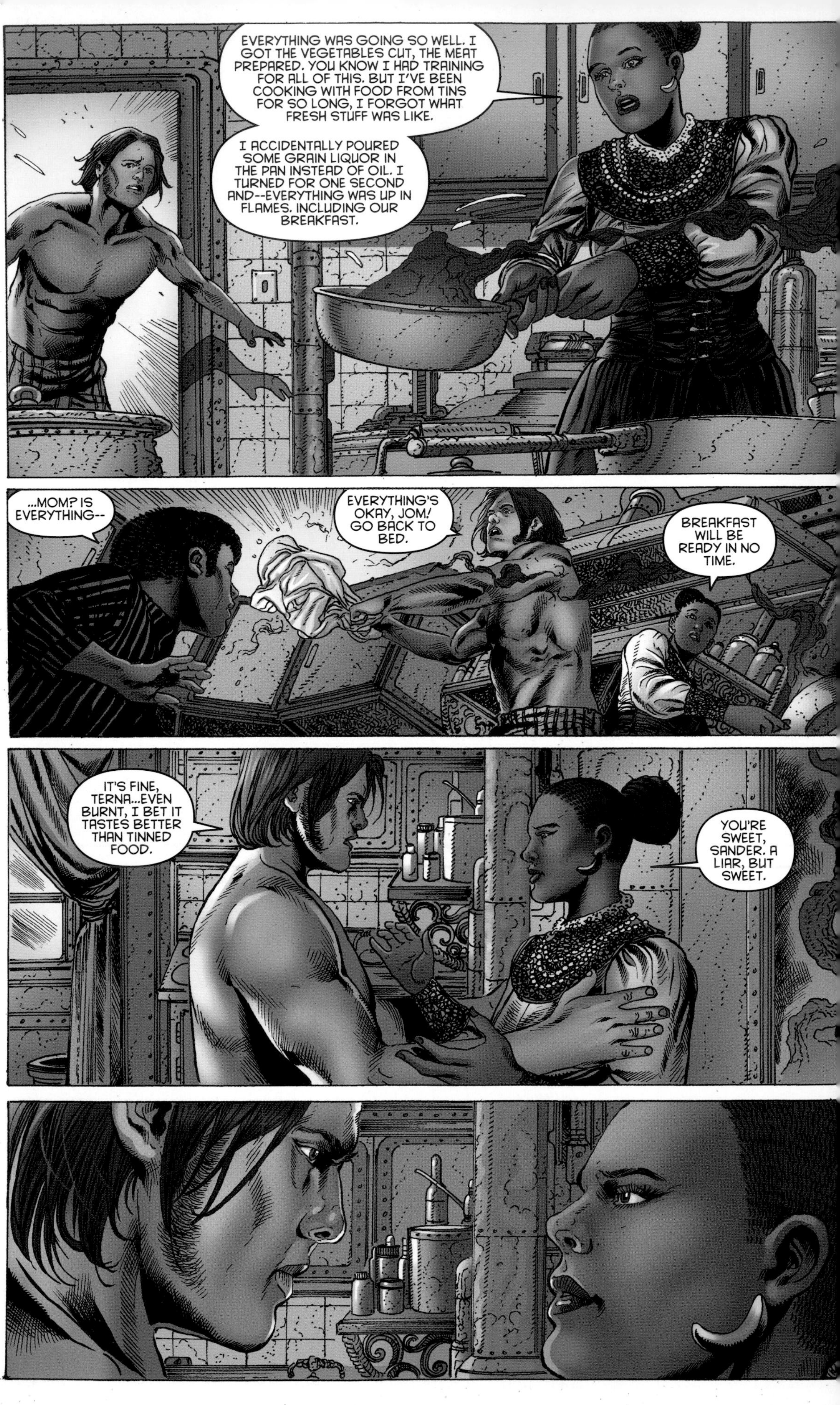
EVERYTHING WAS GOING SO WELL. I GOT THE VEGETABLES CUT, THE MEAT PREPARED. YOU KNOW I HAD TRAINING FOR ALL OF THIS. BUT I'VE BEEN COOKING WITH FOOD FROM TINS FOR SO LONG, I FORGOT WHAT FRESH STUFF WAS LIKE.
I ACCIDENTALLY POURED SOME GRAIN LIQUOR IN THE PAN INSTEAD OF OIL. I TURNED FOR ONE SECOND AND--EVERYTHING WAS UP IN FLAMES. INCLUDING OUR BREAKFAST.
...MOM? IS EVERYTHING--
EVERYTHING'S OKAY, JOM! GO BACK TO BED.
BREAKFAST WILL BE READY IN NO TIME.
IT'S FINE, TERNA...EVEN BURNT, I BET IT TASTES BETTER THAN TINNED FOOD.
YOU'RE SWEET, SANDER. A LIAR, BUT SWEET.

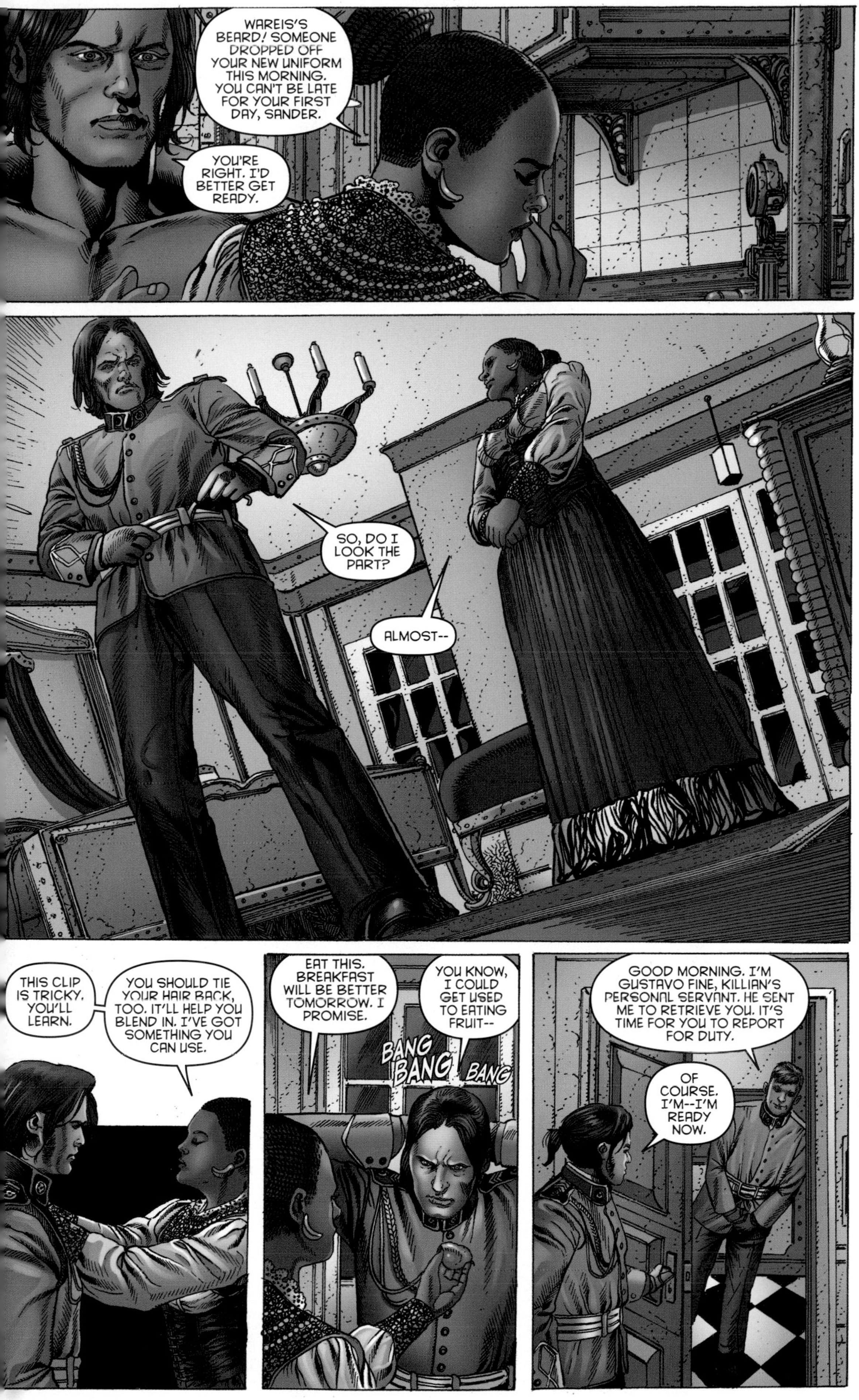
WAREIS'S BEARD! SOMEONE DROPPED OFF YOUR NEW UNIFORM THIS MORNING. YOU CAN'T BE LATE FOR YOUR FIRST DAY, SANDER.
YOU'RE RIGHT. I'D BETTER GET READY.
SO, DO I LOOK THE PART?
ALMOST--
THIS CLIP IS TRICKY. YOU'LL LEARN.
YOU SHOULD TIE YOUR HAIR BACK, TOO. IT'LL HELP YOU BLEND IN. I'VE GOT SOMETHING YOU CAN USE.
EAT THIS. BREAKFAST WILL BE BETTER TOMORROW. I PROMISE.
YOU KNOW, I COULD GET USED TO EATING FRUIT--
BANG
BANG
BANG
GOOD MORNING. I'M GUSTAVO FINE, KILLIAN'S PERSONAL SERVANT. HE SENT ME TO RETRIEVE YOU. IT'S TIME FOR YOU TO REPORT FOR DUTY.
OF COURSE. I'M--I'M READY NOW.

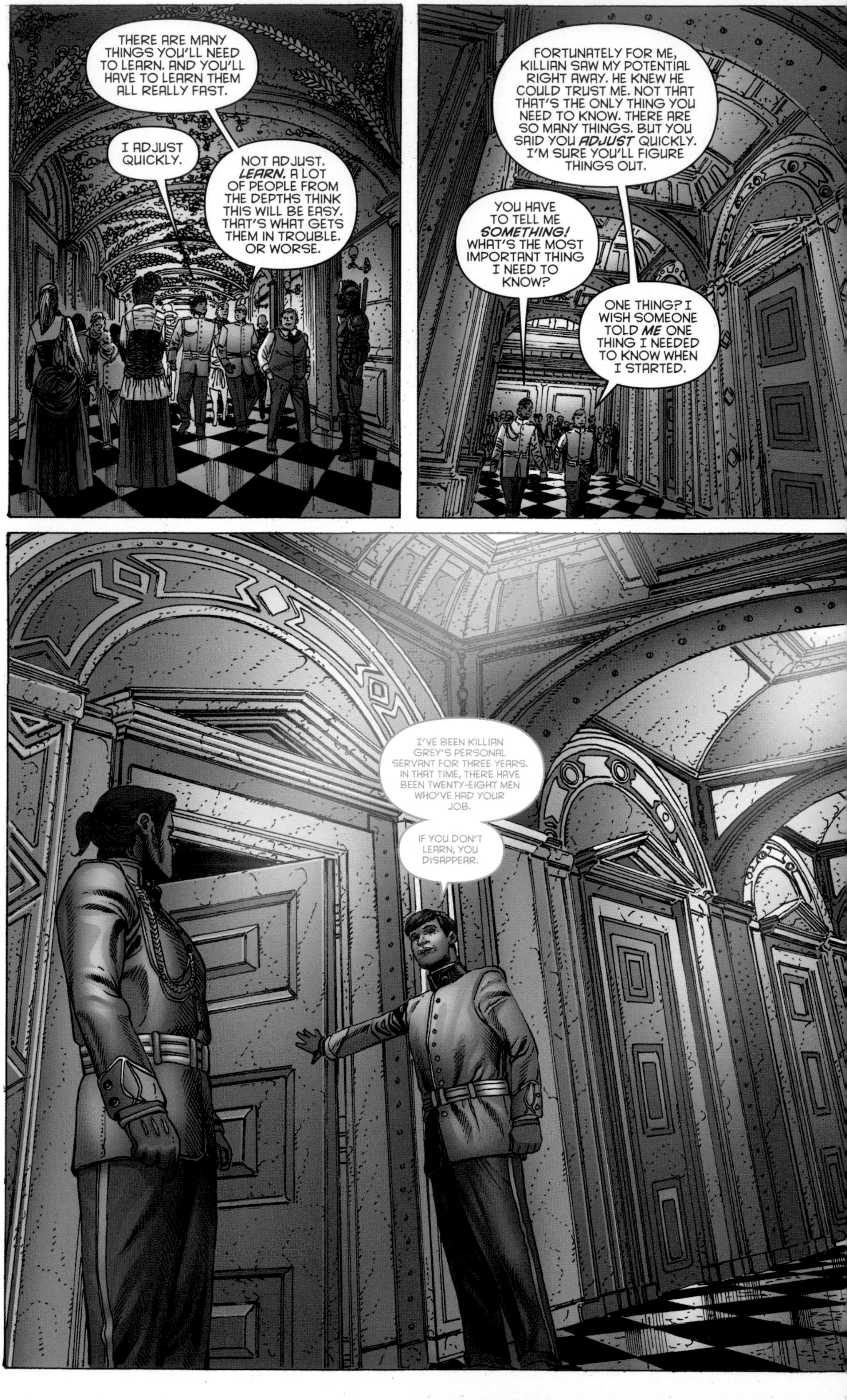
THERE ARE MANY THINGS YOU'LL NEED TO LEARN. AND YOU'LL HAVE TO LEARN THEM ALL REALLY FAST.
I ADJUST QUICKLY.
NOT ADJUST. LEARN. A LOT OF PEOPLE FROM THE DEPTHS THINK THIS WILL BE EASY. THAT'S WHAT GETS THEM IN TROUBLE. OR WORSE.
FORTUNATELY FOR ME, KILLIAN SAW MY POTENTIAL RIGHT AWAY. HE KNEW HE COULD TRUST ME. NOT THAT THAT'S THE ONLY THING YOU NEED TO KNOW. THERE ARE SO MANY THINGS. BUT YOU SAID YOU ADJUST QUICKLY. I'M SURE YOU'LL FIGURE THINGS OUT.
YOU HAVE TO TELL ME SOMETHING! WHAT'S THE MOST IMPORTANT THING I NEED TO KNOW?
ONE THING? I WISH SOMEONE TOLD ME ONE THING I NEEDED TO KNOW WHEN I STARTED.
I'VE BEEN KILLIAN GREY'S PERSONAL SERVANT FOR THREE YEARS. IN THAT TIME, THERE HAVE BEEN TWENTY-EIGHT MEN WHO'VE HAD YOUR JOB.
IF YOU DON'T LEARN, YOU DISAPPEAR.

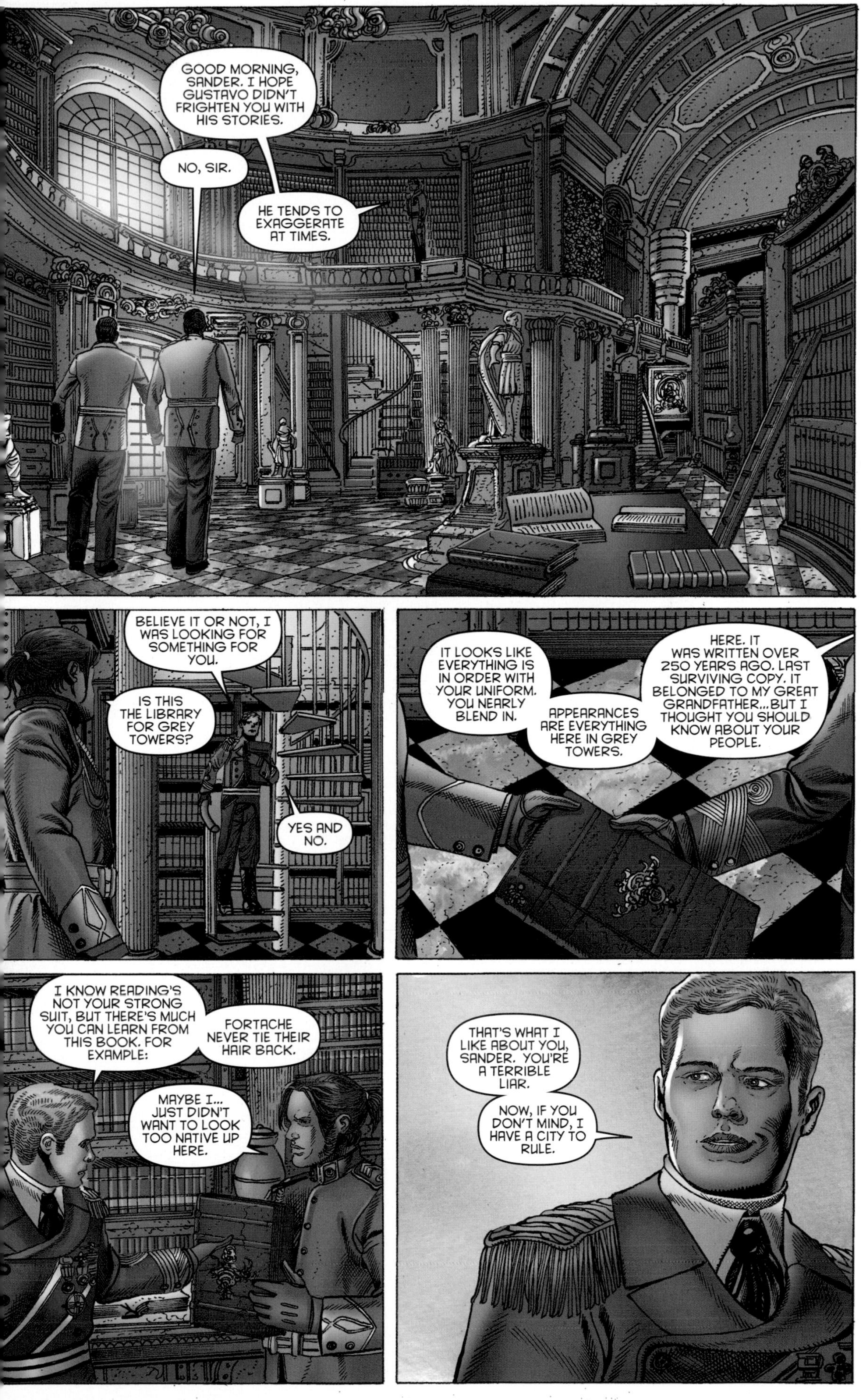
GOOD MORNING, SANDER. I HOPE GUSTAVO DIDN'T FRIGHTEN YOU WITH HIS STORIES.
NO, SIR.
HE TENDS TO EXAGGERATE AT TIMES.
BELIEVE IT OR NOT, I WAS LOOKING FOR SOMETHING FOR YOU.
IS THIS THE LIBRARY FOR GREY TOWERS?
YES AND NO.
IT LOOKS LIKE EVERYTHING IS IN ORDER WITH YOUR UNIFORM. YOU NEARLY BLEND IN.
APPEARANCES ARE EVERYTHING HERE IN GREY TOWERS.
HERE. IT WAS WRITTEN OVER 250 YEARS AGO. LAST SURVIVING COPY. IT BELONGED TO MY GREAT GRANDFATHER... BUT I THOUGHT YOU SHOULD KNOW ABOUT YOUR PEOPLE.
I KNOW READING'S NOT YOUR STRONG SUIT, BUT THERE'S MUCH YOU CAN LEARN FROM THIS BOOK. FOR EXAMPLE:
FORTACHE NEVER TIE THEIR HAIR BACK.
MAYBE I... JUST DIDN'T WANT TO LOOK TOO NATIVE UP HERE.
THAT'S WHAT I LIKE ABOUT YOU, SANDER. YOU'RE A TERRIBLE LIAR.
NOW, IF YOU DON'T MIND, I HAVE A CITY TO RULE.

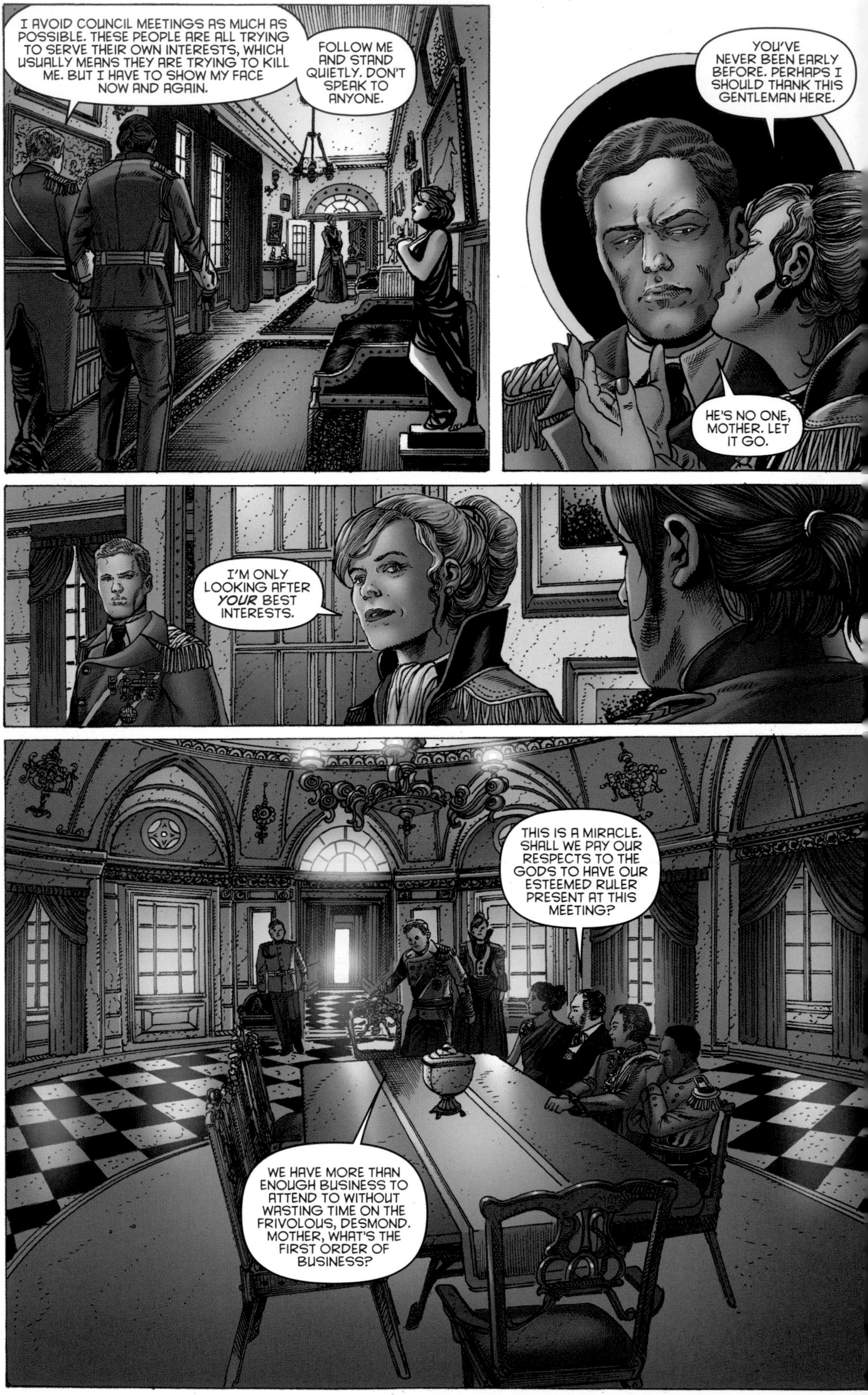
I AVOID COUNCIL MEETINGS AS MUCH AS POSSIBLE. THESE PEOPLE ARE ALL TRYING TO SERVE THEIR OWN INTERESTS, WHICH USUALLY MEANS THEY ARE TRYING TO KILL ME. BUT I HAVE TO SHOW MY FACE NOW AND AGAIN.
FOLLOW ME AND STAND QUIETLY. DON'T SPEAK TO ANYONE.
YOU'VE NEVER BEEN EARLY BEFORE. PERHAPS I SHOULD THANK THIS GENTLEMAN HERE.
HE'S NO ONE, MOTHER. LET IT GO.
I'M ONLY LOOKING AFTER *YOUR* BEST INTERESTS.
THIS IS A MIRACLE. SHALL WE PAY OUR RESPECTS TO THE GODS TO HAVE OUR ESTEEMED RULER PRESENT AT THIS MEETING?
WE HAVE MORE THAN ENOUGH BUSINESS TO ATTEND TO WITHOUT WASTING TIME ON THE FRIVOLOUS, DESMOND. MOTHER, WHAT'S THE FIRST ORDER OF BUSINESS?

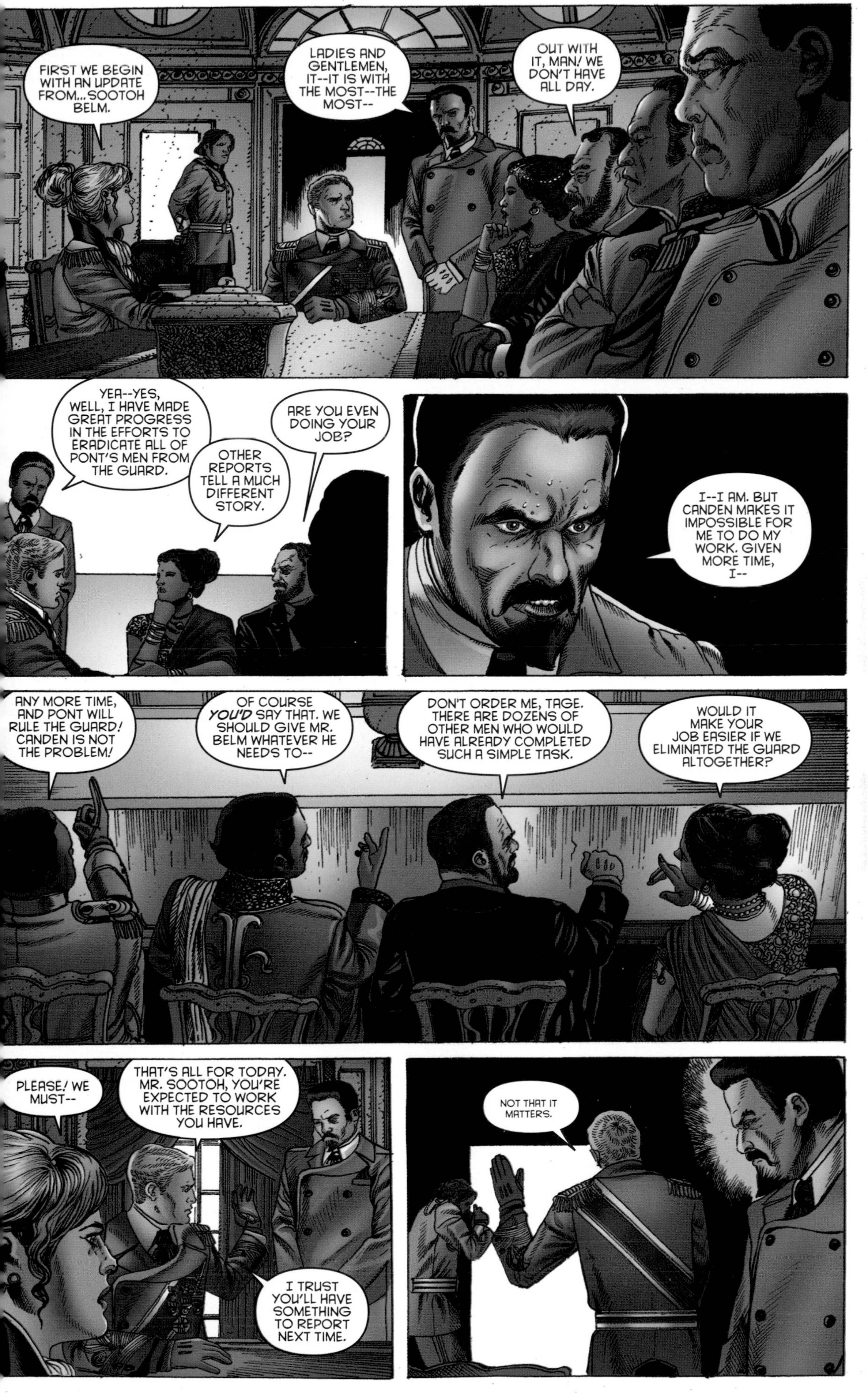
FIRST WE BEGIN WITH AN UPDATE FROM...SOOTOH BELM.
LADIES AND GENTLEMEN, IT--IT IS WITH THE MOST--THE MOST--
OUT WITH IT, MAN! WE DON'T HAVE ALL DAY.
YEA--YES, WELL, I HAVE MADE GREAT PROGRESS IN THE EFFORTS TO ERADICATE ALL OF PONT'S MEN FROM THE GUARD.
OTHER REPORTS TELL A MUCH DIFFERENT STORY.
ARE YOU EVEN DOING YOUR JOB?
I--I AM. BUT CANDEN MAKES IT IMPOSSIBLE FOR ME TO DO MY WORK. GIVEN MORE TIME, I--
ANY MORE TIME, AND PONT WILL RULE THE GUARD! CANDEN IS NOT THE PROBLEM!
OF COURSE YOU'D SAY THAT. WE SHOULD GIVE MR. BELM WHATEVER HE NEEDS TO--
DON'T ORDER ME, TAGE. THERE ARE DOZENS OF OTHER MEN WHO WOULD HAVE ALREADY COMPLETED SUCH A SIMPLE TASK.
WOULD IT MAKE YOUR JOB EASIER IF WE ELIMINATED THE GUARD ALTOGETHER?
PLEASE! WE MUST--
THAT'S ALL FOR TODAY. MR. SOOTOH, YOU'RE EXPECTED TO WORK WITH THE RESOURCES YOU HAVE.
I TRUST YOU'LL HAVE SOMETHING TO REPORT NEXT TIME.
NOT THAT IT MATTERS.

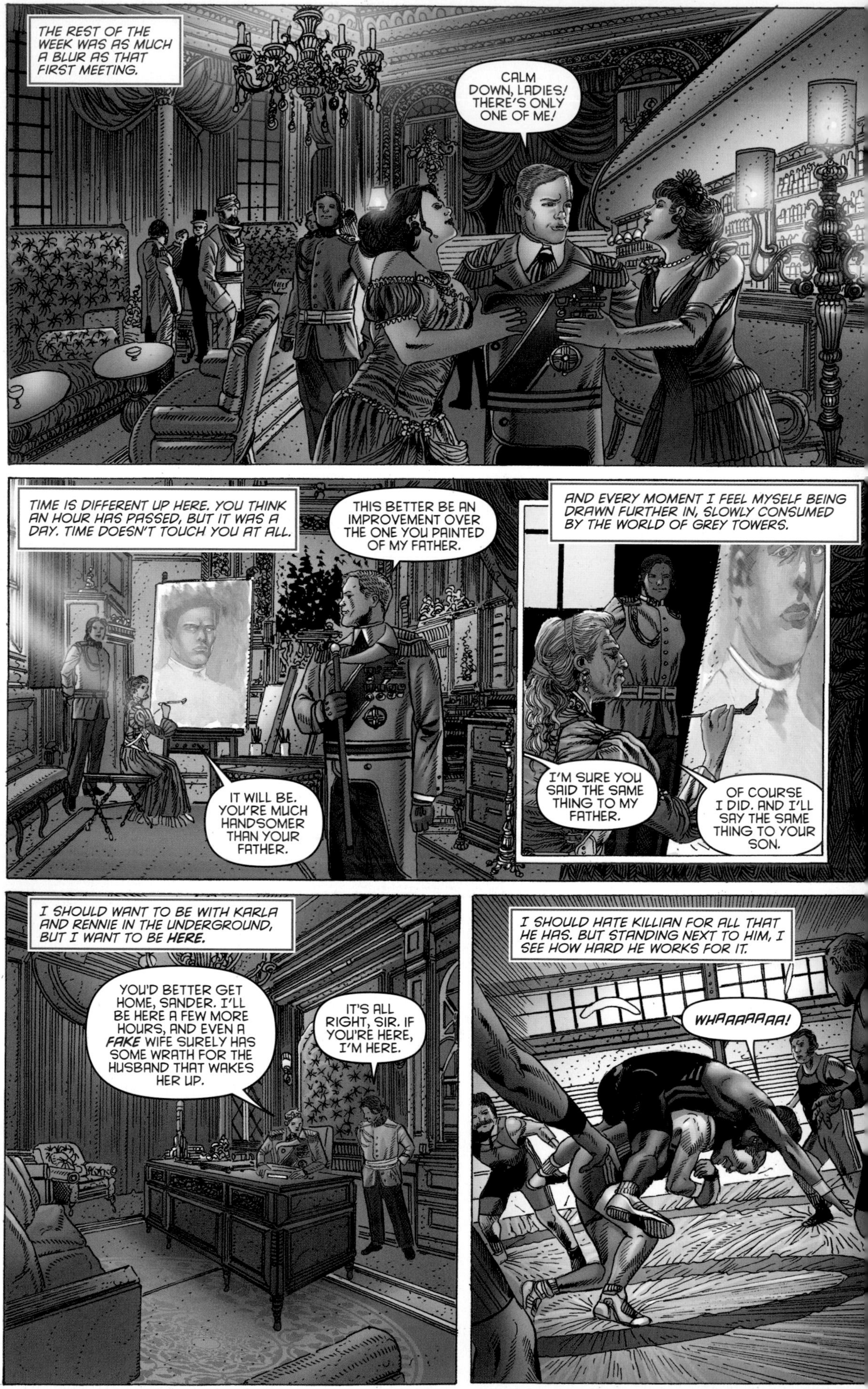

THE REST OF THE WEEK WAS AS MUCH A BLUR AS THAT FIRST MEETING.
CALM DOWN, LADIES! THERE'S ONLY ONE OF ME!
TIME IS DIFFERENT UP HERE. YOU THINK AN HOUR HAS PASSED, BUT IT WAS A DAY. TIME DOESN'T TOUCH YOU AT ALL.
THIS BETTER BE AN IMPROVEMENT OVER THE ONE YOU PAINTED OF MY FATHER.
IT WILL BE. YOU'RE MUCH HANDSOMER THAN YOUR FATHER.
AND EVERY MOMENT I FEEL MYSELF BEING DRAWN FURTHER IN, SLOWLY CONSUMED BY THE WORLD OF GREY TOWERS.
I'M SURE YOU SAID THE SAME THING TO MY FATHER.
OF COURSE I DID. AND I'LL SAY THE SAME THING TO YOUR SON.
I SHOULD WANT TO BE WITH KARLA AND RENNIE IN THE UNDERGROUND, BUT I WANT TO BE HERE.
YOU'D BETTER GET HOME, SANDER. I'LL BE HERE A FEW MORE HOURS, AND EVEN A FAKE WIFE SURELY HAS SOME WRATH FOR THE HUSBAND THAT WAKES HER UP.
IT'S ALL RIGHT, SIR. IF YOU'RE HERE, I'M HERE.
I SHOULD HATE KILLIAN FOR ALL THAT HE HAS. BUT STANDING NEXT TO HIM, I SEE HOW HARD HE WORKS FOR IT.
WHAAAAAAA!

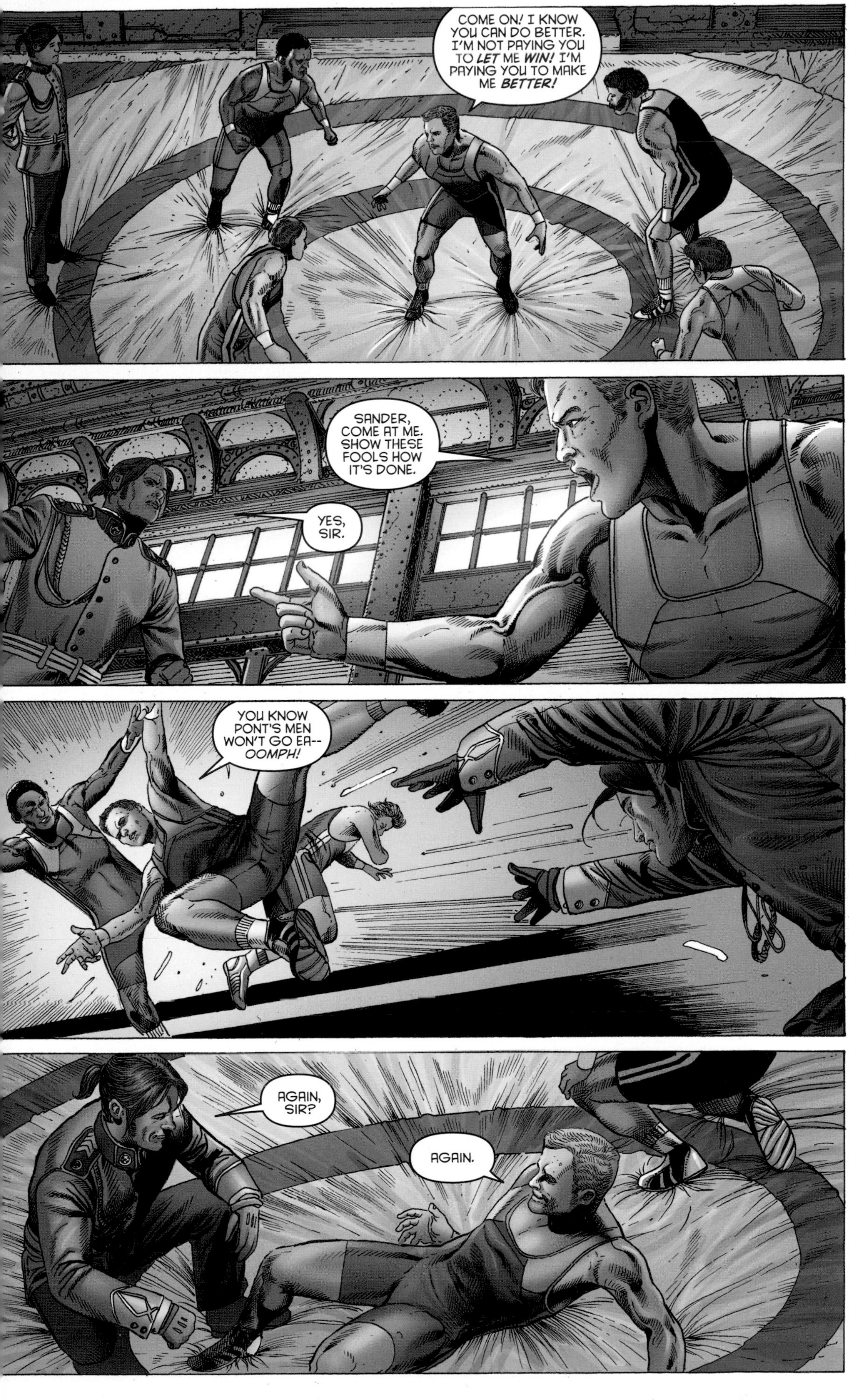
COME ON! I KNOW YOU CAN DO BETTER. I'M NOT PAYING YOU TO LET ME WIN! I'M PAYING YOU TO MAKE ME BETTER!
SANDER, COME AT ME. SHOW THESE FOOLS HOW IT'S DONE.
YES, SIR.
YOU KNOW PONT'S MEN WON'T GO EA-- OOMPH!
AGAIN, SIR?
AGAIN.

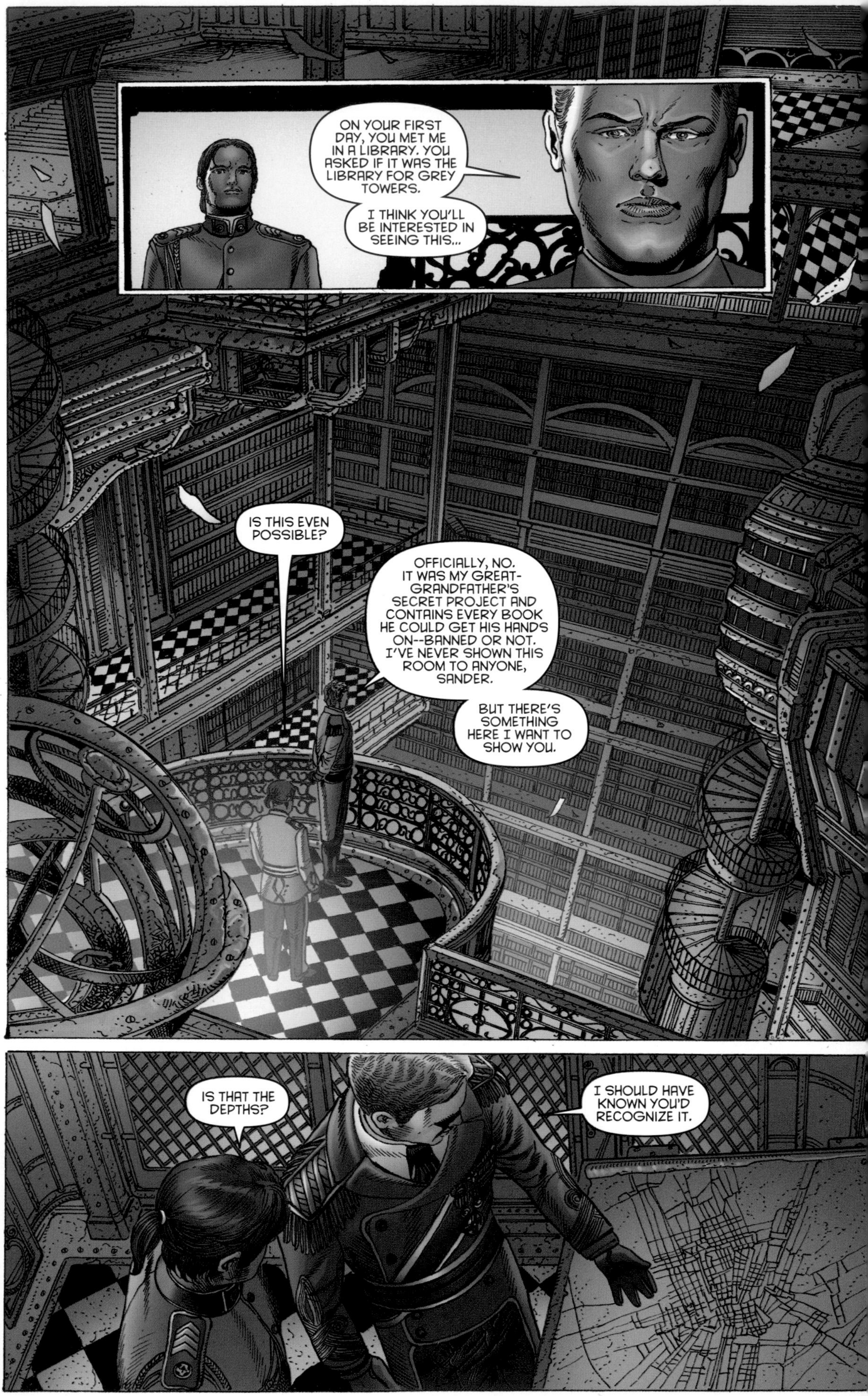
ON YOUR FIRST DAY, YOU MET ME IN A LIBRARY. YOU ASKED IF IT WAS THE LIBRARY FOR GREY TOWERS.
I THINK YOU'LL BE INTERESTED IN SEEING THIS...
IS THIS EVEN POSSIBLE?
OFFICIALLY, NO. IT WAS MY GREAT-GRANDFATHER'S SECRET PROJECT AND CONTAINS EVERY BOOK HE COULD GET HIS HANDS ON--BANNED OR NOT. I'VE NEVER SHOWN THIS ROOM TO ANYONE, SANDER.
BUT THERE'S SOMETHING HERE I WANT TO SHOW YOU.
IS THAT THE DEPTHS?
I SHOULD HAVE KNOWN YOU'D RECOGNIZE IT.

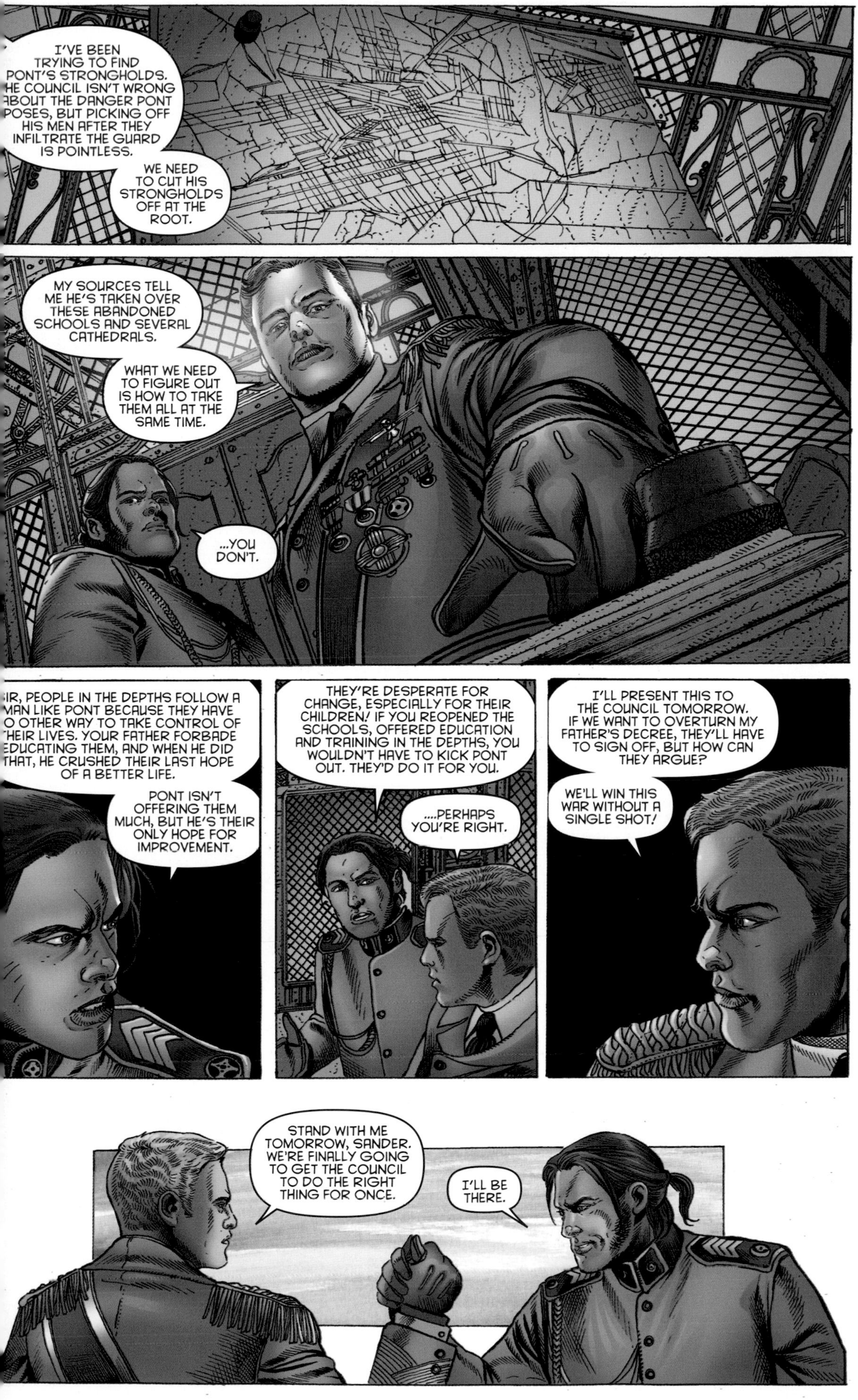
I'VE BEEN TRYING TO FIND PONT'S STRONGHOLDS. HE COUNCIL ISN'T WRONG ABOUT THE DANGER PONT POSES, BUT PICKING OFF HIS MEN AFTER THEY INFILTRATE THE GUARD IS POINTLESS.
WE NEED TO CUT HIS STRONGHOLDS OFF AT THE ROOT.
MY SOURCES TELL ME HE'S TAKEN OVER THESE ABANDONED SCHOOLS AND SEVERAL CATHEDRALS.
WHAT WE NEED TO FIGURE OUT IS HOW TO TAKE THEM ALL AT THE SAME TIME.
...YOU DON'T.
IR, PEOPLE IN THE DEPTHS FOLLOW A MAN LIKE PONT BECAUSE THEY HAVE O OTHER WAY TO TAKE CONTROL OF HEIR LIVES. YOUR FATHER FORBADE EDUCATING THEM, AND WHEN HE DID THAT, HE CRUSHED THEIR LAST HOPE OF A BETTER LIFE.
PONT ISN'T OFFERING THEM MUCH, BUT HE'S THEIR ONLY HOPE FOR IMPROVEMENT.
THEY'RE DESPERATE FOR CHANGE, ESPECIALLY FOR THEIR CHILDREN! IF YOU REOPENED THE SCHOOLS, OFFERED EDUCATION AND TRAINING IN THE DEPTHS, YOU WOULDN'T HAVE TO KICK PONT OUT. THEY'D DO IT FOR YOU.
....PERHAPS YOU'RE RIGHT.
I'LL PRESENT THIS TO THE COUNCIL TOMORROW. IF WE WANT TO OVERTURN MY FATHER'S DECREE, THEY'LL HAVE TO SIGN OFF, BUT HOW CAN THEY ARGUE?
WE'LL WIN THIS WAR WITHOUT A SINGLE SHOT!
STAND WITH ME TOMORROW, SANDER. WE'RE FINALLY GOING TO GET THE COUNCIL TO DO THE RIGHT THING FOR ONCE.
I'LL BE THERE.

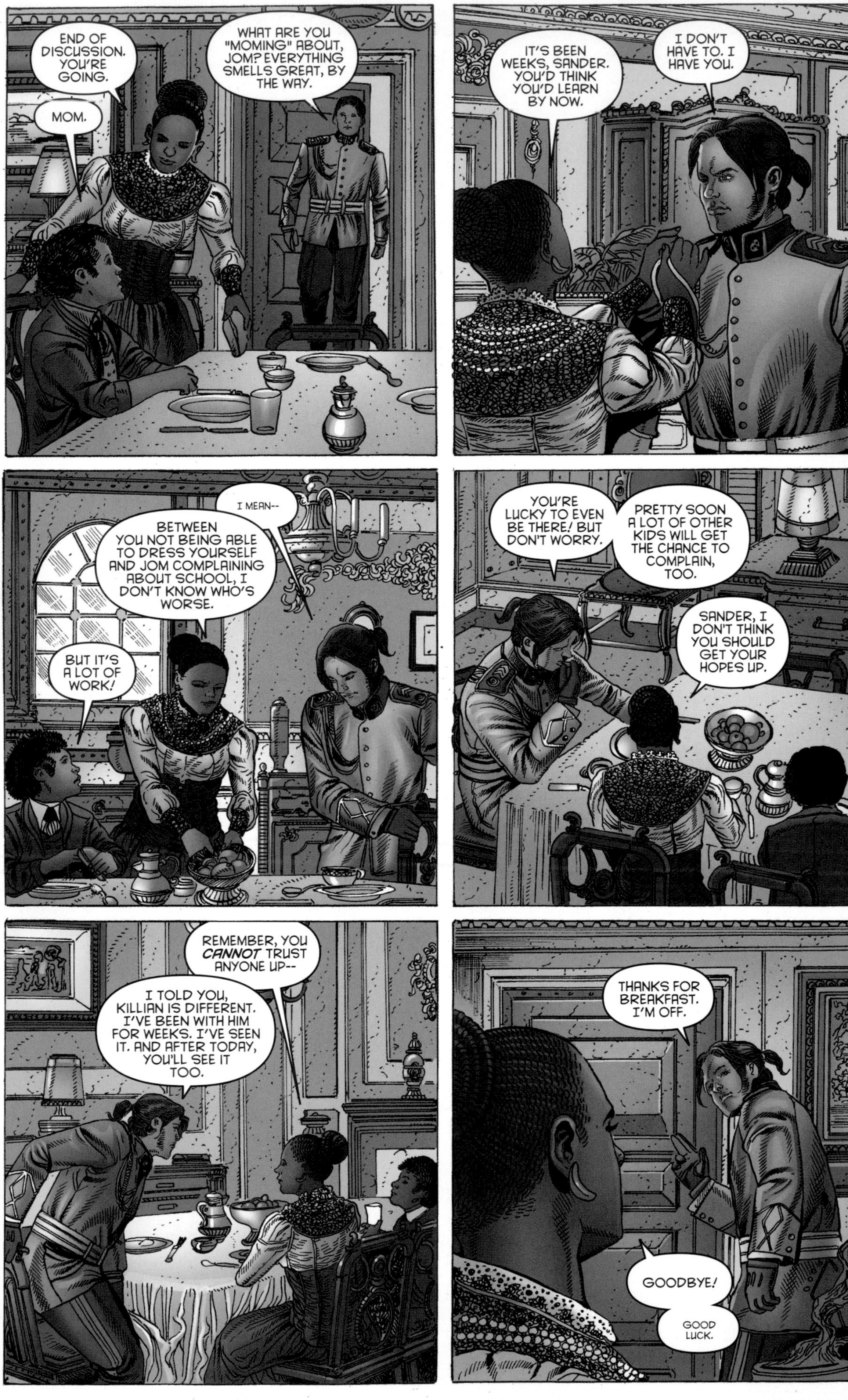
END OF DISCUSSION. YOU'RE GOING.
MOM.
WHAT ARE YOU "MOMING" ABOUT, JOM? EVERYTHING SMELLS GREAT, BY THE WAY.
IT'S BEEN WEEKS, SANDER. YOU'D THINK YOU'D LEARN BY NOW.
I DON'T HAVE TO. I HAVE YOU.
BETWEEN YOU NOT BEING ABLE TO DRESS YOURSELF AND JOM COMPLAINING ABOUT SCHOOL, I DON'T KNOW WHO'S WORSE.
I MEAN--
BUT IT'S A LOT OF WORK!
YOU'RE LUCKY TO EVEN BE THERE! BUT DON'T WORRY.
PRETTY SOON A LOT OF OTHER KIDS WILL GET THE CHANCE TO COMPLAIN, TOO.
SANDER, I DON'T THINK YOU SHOULD GET YOUR HOPES UP.
REMEMBER, YOU *CANNOT* TRUST ANYONE UP--
I TOLD YOU, KILLIAN IS DIFFERENT. I'VE BEEN WITH HIM FOR WEEKS. I'VE SEEN IT. AND AFTER TODAY, YOU'LL SEE IT TOO.
THANKS FOR BREAKFAST. I'M OFF.
GOODBYE!
GOOD LUCK.

LAST MEETING, WE LISTENED TO SOOTOH DISCUSS THE PROBLEMS WITH PONT'S MEN INFILTRATING THE GUARD. THAT'S NOT THE PROBLEM. WE NEED TO CONCENTRATE OUR EFFORTS ON ELIMINATING ANYONE'S *DESIRE* TO OVERTHROW THE GUARD, AND *US*.

I WASN'T AWARE THAT YOU WERE INTERESTED IN OUR AFFAIRS, LET ALONE OUR PRESERVATION. CAN I ASSUME YOU ALSO HAVE A SOLUTION TO THIS PROBLEM THAT PLAGUES *US*?

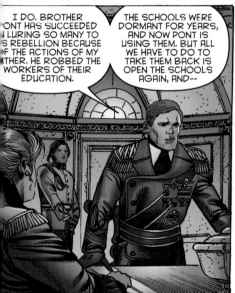

I DO. BROTHER PONT HAS SUCCEEDED IN LURING SO MANY TO HIS REBELLION BECAUSE OF THE ACTIONS OF MY FATHER. HE ROBBED THE WORKERS OF THEIR EDUCATION.

THE SCHOOLS WERE DORMANT FOR YEARS, AND NOW PONT IS USING THEM. BUT ALL WE HAVE TO DO TO TAKE THEM BACK IS OPEN THE SCHOOLS AGAIN, AND--

WHAT? THESE PEOPLE CAN'T LEAD THEMSELVES!

DO YOU REALIZE WHAT YOU'RE SAYING? AN EDUCATED POPULACE IS MORE DANGEROUS THAN BROTHER PONT AND THE NO-SIDE ARMY COMBINED!

THEY'D SELF-DESTRUCT IN A YEAR AND TAKE LANTERN CITY WITH THEM!

IF WE CONTINUE ON THIS SAME PATH, THERE WON'T *BE* A LANTERN CITY.

PERHAPS THERE WON'T BE A CITY FOR *YOU* TO RULE, BUT LANTERN CITY IS AS STRONG AS IT'S EVER BEEN.

PERHAPS THIS IS A CONVERSATION BEST SERVED BY CAREFUL THOUGHT. LET'S TURN TO A MATTER WHERE ALL OUR INTERESTS ALIGN.

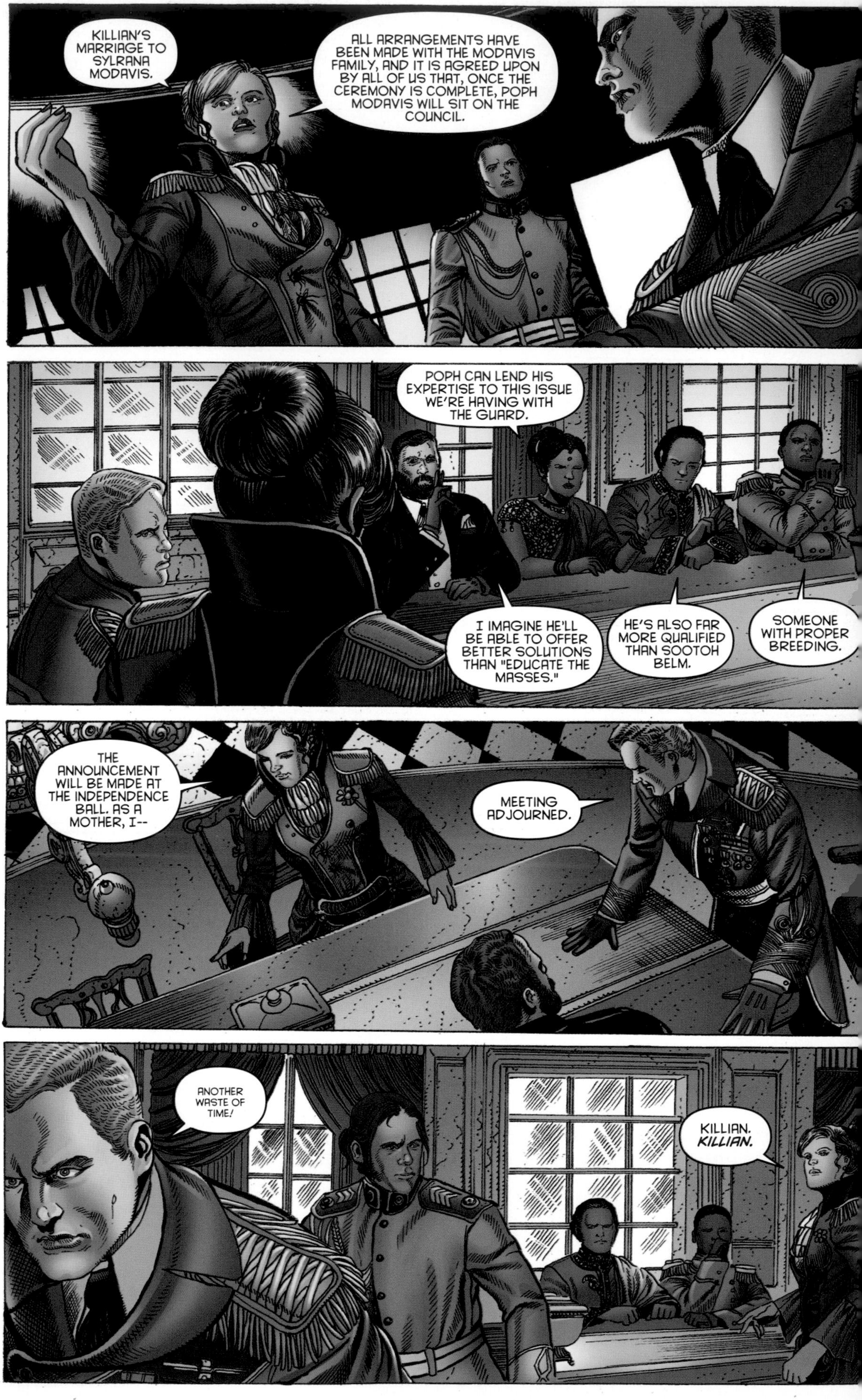
KILLIAN'S MARRIAGE TO SYLRANA MODAVIS.
ALL ARRANGEMENTS HAVE BEEN MADE WITH THE MODAVIS FAMILY, AND IT IS AGREED UPON BY ALL OF US THAT, ONCE THE CEREMONY IS COMPLETE, POPH MODAVIS WILL SIT ON THE COUNCIL.
POPH CAN LEND HIS EXPERTISE TO THIS ISSUE WE'RE HAVING WITH THE GUARD.
I IMAGINE HE'LL BE ABLE TO OFFER BETTER SOLUTIONS THAN "EDUCATE THE MASSES."
HE'S ALSO FAR MORE QUALIFIED THAN SOOTOH BELM.
SOMEONE WITH PROPER BREEDING.
THE ANNOUNCEMENT WILL BE MADE AT THE INDEPENDENCE BALL. AS A MOTHER, I--
MEETING ADJOURNED.
ANOTHER WASTE OF TIME!
KILLIAN. *KILLIAN.*

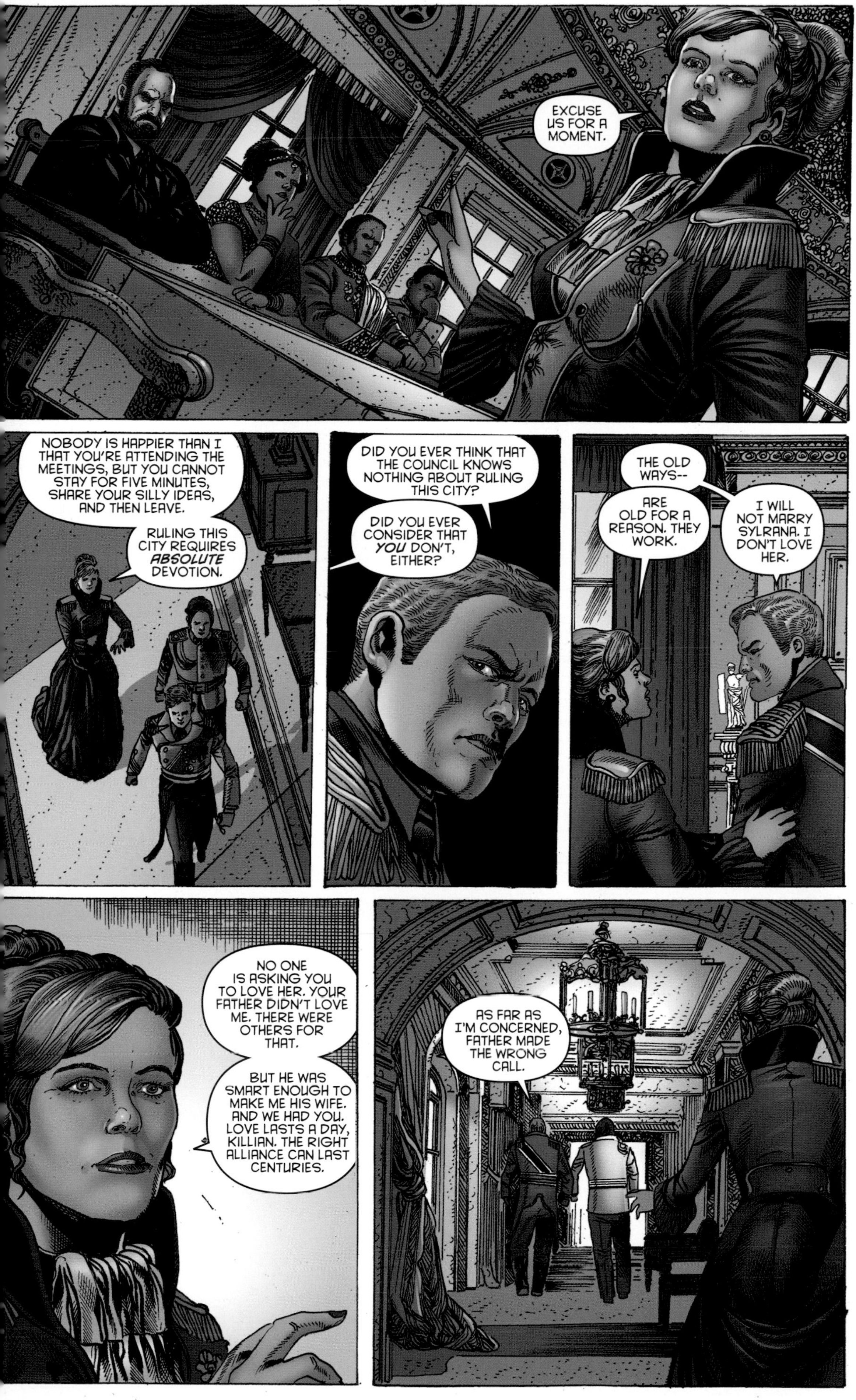
EXCUSE US FOR A MOMENT.
NOBODY IS HAPPIER THAN I THAT YOU'RE ATTENDING THE MEETINGS, BUT YOU CANNOT STAY FOR FIVE MINUTES, SHARE YOUR SILLY IDEAS, AND THEN LEAVE.
RULING THIS CITY REQUIRES *ABSOLUTE* DEVOTION.
DID YOU EVER THINK THAT THE COUNCIL KNOWS NOTHING ABOUT RULING THIS CITY?
DID YOU EVER CONSIDER THAT *YOU* DON'T, EITHER?
THE OLD WAYS--
ARE OLD FOR A REASON. THEY WORK.
I WILL NOT MARRY SYLRANA. I DON'T LOVE HER.
NO ONE IS ASKING YOU TO LOVE HER. YOUR FATHER DIDN'T LOVE ME. THERE WERE OTHERS FOR THAT.
BUT HE WAS SMART ENOUGH TO MAKE ME HIS WIFE. AND WE HAD YOU. LOVE LASTS A DAY, KILLIAN. THE RIGHT ALLIANCE CAN LAST CENTURIES.
AS FAR AS I'M CONCERNED, FATHER MADE THE WRONG CALL.

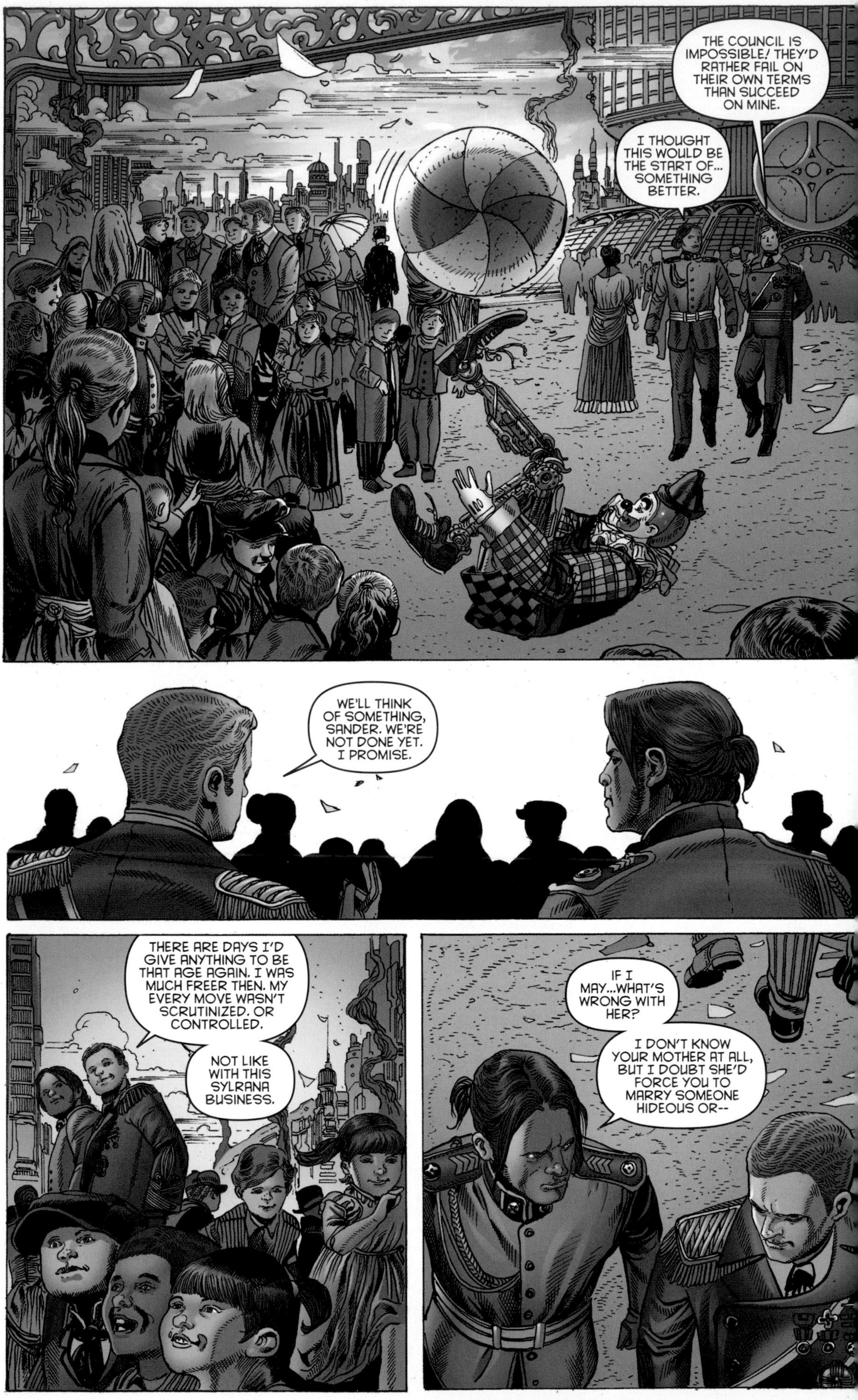
THE COUNCIL IS IMPOSSIBLE! THEY'D RATHER FAIL ON THEIR OWN TERMS THAN SUCCEED ON MINE.
I THOUGHT THIS WOULD BE THE START OF... SOMETHING BETTER.
WE'LL THINK OF SOMETHING, SANDER. WE'RE NOT DONE YET. I PROMISE.
THERE ARE DAYS I'D GIVE ANYTHING TO BE THAT AGE AGAIN. I WAS MUCH FREER THEN. MY EVERY MOVE WASN'T SCRUTINIZED. OR CONTROLLED.
NOT LIKE WITH THIS SYLRANA BUSINESS.
IF I MAY...WHAT'S WRONG WITH HER?
I DON'T KNOW YOUR MOTHER AT ALL, BUT I DOUBT SHE'D FORCE YOU TO MARRY SOMEONE HIDEOUS OR--

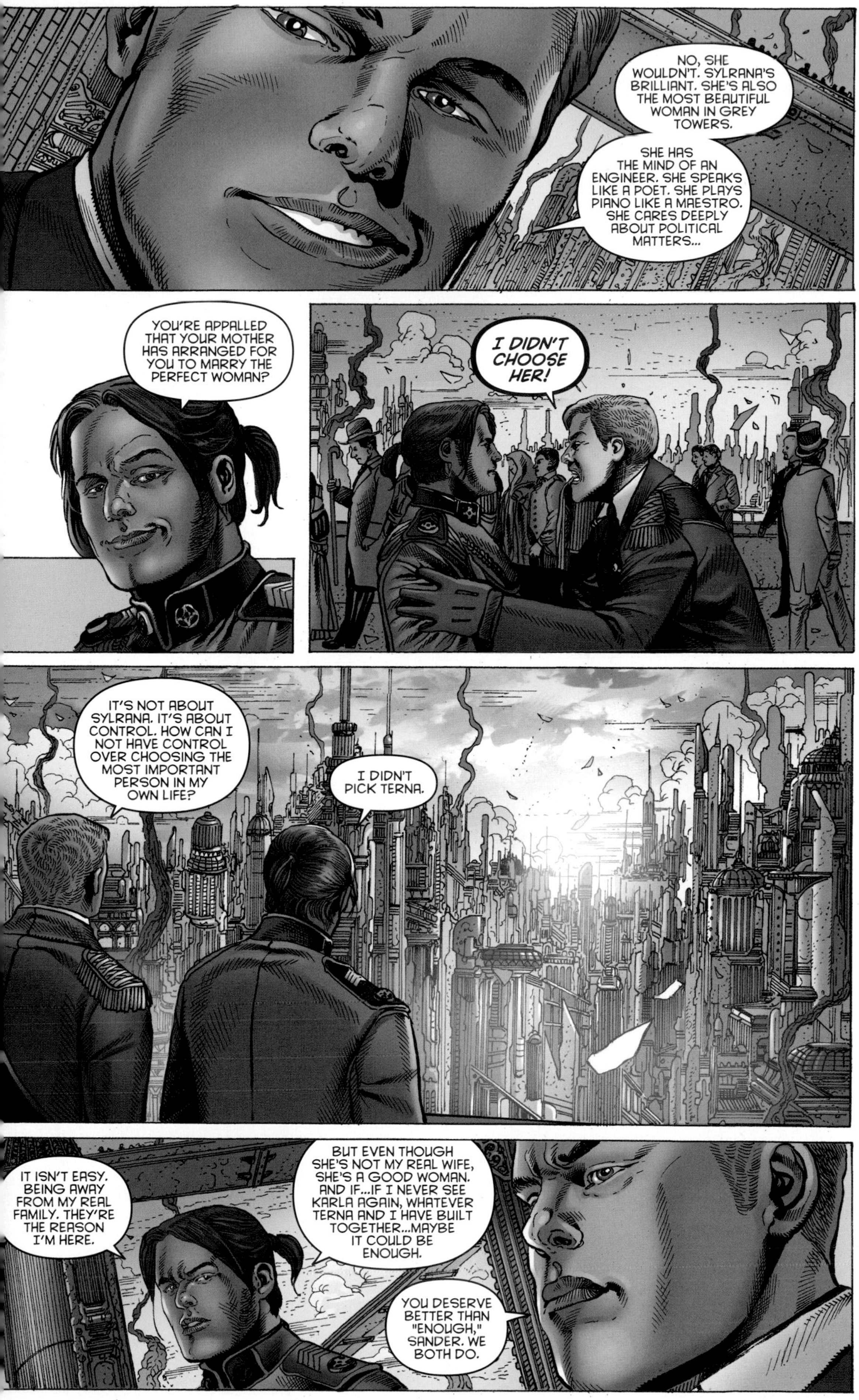
NO, SHE WOULDN'T. SYLRANA'S BRILLIANT. SHE'S ALSO THE MOST BEAUTIFUL WOMAN IN GREY TOWERS.
SHE HAS THE MIND OF AN ENGINEER. SHE SPEAKS LIKE A POET. SHE PLAYS PIANO LIKE A MAESTRO. SHE CARES DEEPLY ABOUT POLITICAL MATTERS...
YOU'RE APPALLED THAT YOUR MOTHER HAS ARRANGED FOR YOU TO MARRY THE PERFECT WOMAN?
I DIDN'T CHOOSE HER!
IT'S NOT ABOUT SYLRANA. IT'S ABOUT CONTROL. HOW CAN I NOT HAVE CONTROL OVER CHOOSING THE MOST IMPORTANT PERSON IN MY OWN LIFE?
I DIDN'T PICK TERNA.
IT ISN'T EASY. BEING AWAY FROM MY REAL FAMILY. THEY'RE THE REASON I'M HERE.
BUT EVEN THOUGH SHE'S NOT MY REAL WIFE, SHE'S A GOOD WOMAN. AND IF...IF I NEVER SEE KARLA AGAIN, WHATEVER TERNA AND I HAVE BUILT TOGETHER...MAYBE IT COULD BE ENOUGH.
YOU DESERVE BETTER THAN "ENOUGH," SANDER. WE BOTH DO.

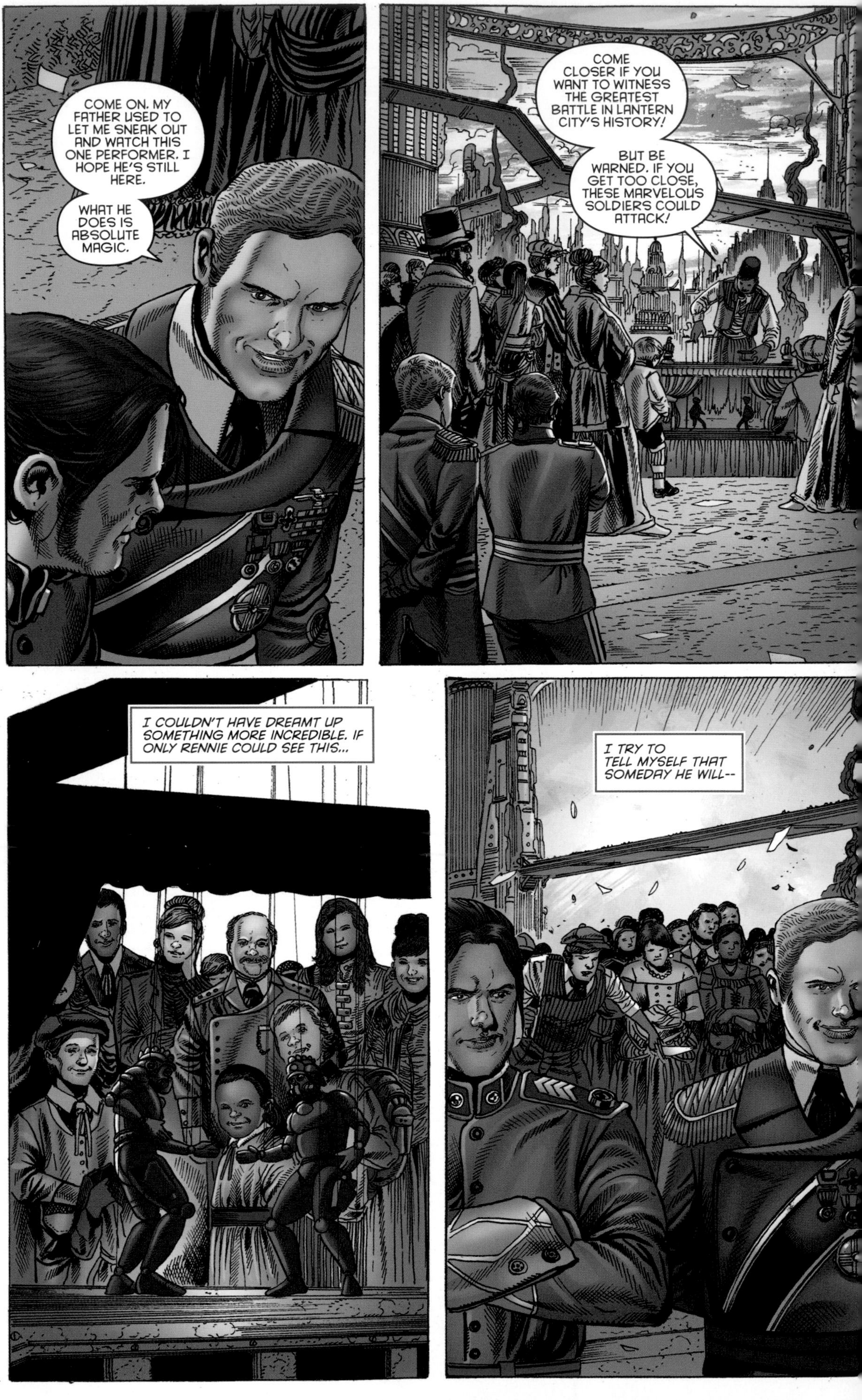
COME ON. MY FATHER USED TO LET ME SNEAK OUT AND WATCH THIS ONE PERFORMER. I HOPE HE'S STILL HERE.
WHAT HE DOES IS ABSOLUTE MAGIC.
COME CLOSER IF YOU WANT TO WITNESS THE GREATEST BATTLE IN LANTERN CITY'S HISTORY!
BUT BE WARNED. IF YOU GET TOO CLOSE, THESE MARVELOUS SOLDIERS COULD ATTACK!
I COULDN'T HAVE DREAMT UP SOMETHING MORE INCREDIBLE. IF ONLY RENNIE COULD SEE THIS...
I TRY TO TELL MYSELF THAT SOMEDAY HE WILL--

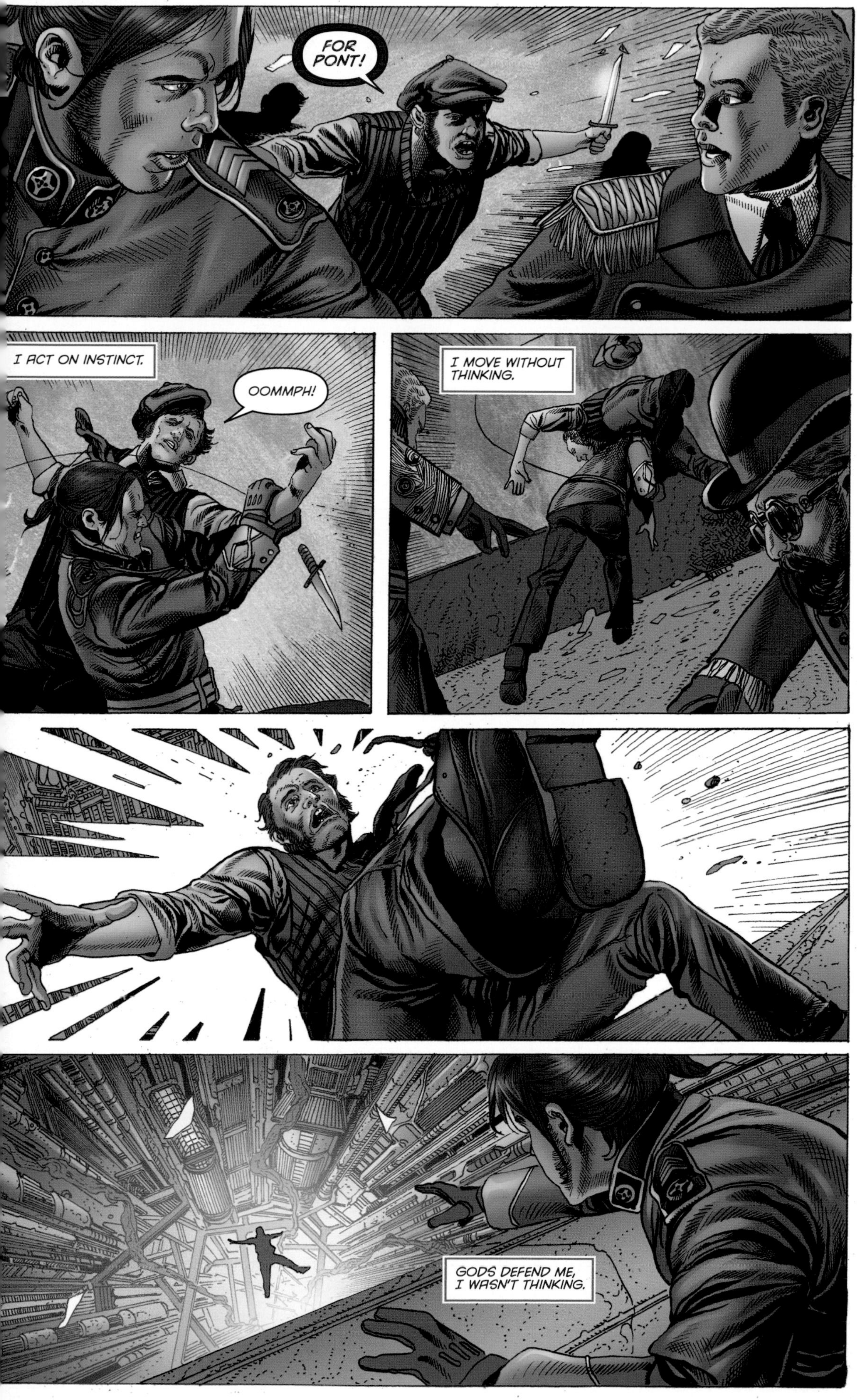
FOR PONT!
I ACT ON INSTINCT.
OOMMPH!
I MOVE WITHOUT THINKING.
GODS DEFEND ME, I WASN'T THINKING.

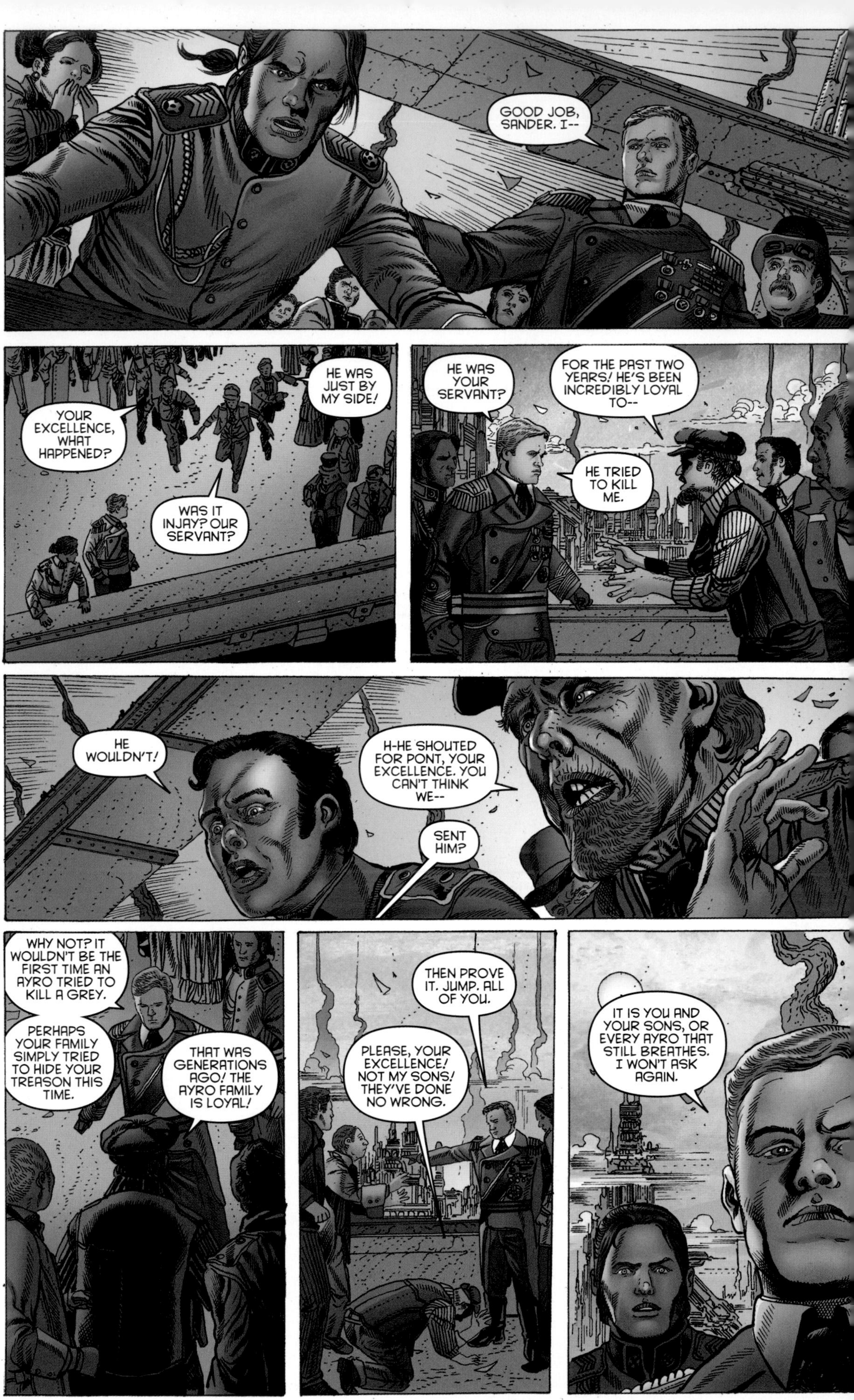
GOOD JOB, SANDER. I--
YOUR EXCELLENCE, WHAT HAPPENED?
HE WAS JUST BY MY SIDE!
WAS IT INJAY? OUR SERVANT?
HE WAS YOUR SERVANT?
FOR THE PAST TWO YEARS! HE'S BEEN INCREDIBLY LOYAL TO--
HE TRIED TO KILL ME.
HE WOULDN'T!
H-HE SHOUTED FOR PONT, YOUR EXCELLENCE. YOU CAN'T THINK WE--
SENT HIM?
WHY NOT? IT WOULDN'T BE THE FIRST TIME AN AYRO TRIED TO KILL A GREY.
PERHAPS YOUR FAMILY SIMPLY TRIED TO HIDE YOUR TREASON THIS TIME.
THAT WAS GENERATIONS AGO! THE AYRO FAMILY IS LOYAL!
THEN PROVE IT. JUMP. ALL OF YOU.
PLEASE, YOUR EXCELLENCE! NOT MY SONS! THEY'VE DONE NO WRONG.
IT IS YOU AND YOUR SONS, OR EVERY AYRO THAT STILL BREATHES. I WON'T ASK AGAIN.

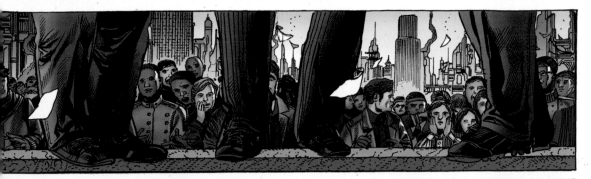

I THINK IT'S TIME WE--

--WHAT IS THAT LOOK FOR?

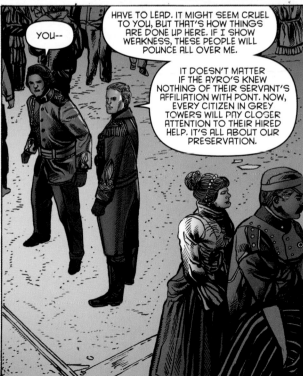

YOU--

HAVE TO LEAD. IT MIGHT SEEM CRUEL TO YOU, BUT THAT'S HOW THINGS ARE DONE UP HERE. IF I SHOW WEAKNESS, THESE PEOPLE WILL POUNCE ALL OVER ME.

IT DOESN'T MATTER IF THE AYRO'S KNEW NOTHING OF THEIR SERVANT'S AFFILIATION WITH PONT. NOW, EVERY CITIZEN IN GREY TOWERS WILL PAY CLOSER ATTENTION TO THEIR HIRED HELP. IT'S ALL ABOUT OUR PRESERVATION.

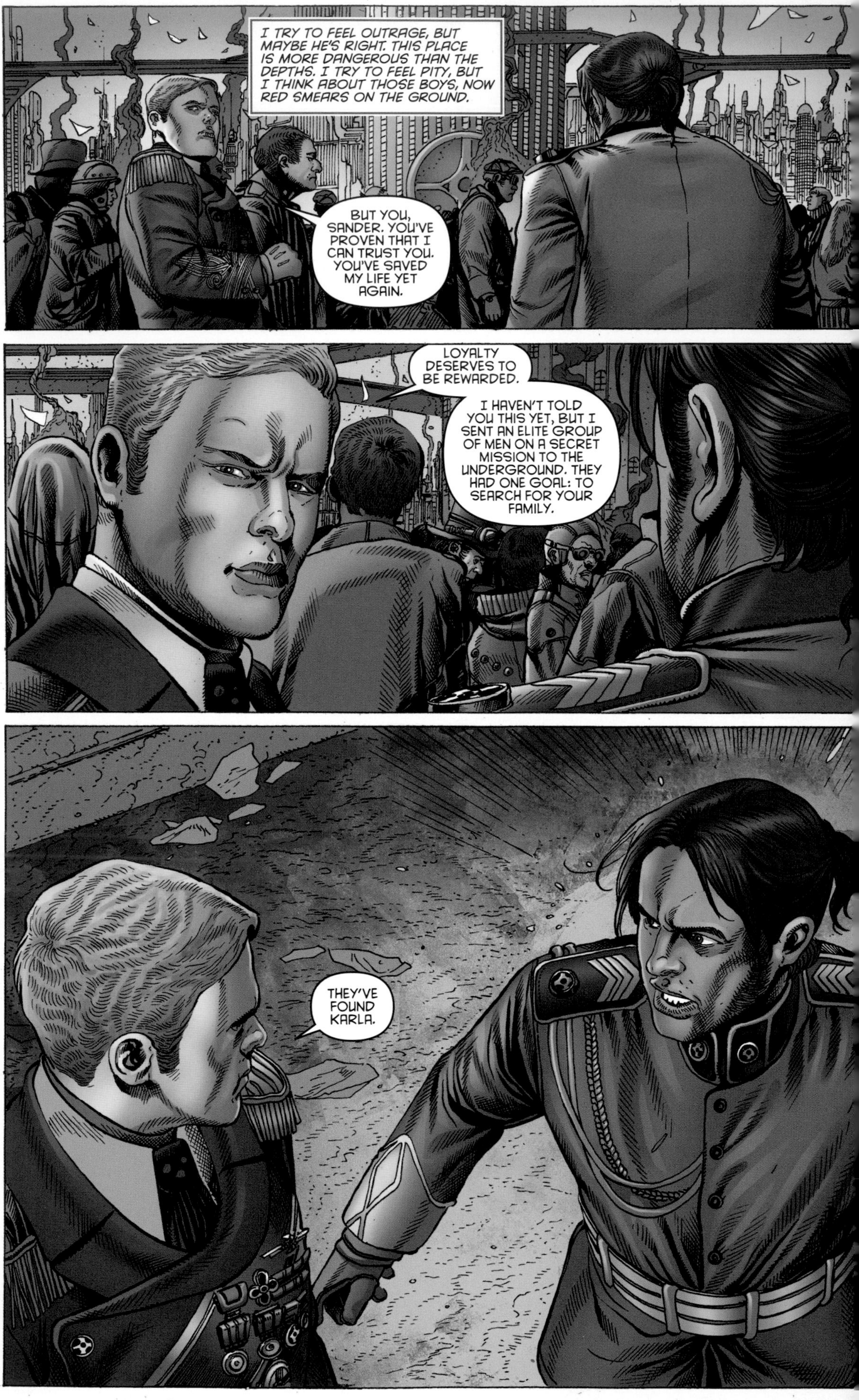
I TRY TO FEEL OUTRAGE, BUT MAYBE HE'S RIGHT. THIS PLACE IS MORE DANGEROUS THAN THE DEPTHS. I TRY TO FEEL PITY, BUT I THINK ABOUT THOSE BOYS, NOW RED SMEARS ON THE GROUND.
BUT YOU, SANDER. YOU'VE PROVEN THAT I CAN TRUST YOU. YOU'VE SAVED MY LIFE YET AGAIN.
LOYALTY DESERVES TO BE REWARDED.
I HAVEN'T TOLD YOU THIS YET, BUT I SENT AN ELITE GROUP OF MEN ON A SECRET MISSION TO THE UNDERGROUND. THEY HAD ONE GOAL: TO SEARCH FOR YOUR FAMILY.
THEY'VE FOUND KARLA.

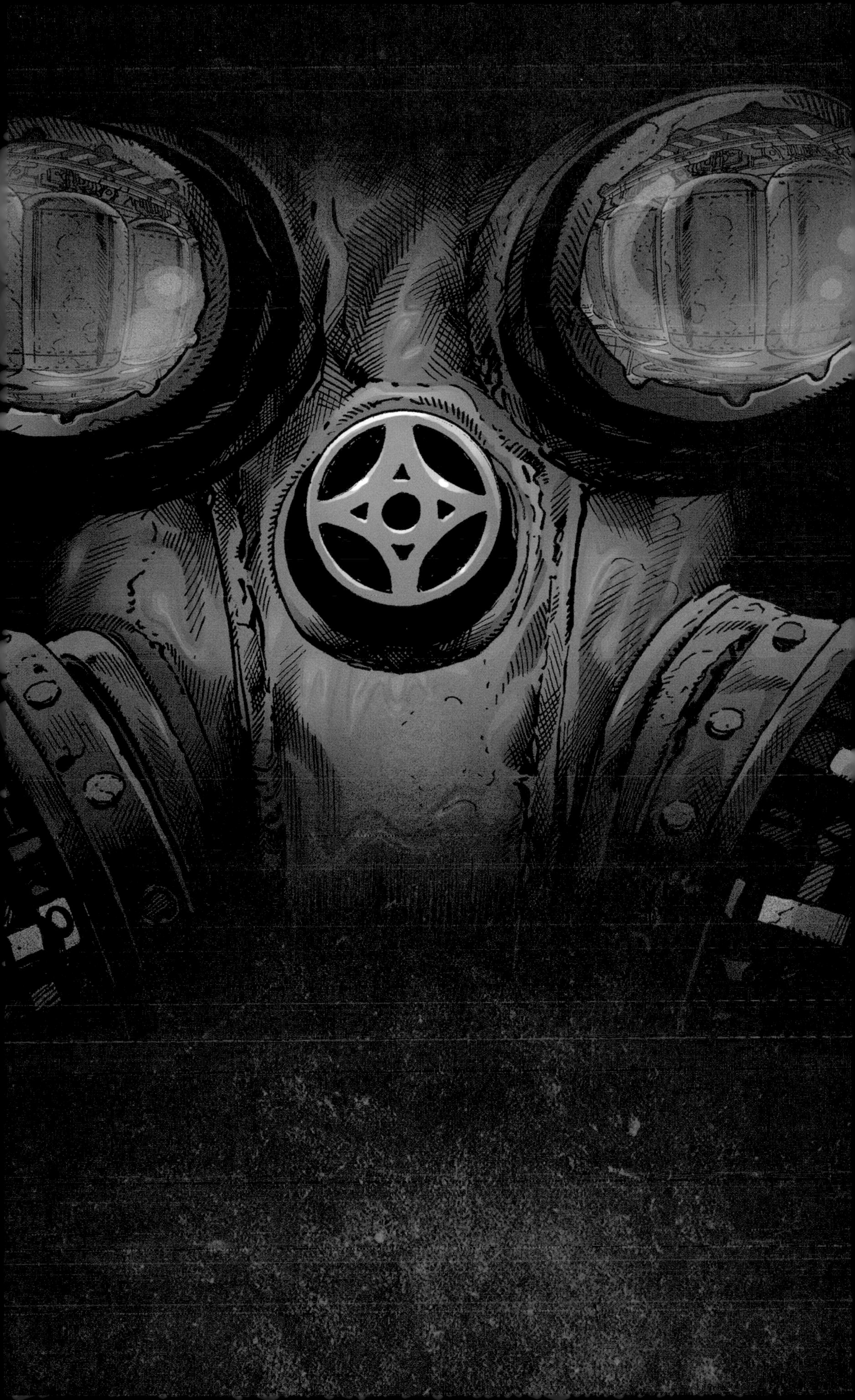

CHAPTER SEVEN

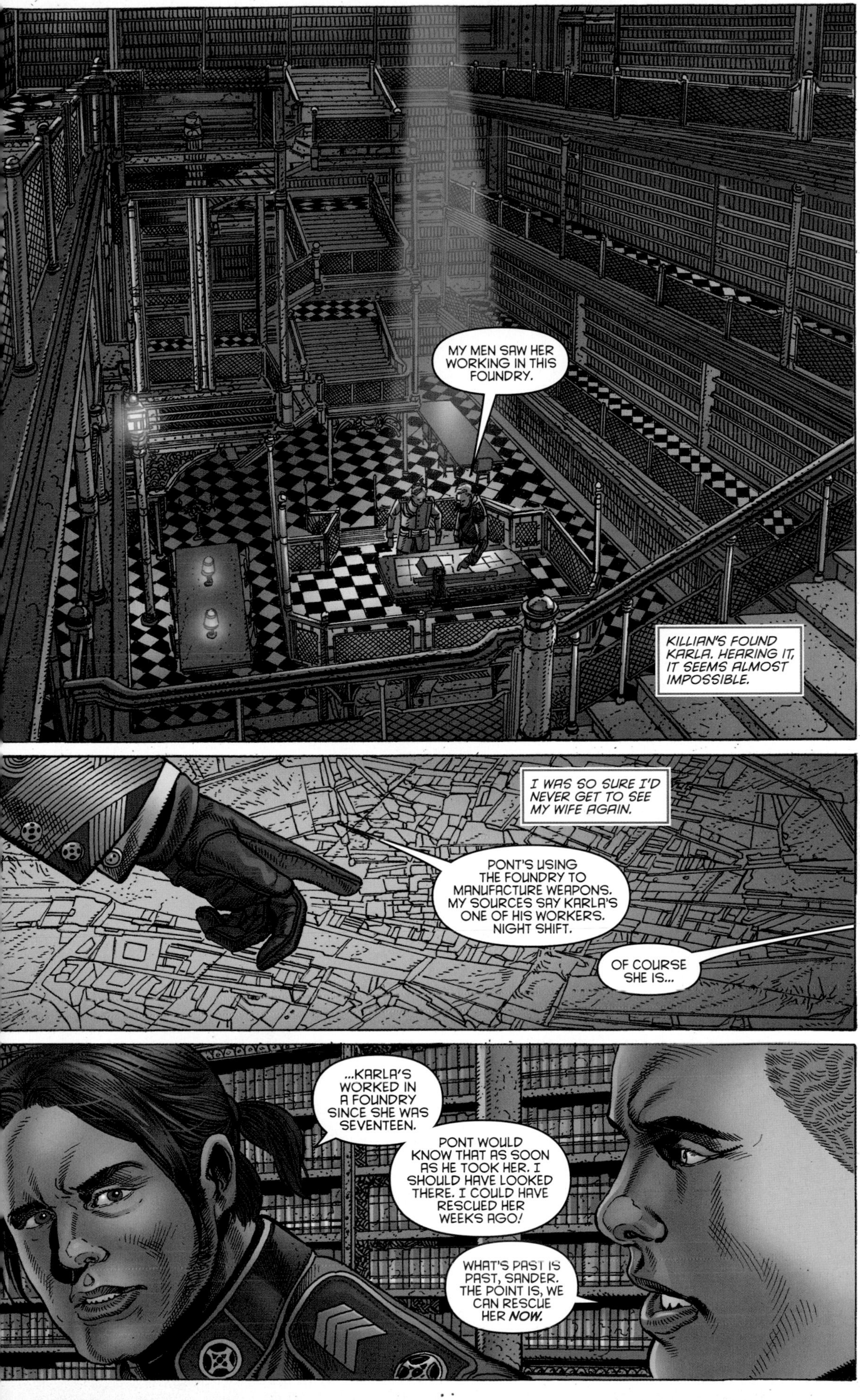
MY MEN SAW HER WORKING IN THIS FOUNDRY.
KILLIAN'S FOUND KARLA. HEARING IT, IT SEEMS ALMOST IMPOSSIBLE.
I WAS SO SURE I'D NEVER GET TO SEE MY WIFE AGAIN.
PONT'S USING THE FOUNDRY TO MANUFACTURE WEAPONS. MY SOURCES SAY KARLA'S ONE OF HIS WORKERS. NIGHT SHIFT.
OF COURSE SHE IS...
...KARLA'S WORKED IN A FOUNDRY SINCE SHE WAS SEVENTEEN.
PONT WOULD KNOW THAT AS SOON AS HE TOOK HER. I SHOULD HAVE LOOKED THERE. I COULD HAVE RESCUED HER WEEKS AGO!
WHAT'S PAST IS PAST, SANDER. THE POINT IS, WE CAN RESCUE HER *NOW.*

I'VE BEEN SO CAUGHT UP IN EVERYTHING--THIS JOB, TERNA AND JOM, LIVING IN GREY TOWERS--I DID THIS FOR *KARLA AND RENNIE,* AND THEY'RE SUFFERING WHILE I'M UP HERE.

SANDER--

--YOU DID THIS TO MAKE A DIFFERENCE, AND YOU *HAVE.* YOU SAVED MY LIFE. YOU OPENED MY EYES TO THE SUFFERING IN OUR CITY.

AND YOU HAVE NEVER, EVER GIVEN UP ON THEM.

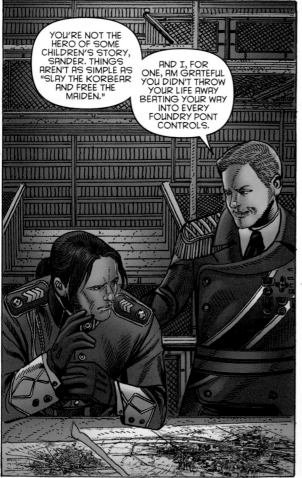

YOU'RE NOT THE HERO OF SOME CHILDREN'S STORY, SANDER. THINGS AREN'T AS SIMPLE AS "SLAY THE KORBEAR AND FREE THE MAIDEN."

AND I, FOR ONE, AM GRATEFUL YOU DIDN'T THROW YOUR LIFE AWAY BEATING YOUR WAY INTO EVERY FOUNDRY PONT CONTROLS.

YOU WOULDN'T HAVE MADE IT THROUGH TWO BUILDINGS WHEN YOU WERE JUST A GUARD. YOU COULD NEVER HAVE DONE THIS WITHOUT *MY* HELP.

FORTUNATELY, NOW YOU HAVE IT.

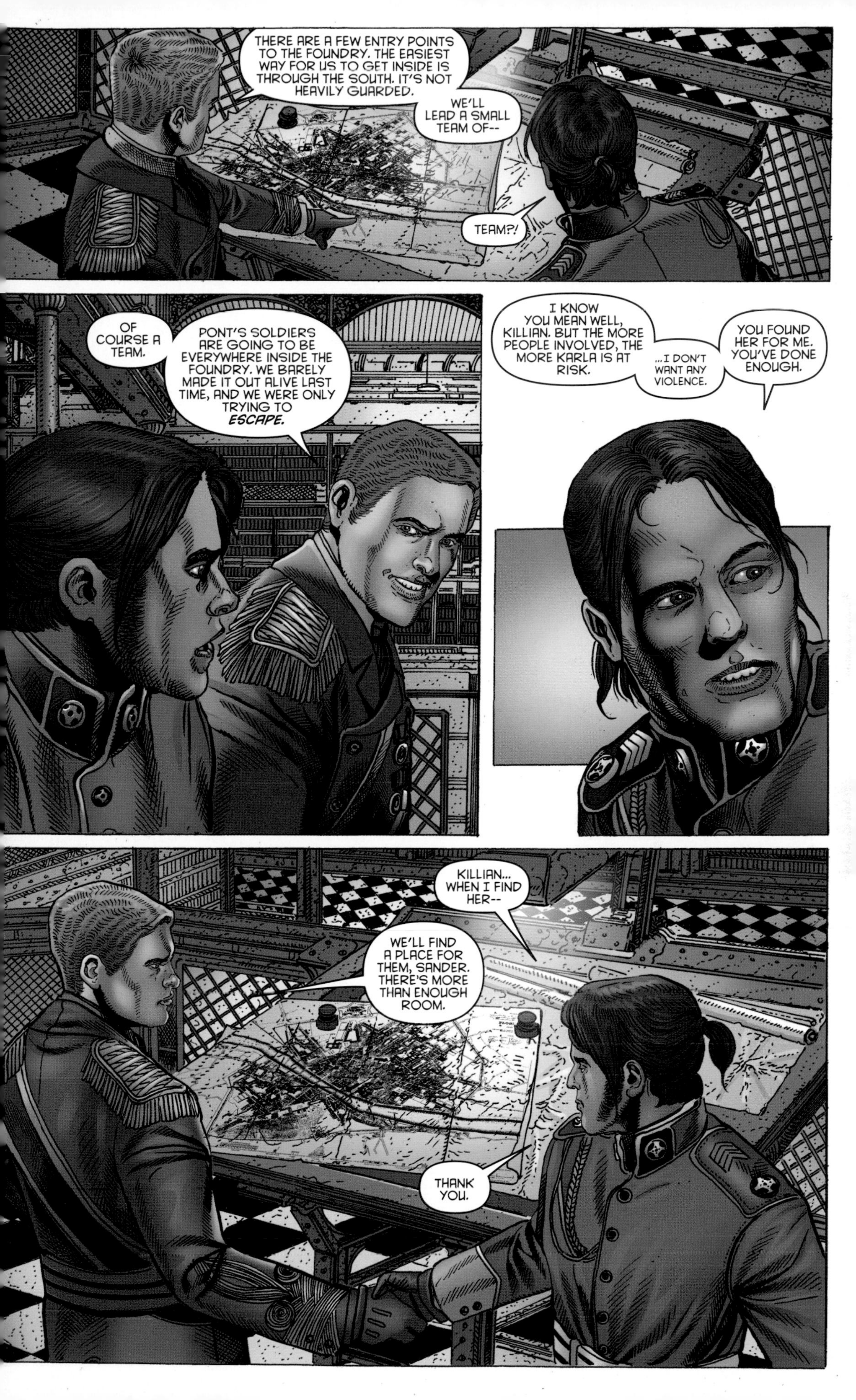
THERE ARE A FEW ENTRY POINTS TO THE FOUNDRY. THE EASIEST WAY FOR US TO GET INSIDE IS THROUGH THE SOUTH. IT'S NOT HEAVILY GUARDED.
WE'LL LEAD A SMALL TEAM OF--
TEAM?!
OF COURSE A TEAM.
PONT'S SOLDIERS ARE GOING TO BE EVERYWHERE INSIDE THE FOUNDRY. WE BARELY MADE IT OUT ALIVE LAST TIME, AND WE WERE ONLY TRYING TO *ESCAPE.*
I KNOW YOU MEAN WELL, KILLIAN. BUT THE MORE PEOPLE INVOLVED, THE MORE KARLA IS AT RISK.
...I DON'T WANT ANY VIOLENCE.
YOU FOUND HER FOR ME. YOU'VE DONE ENOUGH.
KILLIAN... WHEN I FIND HER--
WE'LL FIND A PLACE FOR THEM, SANDER. THERE'S MORE THAN ENOUGH ROOM.
THANK YOU.

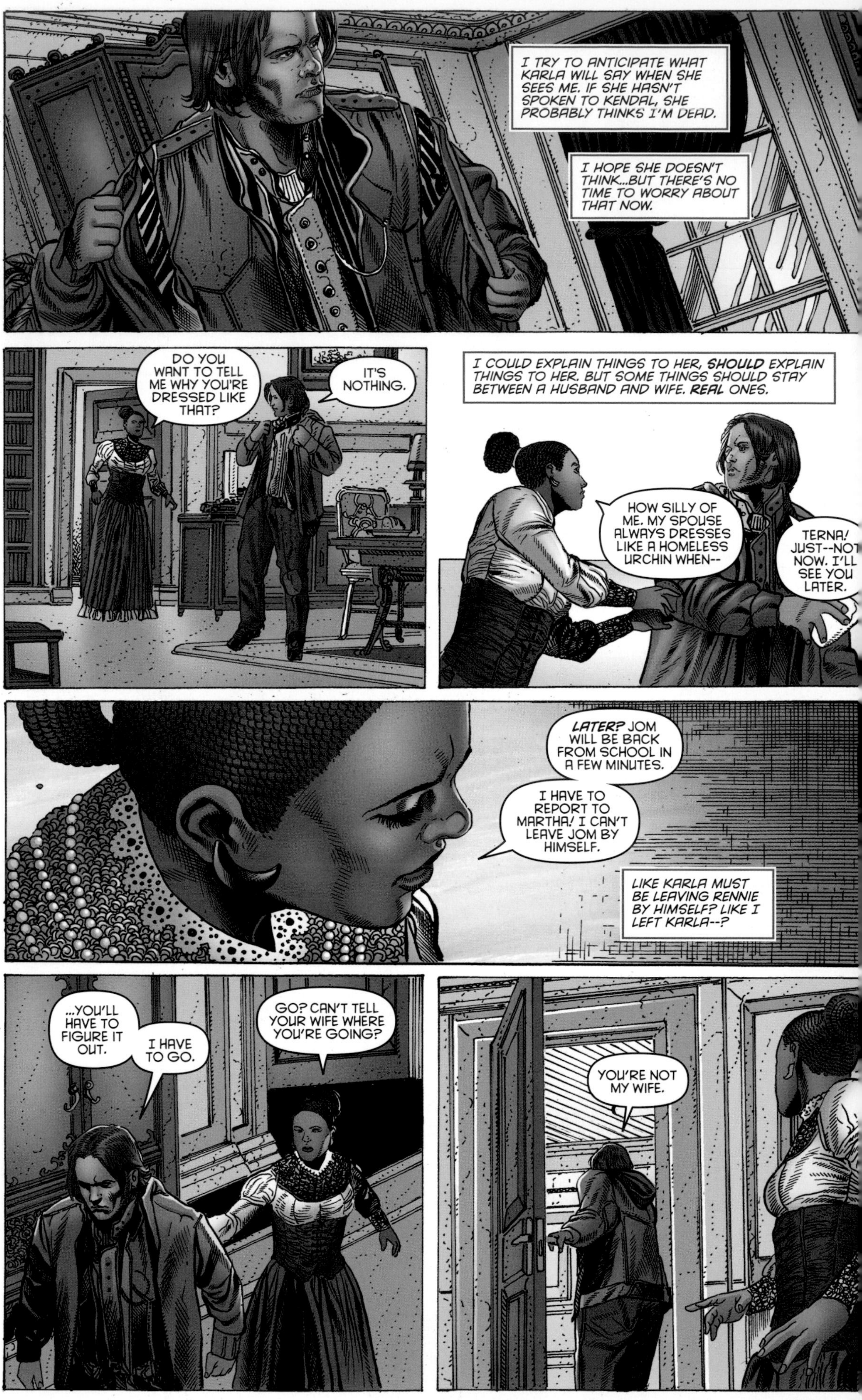
I TRY TO ANTICIPATE WHAT KARLA WILL SAY WHEN SHE SEES ME. IF SHE HASN'T SPOKEN TO KENDAL, SHE PROBABLY THINKS I'M DEAD.
I HOPE SHE DOESN'T THINK...BUT THERE'S NO TIME TO WORRY ABOUT THAT NOW.
DO YOU WANT TO TELL ME WHY YOU'RE DRESSED LIKE THAT?
IT'S NOTHING.
I COULD EXPLAIN THINGS TO HER, SHOULD EXPLAIN THINGS TO HER. BUT SOME THINGS SHOULD STAY BETWEEN A HUSBAND AND WIFE. REAL ONES.
HOW SILLY OF ME. MY SPOUSE ALWAYS DRESSES LIKE A HOMELESS URCHIN WHEN--
TERNA! JUST--NOT NOW. I'LL SEE YOU LATER.
LATER? JOM WILL BE BACK FROM SCHOOL IN A FEW MINUTES.
I HAVE TO REPORT TO MARTHA! I CAN'T LEAVE JOM BY HIMSELF.
LIKE KARLA MUST BE LEAVING RENNIE BY HIMSELF? LIKE I LEFT KARLA--?
...YOU'LL HAVE TO FIGURE IT OUT.
I HAVE TO GO.
GO? CAN'T TELL YOUR WIFE WHERE YOU'RE GOING?
YOU'RE NOT MY WIFE.

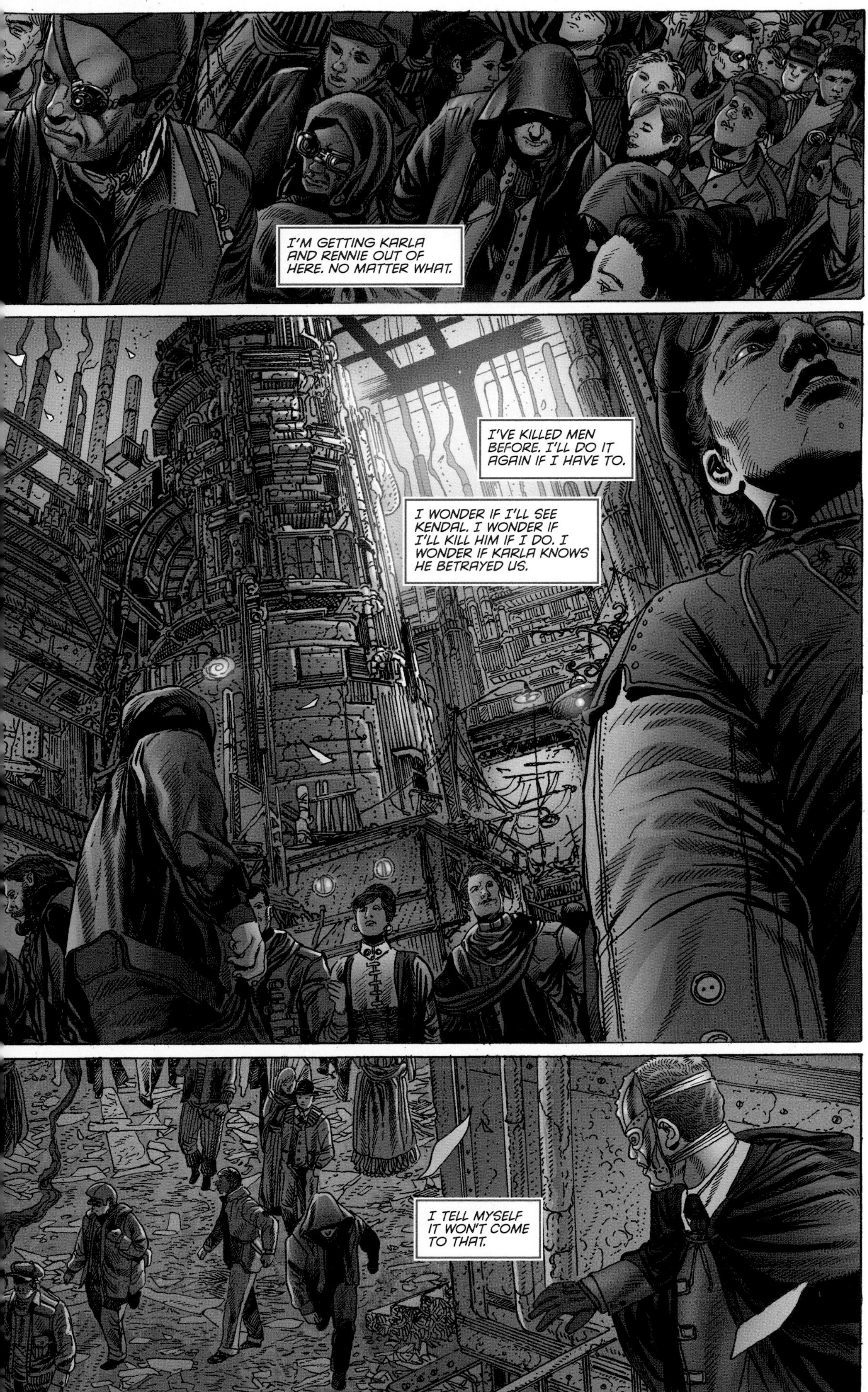
I'M GETTING KARLA AND RENNIE OUT OF HERE. NO MATTER WHAT.
I'VE KILLED MEN BEFORE. I'LL DO IT AGAIN IF I HAVE TO.
I WONDER IF I'LL SEE KENDAL. I WONDER IF I'LL KILL HIM IF I DO. I WONDER IF KARLA KNOWS HE BETRAYED US.
I TELL MYSELF IT WON'T COME TO THAT.

HOW MANY WORKERS ARE INSIDE? HOW LONG WILL IT TAKE ME TO FIND KARLA?

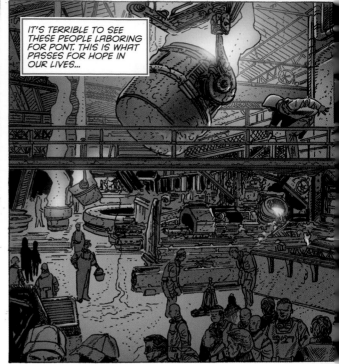

IT'S TERRIBLE TO SEE THESE PEOPLE LABORING FOR PONT. THIS IS WHAT PASSES FOR HOPE IN OUR LIVES...

...SLAVING AWAY FOR A CRIME BOSS WHO ROBS THEM SLIGHTLY LESS OFTEN THAN THE ACTUAL CITY ITSELF.

KARLA...

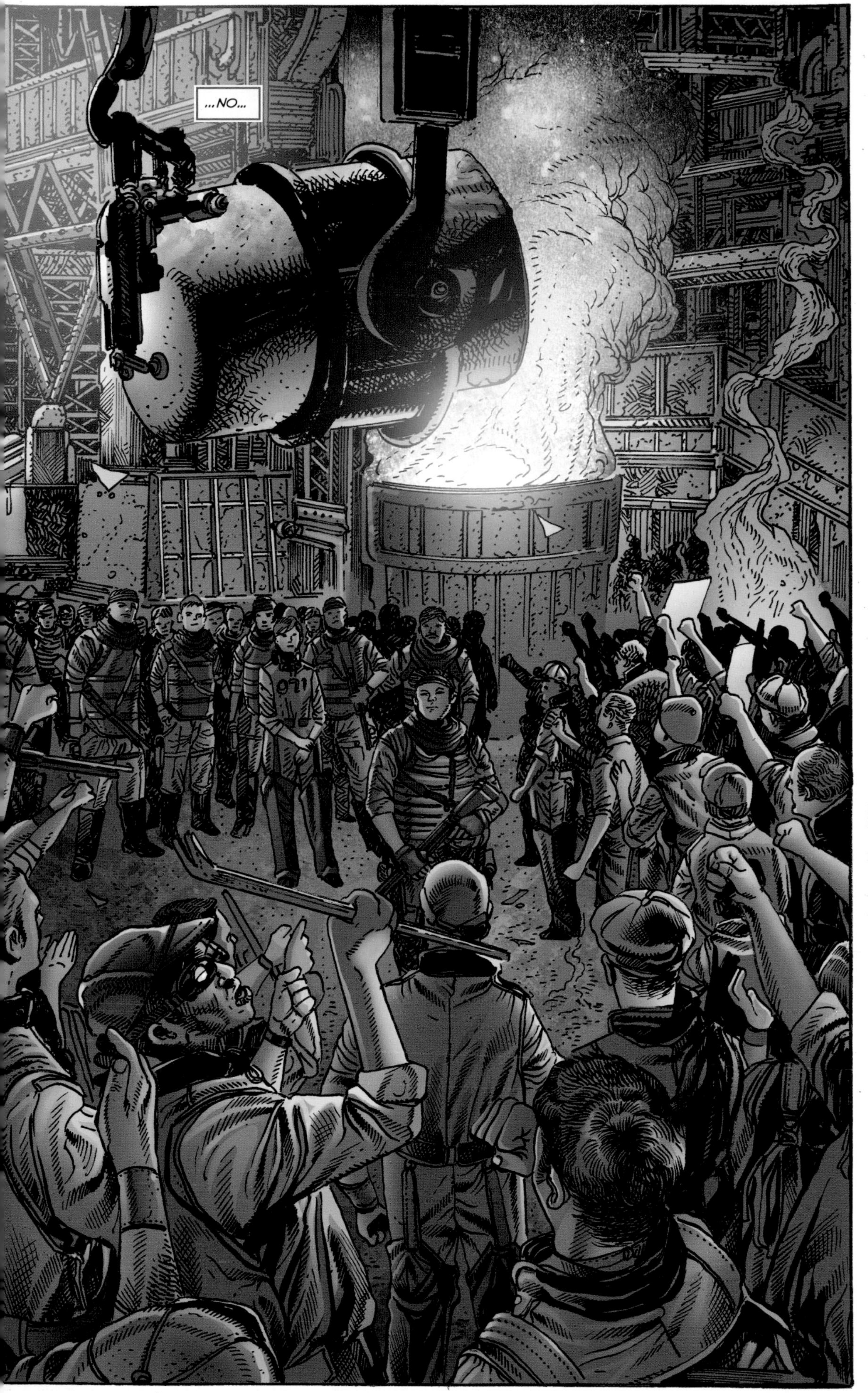
...NO...

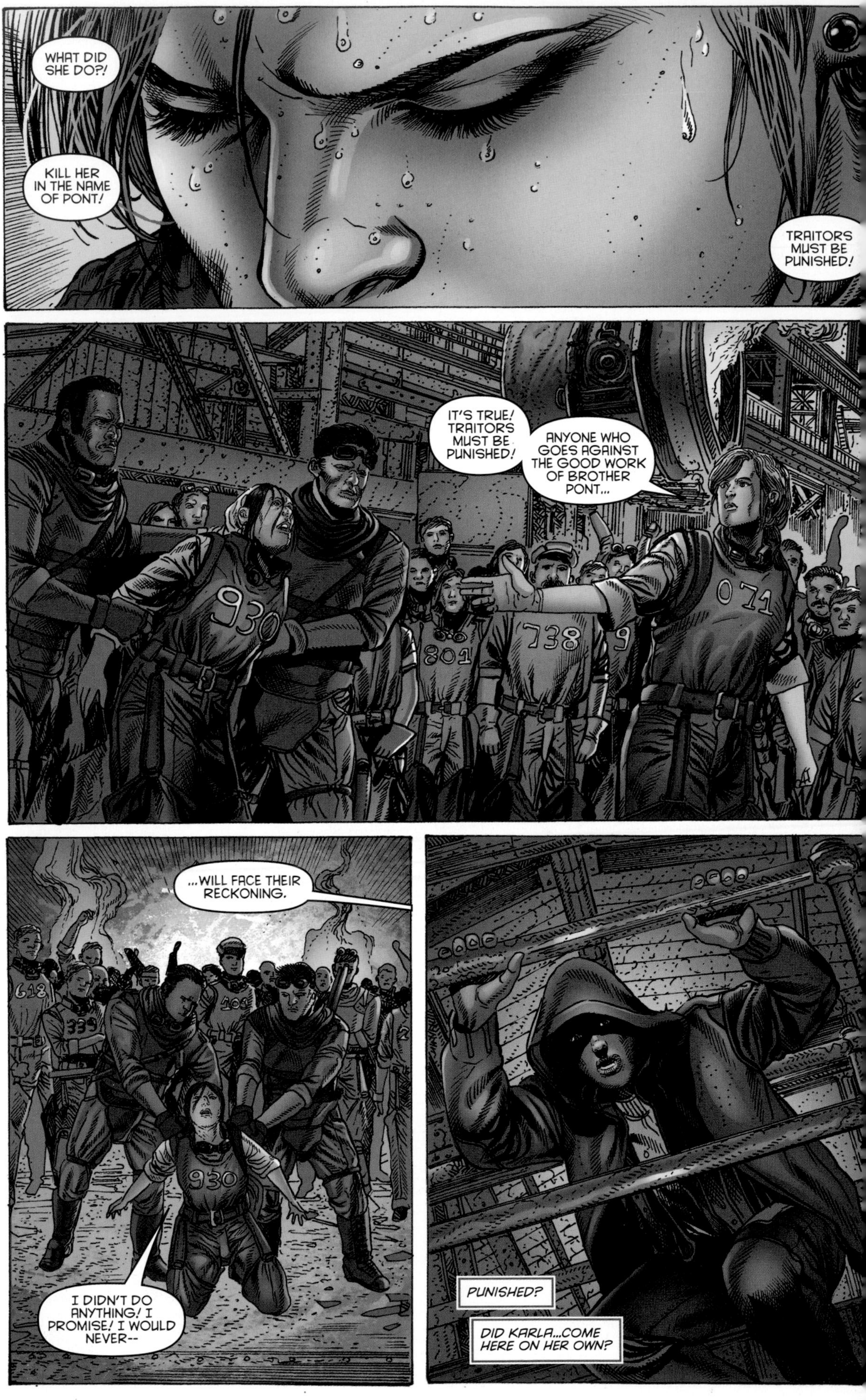
WHAT DID SHE DO?!
KILL HER IN THE NAME OF PONT!
TRAITORS MUST BE PUNISHED!
IT'S TRUE! TRAITORS MUST BE PUNISHED!
ANYONE WHO GOES AGAINST THE GOOD WORK OF BROTHER PONT...
930
801
738
071
...WILL FACE THEIR RECKONING.
I DIDN'T DO ANYTHING! I PROMISE! I WOULD NEVER--
618
339
930
PUNISHED?
DID KARLA...COME HERE ON HER OWN?

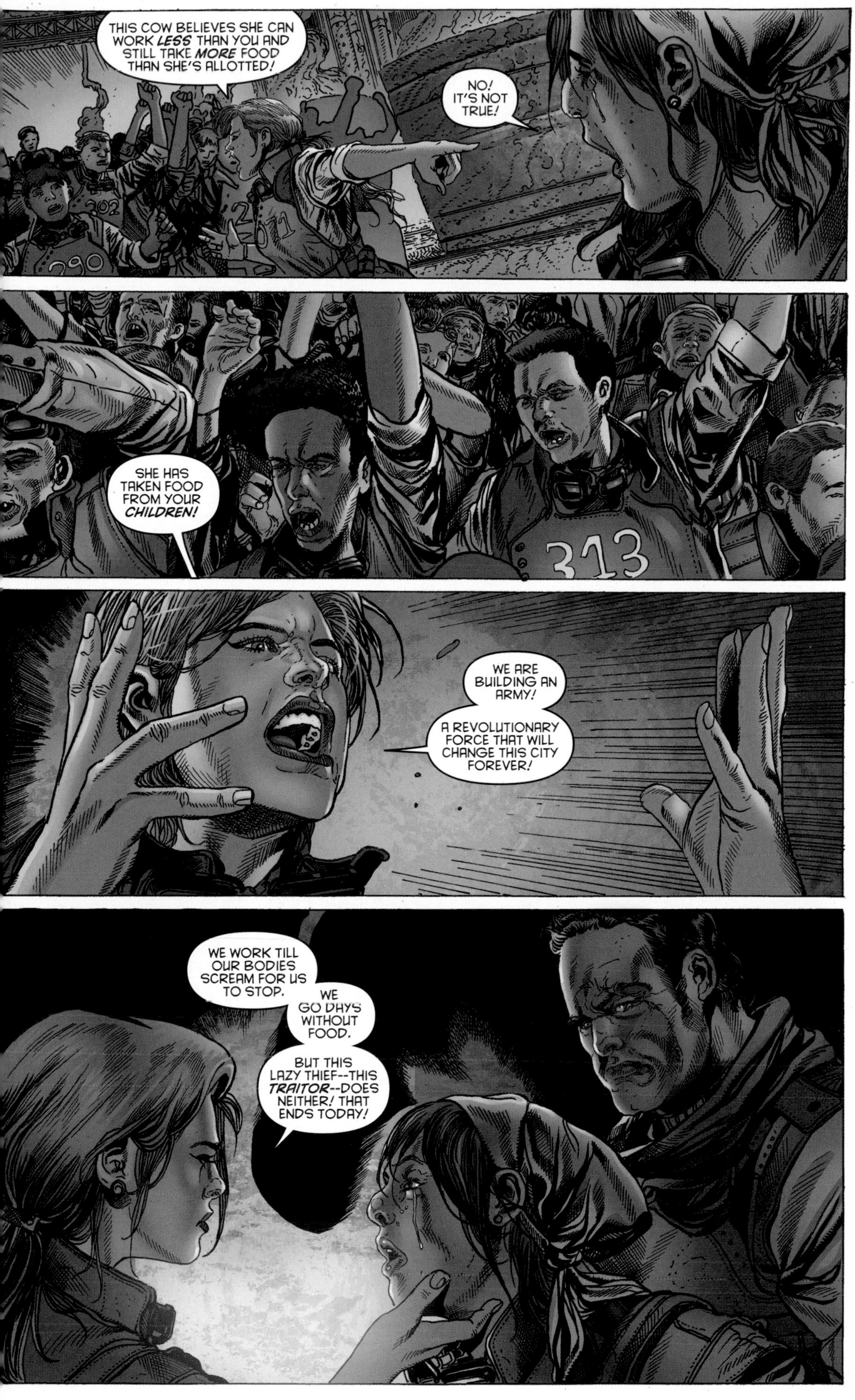
THIS COW BELIEVES SHE CAN WORK *LESS* THAN YOU AND STILL TAKE *MORE* FOOD THAN SHE'S ALLOTTED!
NO! IT'S NOT TRUE!
SHE HAS TAKEN FOOD FROM YOUR ***CHILDREN!***
WE ARE BUILDING AN ARMY!
A REVOLUTIONARY FORCE THAT WILL CHANGE THIS CITY FOREVER!
WE WORK TILL OUR BODIES SCREAM FOR US TO STOP.
WE GO DAYS WITHOUT FOOD.
BUT THIS LAZY THIEF--THIS *TRAITOR*--DOES NEITHER! THAT ENDS TODAY!

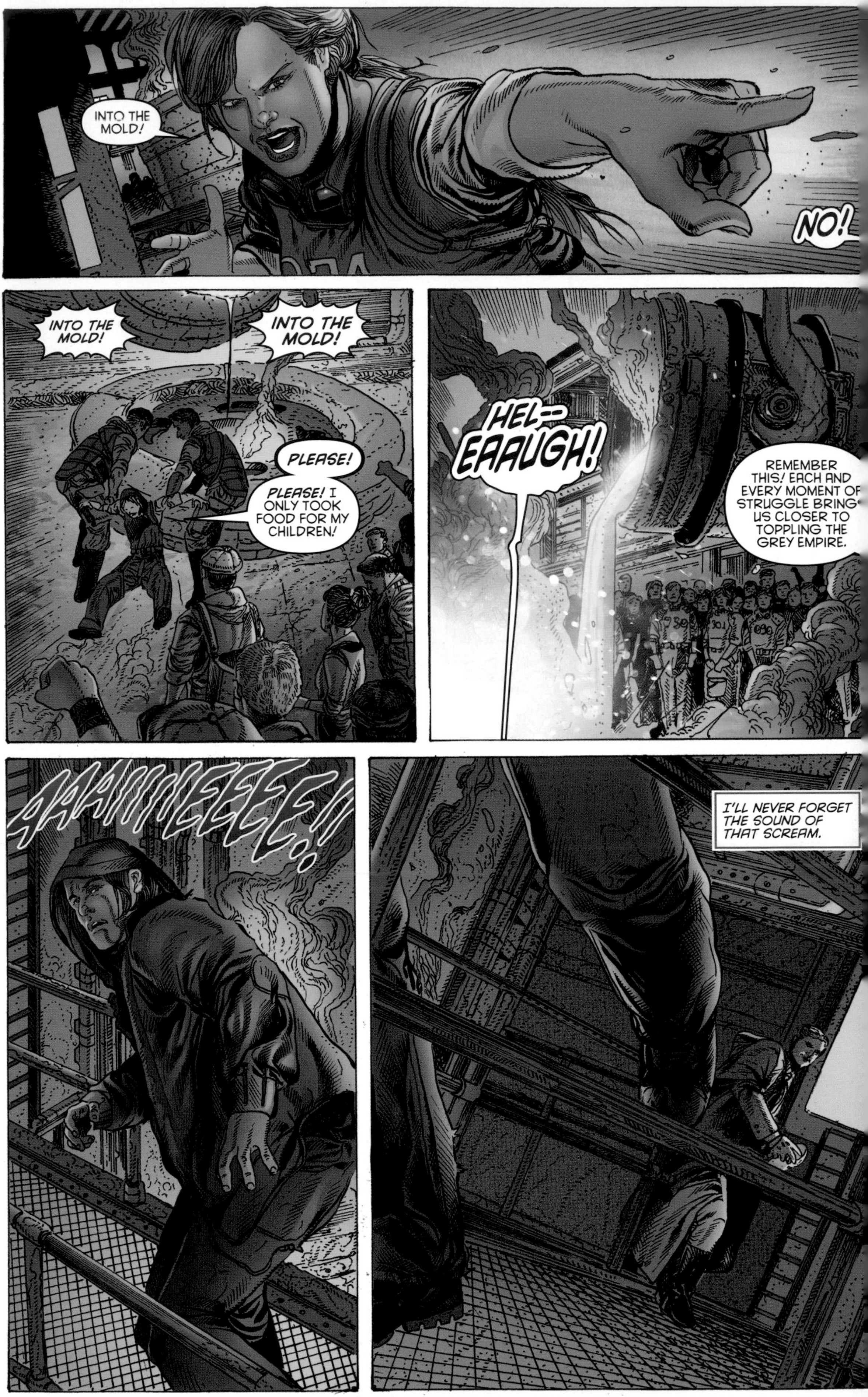
INTO THE MOLD!
NO!
INTO THE MOLD!
INTO THE MOLD!
PLEASE!
PLEASE! I ONLY TOOK FOOD FOR MY CHILDREN!
HEL-- EAAUGH!
REMEMBER THIS! EACH AND EVERY MOMENT OF STRUGGLE BRINGS US CLOSER TO TOPPLING THE GREY EMPIRE.
AAAIIIEEEE!!
I'LL NEVER FORGET THE SOUND OF THAT SCREAM.

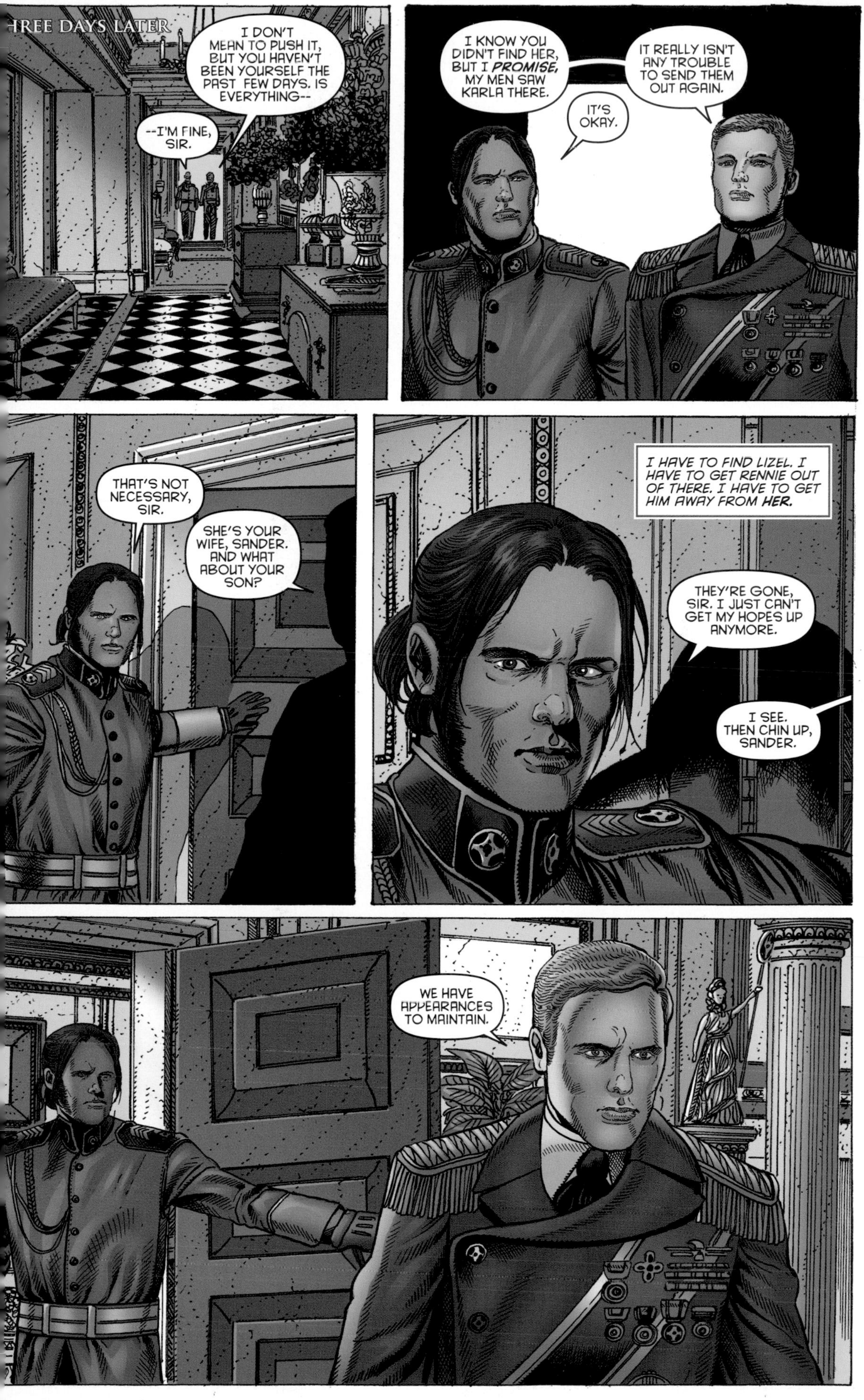
HREE DAYS LATER
I DON'T MEAN TO PUSH IT, BUT YOU HAVEN'T BEEN YOURSELF THE PAST FEW DAYS. IS EVERYTHING--
--I'M FINE, SIR.
I KNOW YOU DIDN'T FIND HER, BUT I PROMISE, MY MEN SAW KARLA THERE.
IT'S OKAY.
IT REALLY ISN'T ANY TROUBLE TO SEND THEM OUT AGAIN.
THAT'S NOT NECESSARY, SIR.
SHE'S YOUR WIFE, SANDER. AND WHAT ABOUT YOUR SON?
I HAVE TO FIND LIZEL. I HAVE TO GET RENNIE OUT OF THERE. I HAVE TO GET HIM AWAY FROM HER.
THEY'RE GONE, SIR. I JUST CAN'T GET MY HOPES UP ANYMORE.
I SEE. THEN CHIN UP, SANDER.
WE HAVE APPEARANCES TO MAINTAIN.

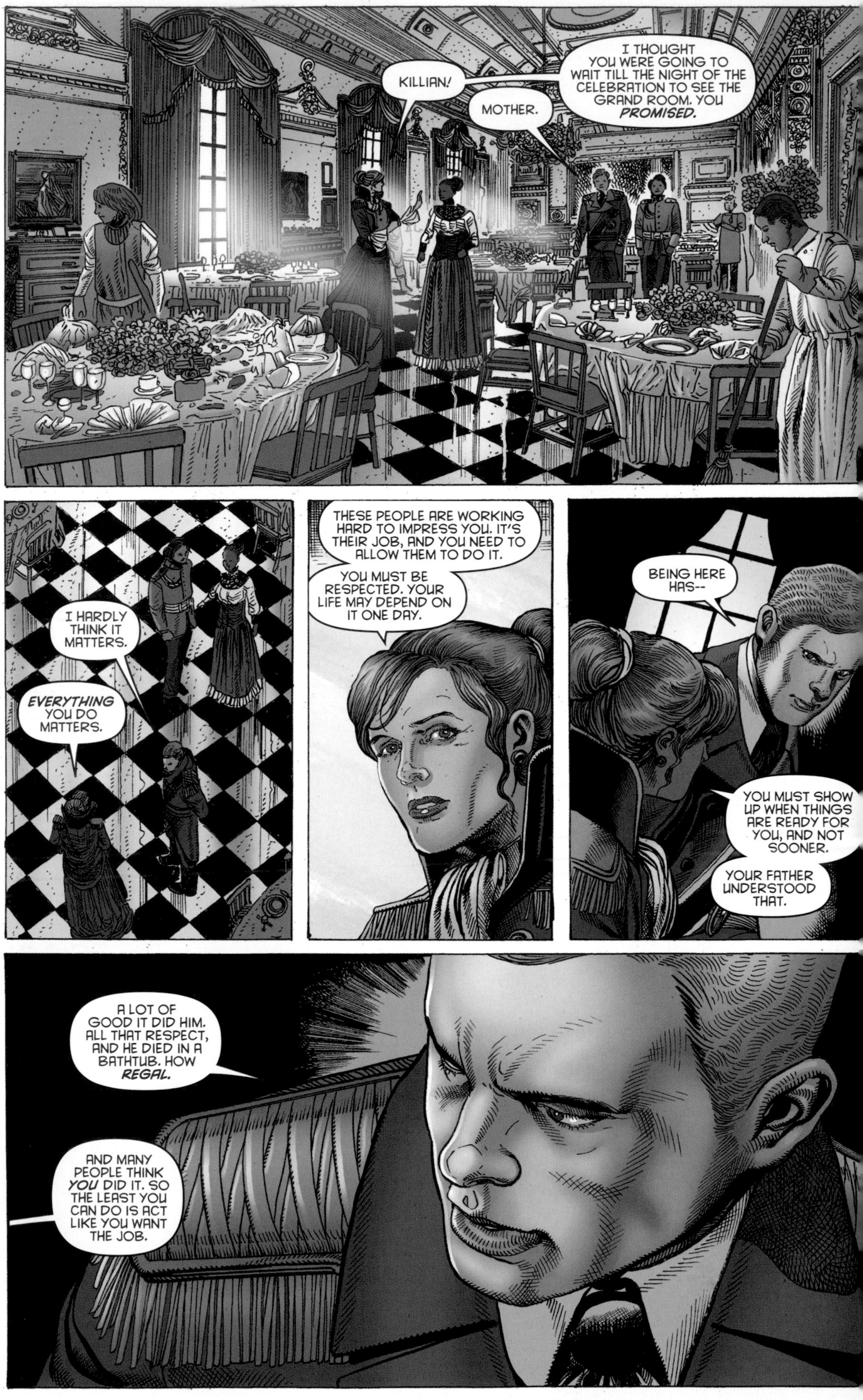
KILLIAN!
I THOUGHT YOU WERE GOING TO WAIT TILL THE NIGHT OF THE CELEBRATION TO SEE THE GRAND ROOM. YOU *PROMISED.*
MOTHER.
I HARDLY THINK IT MATTERS.
EVERYTHING YOU DO MATTERS.
THESE PEOPLE ARE WORKING HARD TO IMPRESS YOU. IT'S THEIR JOB, AND YOU NEED TO ALLOW THEM TO DO IT.
YOU MUST BE RESPECTED. YOUR LIFE MAY DEPEND ON IT ONE DAY.
BEING HERE HAS--
YOU MUST SHOW UP WHEN THINGS ARE READY FOR YOU, AND NOT SOONER.
YOUR FATHER UNDERSTOOD THAT.
A LOT OF GOOD IT DID HIM. ALL THAT RESPECT, AND HE DIED IN A BATHTUB. HOW *REGAL.*
AND MANY PEOPLE THINK *YOU* DID IT. SO THE LEAST YOU CAN DO IS ACT LIKE YOU WANT THE JOB.

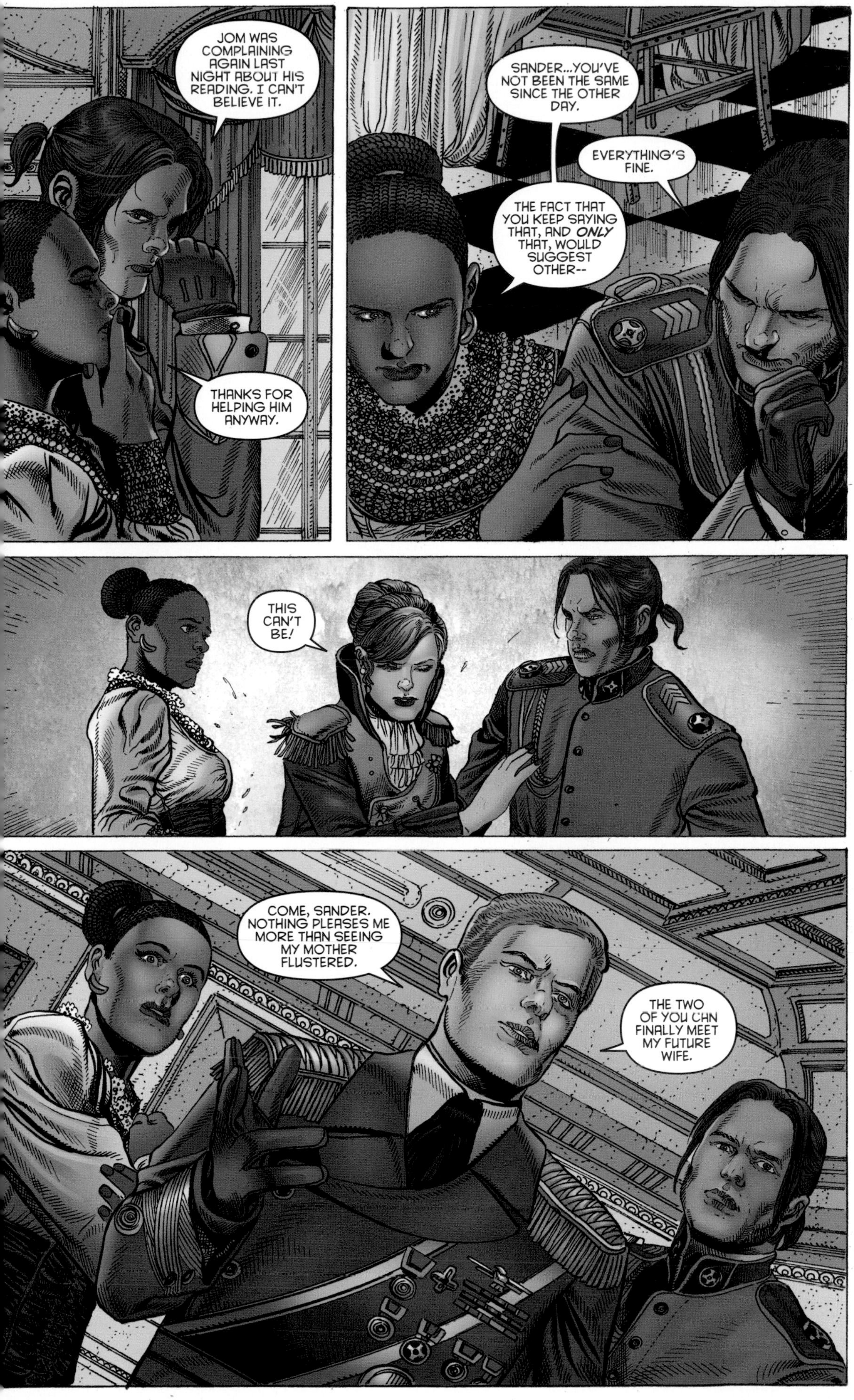
JOM WAS COMPLAINING AGAIN LAST NIGHT ABOUT HIS READING. I CAN'T BELIEVE IT.
THANKS FOR HELPING HIM ANYWAY.
SANDER...YOU'VE NOT BEEN THE SAME SINCE THE OTHER DAY.
EVERYTHING'S FINE.
THE FACT THAT YOU KEEP SAYING THAT, AND ONLY THAT, WOULD SUGGEST OTHER--
THIS CAN'T BE!
COME, SANDER. NOTHING PLEASES ME MORE THAN SEEING MY MOTHER FLUSTERED.
THE TWO OF YOU CAN FINALLY MEET MY FUTURE WIFE.

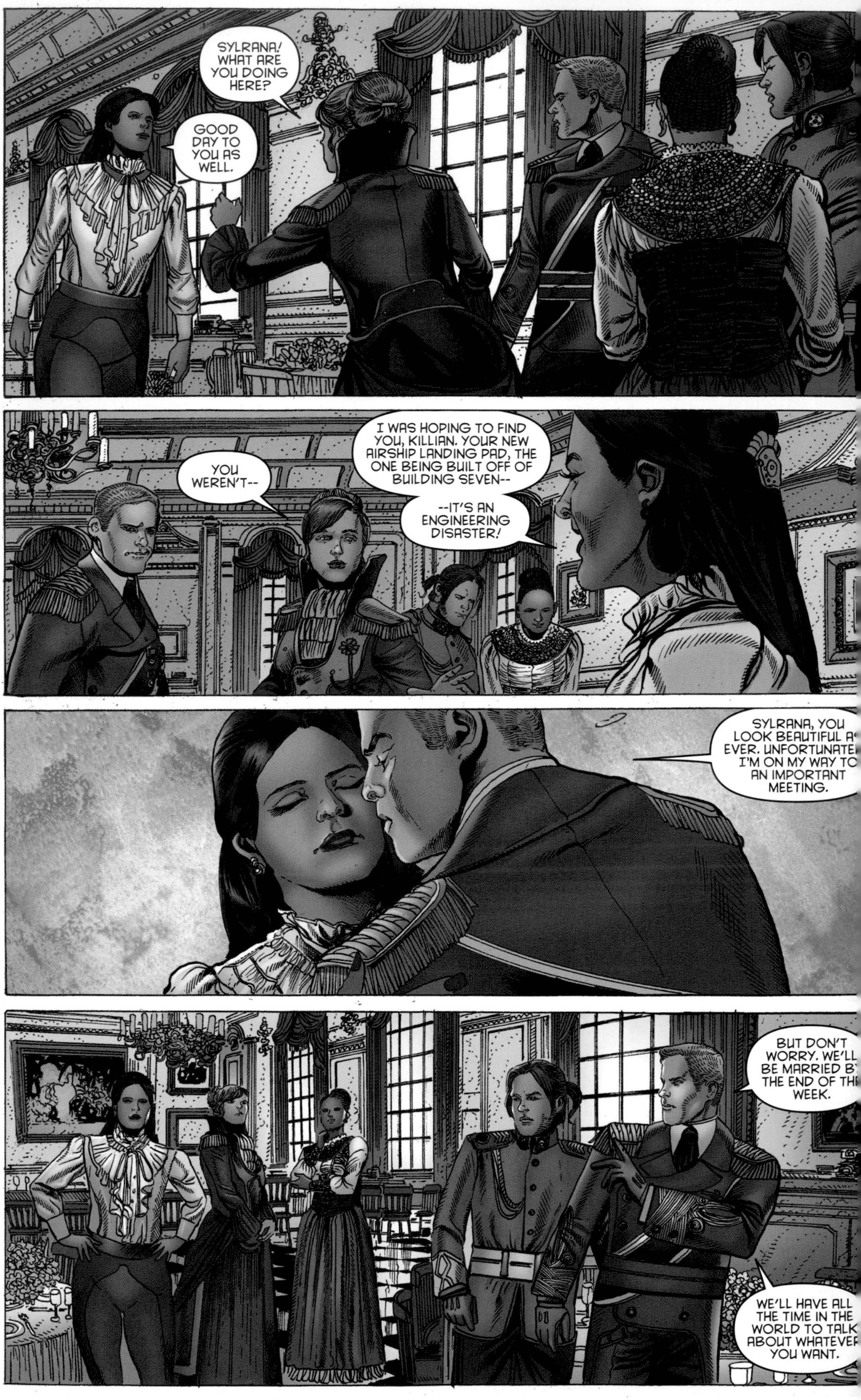
SYLRANA! WHAT ARE YOU DOING HERE?
GOOD DAY TO YOU AS WELL.
YOU WEREN'T--
I WAS HOPING TO FIND YOU, KILLIAN. YOUR NEW AIRSHIP LANDING PAD, THE ONE BEING BUILT OFF OF BUILDING SEVEN--
--IT'S AN ENGINEERING DISASTER!
SYLRANA, YOU LOOK BEAUTIFUL A EVER. UNFORTUNATE I'M ON MY WAY TO AN IMPORTANT MEETING.
BUT DON'T WORRY. WE'LL BE MARRIED B THE END OF TH WEEK.
WE'LL HAVE ALL THE TIME IN THE WORLD TO TALK ABOUT WHATEVE YOU WANT.

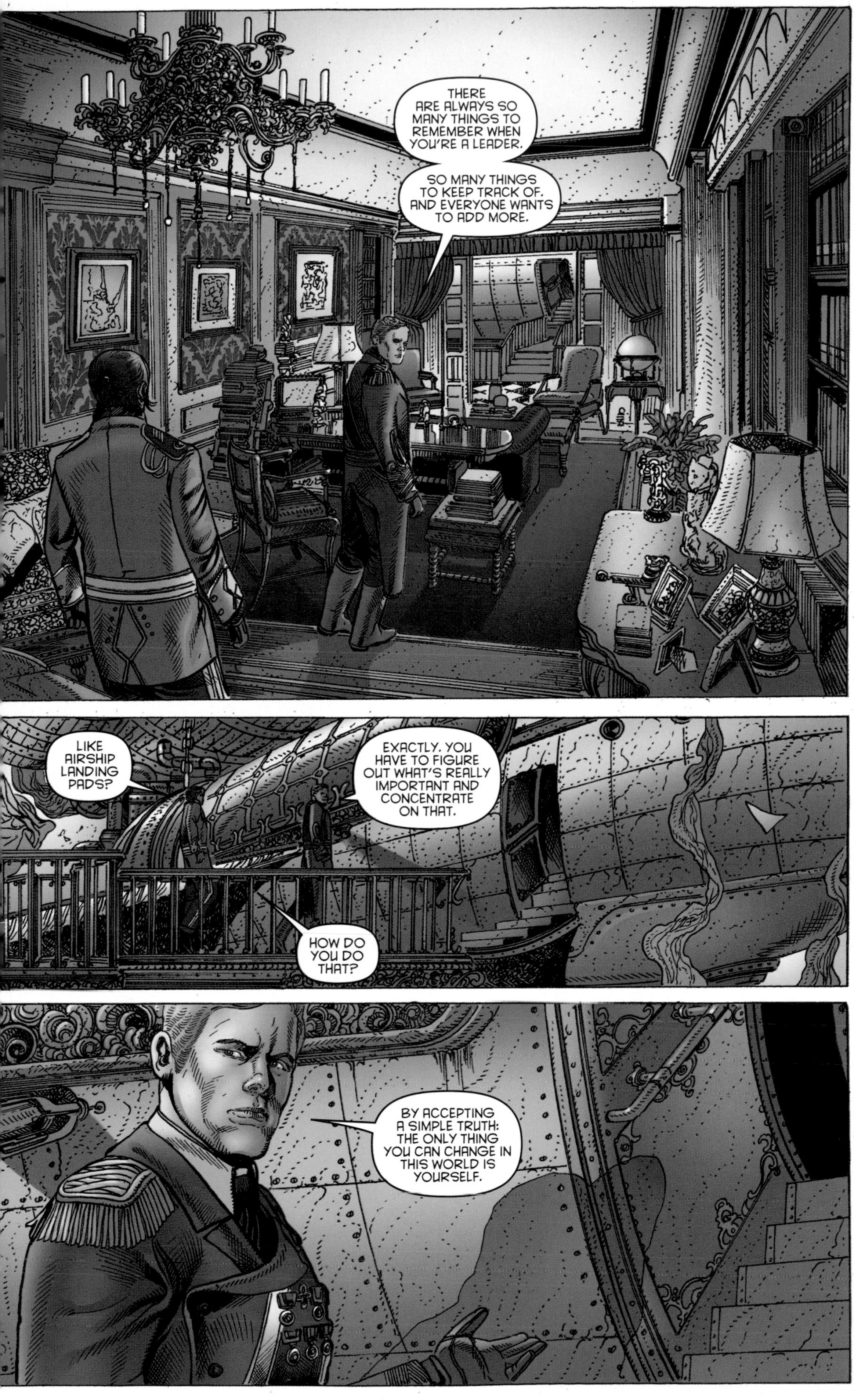
THERE ARE ALWAYS SO MANY THINGS TO REMEMBER WHEN YOU'RE A LEADER.
SO MANY THINGS TO KEEP TRACK OF. AND EVERYONE WANTS TO ADD MORE.
LIKE AIRSHIP LANDING PADS?
EXACTLY. YOU HAVE TO FIGURE OUT WHAT'S REALLY IMPORTANT AND CONCENTRATE ON THAT.
HOW DO YOU DO THAT?
BY ACCEPTING A SIMPLE TRUTH: THE ONLY THING YOU CAN CHANGE IN THIS WORLD IS YOURSELF.

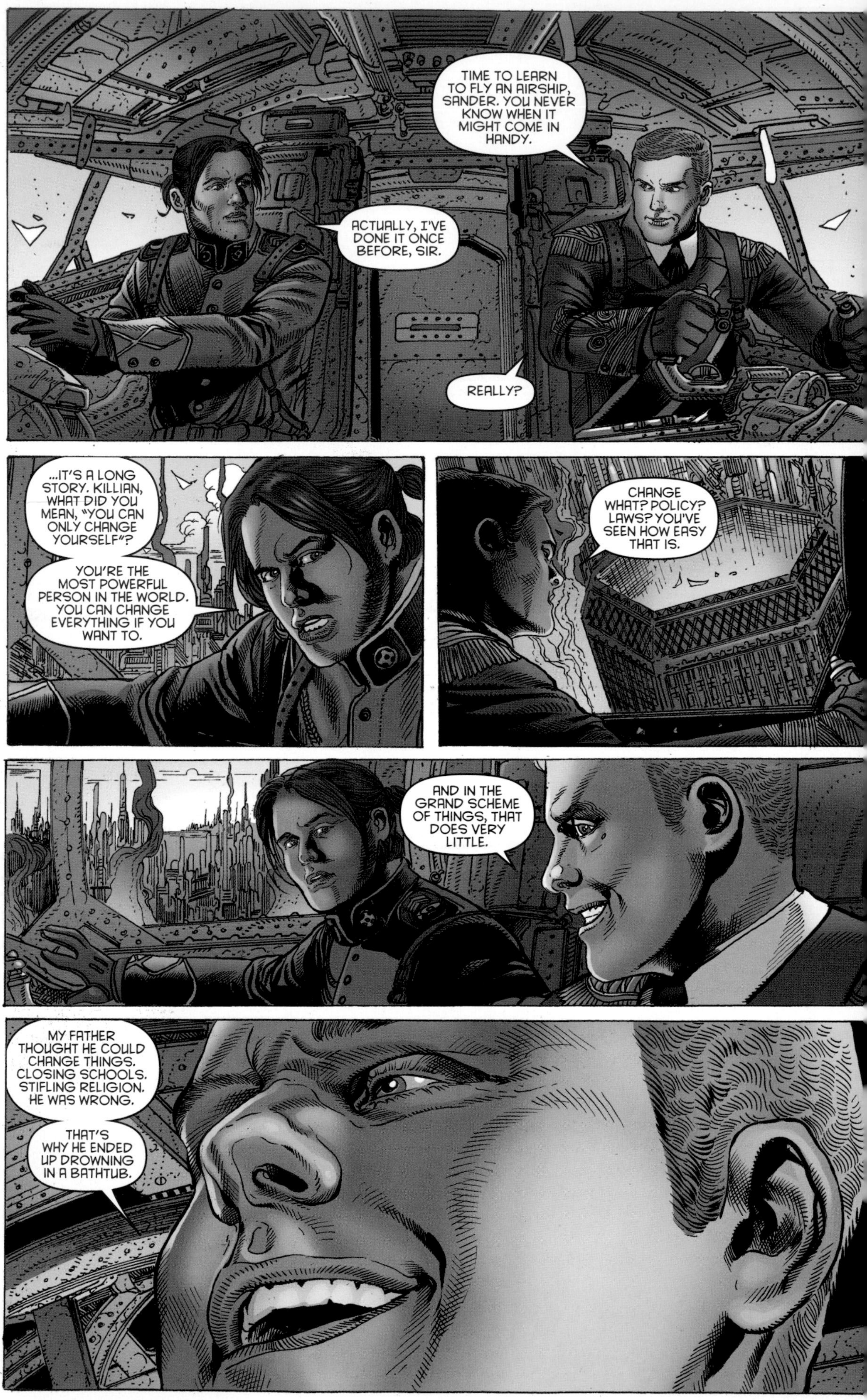
TIME TO LEARN TO FLY AN AIRSHIP, SANDER. YOU NEVER KNOW WHEN IT MIGHT COME IN HANDY.
ACTUALLY, I'VE DONE IT ONCE BEFORE, SIR.
REALLY?
...IT'S A LONG STORY. KILLIAN, WHAT DID YOU MEAN, "YOU CAN ONLY CHANGE YOURSELF"?
YOU'RE THE MOST POWERFUL PERSON IN THE WORLD. YOU CAN CHANGE EVERYTHING IF YOU WANT TO.
CHANGE WHAT? POLICY? LAWS? YOU'VE SEEN HOW EASY THAT IS.
AND IN THE GRAND SCHEME OF THINGS, THAT DOES VERY LITTLE.
MY FATHER THOUGHT HE COULD CHANGE THINGS. CLOSING SCHOOLS. STIFLING RELIGION. HE WAS WRONG.
THAT'S WHY HE ENDED UP DROWNING IN A BATHTUB.

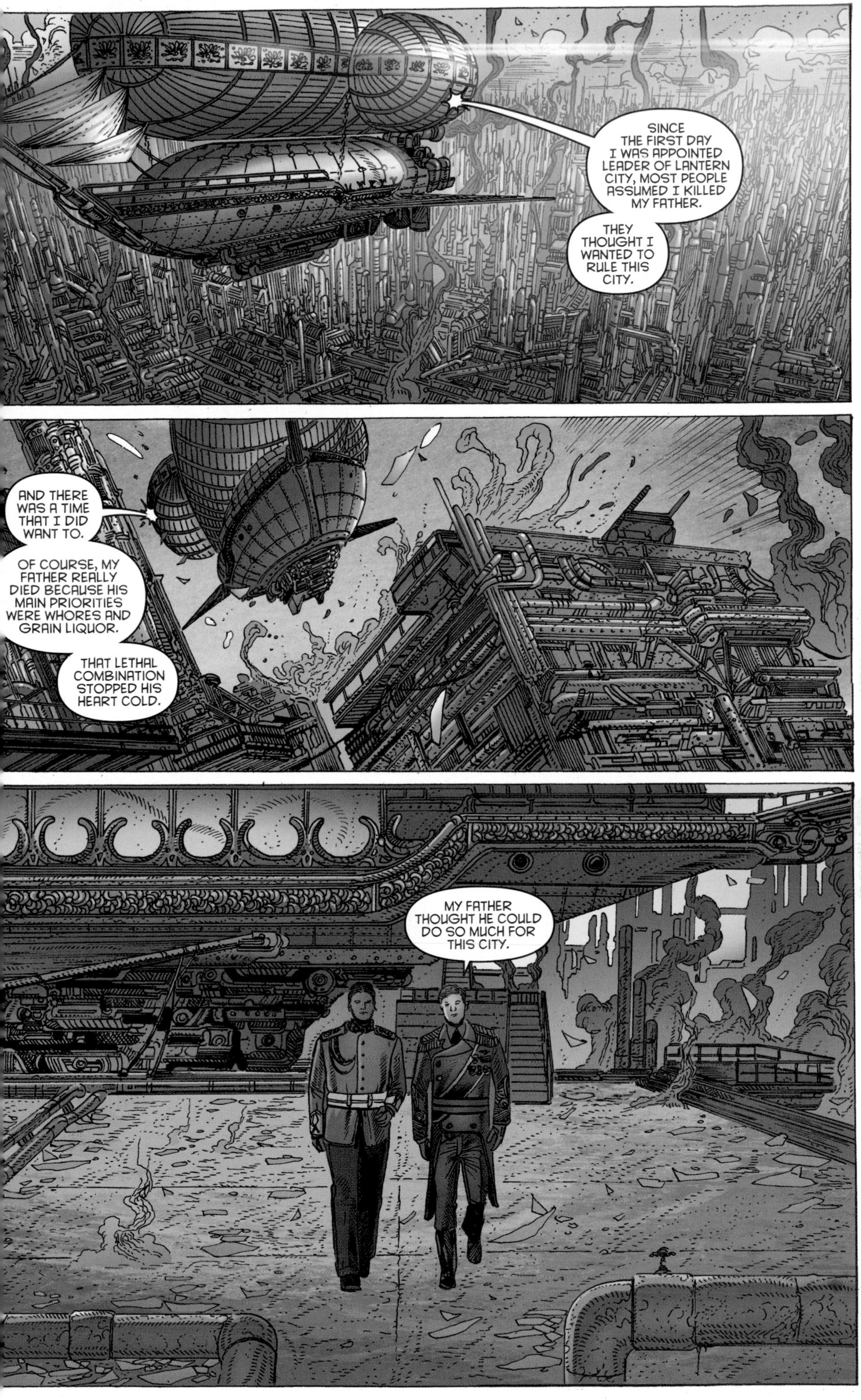
SINCE THE FIRST DAY I WAS APPOINTED LEADER OF LANTERN CITY, MOST PEOPLE ASSUMED I KILLED MY FATHER.
THEY THOUGHT I WANTED TO RULE THIS CITY.
AND THERE WAS A TIME THAT I DID WANT TO.
OF COURSE, MY FATHER REALLY DIED BECAUSE HIS MAIN PRIORITIES WERE WHORES AND GRAIN LIQUOR.
THAT LETHAL COMBINATION STOPPED HIS HEART COLD.
MY FATHER THOUGHT HE COULD DO SO MUCH FOR THIS CITY.

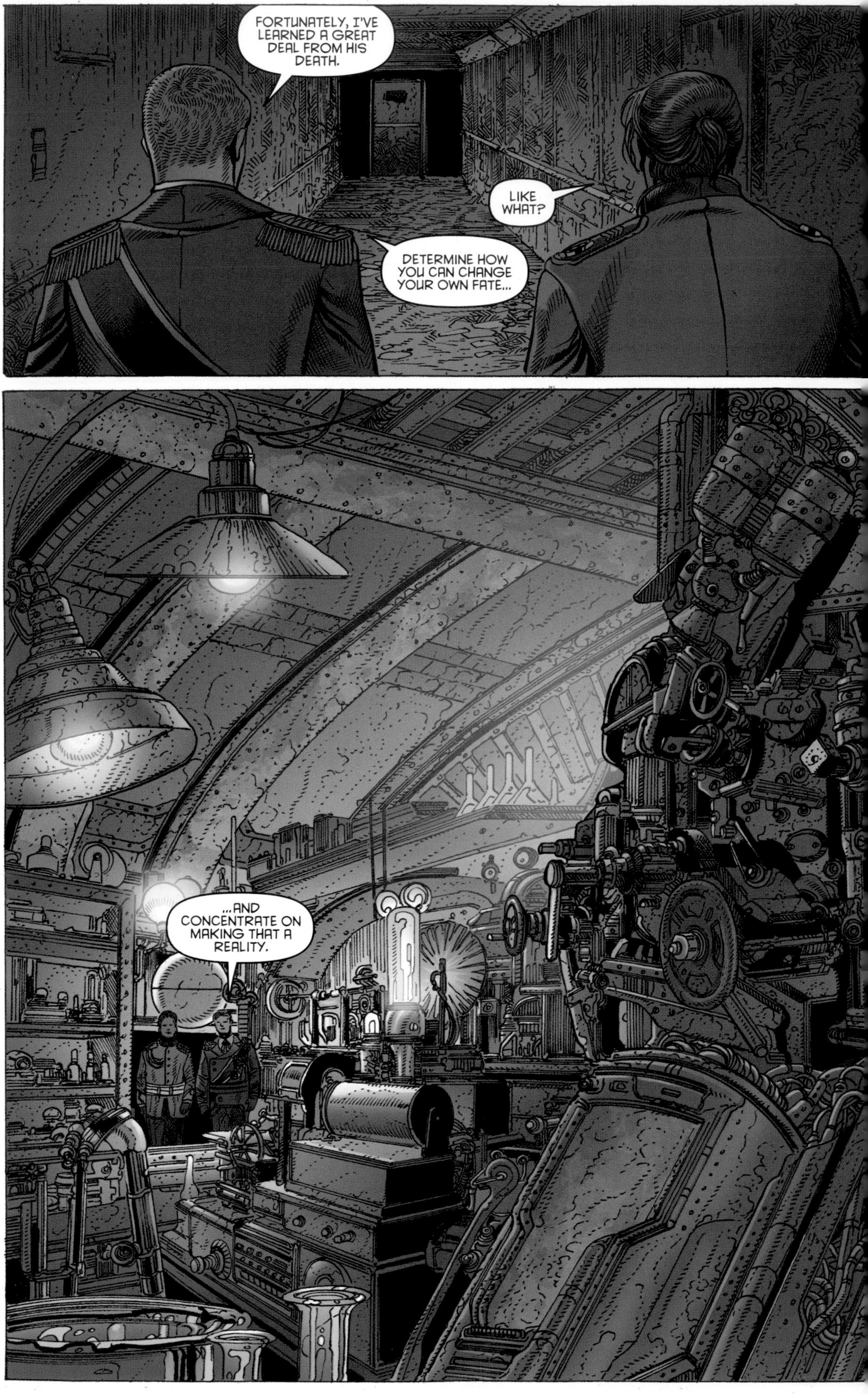
FORTUNATELY, I'VE LEARNED A GREAT DEAL FROM HIS DEATH.
LIKE WHAT?
DETERMINE HOW YOU CAN CHANGE YOUR OWN FATE...
...AND CONCENTRATE ON MAKING THAT A REALITY.

WHAT IS THIS PLACE?

IT'S MY LAB.

MY SALVATION.

NO ONE ELSE HAS EVER BEEN HERE, SANDER. HERE I BUILD ALL THE THINGS THINGS I'VE THOUGHT UP OR FOUND IN FORGOTTEN OLD BOOKS.

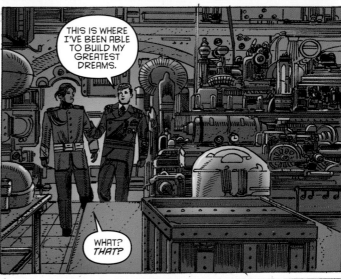

THIS IS WHERE I'VE BEEN ABLE TO BUILD MY GREATEST DREAMS.

WHAT? *THAT?*

YES. THAT IS THE ONE TOOL THAT WILL CHANGE THIS CITY'S HISTORY FOREVER...

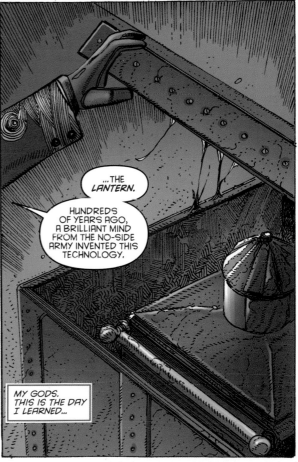

...THE *LANTERN.*

HUNDREDS OF YEARS AGO, A BRILLIANT MIND FROM THE NO-SIDE ARMY INVENTED THIS TECHNOLOGY.

MY GODS. THIS IS THE DAY I LEARNED...

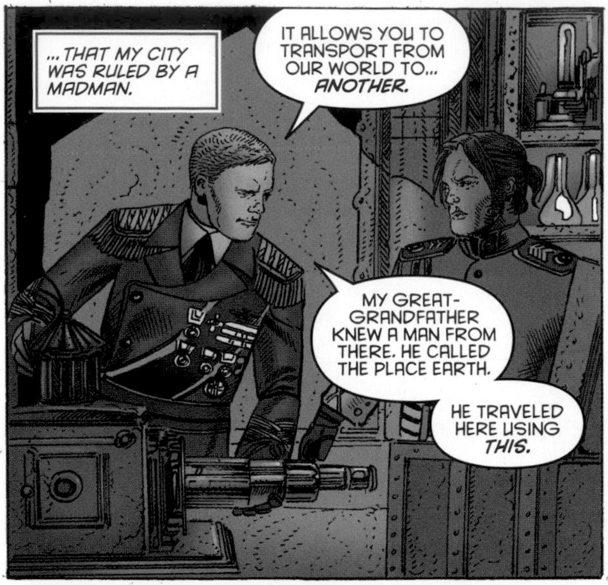
...THAT MY CITY WAS RULED BY A MADMAN.
IT ALLOWS YOU TO TRANSPORT FROM OUR WORLD TO... *ANOTHER.*
MY GREAT-GRANDFATHER KNEW A MAN FROM THERE. HE CALLED THE PLACE EARTH.
HE TRAVELED HERE USING *THIS.*

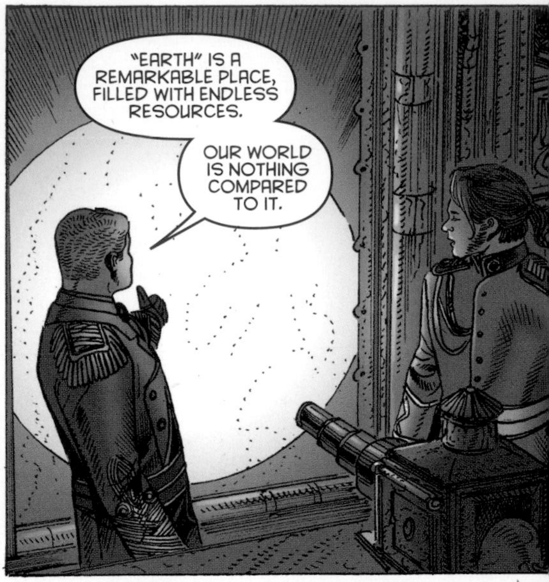
"EARTH" IS A REMARKABLE PLACE, FILLED WITH ENDLESS RESOURCES.
OUR WORLD IS NOTHING COMPARED TO IT.

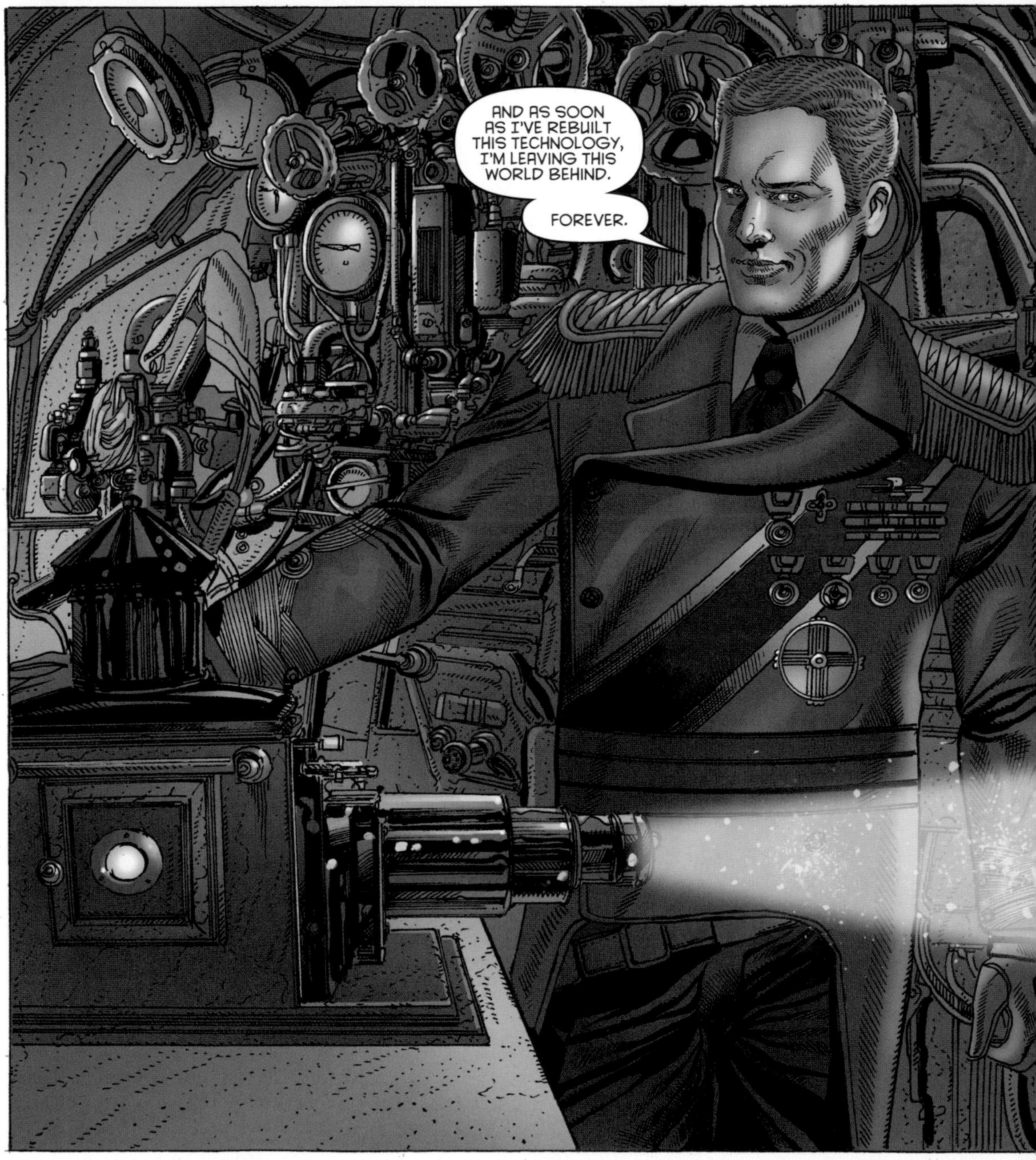
AND AS SOON AS I'VE REBUILT THIS TECHNOLOGY, I'M LEAVING THIS WORLD BEHIND.
FOREVER.

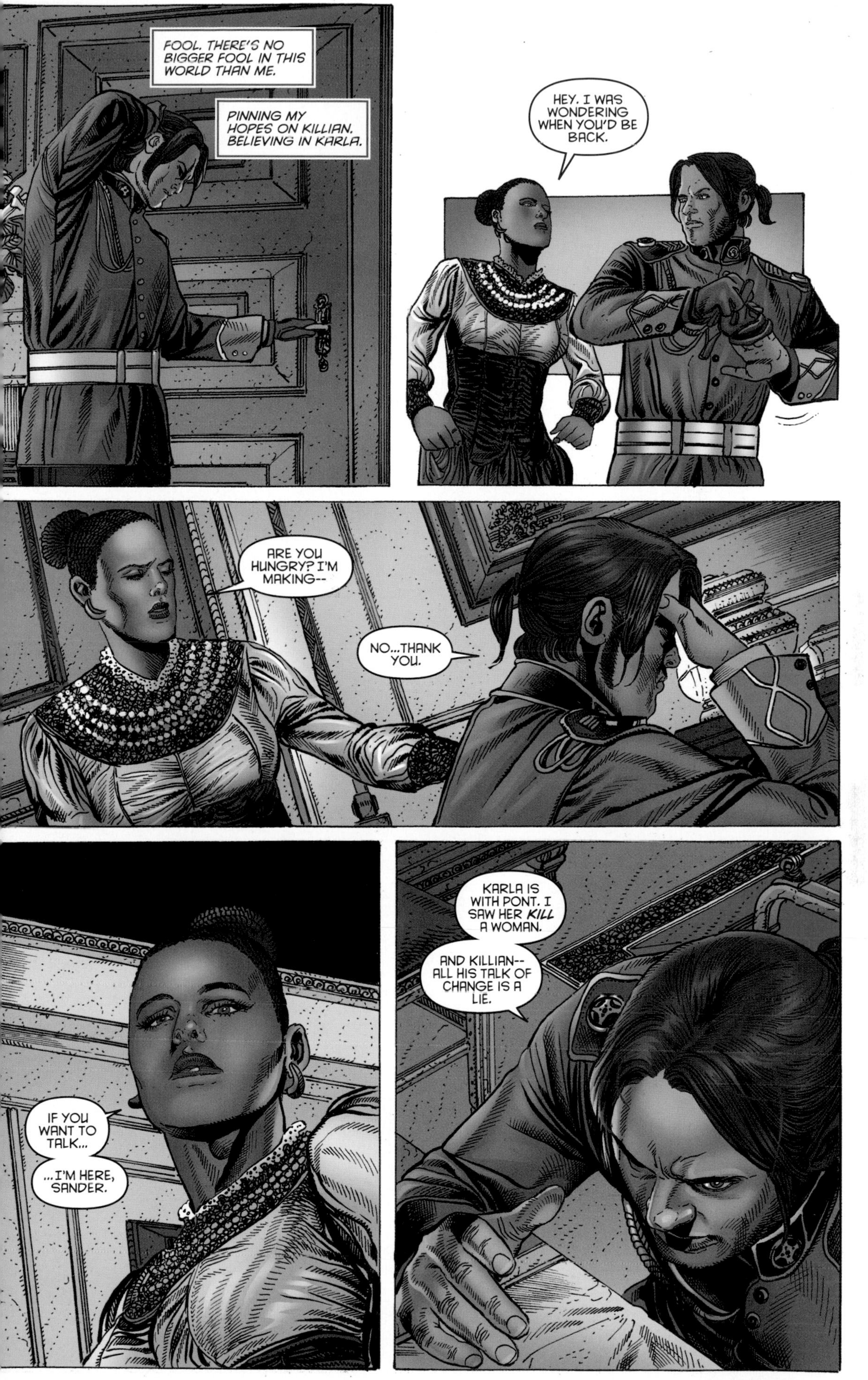

FOOL. THERE'S NO BIGGER FOOL IN THIS WORLD THAN ME.
PINNING MY HOPES ON KILLIAN. BELIEVING IN KARLA.
HEY. I WAS WONDERING WHEN YOU'D BE BACK.
ARE YOU HUNGRY? I'M MAKING--
NO...THANK YOU.
IF YOU WANT TO TALK...
...I'M HERE, SANDER.
KARLA IS WITH PONT. I SAW HER KILL A WOMAN.
AND KILLIAN-- ALL HIS TALK OF CHANGE IS A LIE.

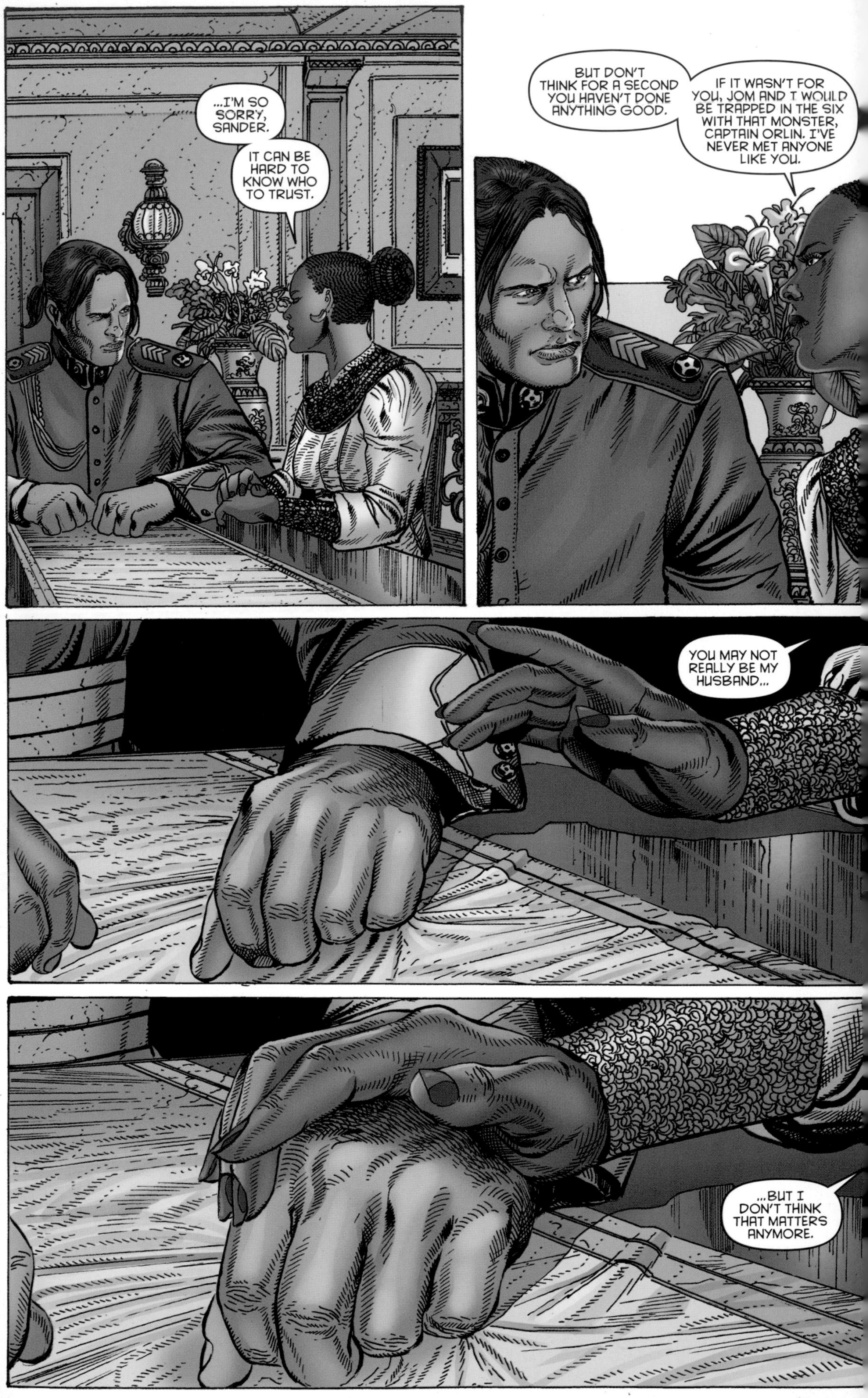
...I'M SO SORRY, SANDER.
IT CAN BE HARD TO KNOW WHO TO TRUST.
BUT DON'T THINK FOR A SECOND YOU HAVEN'T DONE ANYTHING GOOD.
IF IT WASN'T FOR YOU, JOM AND I WOULD BE TRAPPED IN THE SIX WITH THAT MONSTER, CAPTAIN ORLIN. I'VE NEVER MET ANYONE LIKE YOU.
YOU MAY NOT REALLY BE MY HUSBAND...
...BUT I DON'T THINK THAT MATTERS ANYMORE.

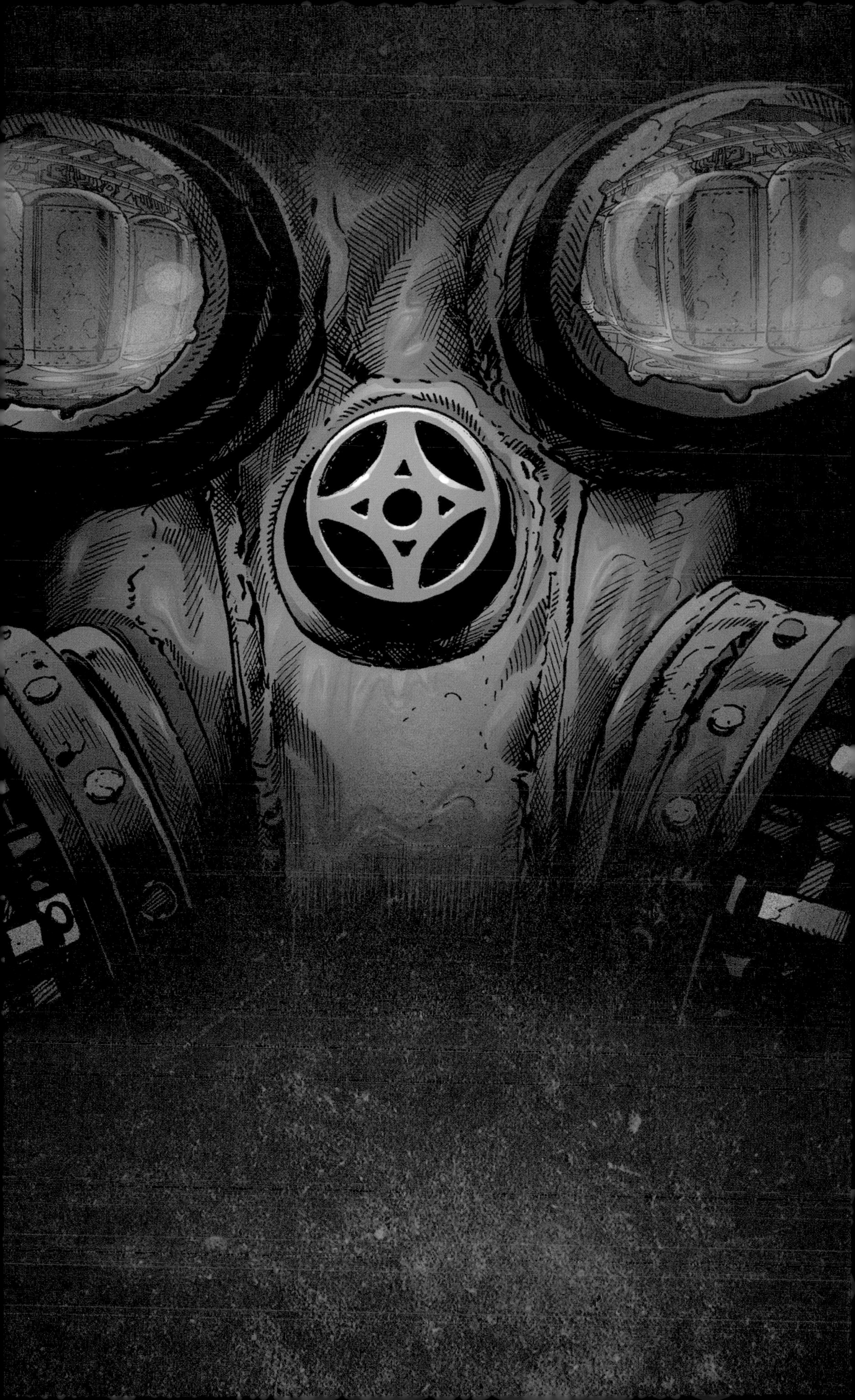

CHAPTER EIGHT

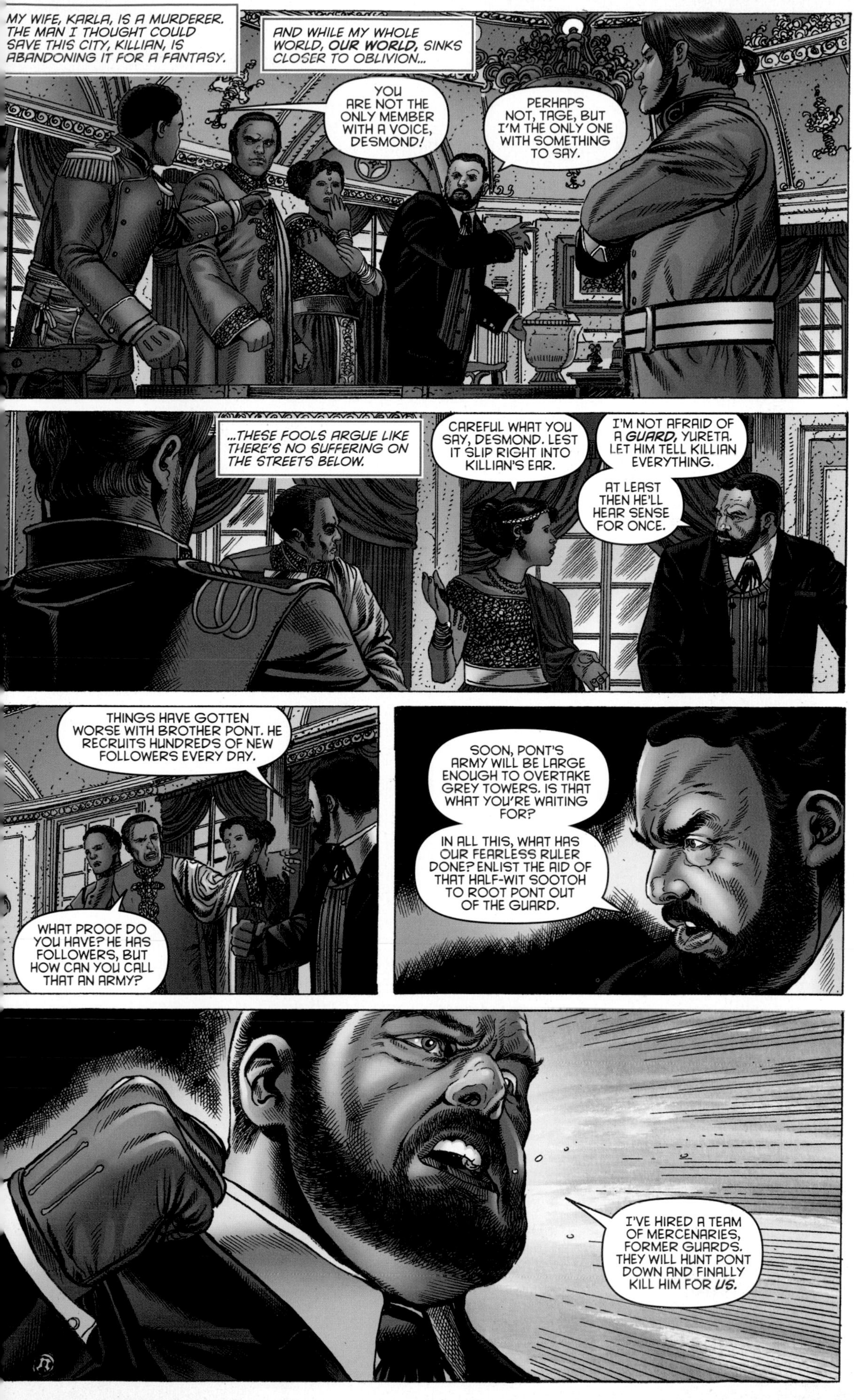
MY WIFE, KARLA, IS A MURDERER. THE MAN I THOUGHT COULD SAVE THIS CITY, KILLIAN, IS ABANDONING IT FOR A FANTASY.
AND WHILE MY WHOLE WORLD, OUR WORLD, SINKS CLOSER TO OBLIVION...
YOU ARE NOT THE ONLY MEMBER WITH A VOICE, DESMOND!
PERHAPS NOT, TAGE, BUT I'M THE ONLY ONE WITH SOMETHING TO SAY.
...THESE FOOLS ARGUE LIKE THERE'S NO SUFFERING ON THE STREETS BELOW.
CAREFUL WHAT YOU SAY, DESMOND. LEST IT SLIP RIGHT INTO KILLIAN'S EAR.
I'M NOT AFRAID OF A GUARD, YURETA. LET HIM TELL KILLIAN EVERYTHING.
AT LEAST THEN HE'LL HEAR SENSE FOR ONCE.
THINGS HAVE GOTTEN WORSE WITH BROTHER PONT. HE RECRUITS HUNDREDS OF NEW FOLLOWERS EVERY DAY.
WHAT PROOF DO YOU HAVE? HE HAS FOLLOWERS, BUT HOW CAN YOU CALL THAT AN ARMY?
SOON, PONT'S ARMY WILL BE LARGE ENOUGH TO OVERTAKE GREY TOWERS. IS THAT WHAT YOU'RE WAITING FOR?
IN ALL THIS, WHAT HAS OUR FEARLESS RULER DONE? ENLIST THE AID OF THAT HALF-WIT SOOTOH TO ROOT PONT OUT OF THE GUARD.
I'VE HIRED A TEAM OF MERCENARIES, FORMER GUARDS. THEY WILL HUNT PONT DOWN AND FINALLY KILL HIM FOR US.

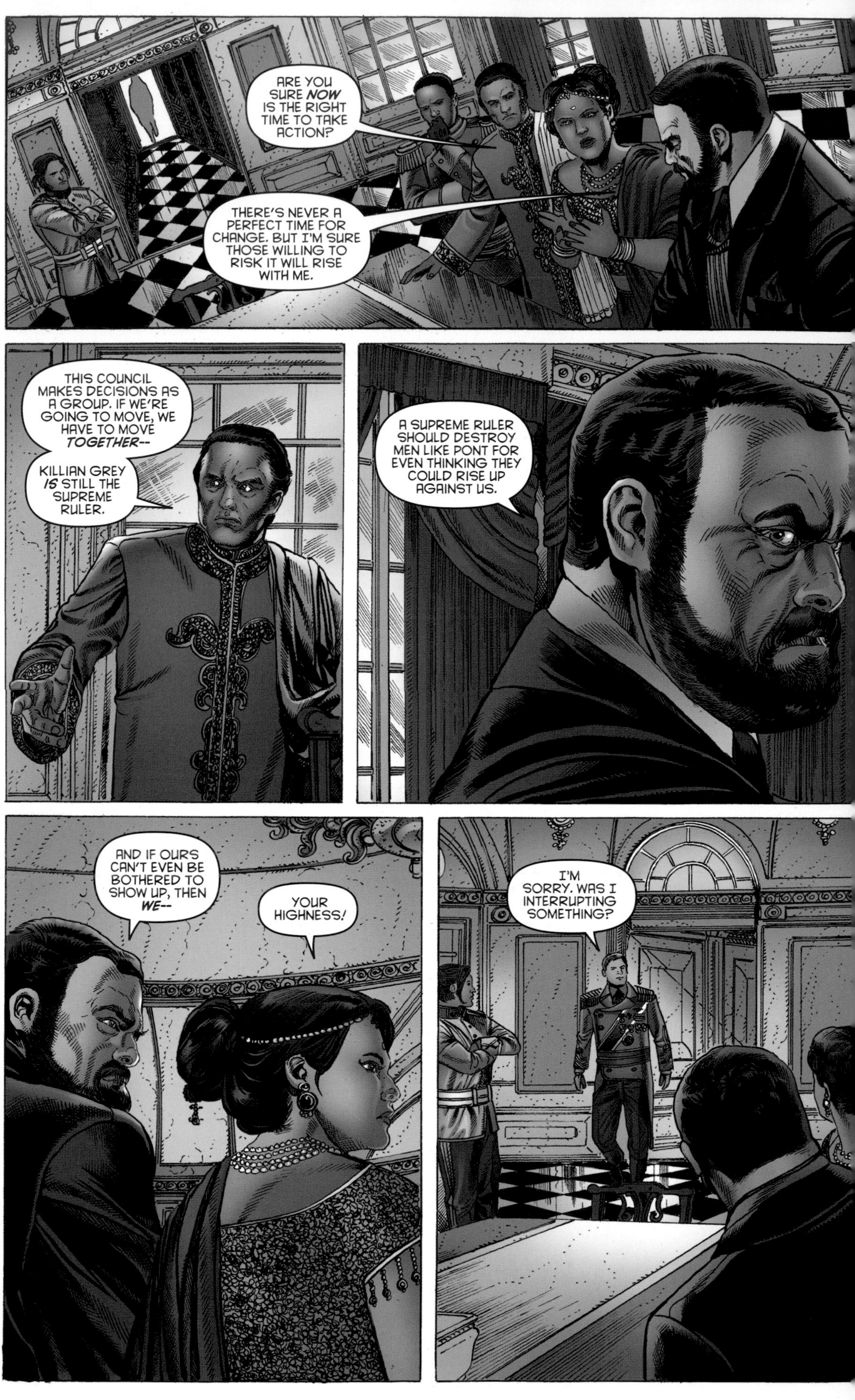
ARE YOU SURE NOW IS THE RIGHT TIME TO TAKE ACTION?
THERE'S NEVER A PERFECT TIME FOR CHANGE. BUT I'M SURE THOSE WILLING TO RISK IT WILL RISE WITH ME.
THIS COUNCIL MAKES DECISIONS AS A GROUP. IF WE'RE GOING TO MOVE, WE HAVE TO MOVE TOGETHER--
KILLIAN GREY IS STILL THE SUPREME RULER.
A SUPREME RULER SHOULD DESTROY MEN LIKE PONT FOR EVEN THINKING THEY COULD RISE UP AGAINST US.
AND IF OURS CAN'T EVEN BE BOTHERED TO SHOW UP, THEN WE--
YOUR HIGHNESS!
I'M SORRY. WAS I INTERRUPTING SOMETHING?

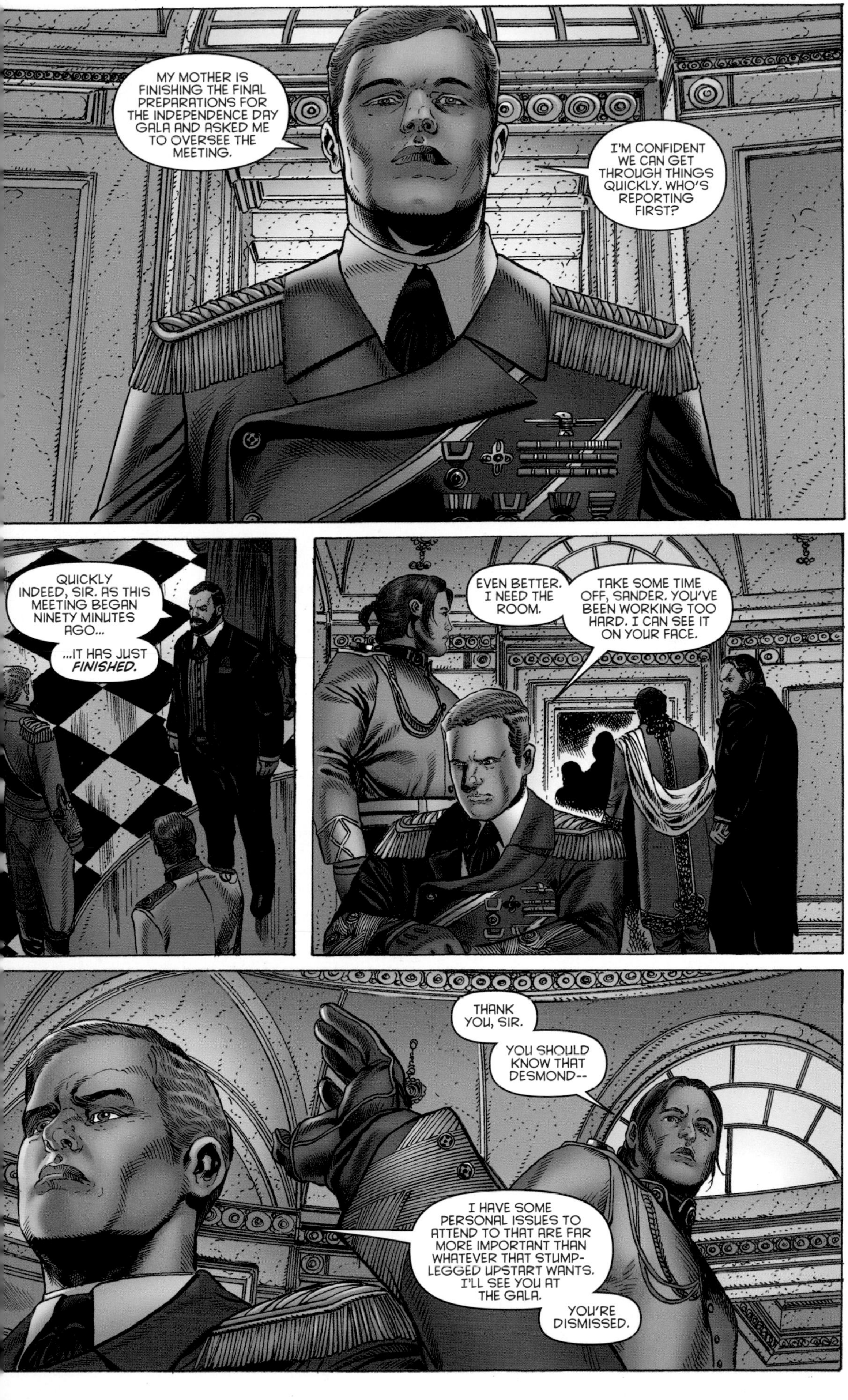
MY MOTHER IS FINISHING THE FINAL PREPARATIONS FOR THE INDEPENDENCE DAY GALA AND ASKED ME TO OVERSEE THE MEETING.
I'M CONFIDENT WE CAN GET THROUGH THINGS QUICKLY. WHO'S REPORTING FIRST?
QUICKLY INDEED, SIR. AS THIS MEETING BEGAN NINETY MINUTES AGO...
...IT HAS JUST *FINISHED.*
EVEN BETTER. I NEED THE ROOM.
TAKE SOME TIME OFF, SANDER. YOU'VE BEEN WORKING TOO HARD. I CAN SEE IT ON YOUR FACE.
THANK YOU, SIR.
YOU SHOULD KNOW THAT DESMOND--
I HAVE SOME PERSONAL ISSUES TO ATTEND TO THAT ARE FAR MORE IMPORTANT THAN WHATEVER THAT STUMP-LEGGED UPSTART WANTS. I'LL SEE YOU AT THE GALA.
YOU'RE DISMISSED.

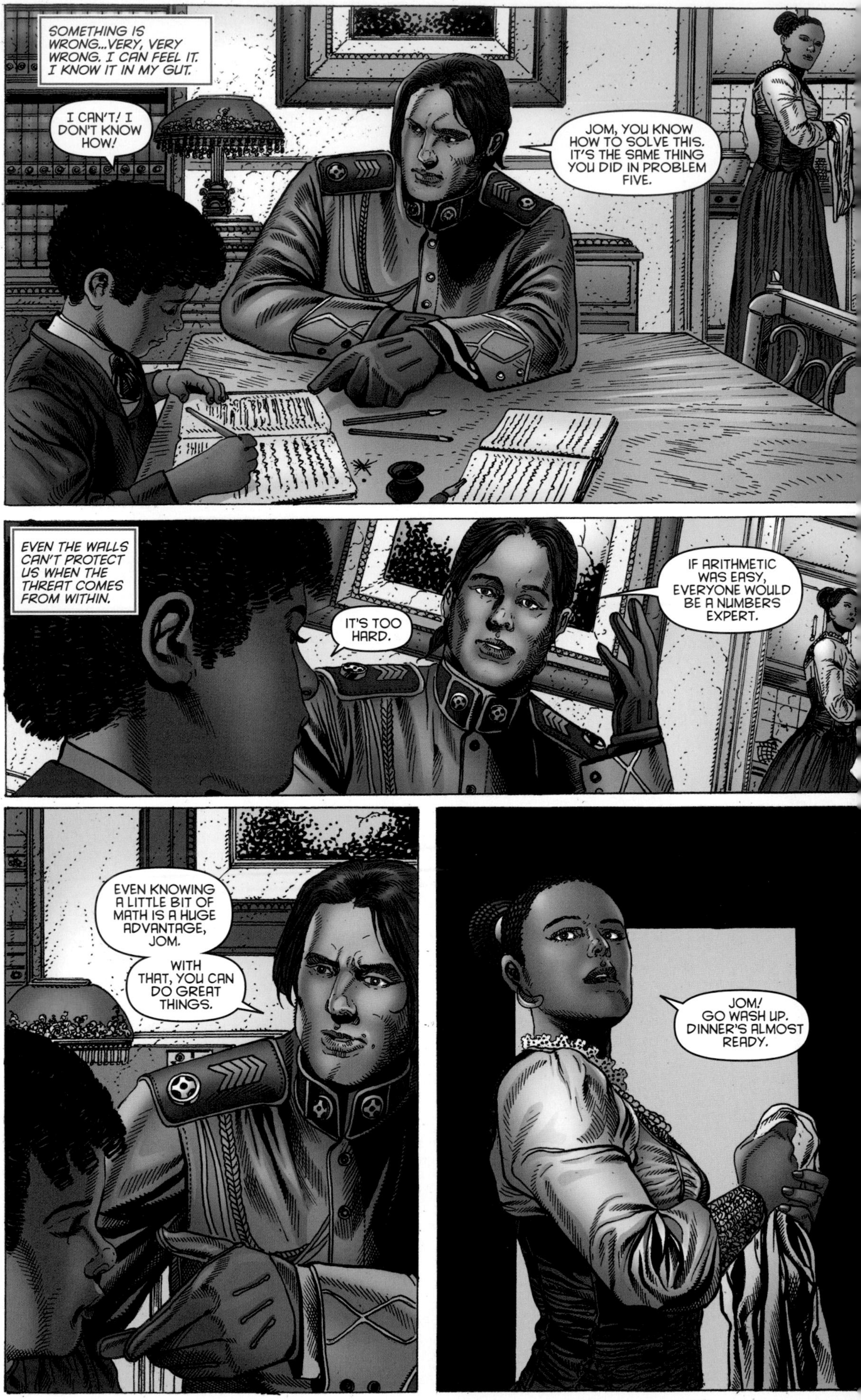
SOMETHING IS WRONG...VERY, VERY WRONG. I CAN FEEL IT. I KNOW IT IN MY GUT.
I CAN'T! I DON'T KNOW HOW!
JOM, YOU KNOW HOW TO SOLVE THIS. IT'S THE SAME THING YOU DID IN PROBLEM FIVE.
EVEN THE WALLS CAN'T PROTECT US WHEN THE THREAT COMES FROM WITHIN.
IT'S TOO HARD.
IF ARITHMETIC WAS EASY, EVERYONE WOULD BE A NUMBERS EXPERT.
EVEN KNOWING A LITTLE BIT OF MATH IS A HUGE ADVANTAGE, JOM.
WITH THAT, YOU CAN DO GREAT THINGS.
JOM! GO WASH UP. DINNER'S ALMOST READY.

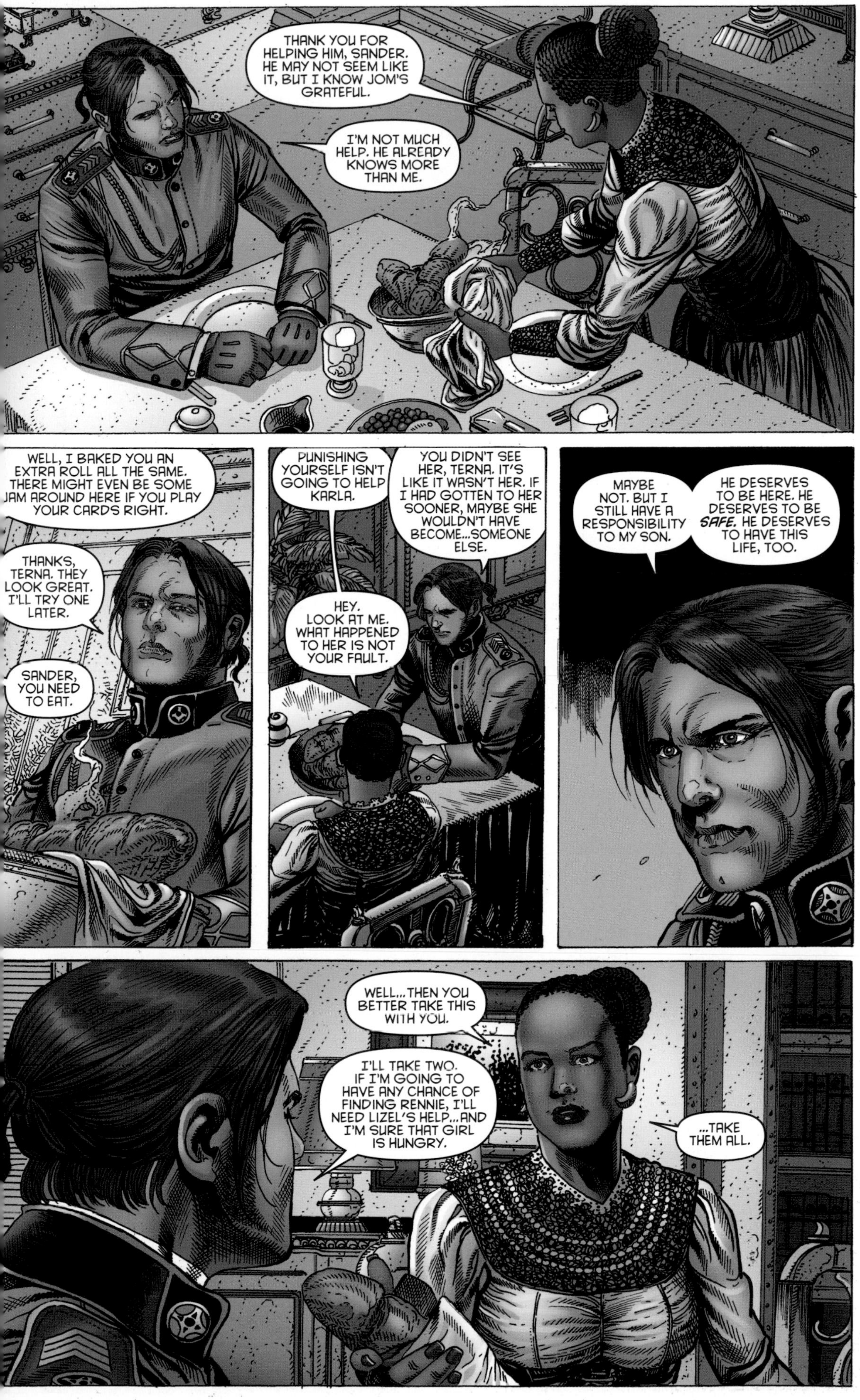
THANK YOU FOR HELPING HIM, SANDER. HE MAY NOT SEEM LIKE IT, BUT I KNOW JOM'S GRATEFUL.
I'M NOT MUCH HELP. HE ALREADY KNOWS MORE THAN ME.
WELL, I BAKED YOU AN EXTRA ROLL ALL THE SAME. THERE MIGHT EVEN BE SOME JAM AROUND HERE IF YOU PLAY YOUR CARDS RIGHT.
THANKS, TERNA. THEY LOOK GREAT. I'LL TRY ONE LATER.
SANDER, YOU NEED TO EAT.
PUNISHING YOURSELF ISN'T GOING TO HELP KARLA.
YOU DIDN'T SEE HER, TERNA. IT'S LIKE IT WASN'T HER. IF I HAD GOTTEN TO HER SOONER, MAYBE SHE WOULDN'T HAVE BECOME...SOMEONE ELSE.
HEY. LOOK AT ME. WHAT HAPPENED TO HER IS NOT YOUR FAULT.
MAYBE NOT. BUT I STILL HAVE A RESPONSIBILITY TO MY SON.
HE DESERVES TO BE HERE. HE DESERVES TO BE SAFE. HE DESERVES TO HAVE THIS LIFE, TOO.
WELL...THEN YOU BETTER TAKE THIS WITH YOU.
I'LL TAKE TWO. IF I'M GOING TO HAVE ANY CHANCE OF FINDING RENNIE, I'LL NEED LIZEL'S HELP...AND I'M SURE THAT GIRL IS HUNGRY.
...TAKE THEM ALL.

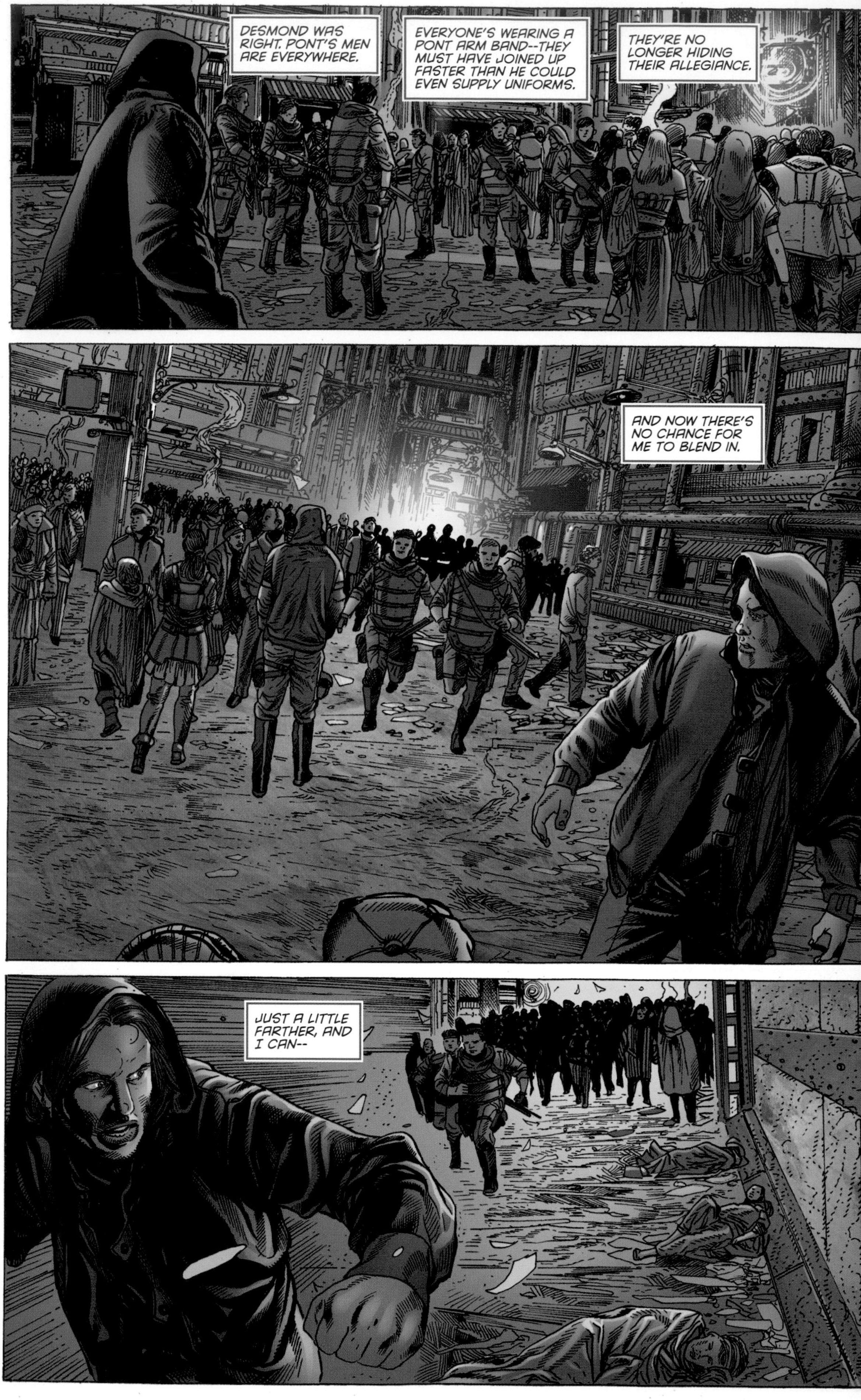
DESMOND WAS RIGHT. PONT'S MEN ARE EVERYWHERE.
EVERYONE'S WEARING A PONT ARM BAND--THEY MUST HAVE JOINED UP FASTER THAN HE COULD EVEN SUPPLY UNIFORMS.
THEY'RE NO LONGER HIDING THEIR ALLEGIANCE.
AND NOW THERE'S NO CHANCE FOR ME TO BLEND IN.
JUST A LITTLE FARTHER, AND I CAN--

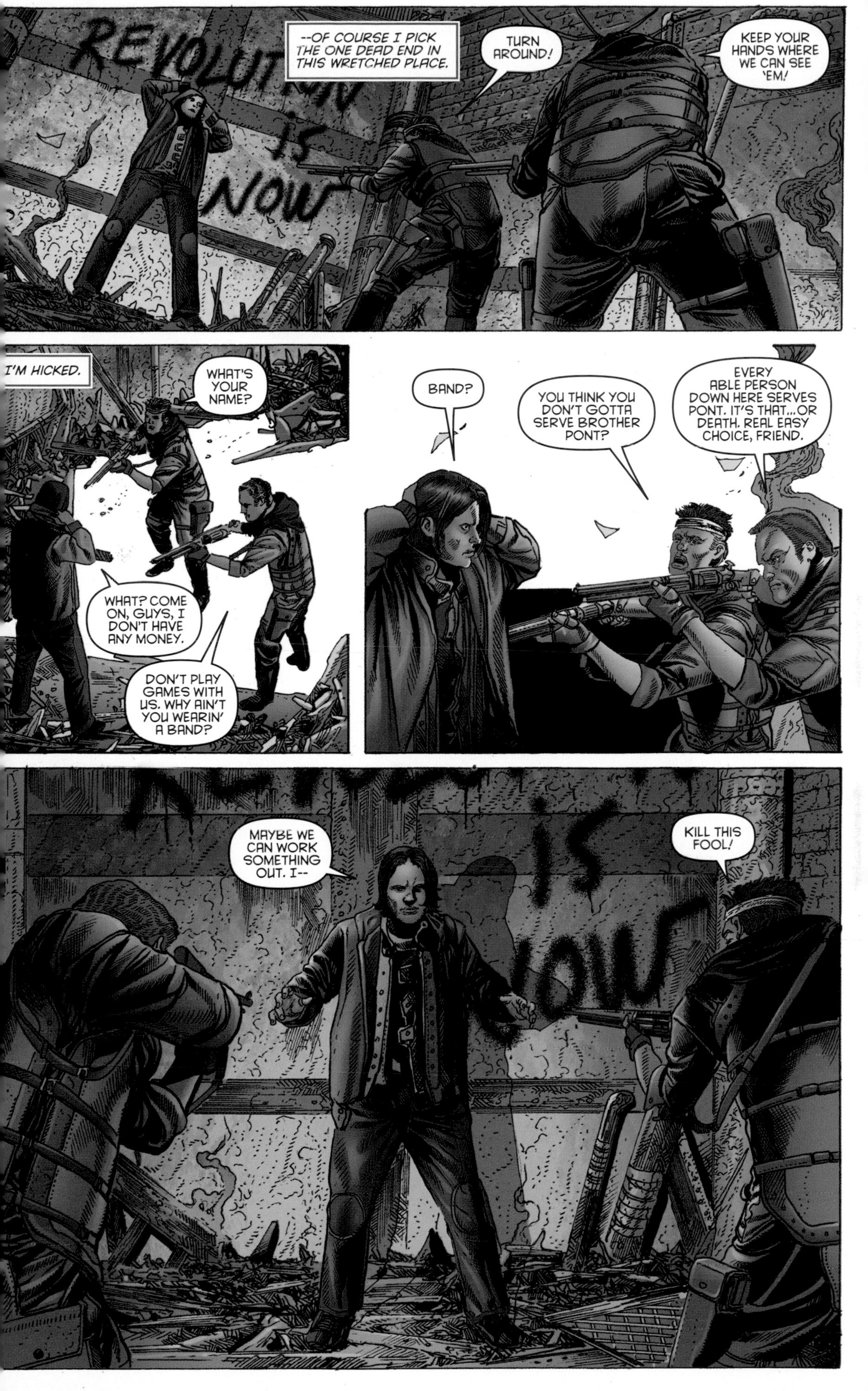
REVOLUTION IS NOW
--OF COURSE I PICK THE ONE DEAD END IN THIS WRETCHED PLACE.
TURN AROUND!
KEEP YOUR HANDS WHERE WE CAN SEE 'EM!
I'M HICKED.
WHAT'S YOUR NAME?
WHAT? COME ON, GUYS, I DON'T HAVE ANY MONEY.
DON'T PLAY GAMES WITH US. WHY AIN'T YOU WEARIN' A BAND?
BAND?
YOU THINK YOU DON'T GOTTA SERVE BROTHER PONT?
EVERY ABLE PERSON DOWN HERE SERVES PONT. IT'S THAT...OR DEATH. REAL EASY CHOICE, FRIEND.
MAYBE WE CAN WORK SOMETHING OUT. I--
KILL THIS FOOL!

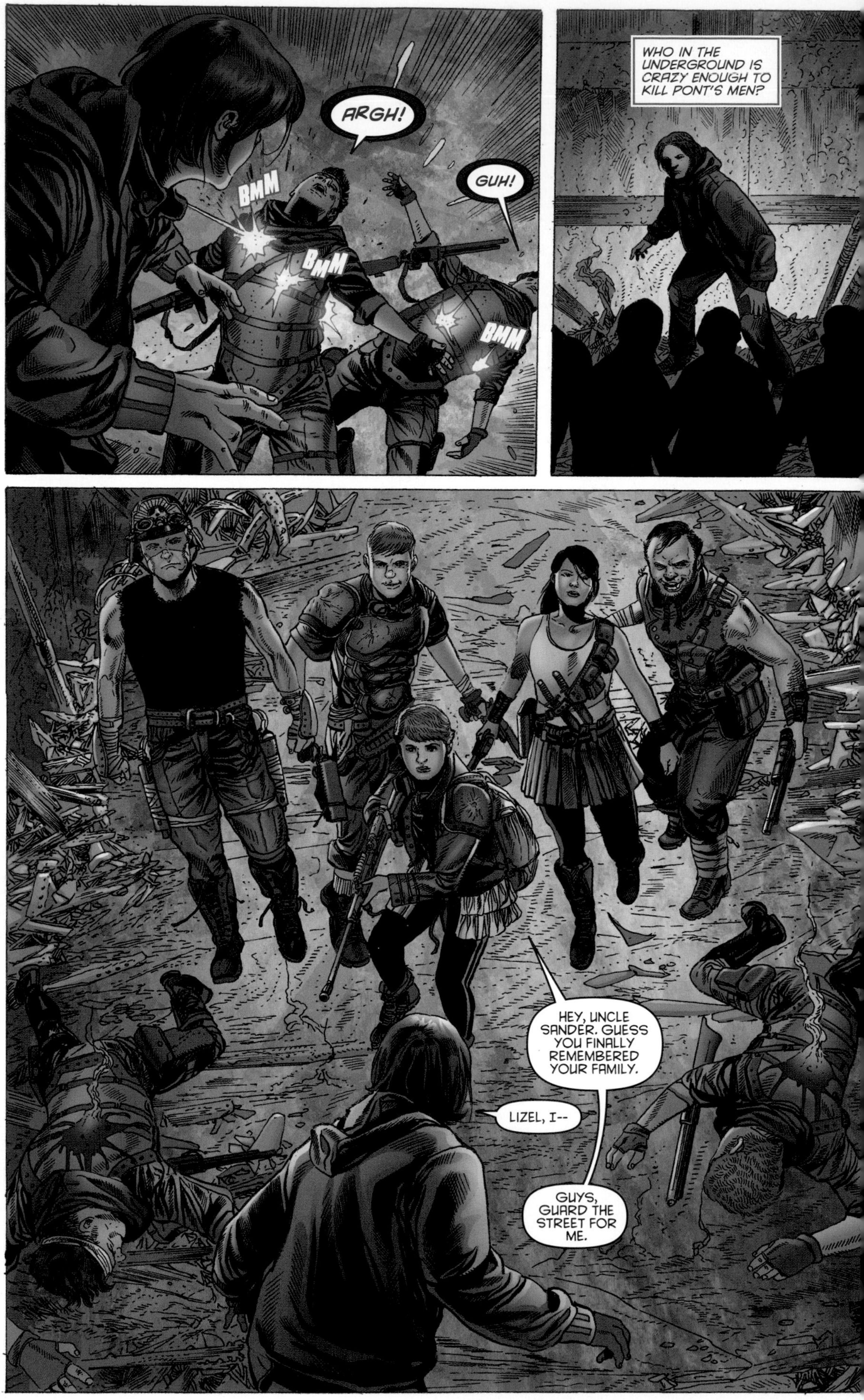
ARGH!
BMM
BMM
GUH!
BMM
WHO IN THE UNDERGROUND IS CRAZY ENOUGH TO KILL PONT'S MEN?
HEY, UNCLE SANDER. GUESS YOU FINALLY REMEMBERED YOUR FAMILY.
LIZEL, I--
GUYS, GUARD THE STREET FOR ME.

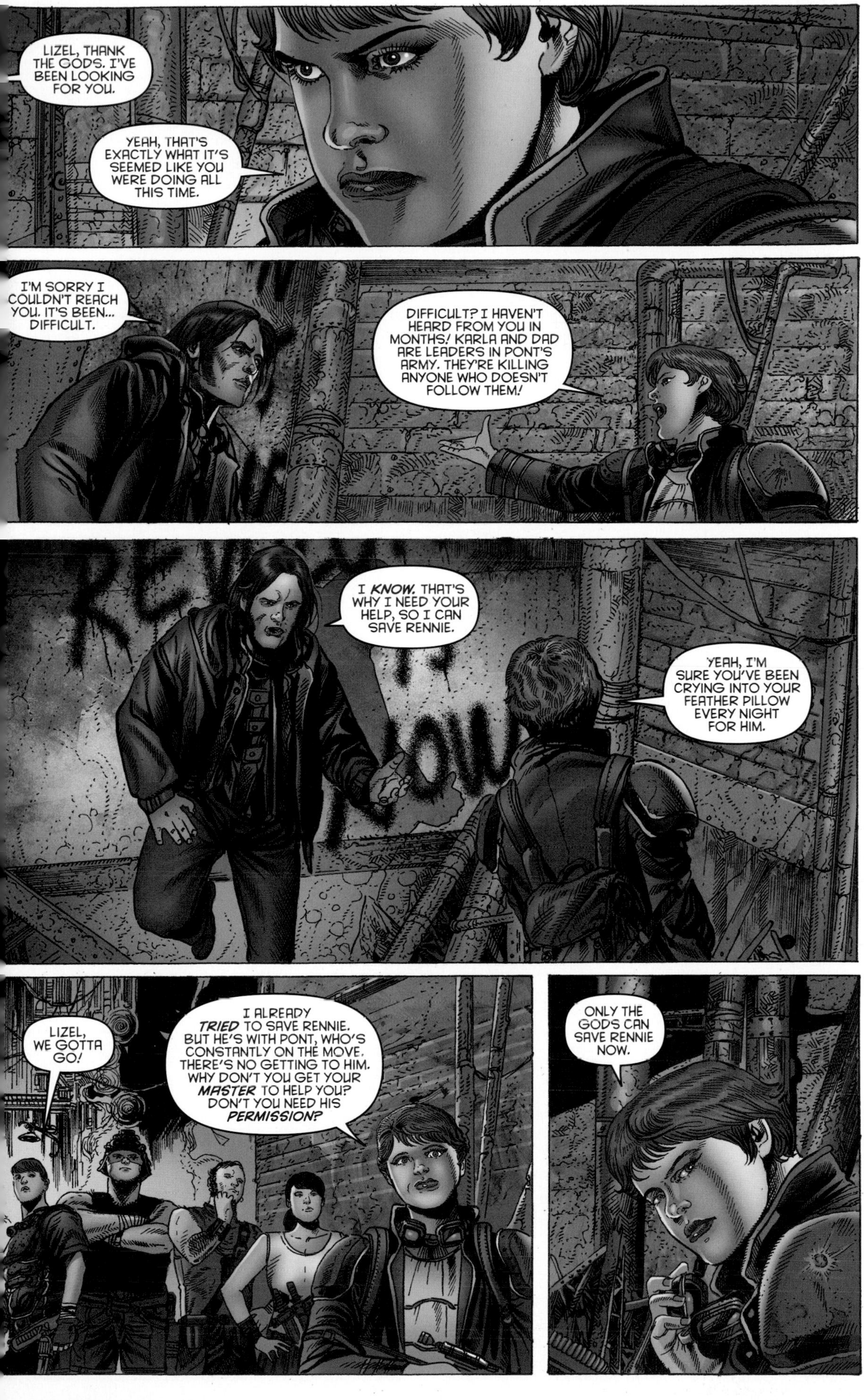
LIZEL, THANK THE GODS. I'VE BEEN LOOKING FOR YOU.
YEAH, THAT'S EXACTLY WHAT IT'S SEEMED LIKE YOU WERE DOING ALL THIS TIME.
I'M SORRY I COULDN'T REACH YOU. IT'S BEEN... DIFFICULT.
DIFFICULT? I HAVEN'T HEARD FROM YOU IN MONTHS! KARLA AND DAD ARE LEADERS IN PONT'S ARMY. THEY'RE KILLING ANYONE WHO DOESN'T FOLLOW THEM!
I KNOW. THAT'S WHY I NEED YOUR HELP, SO I CAN SAVE RENNIE.
YEAH, I'M SURE YOU'VE BEEN CRYING INTO YOUR FEATHER PILLOW EVERY NIGHT FOR HIM.
LIZEL, WE GOTTA GO!
I ALREADY TRIED TO SAVE RENNIE. BUT HE'S WITH PONT, WHO'S CONSTANTLY ON THE MOVE. THERE'S NO GETTING TO HIM. WHY DON'T YOU GET YOUR MASTER TO HELP YOU? DON'T YOU NEED HIS PERMISSION?
ONLY THE GODS CAN SAVE RENNIE NOW.

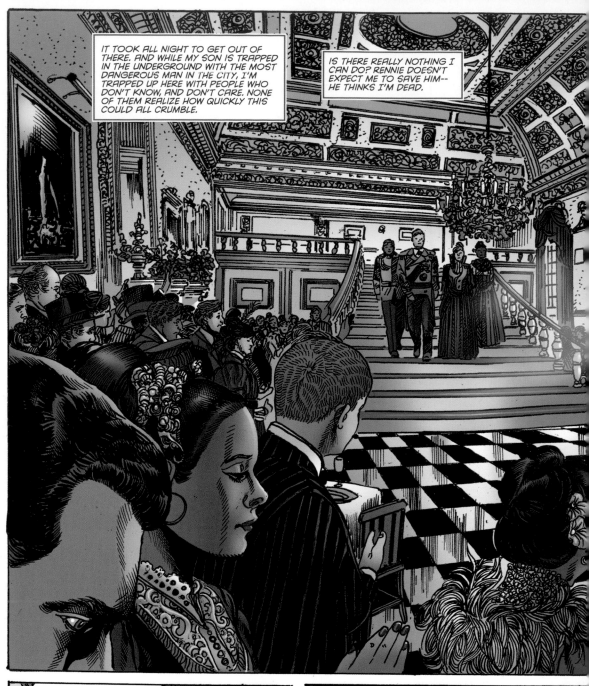

IT TOOK ALL NIGHT TO GET OUT OF THERE. AND WHILE MY SON IS TRAPPED IN THE UNDERGROUND WITH THE MOST DANGEROUS MAN IN THE CITY, I'M TRAPPED UP HERE WITH PEOPLE WHO DON'T KNOW, AND DON'T CARE. NONE OF THEM REALIZE HOW QUICKLY THIS COULD ALL CRUMBLE.

IS THERE REALLY NOTHING I CAN DO? RENNIE DOESN'T EXPECT ME TO SAVE HIM-- HE THINKS I'M DEAD.

DON'T BE SEDUCED BY THE EXTRAVAGANCE. THESE PEOPLE WOULD KILL ME IN AN INSTANT.

YOU'VE OUTDONE YOURSELF, MOTHER.

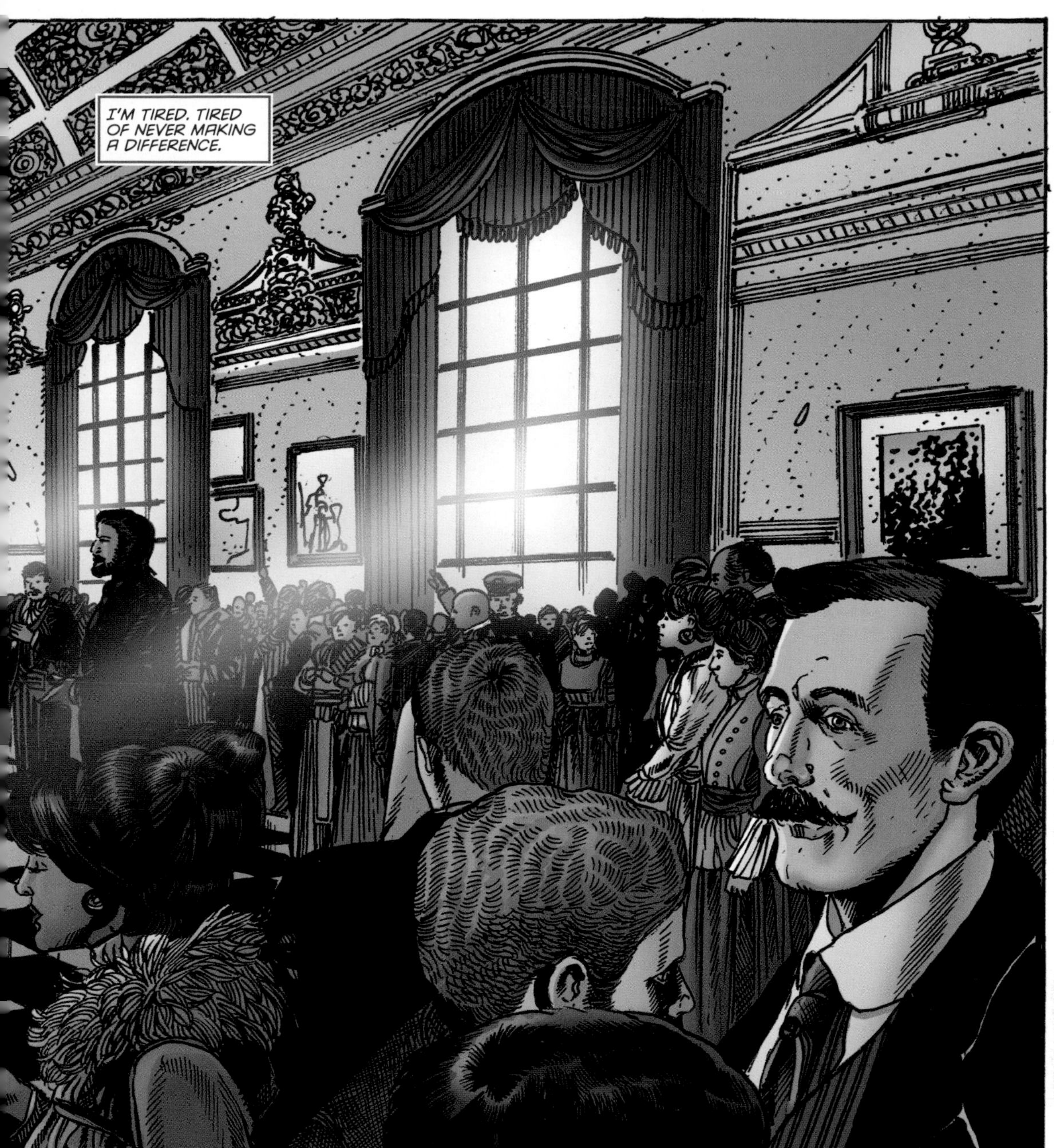
I'M TIRED. TIRED OF NEVER MAKING A DIFFERENCE.

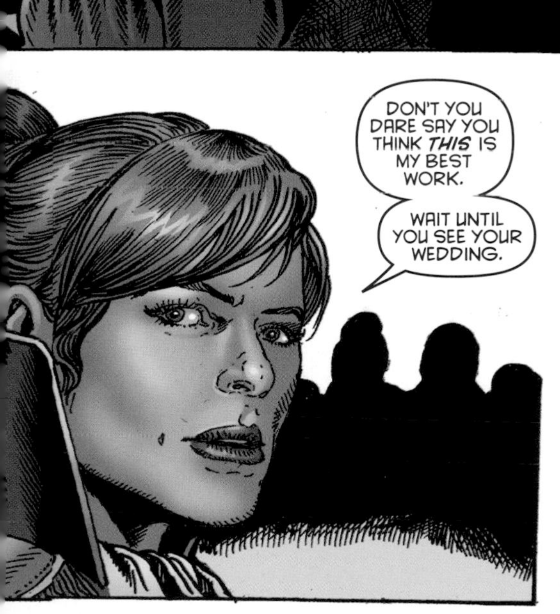
DON'T YOU DARE SAY YOU THINK *THIS* IS MY BEST WORK.
WAIT UNTIL YOU SEE YOUR WEDDING.

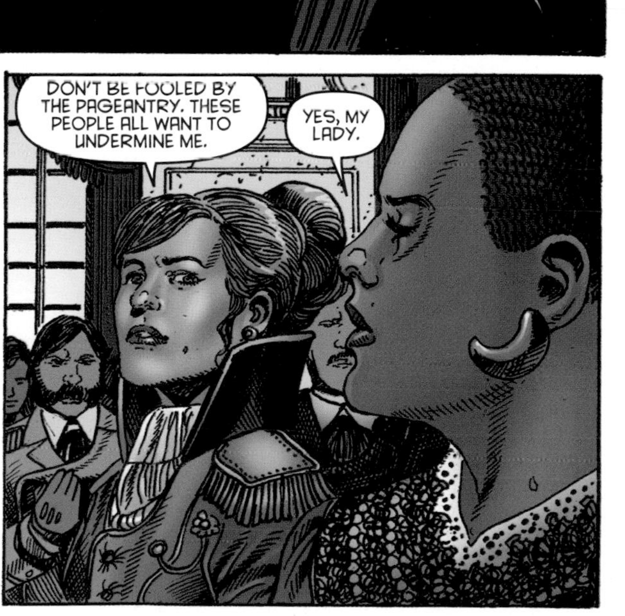
DON'T BE FOOLED BY THE PAGEANTRY. THESE PEOPLE ALL WANT TO UNDERMINE ME.
YES, MY LADY.

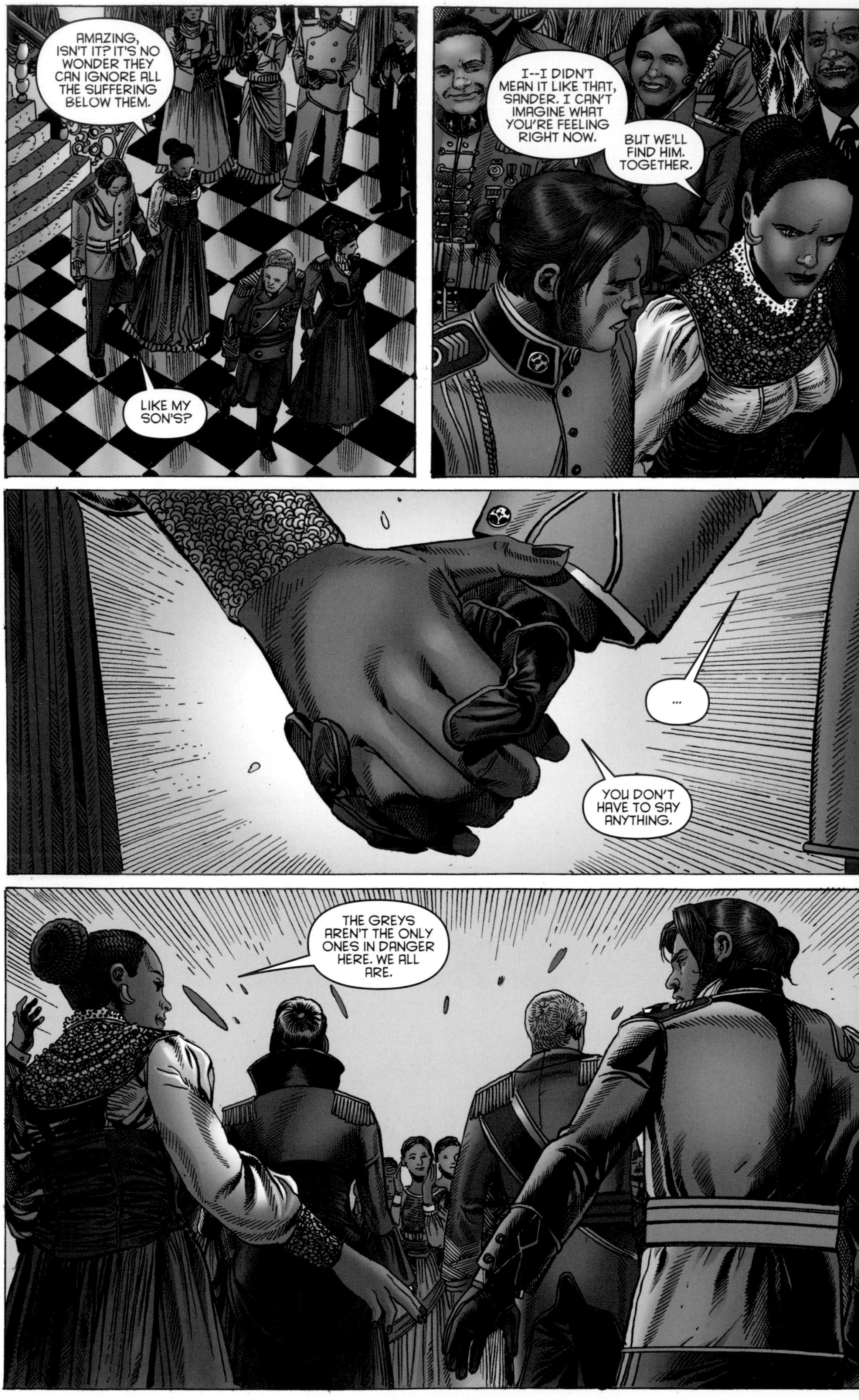
AMAZING, ISN'T IT? IT'S NO WONDER THEY CAN IGNORE ALL THE SUFFERING BELOW THEM.
LIKE MY SON'S?
I--I DIDN'T MEAN IT LIKE THAT, SANDER. I CAN'T IMAGINE WHAT YOU'RE FEELING RIGHT NOW.
BUT WE'LL FIND HIM. TOGETHER.
...
YOU DON'T HAVE TO SAY ANYTHING.
THE GREYS AREN'T THE ONLY ONES IN DANGER HERE. WE ALL ARE.

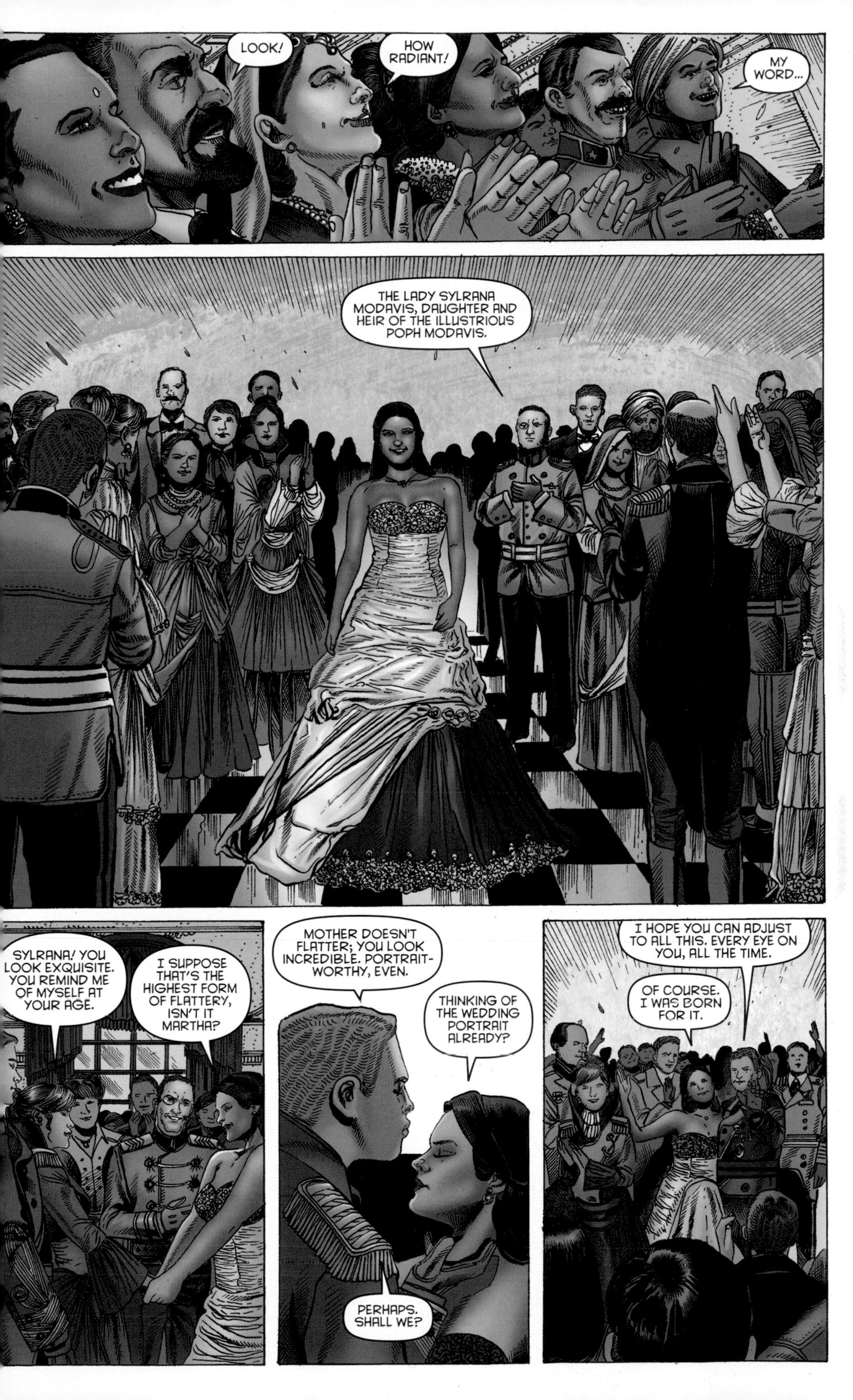
LOOK!
HOW RADIANT!
MY WORD...
THE LADY SYLRANA MODAVIS, DAUGHTER AND HEIR OF THE ILLUSTRIOUS POPH MODAVIS.
SYLRANA! YOU LOOK EXQUISITE. YOU REMIND ME OF MYSELF AT YOUR AGE.
I SUPPOSE THAT'S THE HIGHEST FORM OF FLATTERY, ISN'T IT MARTHA?
MOTHER DOESN'T FLATTER; YOU LOOK INCREDIBLE. PORTRAIT-WORTHY, EVEN.
THINKING OF THE WEDDING PORTRAIT ALREADY?
PERHAPS. SHALL WE?
I HOPE YOU CAN ADJUST TO ALL THIS. EVERY EYE ON YOU, ALL THE TIME.
OF COURSE. I WAS BORN FOR IT.

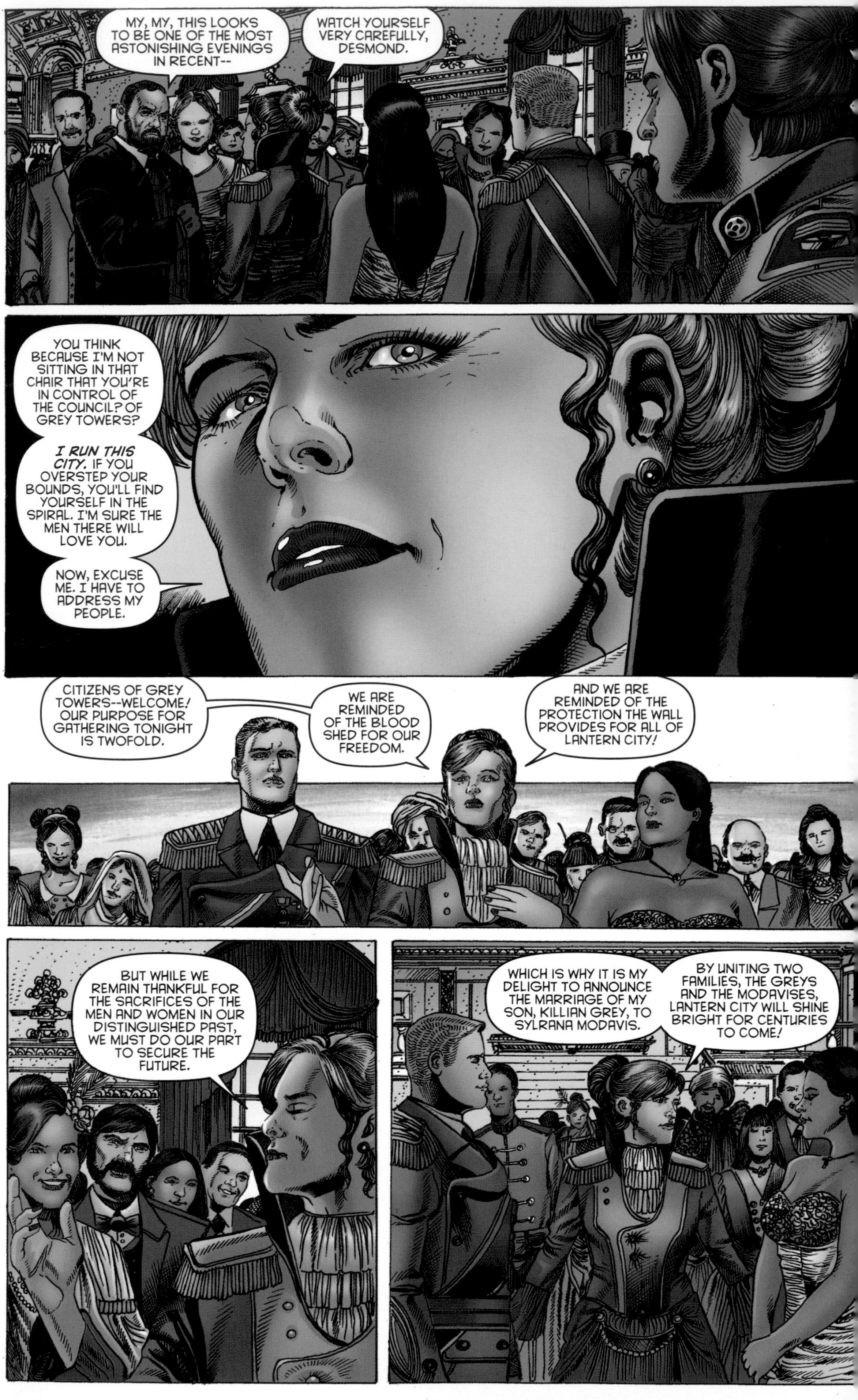
MY, MY, THIS LOOKS TO BE ONE OF THE MOST ASTONISHING EVENINGS IN RECENT--
WATCH YOURSELF VERY CAREFULLY, DESMOND.
YOU THINK BECAUSE I'M NOT SITTING IN THAT CHAIR THAT YOU'RE IN CONTROL OF THE COUNCIL? OF GREY TOWERS?
I RUN THIS CITY. IF YOU OVERSTEP YOUR BOUNDS, YOU'LL FIND YOURSELF IN THE SPIRAL. I'M SURE THE MEN THERE WILL LOVE YOU.
NOW, EXCUSE ME. I HAVE TO ADDRESS MY PEOPLE.
CITIZENS OF GREY TOWERS--WELCOME! OUR PURPOSE FOR GATHERING TONIGHT IS TWOFOLD.
WE ARE REMINDED OF THE BLOOD SHED FOR OUR FREEDOM.
AND WE ARE REMINDED OF THE PROTECTION THE WALL PROVIDES FOR ALL OF LANTERN CITY!
BUT WHILE WE REMAIN THANKFUL FOR THE SACRIFICES OF THE MEN AND WOMEN IN OUR DISTINGUISHED PAST, WE MUST DO OUR PART TO SECURE THE FUTURE.
WHICH IS WHY IT IS MY DELIGHT TO ANNOUNCE THE MARRIAGE OF MY SON, KILLIAN GREY, TO SYLRANA MODAVIS.
BY UNITING TWO FAMILIES, THE GREYS AND THE MODAVISES, LANTERN CITY WILL SHINE BRIGHT FOR CENTURIES TO COME!

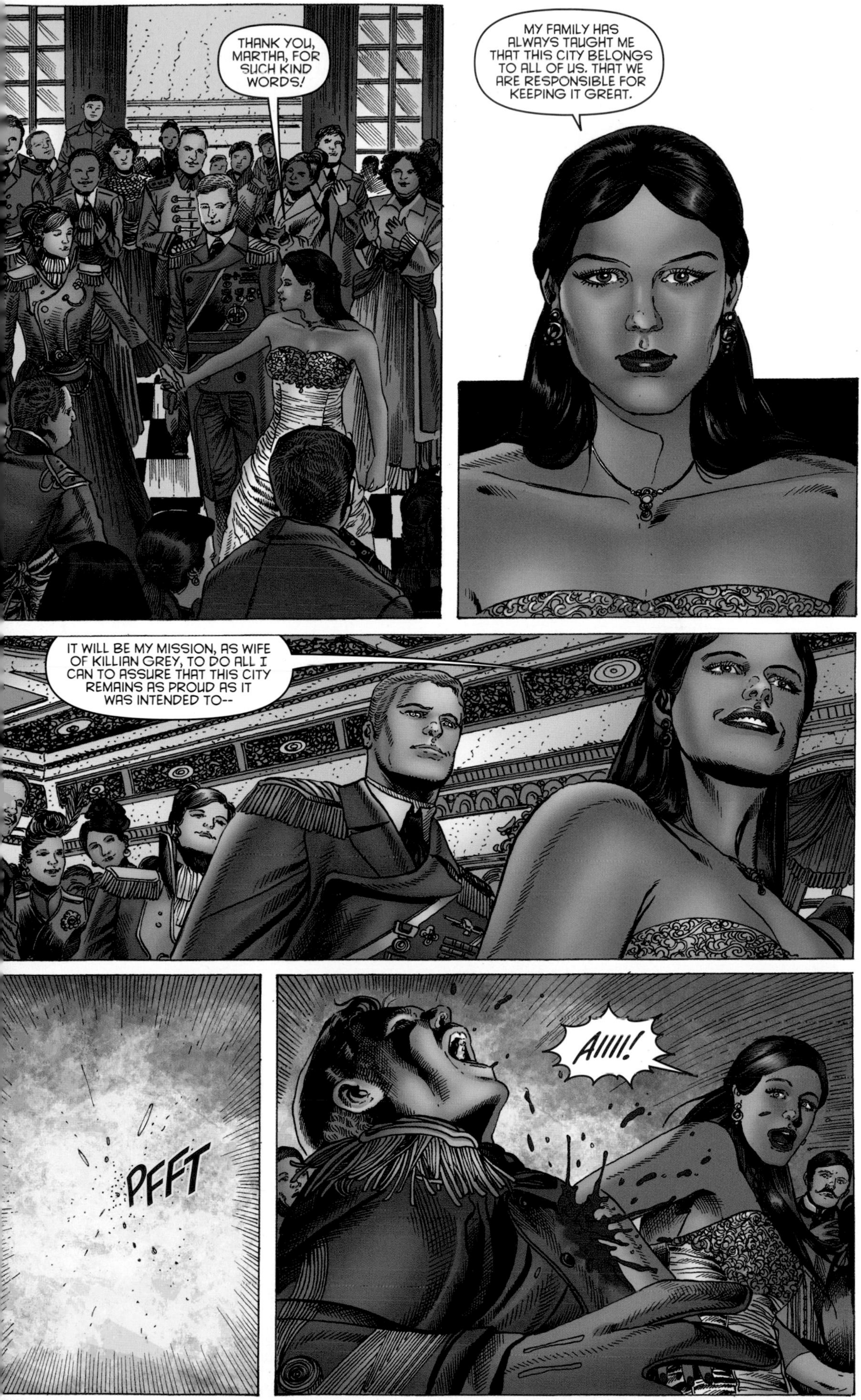
THANK YOU, MARTHA, FOR SUCH KIND WORDS!
MY FAMILY HAS ALWAYS TAUGHT ME THAT THIS CITY BELONGS TO ALL OF US. THAT WE ARE RESPONSIBLE FOR KEEPING IT GREAT.
IT WILL BE MY MISSION, AS WIFE OF KILLIAN GREY, TO DO ALL I CAN TO ASSURE THAT THIS CITY REMAINS AS PROUD AS IT WAS INTENDED TO--
PFFT
AIIII!

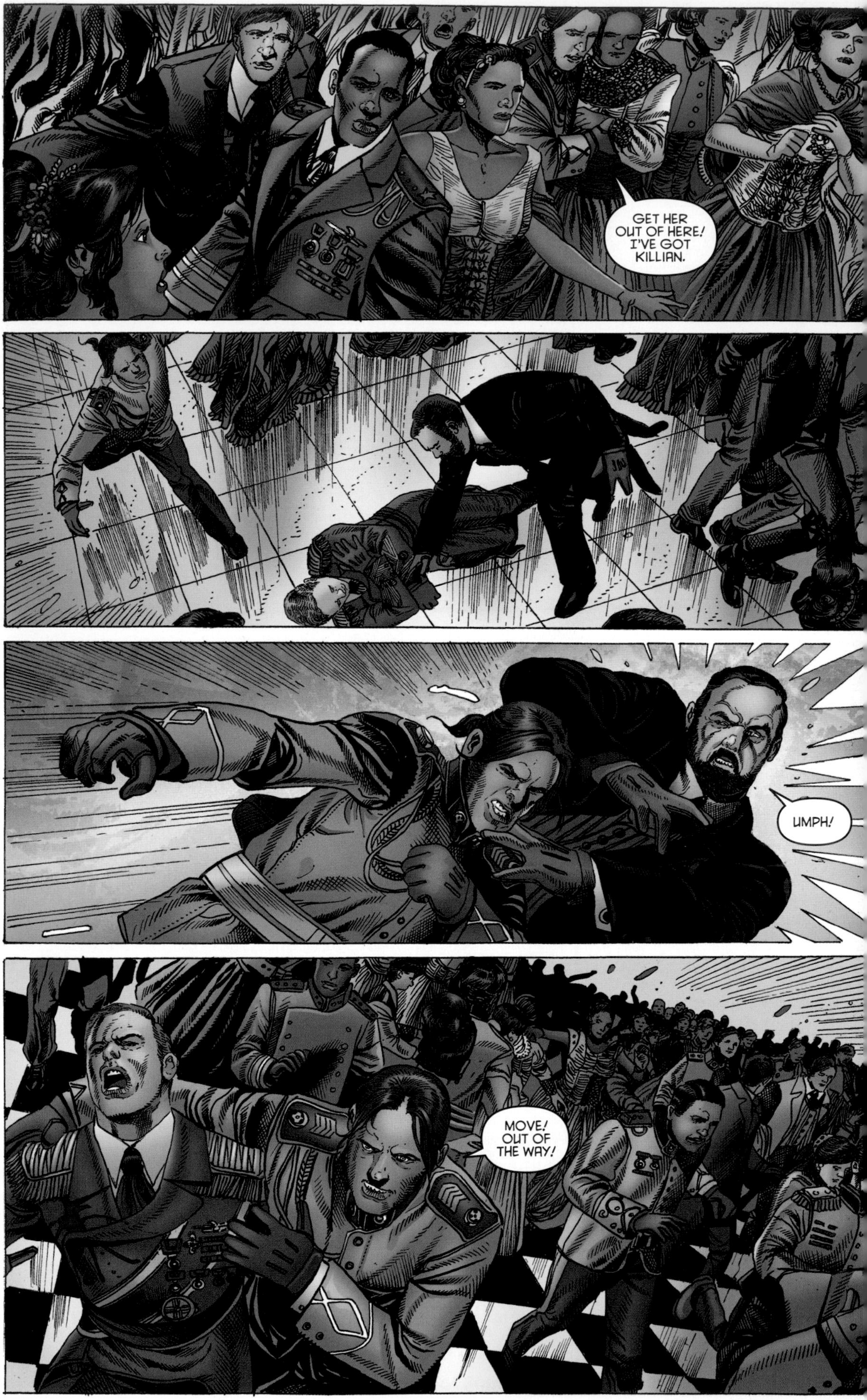
GET HER OUT OF HERE! I'VE GOT KILLIAN.
UMPH!
MOVE! OUT OF THE WAY!

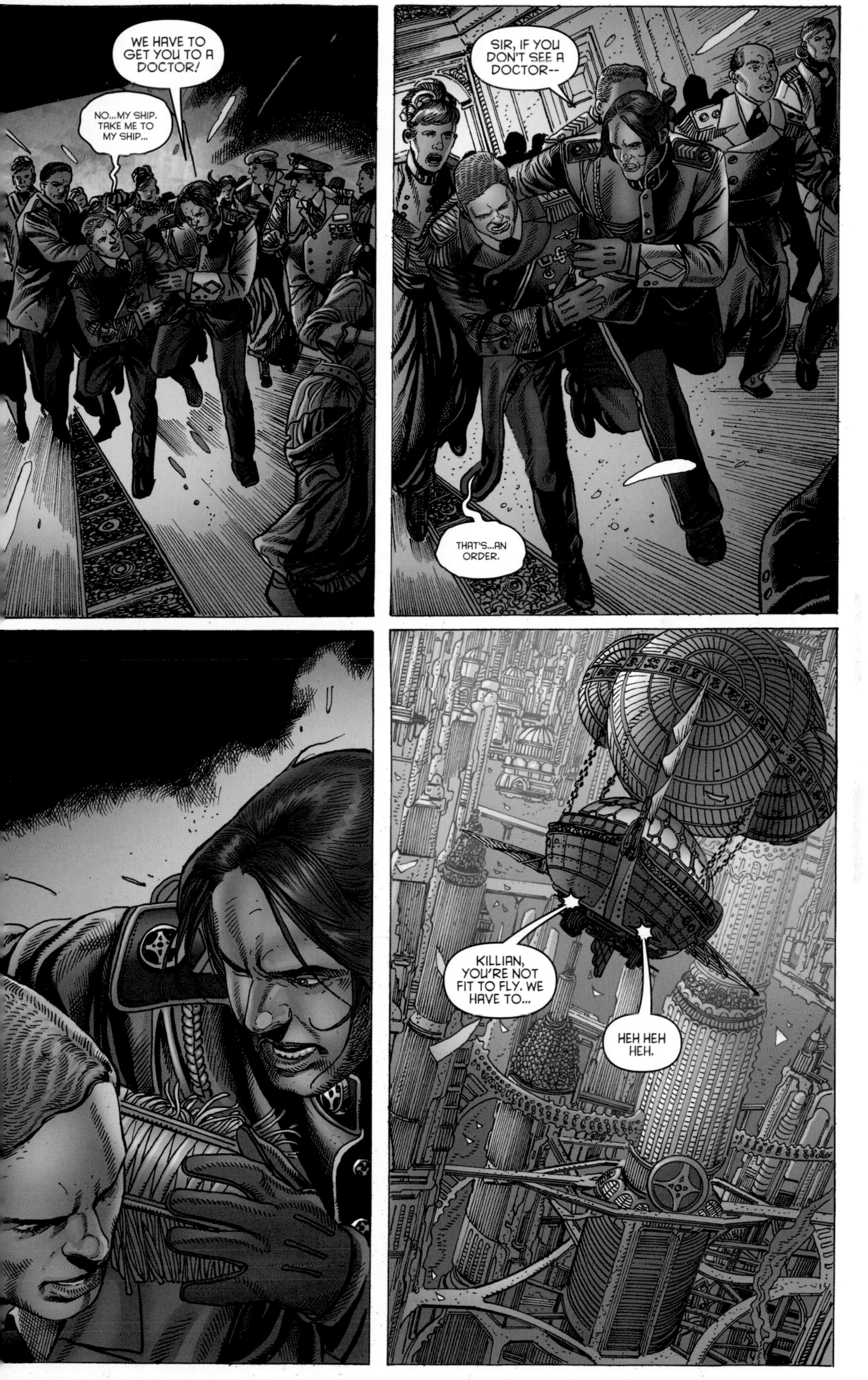
WE HAVE TO GET YOU TO A DOCTOR!
NO...MY SHIP. TAKE ME TO MY SHIP...
SIR, IF YOU DON'T SEE A DOCTOR--
THAT'S...AN ORDER.
KILLIAN, YOU'RE NOT FIT TO FLY. WE HAVE TO...
HEH HEH HEH.

WHAT? HOW?

A PIG'S STOMACH, FILLED WITH PIG'S BLOOD AND SEWN SHUT. VERY EASY TO CONCEAL IN MY JACKET. AND WITH A PRESSURE CARTRIDGE, EASY TO PUNCTURE. ESPECIALLY WITH THE DISTRACTION OF GUSTAVO FIRING A GUN.

I'VE HAD A CHANGE OF HEART, SANDER.

I CAN'T LEAVE THIS WORLD YET. THE LANTERN'S STILL FAR FROM READY.

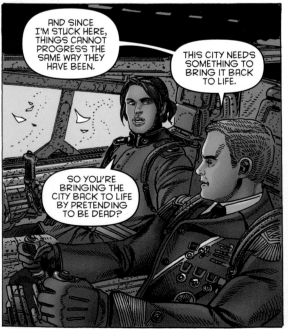

AND SINCE I'M STUCK HERE, THINGS CANNOT PROGRESS THE SAME WAY THEY HAVE BEEN.

THIS CITY NEEDS SOMETHING TO BRING IT BACK TO LIFE.

SO YOU'RE BRINGING THE CITY BACK TO LIFE BY PRETENDING TO BE DEAD?

THERE'S PERFECT LOGIC TO IT. CAN'T YOU SEE?

HE'S EVEN CRAZIER THAN I THOUGHT.

SIR, WE NEED TO GO BACK. WE CAN FIND SOMEONE TO...HELP.

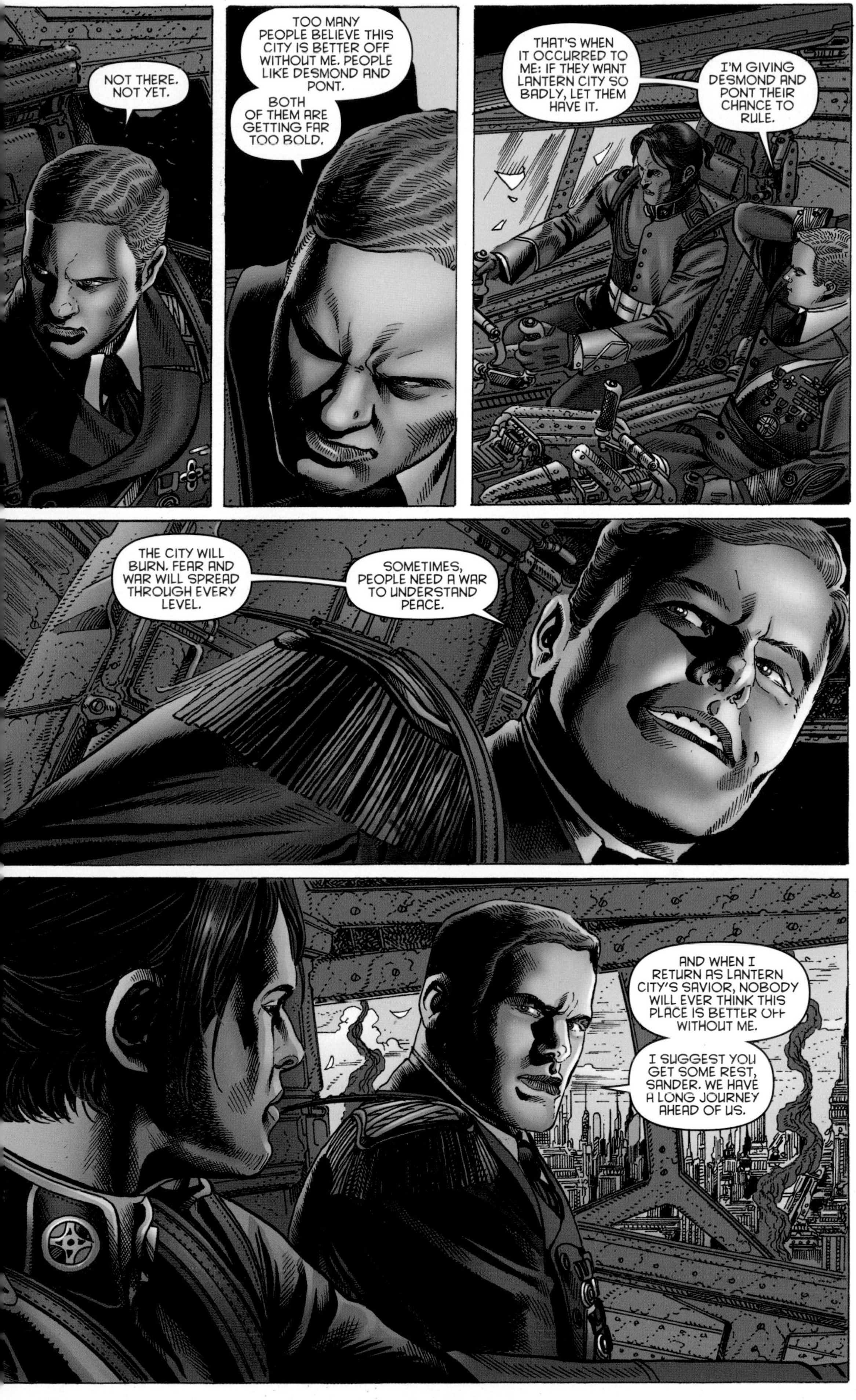
NOT THERE. NOT YET.
TOO MANY PEOPLE BELIEVE THIS CITY IS BETTER OFF WITHOUT ME. PEOPLE LIKE DESMOND AND PONT.
BOTH OF THEM ARE GETTING FAR TOO BOLD.
THAT'S WHEN IT OCCURRED TO ME: IF THEY WANT LANTERN CITY SO BADLY, LET THEM HAVE IT.
I'M GIVING DESMOND AND PONT THEIR CHANCE TO RULE.
THE CITY WILL BURN. FEAR AND WAR WILL SPREAD THROUGH EVERY LEVEL.
SOMETIMES, PEOPLE NEED A WAR TO UNDERSTAND PEACE.
AND WHEN I RETURN AS LANTERN CITY'S SAVIOR, NOBODY WILL EVER THINK THIS PLACE IS BETTER OFF WITHOUT ME.
I SUGGEST YOU GET SOME REST, SANDER. WE HAVE A LONG JOURNEY AHEAD OF US.

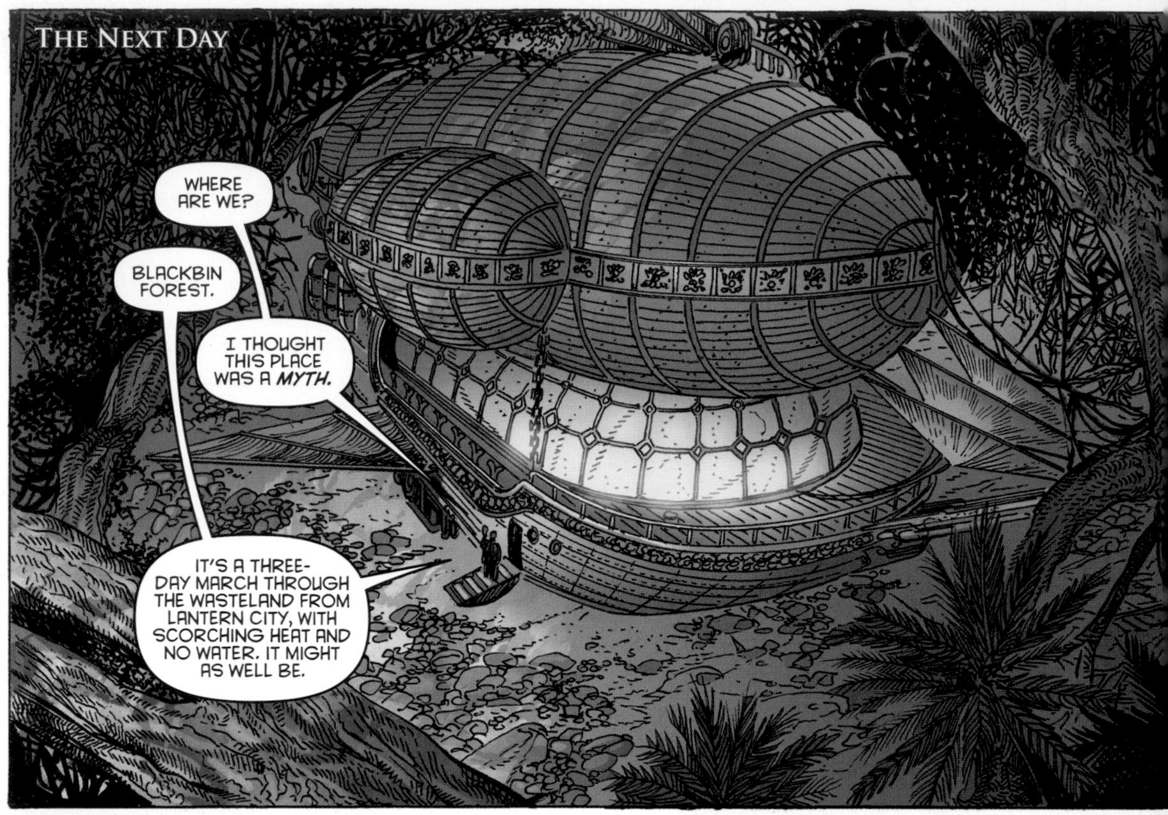
THE NEXT DAY
WHERE ARE WE?
BLACKBIN FOREST.
I THOUGHT THIS PLACE WAS A *MYTH.*
IT'S A THREE-DAY MARCH THROUGH THE WASTELAND FROM LANTERN CITY, WITH SCORCHING HEAT AND NO WATER. IT MIGHT AS WELL BE.

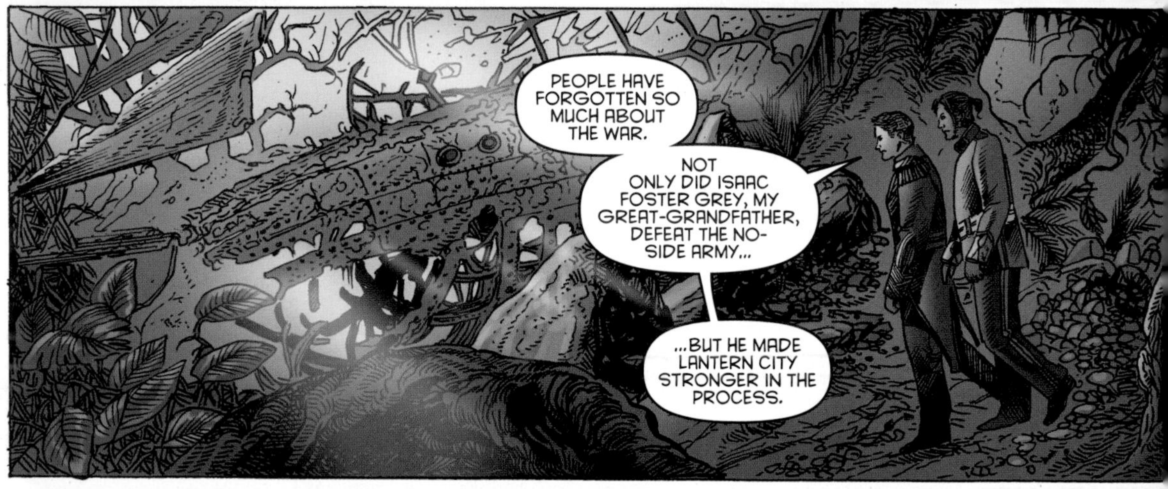
PEOPLE HAVE FORGOTTEN SO MUCH ABOUT THE WAR.
NOT ONLY DID ISAAC FOSTER GREY, MY GREAT-GRANDFATHER, DEFEAT THE NO-SIDE ARMY...
...BUT HE MADE LANTERN CITY STRONGER IN THE PROCESS.

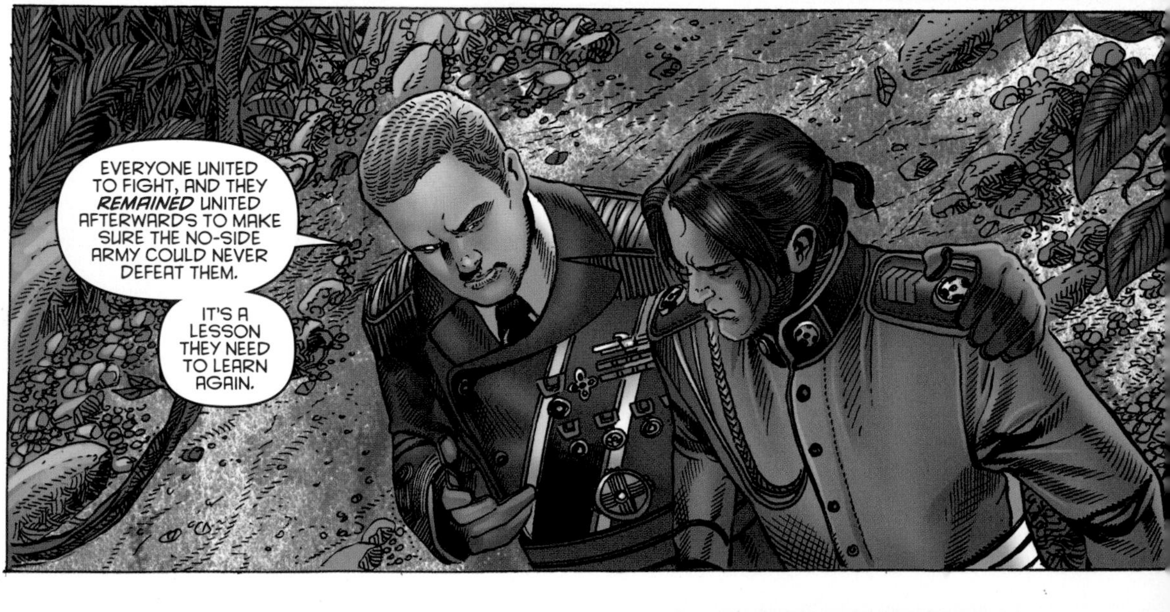
EVERYONE UNITED TO FIGHT, AND THEY ***REMAINED*** UNITED AFTERWARDS TO MAKE SURE THE NO-SIDE ARMY COULD NEVER DEFEAT THEM.
IT'S A LESSON THEY NEED TO LEARN AGAIN.

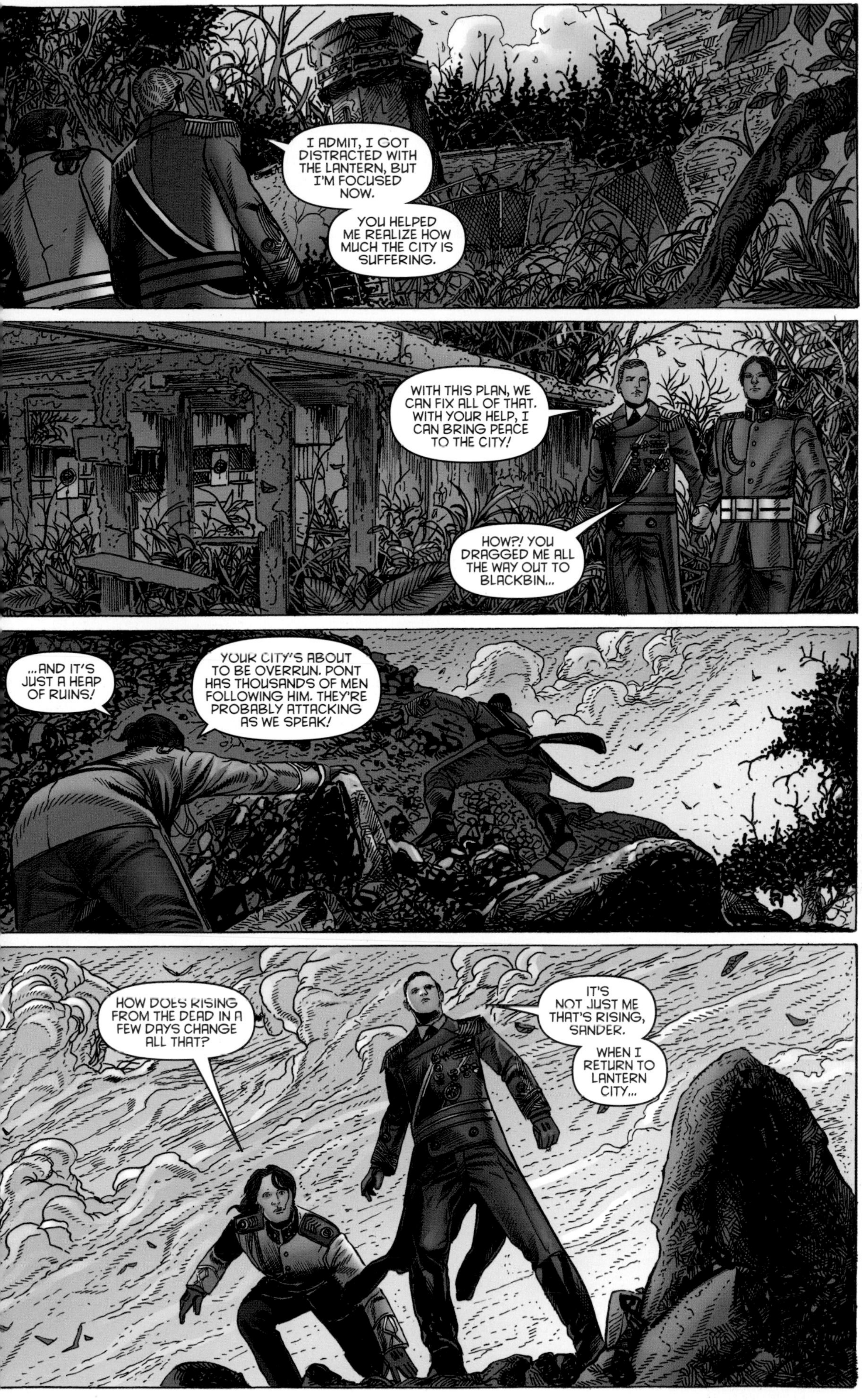
I ADMIT, I GOT DISTRACTED WITH THE LANTERN, BUT I'M FOCUSED NOW.
YOU HELPED ME REALIZE HOW MUCH THE CITY IS SUFFERING.
WITH THIS PLAN, WE CAN FIX ALL OF THAT. WITH YOUR HELP, I CAN BRING PEACE TO THE CITY!
HOW?! YOU DRAGGED ME ALL THE WAY OUT TO BLACKBIN...
...AND IT'S JUST A HEAP OF RUINS!
YOUR CITY'S ABOUT TO BE OVERRUN. PONT HAS THOUSANDS OF MEN FOLLOWING HIM. THEY'RE PROBABLY ATTACKING AS WE SPEAK!
HOW DOES RISING FROM THE DEAD IN A FEW DAYS CHANGE ALL THAT?
IT'S NOT JUST ME THAT'S RISING, SANDER.
WHEN I RETURN TO LANTERN CITY...

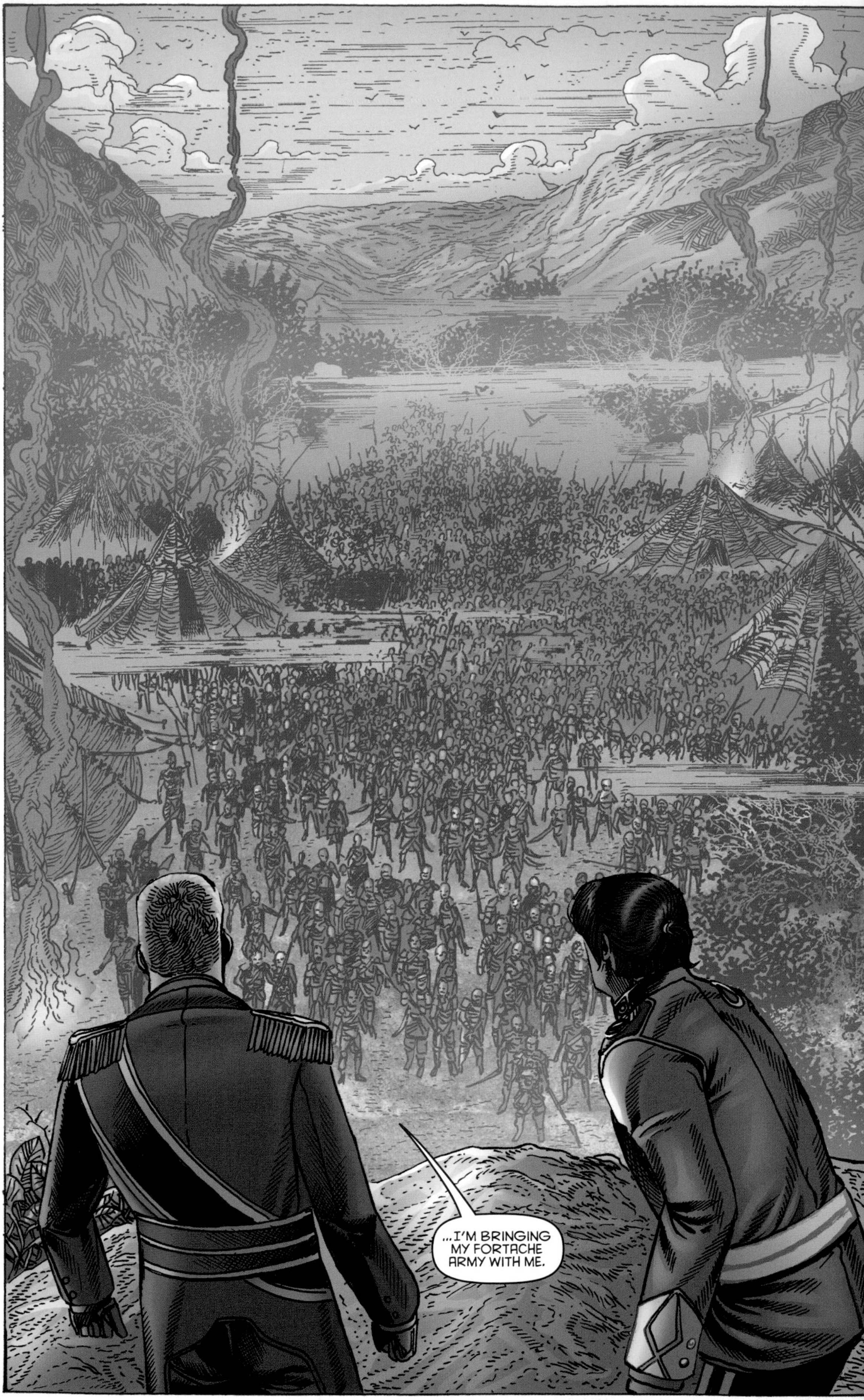
...I'M BRINGING MY FORTACHE ARMY WITH ME.

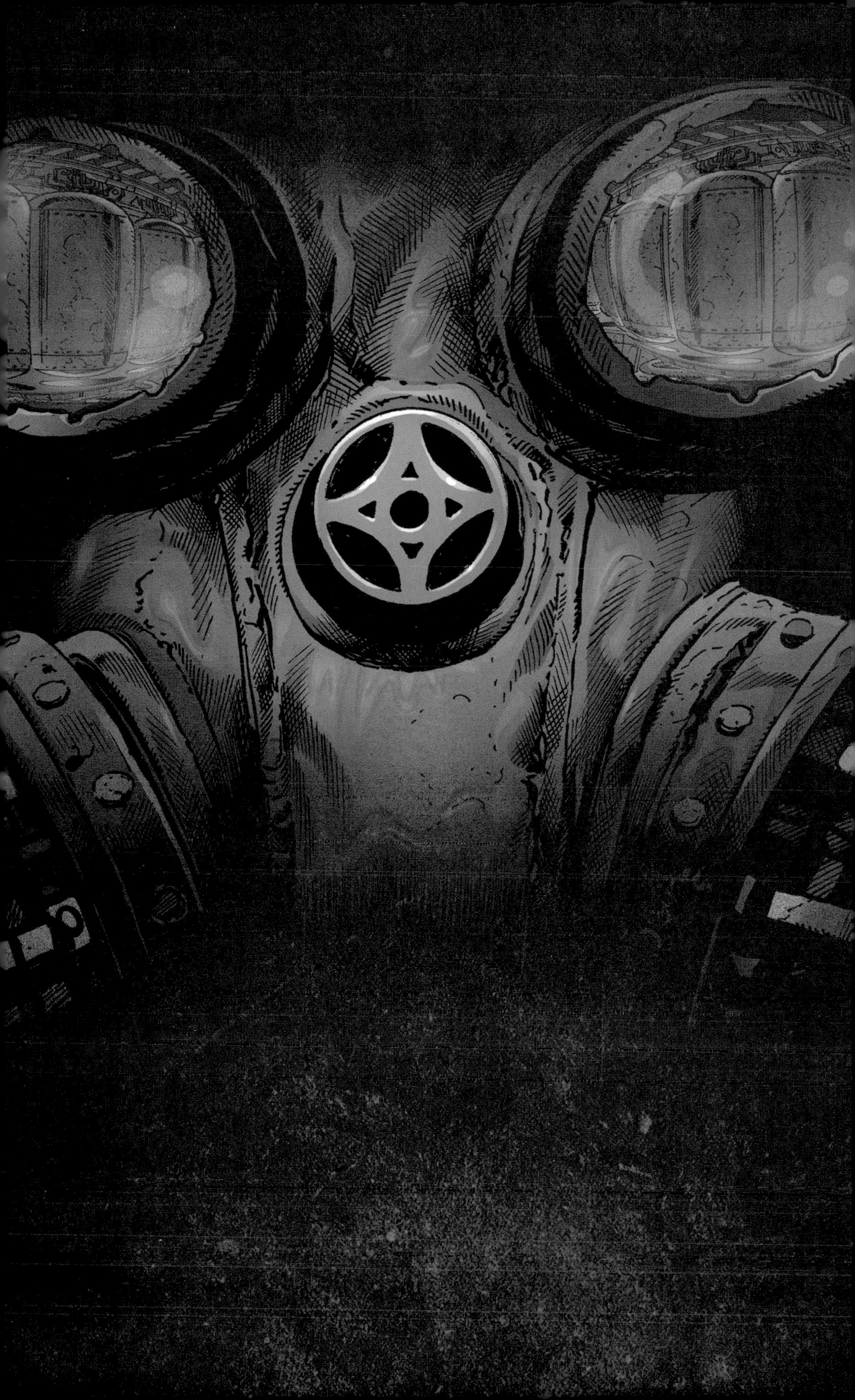

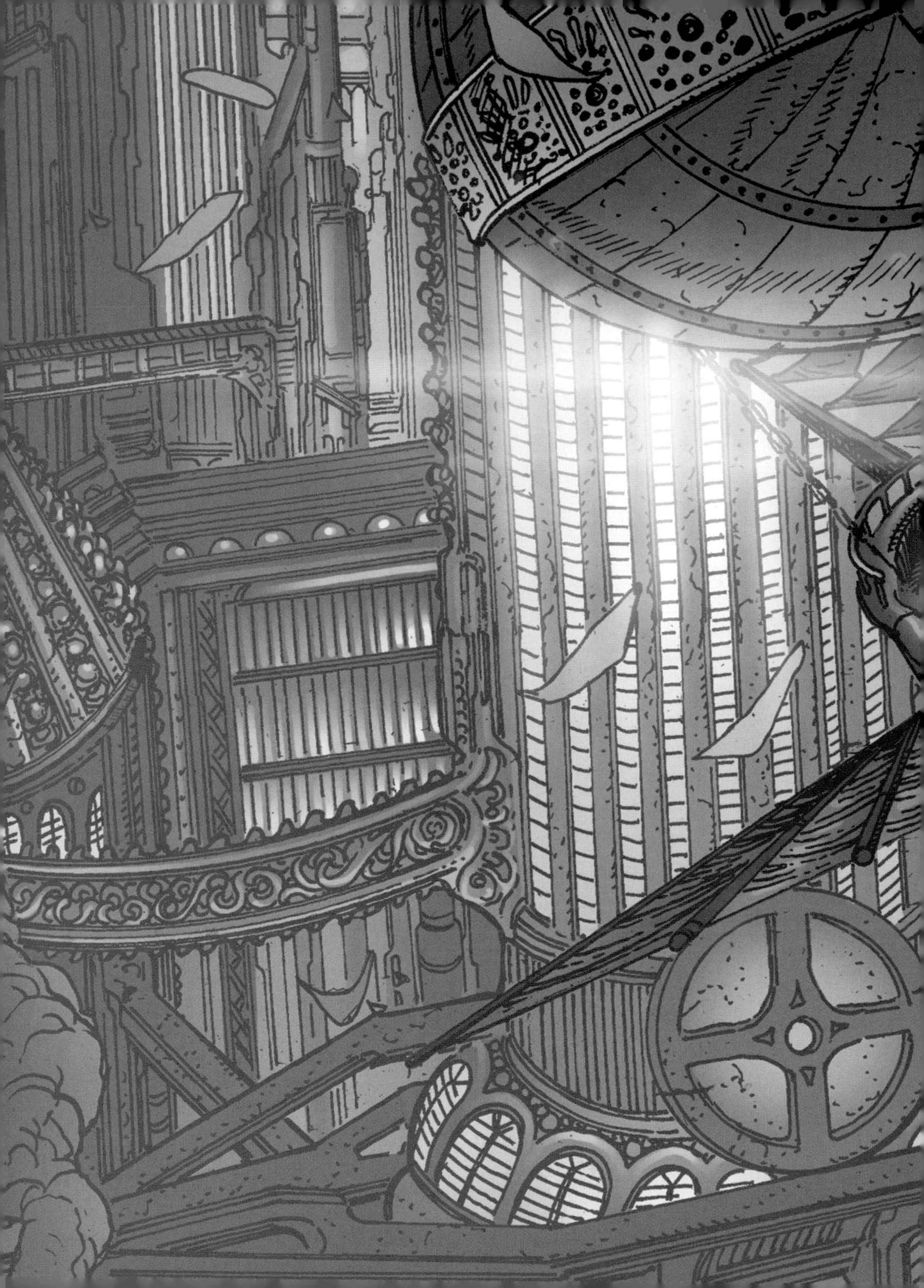

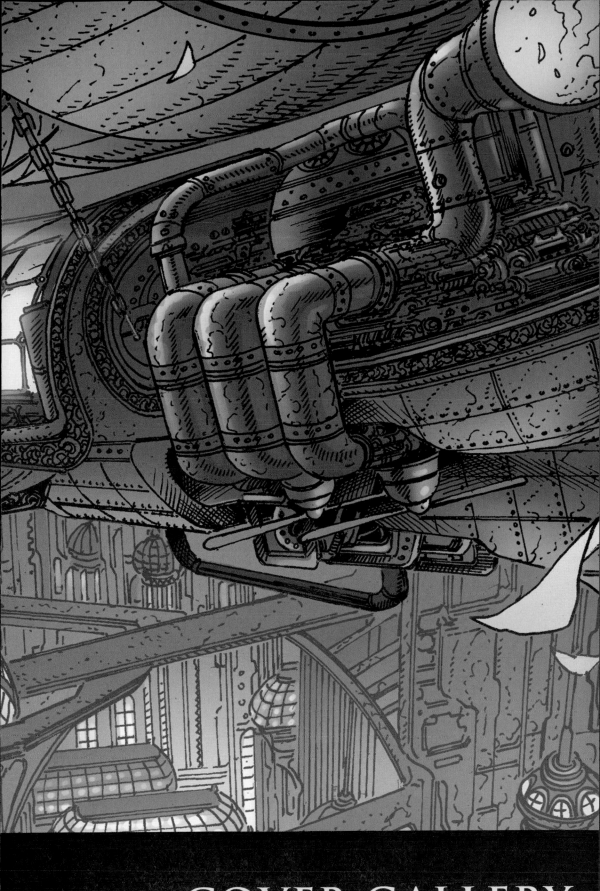

COVER GALLERY

ISSUE FIVE COVER BY
BENJAMIN CARRÉ

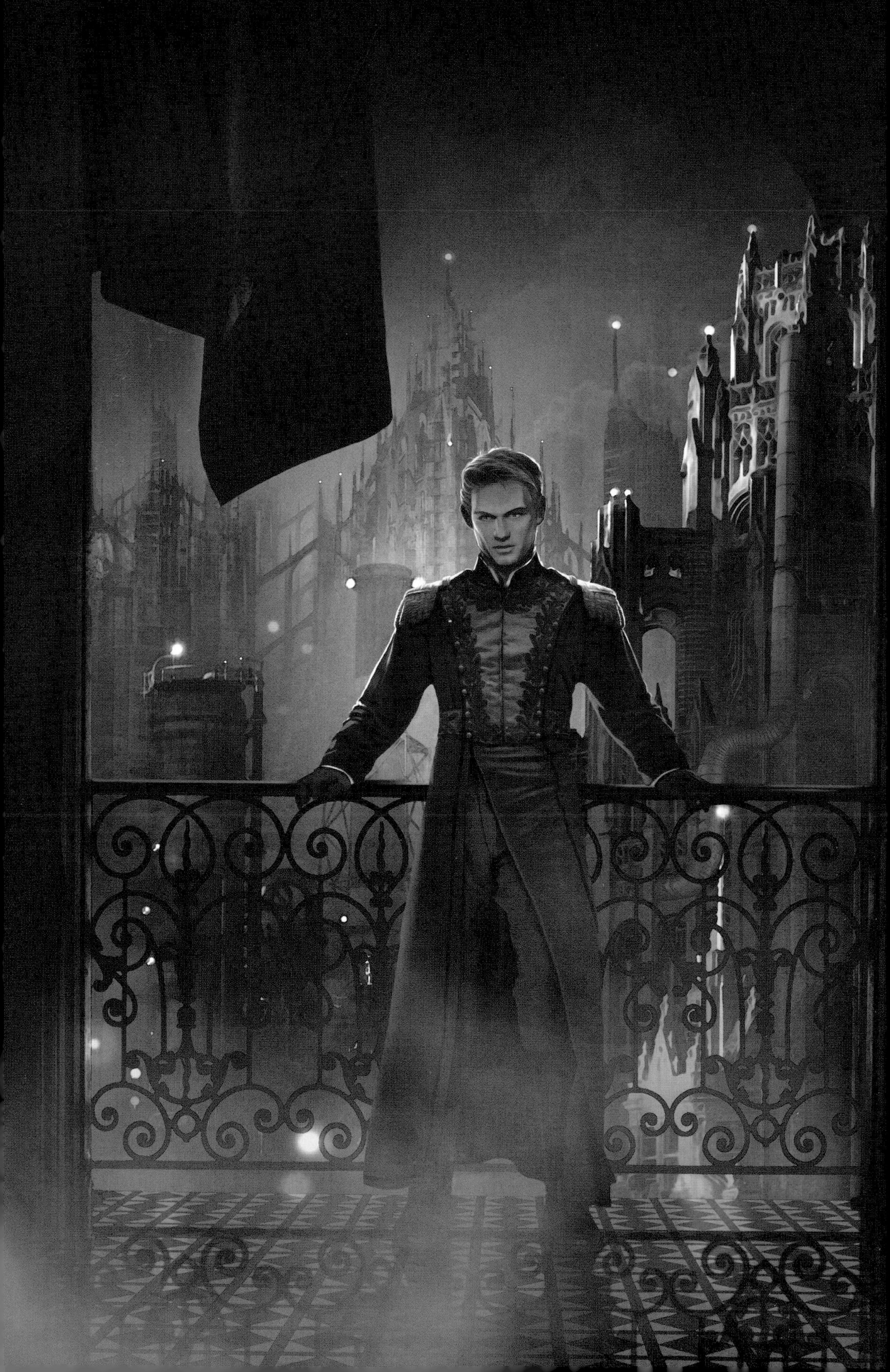

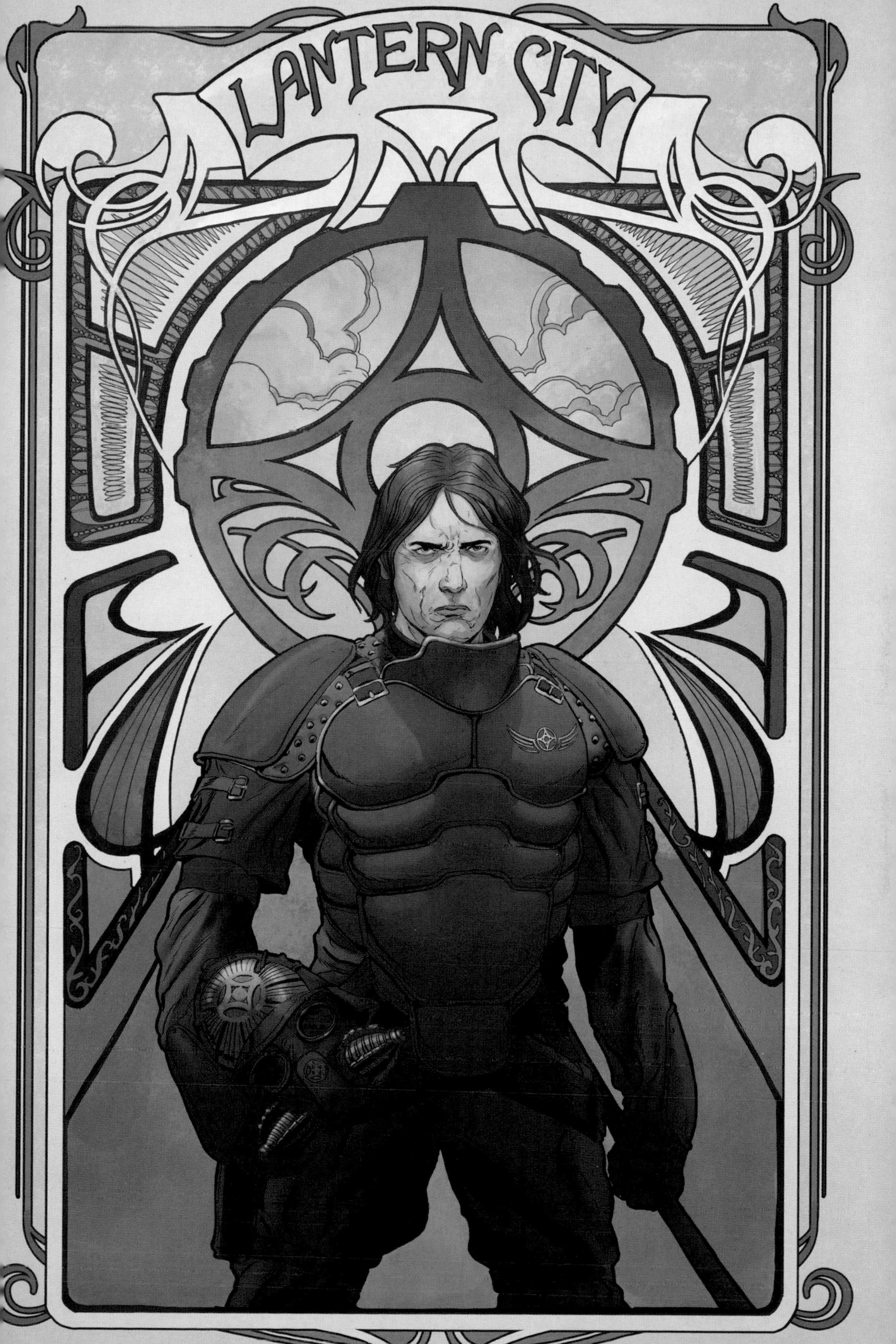
LANTERN CITY

ISSUE FIVE VARIANT COVER BY
ROBERT SAMMELIN

ISSUE SIX COVER BY
BENJAMIN CARRÉ

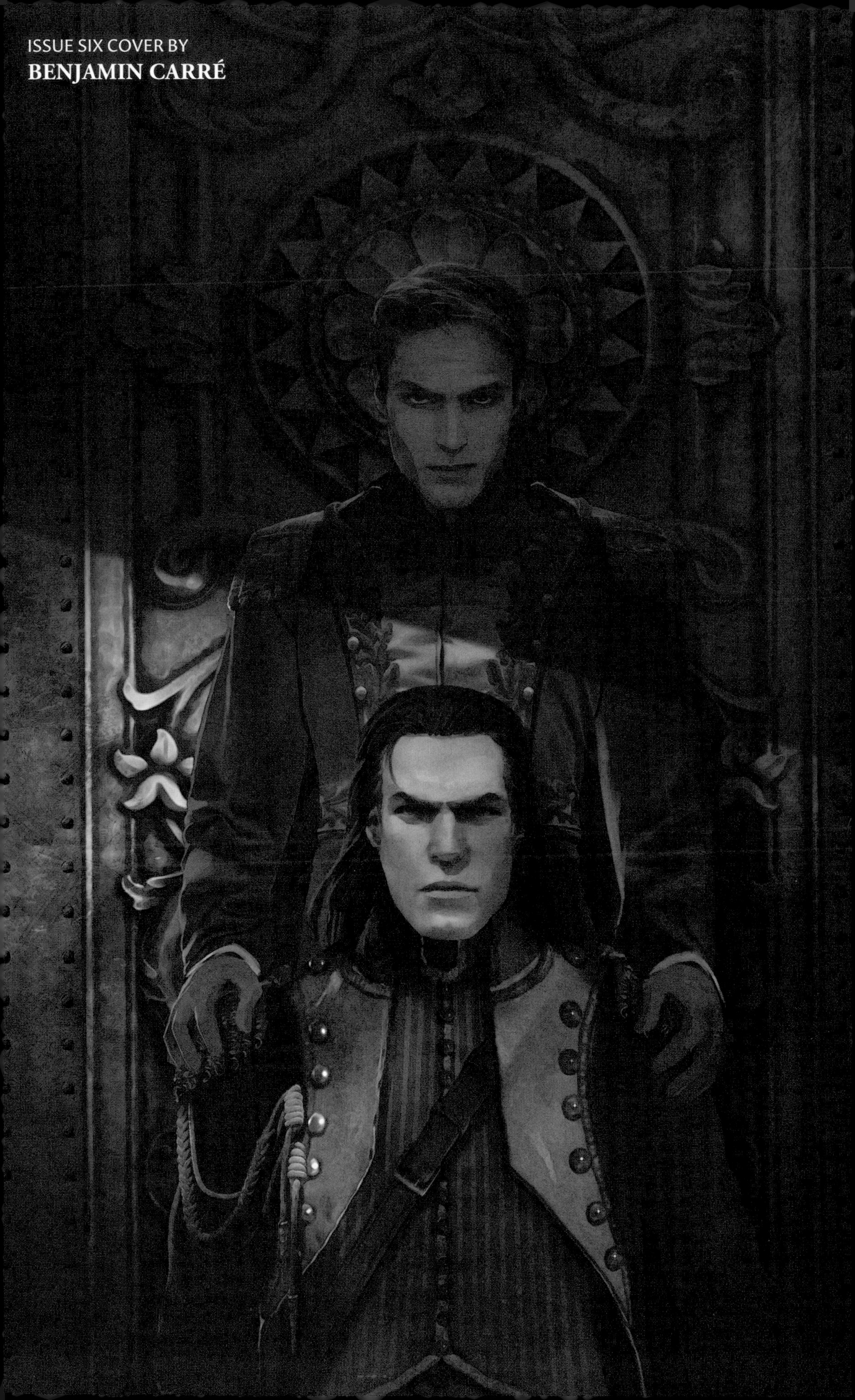

ISSUE SEVEN COVER BY
BENJAMIN CARRÉ

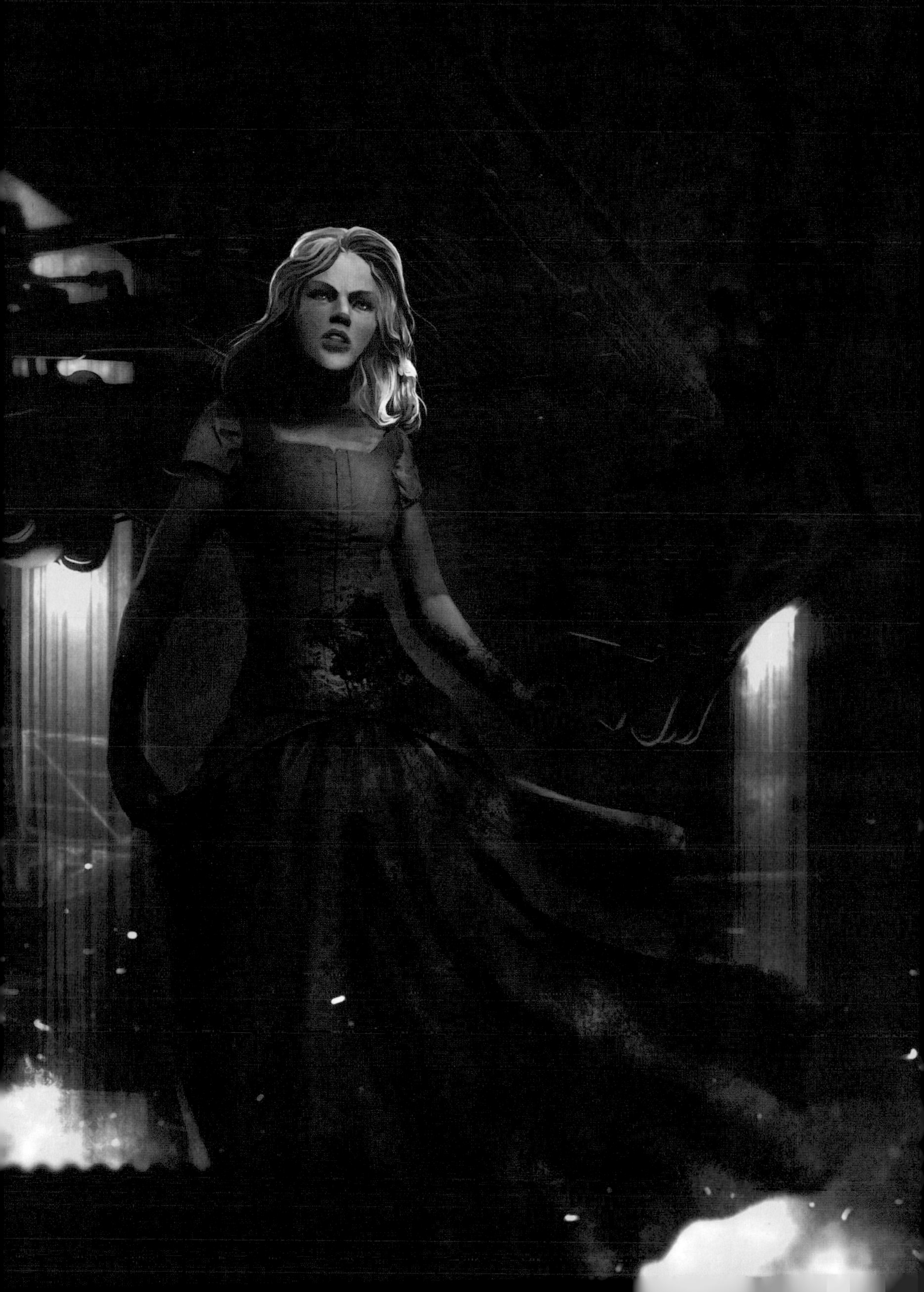

ISSUE EIGHT COVER BY
BENJAMIN CARRÉ

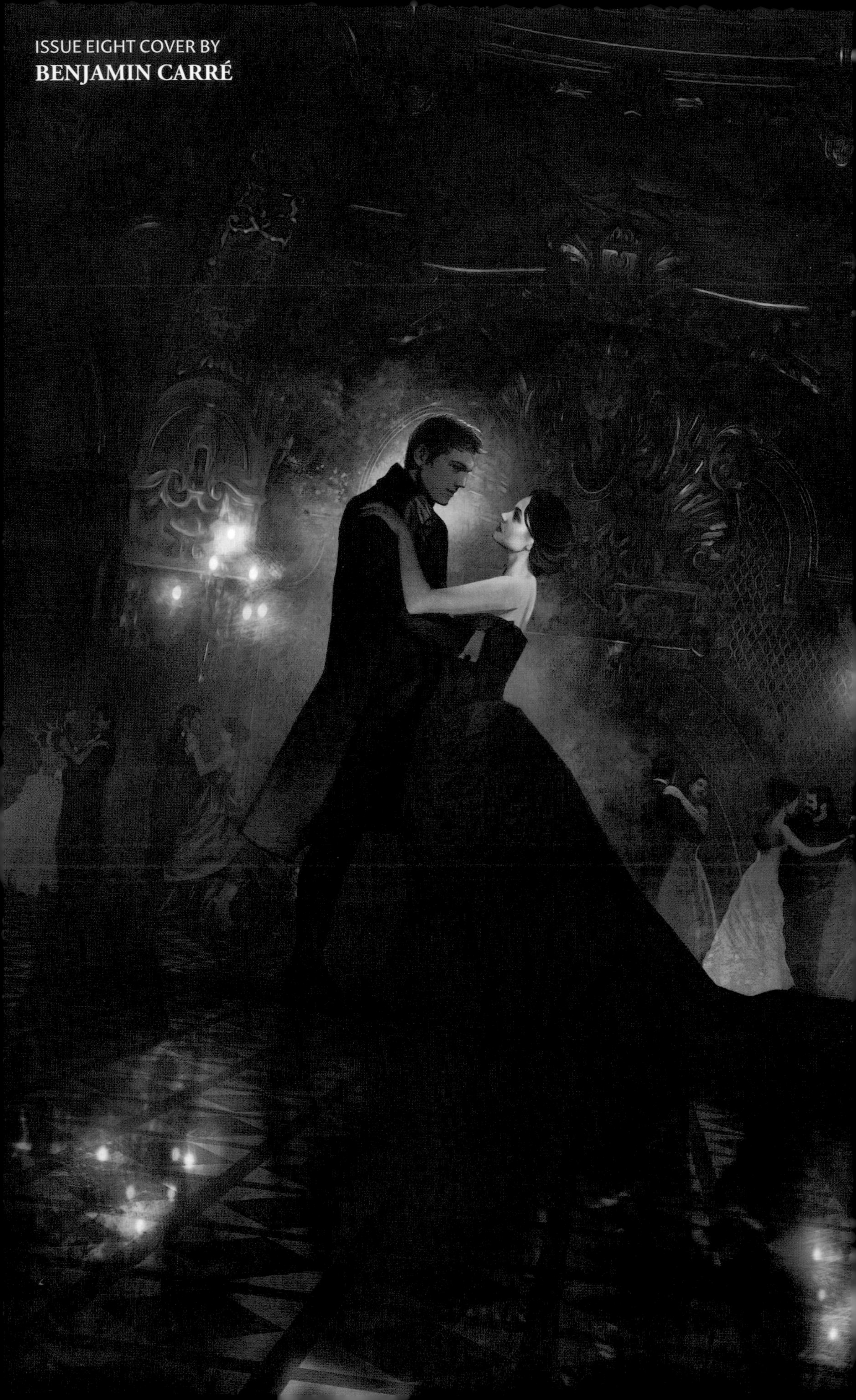

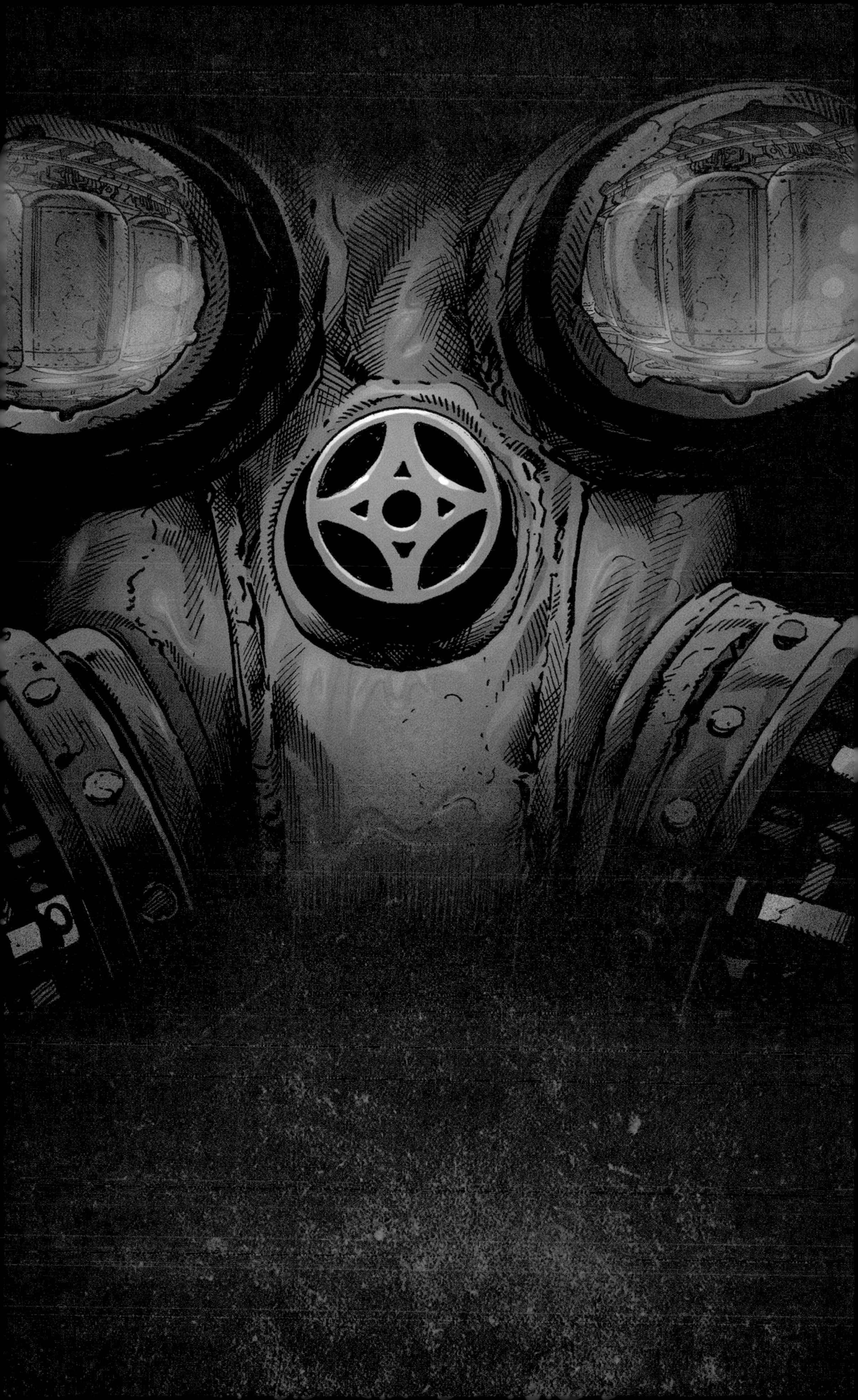

The Devil's Corner

A *Lantern City* prequel story by Matthew Daley

Part I of IV

Everyone in the Devil's Corner knew there was one key to survival: know who you're stealing from. Stealing was a way of life. You wanted to eat, you stole food. You needed a gun, you stole one. You needed a jacket, you used your stolen gun to stick up a guy that had a jacket your size. You needed to sleep, you stole hours from the day. You either adapted to this or died. You could get pushed to the Underground, but if you couldn't cut it in the Devil's Corner, you wouldn't last a second in the Underground. There wasn't anywhere else to go. The Devil's Corner was only a sliver of the sprawling metropolis Lantern City, roughly thirty blocks north-to-south and twelve blocks west-to-east, but it was more overcrowded than any other neighborhood. All of the degenerates, cripples, unemployable, and orphans were quarantined there, fenced off from the rest of the city. It was possible to get out, if you could climb the fifteen stories-tall fence or jump rooftops, but most of the residents didn't bother. They accepted that they would scrounge and rummage through the rest of their existence. For those who wanted more, they figured out ways to survive on the scraps they got or, in the rarest of instances, escaped.

Living a wholesome life in the Devil's Corner was impossible. There were no jobs or stores or cathedrals, only shells of buildings where you could scrape out an existence. A handful of individuals thrived, since they were able to corner the market on food tins or weapons. The Lantern City Guards, the brutal military police force that maintained order throughout the city for the ruling class of the Grey Empire, barely patrolled the streets of the Devil's Corner. There was no need, since so many residents killed each other off or starved to death. Living without the presence of too many Guards was the one advantage of the Devil's Corner.

A small airship flew overhead, looking for a roof where it could land. Much easier said than done, for a majority of roofs had been firebombed; rooftops that weren't damaged from bombings were used by gangs or Lantern City Guards as outposts. Sander Jorve watched the raid airship fly out of sight. They were nothing like the behemoth transporter ships he saw on rare occasions. The transporter ships held hundreds of men and moved slowly across the sky, blotting out the sun. The raid airships were like big-bellied birds, their wings extended out to glide and their midsections were round and covered by metallic grating, akin to an exposed ribcage. The raid airships were painted red and black, just like the Lantern City Guards' uniforms; they were small, holding less than twelve Guards, and their small size allowed them to maneuver quickly— this was the only way to navigate the Devil's Corner. Sander watched the raid airship intently, making sure that it wasn't landing on the building where he was headed. Stealing food would be trouble enough; he didn't want to deal with Guards as well. His mother

Fora always told him that he was better off fighting a Scav or one of Julan Ain's men than a Guard. Local gangs might beat him up, but they'd see him as a potential member, whereas Guards would look at him as nothing more than target practice. In his fifteen years of life, Sander had seen enough deaths at the hand of the Guards, including his own father's, to know that his mother was telling the truth.

He kept close to the side of the red stone building, moving in the shadow of its overhanging roof. Sander stopped for a moment and pinched the side of his shirt. He felt the satchel he'd hidden, tied around the top of his belly. If anyone saw him carrying it, they'd know he was out to steal something and they'd follow him, believing that he knew of a secret stash somewhere. Sander didn't have any inside information on hidden caches of weapons or food. He knew where Julan Ain kept her largest stashes of food tins, but this was common knowledge in Devil's Corner. Sander had never been stupid enough to steal from Ain, but now that his mother had fallen ill, things had changed. Sander was solely responsible for getting their food. They'd gone four days without a morsel to eat and all of the strategizing and planning Sander had done was thrown out the window. They had never been so close to death before. It didn't get any simpler than that. Even with such grim circumstances, Sander obeyed the coda of the Devil's Corner: always know who you're stealing from. In the past, he and Fora avoided anything or anyone that was tied to Julan Ain; that was becoming increasingly more difficult as he grew older and Julan controlled more of his neighborhood, but he and his mother had figured out ways. The times were beyond desperate now and Sander made a decision that could easily result in death. He would steal food from Julan because she had more food than anyone else. There could be easier targets, but searching them out would take time, and that was a resource he did not have.

Julan Ain had two stash houses that everyone knew of and a third that was only a rumor. Sander's goal was optimistic and perhaps unrealistic. He was going to sneak into the buildings nicknamed "Blue Gods" and find Julan's alleged third stash house. The two stash houses that were common knowledge amongst the residents of the Devil's Corner were heavily populated and guarded. If he went there, it would be assumed that he was offering his services to Julan. He was not ready for that, at least not while his mother was still alive. The lifestyle they led was dangerous, but they made their own decisions, independent of a gang leader's whims and desires. Working for Julan would put Sander in constant danger. Ain wanted total control of Devil's Corner and didn't care how she attained it.

On the street below, two young boys chased after a third. They began to pummel the apprehended boy and Sander took advantage of the short distraction. He cut across the street to the nearest Blue Gods building. The four circular-shaped buildings, connected with walkways on various floors, were a sandy blue color broken up by black glass windows. Sander stopped at a door hidden in the shadows, took his knife from his boot, inserted it into the lock, and popped it open by smacking the butt of the knife's handle with his palm. Old locks were easily outwitted. He pulled the door behind him. Darkness enveloped him, and before moving forward, he tied his long black hair into a bun. He guided himself by hand, moving from one black windowpane to the next. All he heard was rats and his own footsteps. Eventually he maneuvered to a stairwell and then to the first walkway and guiding light. The walkways, once proud structures of glass and steel, were now dangerous bridges, weakened by fire bombings. Light streamed through, providing Sander enough visibility to see into the next building. This is where Julan's stash house was alleged to be. Sander saw no signs of life, half-expecting the walkway to be patrolled by Julan's men. He looked to the street below. Did anyone see him? Would it matter if they did? What if Julan placed men on the street to guard her stash house? Sander tried not to think of all the things that could go wrong. He ran across the bridge; each step he took rained shards of glass on the ground below.

The opposite side of the walkway brought more darkness. Sander crouched against the window and listened to his breathing. After a few moments, he heard something else. Voices. Footsteps. Clanking tins. Julan Ain's third stash house was not a rumor. Sander inched closer and closer to the voices, trying to determine how many men were present. He could only distinguish two. Sander was starting to feel like he could get away with this. The voices were muffled through the walls. Laughter. Clanking. Talking. Sander crept closer to the room where the voices came from, hugging the wall, trying desperately not to make any noise. Once he knew which room the voices were working in, he opened up the adjoining room.

It was filled with things he'd never seen: laboratory equipment, tools, journals. It was a space for scientific inquiry and research, though it hadn't been used as such for over a century. Sander didn't waste time wondering what everything was or what it was used for; instead, he got to work. He unbuttoned his shirt and removed his satchel. Inside he found the three small bottles he and Fora had mixed earlier. She knew how to concoct the most potent mix of Measirk and taught Sander accordingly. One bottle was enough to blow a good-sized hole through a wall. Sander needed a little more than that. He sealed the fuse in each bottle, and then tied them all together. He placed them throughout the room, listened for laughter next door, then struck a match. Sander lit the fuse, watched as the fire chewed through the line, and ran from the room. He ran past the stash room and took cover in the next adjoining room.

Muffled voices. Clanking tins. Laughter. Silence. Silence. Silence.

Sander crouched in the far corner, covering his head. The explosion shook the room. The two men screamed and ran about. Sander heard them flee the building. He waited a few extra moments before leaving his hiding place. Smoke wrapped around his head in thick clouds and choked him. He squatted to move beneath it. He entered the stash room and fell over a pile of food tins. There were thousands of tins in the room, all of which would be used as lures for desperate people to join Julan. For the moment, all of them belonged to Sander. He hadn't expected his plan to work and he now regretted doubting himself—if he had brought three or four satchels instead of one, he and his mother would have had enough food for months, or at least enough to trade for medicine. He stuffed thirty tins into his satchel as he thought of his ailing mother and wrapped the strap around his shoulders. He was surprised by the weight of it. A few tins, which is all he'd ever held at one time, weighed next to nothing, but now that there were so many in his satchel, it felt like something substantial.

Sander climbed down a newly formed hole in the floor and found himself in a room that looked similar to the one he just destroyed. He wondered if any of the vials or tools were of use, but he had to flee the Blue Gods before Julan's men returned. His plan was to exit from the same door he had entered, but he worried about wasting time; the longer he stayed in the building, the more likely it was that he'd get caught. Sander also thought about the food. It would be a waste to let it burn. He searched around the lab until he found a mallet. It weighed more than he expected, which was perfect. He hurled it through the black glass. He leapt through the partially open frame and crashed to the street below. Jagged daggers of black glass pierced his palms and fingers. He tried to clear the glass, but he only made it worse. The dozens of people gathered near the building were hoping to learn what had happened.

"There's food! On the next floor. You can climb up from right in there!" said Sander.

The bystanders fought each other as they climbed through the open window. Sander raced away from the action, not looking back. Eventually he found a safe place to hide: a crashed airship. It was one of the small raid airships the Lantern City Guard used throughout the Devil's Corner. The ship had been dragged to the back of a dead-end street. Two men, either dead or sleeping, were propped up against the front of it. Sander climbed in and carefully removed all of the black glass from his hands. At first it was difficult to use his fingers to remove the shards, since they too were covered in glass, so he used his teeth. Sander pushed the skin down with the front of his teeth, then bit down on the shards to grip them. Each piece hurt more than the last. Tears ran down his face. He didn't have to hide them from anyone. Once all of the glass was removed, his hands wouldn't stop shaking. Sander took his knife, and with all his strength, gripped the handle just long enough to cut two swaths of cloth from the bottom of his pants. He used the cloth as bandages and tied them around his hands. He needed to get back to his mother, but he was too weak to move. He'd be safe inside the airship for a few hours. He closed his eyes and tried to think of anything but the pain.

Sander hadn't meant to fall asleep. He didn't realize how tired he was. In the four days since he and Fora last ate, he spent countless hours trying to get them food. He had hardly slept. The fatigue, combined with the numbness from his hands, shut his body down. The sky above held the bluish dark of the early morning. He panicked and raced from the airship. Fora had been left alone for over twelve hours.

Fora was housed in a building twelve blocks from the Blue Gods. She and Sander had holed up in the building for weeks, their longest stretch in any one place. The only reason they hadn't been bothered was because she had ebys. People were afraid of all of the diseases that stalked through Lantern City, and in most circumstances, a sick woman would be left alone—especially one with ebys. Sander didn't know exactly what ebys did to the body, but Fora, never one to complain, talked incessantly about constant pain in her chest and joints; she could barely sleep or eat as the sickness slowly crushed her body. She was, more often than not, unrecognizable to Sander. Fora didn't have much time left, since the remedy concocted by ruling class doctors rarely made it down to the Depths. Sander tried to face the fact that he would soon be alone, left to fend for himself. Between what Fora taught him and what he picked up on the streets, he figured he could survive. It's all he could expect from the world, even though he knew he wanted more.

Sander slowed down as he approached the brown brick building. He hadn't been followed, and the eyes that fell on him as he entered would have looked at him even if he wasn't carrying a satchel of food tins. Immediately inside the building, two men were holding a woman while a third man was holding a knife to her face. She pleaded that she hadn't seen the man they were looking for. Sander knew better than to interfere. He climbed the stairs to the third floor and walked toward the end of the hallway. The door to his apartment was open. He cursed himself for leaving it open. There was no way that Fora had the energy to leave. Sander pushed through the door and found his mother face down on the floor; her left arm was reaching up, as if to grab the door handle.

"Mom! No!" said Sander.

He pulled her away from the door and kicked it shut. The lock was broken, and the door swung back open. Sander had no time to worry about that. He fell to the floor and cradled her in his arms. She weighed nothing. Her once-radiant olive skin was now like leather. Her long black hair, a source of pride, was dirty and matted to her face. He pulled it from her cheeks. He looked like his mother, at least according to what others told him, and he knew what they meant: their skin complexion, black hair, dark eyes, and defined jawlines were identical. Fora peered at him through yellowing eyes surrounded by dark purple skin. All of her beauty was gone. Sander fought back tears. She opened her mouth as if to speak.

"I got us food. I got it," said Sander.

Sander reached into his satchel. Fora grabbed his hand to stop him.

"I got it. You just need to—"

"Stop," said Fora, her voice barely a whisper.

"You can eat some of this and then I can trade most of it for medicine. I can get more food! I—"

"Sander, please. I'm already gone," said Fora.

"No. If you eat you'll be—"

"I love you. I want you to do anything you can to get out of here. It's the only way," said Fora.

"There's nowhere to go!" said Sander.

"There is. There always is," said Fora.

"Mom, no, just—"

"Our people weren't born inside these walls. We don't have to die here either," said Fora.

Fora's breathing sped up, her chest heaved, and then she gave the world her final breath. Sander shook her

and screamed. He held her tightly and cried till his arms were limp. He set his mother down gently. Her lifeless eyes stared up at the ceiling.

He couldn't keep her here. She told him time and time again, especially as death drew closer, that she wanted her body burned to honor the gods, Wareis and Uryston. It was the last thing Sander wanted to do, but it was exactly what he had to do. He lifted her and carried her from the apartment. As soon as Sander reached the hallway, he sensed that something was wrong, but before he could do anything, a door opened and a figure emerged. Sander turned to get a good look at the kid, but he was punched on the left side of his jaw. He dropped Fora's body and stumbled backwards—it was the worst hit he'd ever taken. The kid put him in a headlock and dragged him into an apartment. Sander punched the kid's arms, but he absorbed the blows. If only I could reach my knife, Sander thought.

"I'm not here ta' kill ya' or take what ya' got in the bag," said the kid. "I'll let ya' go but don't hit me."

Sander slipped out from the headlock. He stared down the kid. The kid wasn't much older than him; he had light brown skin, freckles under his eyes, and a shock of auburn hair that added six inches to his height. One of his green pants legs was cut off at the knee and his shirt, once white, was yellow. He wore the same arm protectors as Lantern City Guards.

"I don't know you," said Sander.

"Be glad you do," said the kid. He raised his pointer finger to his lips. Sander didn't understand. "Trust me."

Voices filled the hallway. Sander reached for the door and the kid grabbed him and held him tightly. Sander tried to break free; the kid tackled him to the floor. Gunshots broke through Sander's screams. Bullets cut through the walls. Both boys covered their heads. Sander's ears rung long after the shots ceased. The kid helped him to his feet and pulled him toward an open window. Sander broke free and ran to the door. He opened it and saw bodies in pools of blood. Two of them were Lantern City Guards, three were Julan Ain's men, and one was his mother. Her head was tilted toward him. The kid grabbed his arm again and dragged him toward the window.

"My mom is—"

"When there's dead Guards there's always more on the way!" said the kid.

They went to the open window and climbed up to the roof using two jagged pipes that ran parallel from rooftop to street level. Sander expected to stop when they reached the roof, but the kid ran and hopped to the nearest roof. Sander had made the same move many times before, but for some reason he didn't think he'd make it. The kid looked back.

"Come on!" said the kid.

Sander sprinted toward the edge of the roof and leapt. He was weighed down by the tins of food. He slammed into the side of the building and caught the lip of the roof. Pain erupted in his hands. He struggled to pull himself up. The kid grabbed him underneath the arms and hoisted him up. Sander fell onto the roof. The kid was ready to go.

"This ain't no place ta' rest," said the kid.

"Wha—what are you doing?" said Sander.

"Tryin' ta' help ya' live. Ya' wanna' live?" said the kid. Sander nodded.

"I don't know you," said Sander.

"Bet you're glad ya' do though, ain't ya'? If ya' didn't, you'd be drinkin' up your own blood right now," said the kid.

"Why'd you help me?" said Sander.

"Figured we could help each other," said the kid.

"How?" said Sander.

"I seen ya' before. Ya' seem smart," said the kid.

"You followed me?" said Sander.

"What's it matter? I just saved your life. Now come on," said the kid.

"Who are you?" said Sander.

"The name's Mack Davey. I'm tha' only Scav you can trust in tha' Devil's Corner," said Mack. He extended his hand to Sander.

"Sander Jorve," said Sander.

Mack helped Sander to his feet.

"I'm not one for dyin'. Why don'tcha' follow me," said Mack.

"Where are we going?" said Sander.

"Somewhere Julan Ain can't touch us," said Mack.

Mack headed to the next roof. Sander followed him.

Part II of IV

Mack pulled a small, curved blade from his boot and pierced the food tin, then cut around the top just enough for him to slip two fingers inside and peel the lid off. He pulled three bulbs from the tin and munched on them.

"Onions," said Mack. "Hope ya' stole some galrabbit or steer tongue."

Sander shrugged his shoulders. The two boys were atop a roof that rested in the shadow of the massive wall that ran the perimeter of Lantern City. The wall was so tall that it blocked the sun from reaching most

of the Devil's Corner. Sander didn't know what was beyond the wall, though he'd been told it was built to protect citizens from the No-Side Army. In his short lifespan, there were never any attacks; whether that was due to the wall or not, he didn't know, and it was a fool's game to think about it too much. As far as Sander knew, the wall had always been there, and it would remain long after he died. He sat with his back against the door that led inside the apartment building. Mack said they'd be safe there, that he and his gang always used this roof. Sander understood why: half of the roof was missing, destroyed in a firebombing years earlier. A stone carving of a shirtless, muscular man was set on the one corner of the roof that hadn't been destroyed. The man had long hair and held a sword above his head. Sander had passed this building dozens of times and never noticed the man before. Mack nudged Sander with his boot.

"Ya' know who that is?" said Mack.

"No," said Sander. Mack handed him an open tin of onions. "Thanks."

"Your dad, ain't it?" said Mack, laughing so hard he choked on an onion bulb.

Sander took one bite of onion then put the tin down. After seeing his mother's lifeless eyes, he didn't expect to have an appetite ever again. Mack nudged him again.

"Gotta' eat," said Mack.

"I'm not—"

"Yeah ya' are. I know tha' hungry look. I got it most days myself. Havin' a dead mother don't mean ya' don't gotta' eat," said Mack.

Sander held the tin to his lips and tipped it back. He hated onions and never acquired a taste for them after years of subsiding on them. They were the easiest thing to get in the Devil's Corner, and if you didn't eat them, you didn't eat. On rare occasions, you'd get galrabbit or carrot tips, but it could be months before you tasted something other than onion bulbs. Mack sat next to him.

"I'm sorry 'bout your mom. Really," said Mack.

"She was sick. I knew she was going to die, but I still can't believe it happened," said Sander.

"Yeah well, I'll tell ya', ya' get over it. That's how life is," said Mack.

"I need to burn her body," said Mack.

"Sure ya' do. Just not now," said Mack. "Tell me. Who ya' been stealin' from?"

"All sorts," said Sander.

"If ever once ya' stole from Ain, she'll know and make sure ya' pay one way or tha' other," said Mack.

"That's where these tins came from," said Sander.

"It's a good thing ya' met me. I don't take nothin' from Ain. Me and my Scavs don't take nothin' from no one in Devil's Corner," said Mack.

"Then you're a ghost, because there's no other way to live," said Sander.

"My guess is ya' don't get out of Devil's Corner much, do ya'?" said Mack.

"I do. All the time," said Sander.

"Where do ya' go?" said Mack.

"Anywhere I want," said Sander.

Mack laughed and punched Sander in the arm. He stood up and grabbed another tin from Sander's satchel. He cut it open. His face lit up.

"Here, here," said Mack, holding the tin in front of Sander's face. It was salted galrabbit. Sander took a hunk of the dark meat and chewed on it.

"I get this stuff all tha' time. But that's not somethin' you'd know about."

"What do you mean?" said Sander.

"I can tell ya' never been out of Devil's Corner. Anybody that says they go anywhere they please is full of it. There's only a couple places ya' get to once ya' get over this fence. But I don't mind ya' havin' soft hands. I can still use ya' in my gang,"

"What makes you think—"

Before Sander could finish his sentence, he was thrust forward by the opening door. He was sprawled out on his belly and turned quickly. Three guys, all his age, stared him down. He was in a helpless position and the three guys were ready to exploit that, but Mack stepped in.

"Boys, boys, boys, meet our newest Scav. Goes by the name of Sander," said Mack.

"We ain't takin' on nobody more," said the first boy. The left side of his face was marred by bad burn marks; his long blonde hair couldn't hide the scars. He wore a blue shirt and black pants that could be mistaken for clean and new. He carried a gun that was too big for his hand.

"Relax, Tenny," said Mack, grabbing Tenny's arm. "We always got room for one more."

The biggest boy pushed Mack and Tenny aside to get a look at Sander. The boy was bigger than most men, yet had the face of an innocent child. He spit on the ground in front of Sander's feet. His two front teeth protruded outward, like someone tried to yank them out but failed. He squinted his narrow eyes and scrunched his forehead to get his straight black hair out of his plane of vision. Mack pushed Tenny aside and clapped the big boy on the chest.

"Kilks, is that any way to introduce yourself?" said Mack.

Kilks made a popping sound using his tongue and bottom lip. Sander stood up and brushed himself off. Kilks wanted to fight him and he wasn't going to lay down and wait for it to happen. Kilks was bigger, but Sander knew that he could take him. It was exactly the type of attitude someone in the Devil's Corner needed to survive. As soon as you thought people could break you down, they would.

"You first," said Sander.

Kilks spit over Sander's shoulder. Sander composed himself for a moment, making it seem like he wasn't going to retaliate, and as soon as Kilks let his guard down, he jabbed him in the throat. Kilks stumbled backwards, grabbing his neck in dramatic fashion. Sander didn't hit him hard enough to do any real damage; all he wanted to do was send a message.

The third kid, whose pale skin and fair hair made him look like a ghost, spoke as he dumped the food tins from Sander's satchel.

"We never took on a fifth because that means we gotta' split things five ways instead of four. Four is tough enough already," said the kid.

Mack pushed the kid up against the door.

"Those ain't yours, Umo," said Mack.

"No?" said Umo.

"No. Sander took 'em and he decides who gets them," said Mack.

"But you're sayin' he's one of us now and we didn't have no say in that, so I don't think he should have a say in who eats his food," said Umo.

"I don't care. Eat them. They weren't for me anyway," said Sander.

"Like I was sayin'," said Umo. He tossed tins to Tenny and Kilks.

"Ya' need this to open them," said Mack, holding the knife. Umo tried to grab it, but Mack pulled it back.

"Instead of thinkin' like ya' got no sense and believin' that five guys ain't better, think of it like this: yeah we gotta' split our finds five ways, but we can get more when there's five of us. This kid's good. We can use him, and since I'm runnin' things, I say he stays."

"How we know he can grab things?" said Tenny, salivating over his tins.

"Tell 'em where ya' got this food," said Mack.

"From Ain's stash house in the Blue Gods," said Sander.

"Can't," said Umo. "There ain't none there."

"It's not there any more, but it was yesterday," said Sander.

"I seen smoke there," said Kilks.

"That's because of him, right?" said Mack, directing his gaze to Sander.

"I used three bottles of Measirk," said Sander.

"You know how's to make it?" said Tenny.

Sander nodded.

"Why didn't you say so?" said Umo.

The Scavs laughed. Mack handed the knife to Umo. He cut into his tins, then passed the knife around. The Scavs ate like wild animals.

"Fill up boys. We got a run ta' make tomorrow," said Mack.

———

The Scavs knew the roof-route out of the Devil's Corner so well that they could run it blindfolded. Sander ran fourth in line, followed closely by Umo. Sander had known there was a way out, but he never trusted leaving. Yes, the Devil's Corner was bad, but it was an evil he knew; there was an inherent fear in what he didn't know. Besides, getting out and back in was only part of his concern. If a Lantern City Guard caught him outside of Devil's Corner, he'd be killed on the spot or sent to the hellish prison, the Spiral. The Scavs were confident in not being caught and he had no choice but to trust them. Sander had nothing else to lose.

They reached the final rooftop in the Devil's Corner, hopped on top of the fence, and quickly scurried over before being seen by the Guards below. Sander's hands throbbed with pain as he'd grabbed onto the fence, but he didn't let it slow him down. They leapt to the next nearest rooftop, and continued onward. Eventually, they descended into a building, racing down the stairs, maintaining a brisk pace. Just before they reached the building's entrance, Mack stopped them. He stepped outside and a few moments later, opened the door for the other Scavs to follow.

"We're clear! Hurry!" said Mack.

Sander wanted to soak in the surroundings of the neighborhood, but they were moving too quickly; besides, if he stopped, it would be obvious to the locals that he was an outsider. They were approaching a wide footbridge that was patrolled by two Lantern City Guards. Mack diverted their path and they took a side street that came to a dead end. Mack led them through the narrow building and down to the basement and out to the flowing Faudnice River. The Guards were a few hundred yards away. Sander was nervous. He couldn't swim.

"Swim hard. Don't get pulled too far. You'll end up in tha' Silver Sea," said Mack.

The Scavs were ready to dive into the water. Sander looked all around for an alternative route. If I don't find another way, I'll drown, Sander thought. He continued to look as he blurted out:

"Wait! It'll take too long to swim," said Sander.

"Less you know a way to fly, there ain't no other way," said Umo.

Sander's eyes darted every which way.

"Swimming will also get our clothes wet. That'll slow us down. We have to be as fast as we can," said Sander.

"Ya' got a point if ya' got somethin' else in mind," said Mack.

Sander noticed the river dropping off a few hundred yards away.

"How about down there?" said Sander.

"You want us to go farther out? We already far!" said Tenny.

Sander ignored the comment and ran along the Faudnice. He discovered a broken dam. Hunks of rock remained, washed over by the powerful river. The other Scavs caught up to him. Mack looked it over and nodded his head.

"Guess this is better than swimmin'," said Mack. "It's your idea, Sander. You take us over."

Sander led them across a series of rocks, each one less stable than the last. All five of them made it over without falling in the river.

"Smart thinkin'," said Mack.

Sander felt proud.

"I kinda' wanted to swim," said Kilks.

"Then come back here on your own time," said Mack.

"I'm only sayin'," said Kilks.

"So am I," said Mack. "Let's keep it movin'!"

They climbed the wall quickly and dashed ahead to the trolley station. Thousands of people were coming back from work. The Scavs pushed through the crowds and hung on to the side of a departing trolley. Sander held on for dear life while the other Scavs fought and joked, having done this many times before. They were nearing a station when Mack and the other Scavs hopped off effortlessly. Sander hesitated, then let go. He stumbled forward and fell.

"How's he gonna' carry anything if he can't ride?" said Umo.

"Yeah. Them bandages ain't good either," said Kilks.

Mack helped Sander to his feet.

"He's good. Everyone trips their first time," said Mack.

The Scavs traveled down a series of dark alleyways until they reached Ricass. It was the nicest neighborhood in all the Depths; residents of Ricass worked inside Grey Towers as cooks and servants and barbers and tailors and anything else the ruling class needed. These were the most coveted jobs in all the Depths, the closest thing to upward mobility that existed, and most were gained by birthright. While the members of the ruling class did not care at all for any residents of the Depths, they made sure that those in Ricass lived better than everyone else. It was a small gesture to fool the Ricass residents into believing that they were special. The streets were paved and lined with shops. The clothing, while still the garb of the working class, was handsomer and cleaner. Mack stepped back into the shadows of the alleyway as four Lantern City Guards passed. Their helmets and facemasks made them look inhuman, and combined with their blood red armor, they looked more like machines than men. Mack turned to face the Scavs.

"New building. Right across tha' way. Scoped it out a couple days ago. Follow me close. We're goin' straight for the second floor. Couple of apartments there don't have locks. All we need is weapons. We gotta' get out as quick as we get in. Got it?" said Mack.

"Think we got time to meet some girls?" said Kilks.

"If ya' think like that, you'll have a Guard's boot pushing your head through tha' street," said Mack. "Stay smart and follow me."

Mack waited a few minutes until the patrolling Guards passed again. It felt like an eternity. The adrenaline of escaping the Devil's Corner and traveling to Ricass had worn off. Sander's hands were throbbing. He doubted that their plan would succeed. He'd already pulled off one impossible task in the Blue Gods and didn't think he had any luck left. Without uttering a word, Mack took off. The Scavs followed him right into a white stone building. The floors were tiled and the railing a shiny brass. Sander was in awe and had to fight against the distractions. As soon as they reached the second floor, Mack stopped them and pointed out which apartments were open, then assigned Umo to one, teamed Kilks and Tenny up for another, and expected Sander to follow him.

"Only weapons," he whispered.

The Scavs went to work. Sander followed Mack into an apartment. Sander couldn't help but stop as soon as he entered. There was furniture and a stove and pots and books. Mack crawled under the bed and emerged with two rifles. He opened up the stove and found four pistols. He handed two pistols to Sander.

"In tha' front and back of your pants, like this," said Mack. Mack demonstrated how to holster the guns in the waistline of his pants. Sander did the same.

"Carry one of these too?" Mack held a rifle out to Sander. Sander took it without hesitation. "Easy, right?"

They returned to the hallway. Mack snapped his fingers in a pattern: first three times, then twice. The other Scavs emerged. Kilks held one pistol and a rifle. Umo had three pistols. Tenny was empty handed.

"Nothin'," said Tenny.

Mack raised his pointer finger to his lip. Tenny threw his hands up in frustration, then pointed to another door. Mack shook his head. Tenny nodded.

"It's open," Tenny whispered.

"No!" said Mack.

It was too late. Tenny pushed the door open and stepped inside. Shuffling. Yelling. Thump. Tenny flew back into the hallway, a small harpoon through his forehead.

"Guards!" said Mack.

Mack, Sander, Kilks, and Umo took off running. Two Guards emerged from the apartment. They fired their pistols at the boys, but the boys had made it to the stairwell before any of them were hit. Tenny had stumbled upon one of the many Guard stations hidden throughout the apartments of the Depths.

The four boys raced out of the building. Guards were coming from up and down the street. The alleyway from which they came was blocked. Kilks and Umo took off toward a narrow street near the building they just fled. Mack hesitated for a moment, then led Sander toward a cathedral. Bullets whizzed past their heads. They made it inside. A ceremony was underway. A young man and woman stood together at the front of the church while hundreds sat in the pews. The Scavs headed straight to the back, pursued by Guards. Sander kept pace with Mack, not wanting to let the boy out of his sight. The Guards tore through the cathedral, knocking over bystanders.

Mack and Sander made it to the catacombs beneath the church, which led to a series of tunnels. It was dark and cold, and they were lost, but they didn't stop moving. They could hear the Guards getting closer and closer. Eventually they made it to a stairwell, ran up, and broke through the door at the top. They were in the station and a trolley was departing. Mack and Sander pushed through the crowds and made it to the moving car. They grabbed on and climbed around to the outside, avoiding the Guard's gunfire. They'd lost their rifles along the way, but they both had two pistols each. Sander wondered if they could get much for the guns, knowing that whatever they traded for them, be it food or medicine or other weapons, wasn't worth the price that was paid: the life of Tenny. They hopped off the trolley and raced toward the footbridge, which was now unguarded. Mack pushed onward, harder and harder; Sander was in stride with him the entire time.

Once they hopped back over the Devil's Corner fence, Sander expected that they'd take a short break to catch their breath, but Mack continued onward. They roof-hopped all the way back to where the other Scavs met them earlier. Mack collapsed and fought back tears.

"I told him, I told him, I told him, I told him, I told him!" said Mack.

Sander sat down, giving Mack space. He'd seen more death in one day than he could handle. He couldn't stop seeing his mother's lifeless eyes. He began to cry uncontrollably. Mack stood and paced around. Once Sander stopped sobbing, Mack stood still.

"It's gonna' be okay," said Mack. "We'll wait for Umo and Kilks here. This is where they'll come."

"Do you think they'll—"

"They'll make it! They know how ta' get out! I showed 'em," said Mack.

Sander's hands were shaking. He couldn't stop them.

"I can't do this," said Sander.

"But ya' are," said Mack.

"It's not that easy," said Sander.

"It's gotta' be. No other way," said Mack. "We slow down for a second, we get caught or die."

"Well put," said a voice from inside the door. A tall woman stepped onto the roof, flanked by two armed men. Her pale skin was accented by the starless night coils of hair that draped her shoulders. Her green shirt, navy pants, and black boots were identical to the men who bookended her. Her face was youthful, beautiful, and devastating. She grinned, knowing that, in that moment, she had all the power in the world.

"It seems like you've been stealing from me. Or stealing from others without my permission. Either way, you've done something terribly wrong. I'll give you boys an option," she said. She waved her men forward with one finger. One of her men held a gun to Mack's head and the other held a gun to Sander's. "You can die right now or you can pay for your mistakes."

Part III of IV

Julan Ain stood over Sander and Mack. Her offer, work for her or die, was an easy decision for Sander. He hated agreeing with anything she said, especially since his mother taught him to avoid her at all costs, but now that his mother was dead, he had to figure things out on his own. Mack had saved his life, and he followed him and his band of Scavs into a situation he never expected to find himself: with a gun to his head, at the mercy of the most feared person in the Devil's Corner. He had never seen her up close before and had only caught a glimpse of her once, but her legendary brutal status did not match her appearance. She had a regal air about her and in different clothes, she could pass for a member of the ruling class. Not that Sander had ever seen anyone from the ruling class, but at least what he imagined one to look like. She had a beauty

to her that almost distracted him from the fact that he had the cold barrel of a gun pressed to his forehead. The man holding the gun to Sander's head kicked him in the chest. This wasn't a fight he could win.

"Hey!" said Mack, trying to defend Sander.

Mack shouldn't have opened his mouth. Both men pummeled him in a short outburst of fists and boot heels. Mack lay bleeding near Sander. The men took the guns from the boys.

"Get up," said Julan Ain.

Her voice was soft and inviting, both of which clashed with the intent behind her words. Sander stood first, not allowing the burning pain in his chest to affect him. Mack was slower to rise; he wiped the blood from his nose and lip, then spit off the side of the roof. Blood ran down his chin.

"How'd you know where we were?" said Mack.

"I do the talking," said Ain.

One of her men moved in quickly and kicked Mack in the lower leg. Mack could have avoided the hit, but he took it and tried not to flinch.

"You think you're smart. You're mistaken. You and every other Scav in this burn hole think you're a step ahead of me. You think you've been stealing from and selling to people with no connection to me. *Everyone* is connected to me," she said. "I have eyes everywhere. I have ears everywhere. I let you go for so long because I had good instincts about you. Both of you."

"Maybe they ain't so good," said Mack. "Got one of my Scavs killed today."

"You get used to it," said Ain. She turned her attention to Sander. "You owe me more than he does. He's stolen here and there, never much. He gets his takes elsewhere. You and your act of charity the other day cost me a lot. I bet you thought you got away with it. But I've got eyes everywhere. Didn't your mother teach you that? Or did she only show you how to lay down and die?"

Sander stepped forward, with a white-hot rage, but was knocked to his knees by a succession of blows from both of Ain's men. He didn't feel them. He was numb from the anger racing through his body.

"Looks like you both want to die," said Ain.

"We don't," said Mack.

"You speak for both of you?" said Ain.

"I don't want to die," said Sander, finding the confidence in his voice.

He contemplated grabbing one of the guns from Ain's men and changing the power dynamics of the situation, but he wasn't a killer and hadn't used a gun before. He would be killed and he preferred taking a chance by working with Ain than defying her.

"Since the two of you are so resourceful, I believe you can get me the one thing I don't have," said Ain. "An airship."

Mack laughed. He couldn't help it. Sander looked at him, hoping that he would stop. Ain stared at Mack with icy indifference.

"Yeah? That's it? I thought ya' was gonna' ask us for somethin' easy, like bringin' ya' Killian Grey," said Mack.

"Eventually," said Ain.

She cocked her head to the right, ever so slightly, indicating that she was absolutely serious.

"I can't fly," said Sander, surprised by the sound of his own voice.

"You'll learn," said Ain.

"There's a lot a things we could get for ya', even things ya' might not think ya' need, but ain't nobody got a way to get an airship 'less you're in the Guard or livin' in Grey Towers," said Mack.

"I need one. You want to live, you'll get me one," said Ain.

"I—"

"Why don't I make it easier for you? I want one of the raid airships the Guards love to use around here. There's a lot of those for you to take. I'm not asking for a transporter ship, now am I?" said Ain.

"You're serious," said Mack.

"As serious as a bullet through your head," said Ain.

Mack exhaled loudly and shook his head.

"What would we do with it if we got it?" said Sander.

"When you get it, you'll fly it to the rooftop of Mevin Ladies. You know those three tall buildings over off Sixth?" said Ain.

"On Mevin?" said Mack, lacing his rhetorical question with sarcasm.

"We know it," said Sander, deflecting everyone's attention to him, sparing Mack another beat down.

"Good. I've got men waiting there. You two have till morning to get my airship. And before the thought of trying to flee dances through your head, remember, I've got eyes everywhere," said Ain.

She and her men left. Sander looked at Mack; the life was drained from his face.

"We have to do something," said Sander.

"Steal an airship is all, right?" said Mack. "I say we run."

"To where? There's nowhere in Devil's Corner Ain doesn't control, and we won't last more than a few days outside these fences. See what happened to Tenny? We couldn't ever stop moving, and I know this city is big, but it's not big enough for us to hide forever," said Sander.

"Then we figure out a way ta' get outside tha' wall. I heard there's places in tha' Underground that lead to tha' world outside," said Mack.

"You know what's out there?" said Sander.

"They got fields. That's where they grow food," said Mack.

"All protected by the Guard. Has to be," said Sander. "And after that, nothing. There can't be anything. If there was something, we would know. Everybody would try to get out."

"It was an idea," said Mack.

"The only way we stay alive is by taking an airship," said Sander.

"There's no way we live if we try that," said Mack.

"There's no way we live if we don't," said Sander.

"That's one way of puttin' it," said Mack. "Ya' got a plan?"

"I—sort of. It's not much of one, but I know where most of the raid airships are," said Sander. "There's always three or four outside the main fence. That's where the Guards land before they come inside. They get transported in the big ships, then come through the main gate. I've never seen Guards dropped in any other way."

"Everywhere else in tha' city they do. They land tha' big ships or drop outta' them on ropes. Not here," said Mack.

"It might have to do with Julan Ain," said Sander. "She'd probably shoot down any big airships."

"She would," said Mack.

"That's why they use the raid airships. They're small, fast, tough to shoot down. At least that's my guess. The Devil's Corner isn't so big that they need to drop in on those transporter ships. But if they need to get somewhere quick, they got the raid ships. There might be another place in Devil's Corner they keep them, but I've never seen them. You?" said Sander.

"Nah," said Mack.

"If Ain wants a raid ship, we have to somehow get outside the main fence, which is the most guarded area in Devil's Corner, steal a ship right from under the Guards, and learn how to fly," said Sander.

"Well ya' should'a said so before. That's easy," said Mack, making himself laugh. Blood ran down his nose and he caught it with his tongue.

"You know how to get over the fence," said Sander.

"But never at tha' main fence. We avoid that," said Mack.

"Is there a way? Some roof near there?" said Sander.

"Sure. Yeah," said Mack. "And maybe gettin' over ain't tha' hardest thing to do, let's just say. The problem is we'd be droppin' in on a nest of Guards."

"So we distract them," said Sander.

"With what? Ya' got a song and dance?" said Mack.

"No. Something better," said Sander.

He spoke with enough confidence that Mack had to concede leadership to him. If they were going to steal an airship, Sander would figure out a way to make it happen. He led them across five roofs, then down through a building and out to street level. They were both exhausted, but they couldn't think about how tired they were, because they wanted to live and that was enough to propel them forward. A couple of Guards were blocking the entrance to Sander's building. Instead of getting into a confrontation, which only would have slowed them down, Sander led them to a side alleyway. They climbed up to the third floor and in through an open window. A couple lay sleeping in the corner. They barely stirred as Sander and Mack walked through their apartment. Sander broke into the apartment directly above his and dropped through a gaping hole to his apartment below.

"Probably not a great idea, us bein' here," said Mack.

Sander ignored the remarks and reached his hand into a hole in the wall. He didn't think he'd find what Fora had hidden in there, but it was worth the risk of returning to his building. His hand felt around until his fingers touched the jar. He unveiled it to Mack. Mack didn't know what to make of the brownish orange liquid.

"That's piss?" said Mack.

"Mmm-hmm. I thought you'd want to see where I kept my pee," said Sander.

"What the hick kind of joke is—"

"It's Measirk," said Sander.

Mack took the jar and turned it gently in his hands. He was in awe.

"This enough to take down a building!" said Mack.

"Or a fence," said Sander.

"Yeah, but—"

"We'll figure it out. Can you get me to the closest roof?" said Sander.

"Yeah. I know exactly tha' one," said Mack.

"Good. I have something to take care of first," said Sander. "Come with me."

Mack followed Sander into the hallway. The Guards' bodies were gone; Ain's men remained. Sander picked up his mother's body and marched toward the stairs. His legs were tired, but he ignored the pain and discomfort. They reached the rooftop and two men were passed out near the ledge, two bottles of grain near their feet. Without Sander having to say a word, Mack knew to get rid of the men. He woke them and the men were so startled that they didn't protest. Sander laid Fora on her back and shut her eyelids. Sander leaned over her body.

"Go back to our people. When you get there, you can show me the way. That's where we'll meet again," said Sander.

He dropped one small dab of Measirk on her dress, lit a match, and flung it at Fora. Flames engulfed her instantly. Fora transformed into black smoke and rose into the sky high above the city's wall.

———

They waited till nightfall to make their move.

The building nearest to the main fence was only used by Guards. Two of them were on the roof with rifles, ready to shoot anyone that looked suspicious. Sander and Mack were crouched low on the building behind it, hidden from the Sniper Guards. Half of the building was missing, victim of a firebombing. Sander used Mack's curved knife to bore a hole in the top of the jar. He slipped the short fuse into the Measirk.

"We too far," said Mack. "We ain't gettin' to that fence."

"We don't need to blow up the fence. All we need is a distraction to get *over* the fence," said Sander.

"You said we was gonna' take out tha' fence," said Mack.

"And I told you to get us closer to the main fence. You brought us here, when you should have taken us there," said Sander, pointing to a building on the other side of the street.

"I thought that was the Guards' building," said Mack.

"It is. So is that. And the one behind us," said Sander. "They don't need Guards patrolling all the rooftops."

"So what're we gonna' do? That jar makes me nervous," said Mack.

"Measirk is only dangerous when it gets near fire," said Sander, digging a match out of his pocket. "This is what should make you nervous."

"My gods, this ain't gonna' work," said Mack.

"How fast can we make it to that other building?" said Sander, indicating the other Guards' stronghold on the other side of the street.

Mack peered over the roof, looking at different options for routes. He thought carefully before responding.

"A minute. Less if we real quick. More if a roof's out," said Mack.

"This can buy us a couple of minutes," said Sander, tapping on the jar.

Sander adjusted how he was sitting to look through the fence. Dozens of Guards were on the opposite side of the fence. Four raid airships were parked just beyond them.

"We'll only have about two to three minutes before they figure out what's going on. That's a minute to make it to the other building, a minute to climb down the fence, and a minute to get the airship," said Sander.

"I don't know, man. That's not good," said Mack.

"It's either this or nothing else," said Sander.

"Maybe we take that and blow up Ain," said Mack.

"We'd never get close enough. Besides, there's too many people loyal to her. We'd get killed one way or another," said Sander. "You want to live. I want to live. We don't have time to figure out anything else."

"Alright. I'm trustin' ya on this," said Mack.

"As soon as I light this, take off running. Don't look back. I'll be one building behind you," said Sander. "Ready?"

Mack thought about the simple question, then nodded. Sander swiped the match against the side of the wall. The small flame swayed as Sander held it to the fuse. The fuse sparked and Mack took off running. The Guards on the nearby rooftop fired at him, but Mack was too elusive. Sander watched as the flame ate away at the fuse and just as it slipped inside the lid, he stood and threw it toward the Guards. They dove for cover as Sander sprinted toward the next building, following Mack's lead. The explosion sucked all of the surrounding sound and air in a ten-block radius and sent them to the heavens. Sander was thrown from his feet and felt the heat from the blast surround his body. He got up and continued after Mack. The building and nearby fence crumbled as ash and smoke blanketed the entire block. Sander squinted to see ahead of him, to try to make out Mack's figure. At last he made it to the building where they should have been, and Sander leapt over the fence. He caught the top and swung his legs over. The metal fence cut into the barely-healing wounds of his hands. Mack followed him, but slipped, catching himself halfway down the interior side. Sander yelled for Mack to hurry. His voice was lost in the rumble and chaos. Guards were pouring into the Devil's Corner, determined to punish anyone and everyone. Sander descended the fence as soon as Mack reached the top. Just then, the fence started to give. The explosion rocked it to its foundation. It tilted backwards. If they didn't reach the ground fast enough, the fence would fall on top of them. Sander was moving so quickly that he felt like he wasn't moving at all. He kept looking down, making sure no Guards were waiting for them. They hit the street and ran toward the first airship. The fence collapsed on top of it, crushing it completely. Sander pointed toward the farthest one and they raced toward it. The heat and ash continued to fill the air, stifling their breathing.

They climbed inside the airship and closed the hatch. There were eight cubbies for Guards, explosives, weapons, and rappelling ropes. There didn't appear to be any navigation equipment or seat for a pilot.

Mack spotted the ladder first and pointed to it. Sander climbed up to the flight deck. Two pilot seats awaited them. There were gears and levers and switches all around them. They could see the chaos they created through the window.

"We have to fly. We have to fly," said Sander.

"We told her we couldn't," said Mack.

"We can't sit here forever," said Sander.

"We can't sit here for a *minute*," said Mack. "I'm still puttin' my trust in ya'. Fly this thing!"

Sander looked at all of the switches in front of him, then to the lever next to his chair, then to the wheel in between both seats.

"You know how to read?" said Sander.

"Do I sound like a guy that spends time readin' books?" said Mack.

"I think I know what some of these words are," said Sander.

He squinted his eyes, tricking himself into believing that this way he could better understand words he couldn't read. The word began with an "I" and the letters were in red. Sander flipped the switch. The airship came to life. It lurched forward slightly. He flipped the other two red-lettered switches and they started to lift off the ground. Sander pulled back on the lever next to his chair. The nose of the airship pointed upward as they throttled toward the last building they stood upon.

"The wheel!" said Sander.

Mack cranked the wheel to the right and they flew in circles. Mack fell out of his chair. Sander steadied the wheel as Mack got back to his seat.

"We need to get higher," said Mack.

"Try your lever," said Sander.

Mack cranked his lever forward. They dipped thirty feet.

"Pull up!" said Sander.

Mack didn't need Sander's instructions to know what to do; he pulled the lever back to position and the airship steadied. People on the street below were diving out of the way. Sander pumped his lever back and forth and they climbed steadily. Once they were safely above the rooftops, they determined the proper course: forty-five degrees to the northeast. The navigation dials spun and the needles read coordinates they didn't understand. It didn't matter. They knew how to reach the Mevin Ladies easily. They were three tall, thin buildings, some of the tallest in the Devil's Corner, and their graying white exterior clashed with the dark tones of the other nearby structures. Once the Mevin Ladies became visible, Mack sat forward in his seat.

"Ya' know this is crazy," said Mack.

"What?" said Sander, trying to focus on flying the airship.

"This, ain't it? Your whole plan. That ya' thought of it and we did it and we about to have our lives for another day," said Mack.

"I wasn't ready to die," said Sander.

"I guess a guy that keeps a jar of Measirk in his wall can make a decision like that," said Mack.

Sander smiled.

"I got this thing off the ground, but that doesn't mean I can land it," said Sander.

"What's that supposed to mean?" said Mack.

"I could crash this thing and kill us both," said Sander.

"No. It'd be me," said Mack, smacking his palm against the top of his lever.

They were close enough to the Mevin Ladies to see that Ain's men had set up camp on the nearest tower. Sander started to worry about landing, not believing the roof offered enough space to set the airship down; at least, not enough room for him. Even if they got it close, Ain and her men could see that they got the ship. If they had to touch down on street level, she could get someone else to take it up to the roof. They hovered above the roof.

"Drop it slowly," said Sander.

Mack eased the lever and they lowered. Ain and her men made a circle for the airship. Sander held the wheel, steadying the ship. He wondered what would happen next: would Ain let them live, or would she kill them as soon as they stepped out of the ship? And if she let them live, what would she expect them to do next? Getting an airship was close to impossible. How could they outdo themselves?

"More?" said Mack.

"No. Slow," said Sander.

Something thumped against the airship. Then another. And another. The right side of the window shattered in a spider web.

"Someone's—"

A platoon of Guards stormed the next tower of Mevin Ladies. Ain and her men went into combat mode, but it was too late.

"Pull up!" said Mack.

Sander pumped the lever. Dozens of Lantern City Guards poured onto the roof with Ain and her men; the swarm of Guards was too much for Ain. She never had a chance.

The Guards continued to fire at the stolen airship. Sander pumped his lever and Mack cut the wheel to the left. They flew out of the Guards' range. They had nowhere to go but up.

Sander pumped and pumped the lever till the airship was halfway up the ominous wall that surrounded the city. Wind ripped through the broken window. Mack held on to the wheel with all his desperate energy.

"Stop! Stop! Stop!" said Mack.

The airship pointed upward until Mack moved his lever. They leveled the ship and looked at the Devil's Corner below them. It was nothing more than specks of buildings divided by pencil-thin streets. Both boys eased back in their chairs; in that moment, they wanted nothing more than to hover above their neighborhood.

"How long ya' think we can fly for?" said Mack.

"Not as long as we need," said Sander. "We can't go back."

"Maybe we can go over the wall," said Mack.

"I'd like to, but I don't think this ship can make it. It's not built for that," said Sander.

"How about Grey Towers?" said Mack, grinning.

"If we land there I'm sure they'd make us the personal pilots to Killian Grey," said Sander.

"He might like us. By all them posters they got hangin' everywhere, I'd say he ain't much older than us," said Mack.

"He's probably a hundred. They want us thinkin' our ruler's young. That way we don't think of overthrowing him," said Sander.

"Wouldn't it be somethin' ta' just fly up to Grey Towers and land there? Just ta' see how'd they'd react," said Mack.

"I can tell you what they'd do," said Sander. "They'd throw us back to the Depths. That fall's a couple hundred feet."

"It's a thought," said Mack. "I don't know ya' long, but I gotta' say ya' look a little different than most of tha' guys I see."

"Same with you," said Sander.

"I'm serious. Maybe it's tha' long hair or I don't know," said Mack.

"My mom always told me we got Fortache blood in us," said Sander.

"Ha! You're tha' last of a breed," said Mack. "Me, I had a dad somewhere that filled my mom up with me and I've been in Devil's Corner since I can remember. There ain't no history ta' that. This is tha' closest I've ever been ta' somethin'."

"I'm glad to share it with you," said Sander. "Now where can we land this thing? You know places outside the Devil's Corner."

"Alright, alright, I'll think. Not Riccas. That's too

fancy. How about Culstat? Ya' been there? Of course ya' ain't! But I'm tellin' ya', it's the place. Terrible for a Scav, but great for an airship. It's mostly factories there. A couple of buildings that used to be schools, but mostly factories. It's easy for ya' ta' see the smoke towers from Devil's Corner. They got a lot of Guards there, but they wouldn't think nothin' of an airship landin'," said Mack. "Probably we can hide in a factory till we figure tha' rest out."

"How do we get there?" said Sander.

"We gotta' drop closer ta' tha' roofs. It's tha' only way I know," said Mack.

The airship slowly dipped closer to the tall buildings below. They passed underneath a transporter airship and were dwarfed by its size. Sander could see the factories a quarter of a mile away. He was confident that they could land on the side of a factory without being noticed. They could slip into the darkness and make plans from there. Figuring out where to go and how to live outside of the Devil's Corner wouldn't be easy, but they could do it. If things turned bad quickly —or worse than they already were—they could always disappear into the Underground. It was a cutthroat world in the city-beneath-the-city, but they were, as Ain put it, "resourceful", and they'd learn to survive. Sander and Mack had just met and proved they were a formidable team. People that went into hiding in the Underground never returned to the Depths, but that didn't mean they weren't alive.

"You feel that?" said Sander.

The airship dropped.

"That wasn't happenin' before," said Mack.

The airship dropped again.

"We're not going to make it to Culstat!" said Sander.

"Pump the lever!" said Mack.

"I am!" said Sander.

Nothing the young pilots did made a difference. They were spinning out of control and falling from the sky at a terrifying rate. Sander leaned forward and flicked the switches up and down. This helped for a moment, as the airship thrust upward. Mack grabbed the wheel to stop them from spiraling out of control. They were aimed directly at an apartment building. Sander pumped the lever as Mack turned the wheel to the right. They brushed the side of the building and plummeted to the street below. People scattered out of the way. Both boys flew out of their seats, collided with the ceiling, and collapsed back to the floor. Sander was in more pain than he had ever felt before. He forced himself to stand. He stumbled toward Mack and helped him to his feet.

"We can't stop," said Sander.

"Wha—" said Mack.

Sander pulled his partner through the broken window. Mack was bloodied and bruised and limped so badly he could barely walk. Factory workers milled about on the street, either coming or going from their shifts. It wasn't every day that an airship crashed on their block, but they knew better than to stand around and make a scene. Sander didn't know what to make of all the staring people. An elderly woman approached them.

"They'll come from that way," she said, pointing to the east.

"Thanks," said Sander, knowing that she meant the Guards.

His legs remembered how to run. Each step felt like it could be the last. He fought through it, pulling Mack behind him. Shouts. Gunfire. Boots running. Sander glanced backwards. Five Guards were after them. He had to find a place to hide. In the upheaval of the moment, every building looked the same, and all of them were deathtraps. Sander hated the Devil's Corner, and yet in the moment, he missed it. If he was being pursued around familiar streets, he'd know where to go.

Mack yanked his arm free and stopped moving. Sander nearly fell trying to stop.

"I can't. Go," said Mack.

"You have to keep moving," said Sander. "There's no reason to—"

"No," said Mack.

Sander grabbed Mack's arm.

"Go," whispered Mack.

Mack shoved Sander. He'd gone as far as he could. Maybe Mack was nothing more than a Scav; the only way he understood life was by taking from others. That was the way of life in the Devil's Corner, but in all the other neighborhoods, people didn't stand for it. He was tough, but he couldn't survive outside his neighborhood. After they'd been caught by Ain, Mack hadn't expected to live for long. Maybe the Guards would spare him and send him to the Spiral. Maybe they'd show a sliver of mercy. Sander wasn't ready to quit. He didn't know what was up around the next street corner, let alone what life held for him in the next five minutes, but he wasn't ready to stop moving. He wanted to heed his mother's final words. Sander ran ahead, turning back to see the Guards surrounding Mack. Mack looked at Sander and nodded his head. At first he couldn't understand why Mack gave up, but then he realized Mack wasn't quitting; he was buying him time to live.

Sander looked above the buildings to the smoke

stacks. If only he could make it to a factory, he'd find a place to hide. He felt like the workers on the street were encouraging him to push harder, run faster, ignore the burning in his lungs, and do something all of them wished they'd done: foil the Guards. By the time he reached Culstat, no Guards were following him. The monolithic factories loomed overhead. Guards were everywhere, but so were workers. Sander did his best to blend in. He found a narrow passageway between two factories and slipped down it, hoping to find an entrance. There were no doors. There were, however, second-floor windows open. He jumped up and pulled himself in through the window. He was behind a series of furnaces and he crawled underneath the nearest one. There were divots in the floor, lined with grating. He watched booted feet walking to-and-fro, always in constant motion. Nobody knew he was there. Sander tried to sleep; he kept seeing Mack surrounded the Guards and wondered if he should have done more to save his friend, but sleep came eventually and held him for hours.

His clothes were soaked from sweat. His mouth was dry. Sander's head was swirling. He had no sense of time, no idea how long he had slept. Booted feet continued dancing about on the other side of the furnaces. He pulled himself back to the landing where he had dropped in the night before. Two workers were standing thirty feet away. Sander scrambled up to the window and dropped back to the street. He landed awkwardly on his ankle and limped along as he walked. The air was cold and his clothes clung to him. He needed water and new clothes. He needed food. He didn't know where to get anything. His natural instinct was to steal them, but from where? Standing around and contemplating would make matters worse. He had to move. He couldn't stop moving. When he reached the main street, he tried to mask his limp, but couldn't. He scoped out where all the Guards were positioned. They were on every corner, waiting for someone to make the wrong decision. Sander looked different than most everyone else. His tattered clothes were not like the brown and beige uniforms most of the workers wore. How long would it be till a Guard noticed? He stuck to the middle of the street, moving constantly with the largest swaths of workers.

Then, his eyes caught something. A few boys his age, following behind a red-headed gentleman. They couldn't be factory workers. They moved with a different purpose. Sander, gritting his teeth through

the pain in his right ankle, caught up with them and trailed closely behind them. They detoured down a narrow street, passing Guards like they had nothing to fear. Sander was now in stride with them, hoping they wouldn't notice or say anything. They went down another street and another, finally reaching a run-down neighborhood. It wasn't as bad as the Devil's Corner, but it wasn't much better. The buildings were falling apart, trash was everywhere, and broken pipes jutted out in every direction. Guards were stationed randomly about. The red-headed man, youthful and handsome and decked out in clean clothes and shined boots, held the door for the boys. They filed into the building one-by-one. Two Guards approached just as Sander was about to pass through. The man held up his hand to stop Sander.

"Sorry kid, but—"

One of the Guards grabbed Sander and held his hands behind his back. Sander thought it was over; he looked at the red-headed man, pleading for him to help. The red-headed man looked away from Sander. The second Guard stood right over the red-headed man.

"This kid's the kid we're looking for. You know him?" said the Guard.

"Why are you looking for him?" said the man.

"Stole an airship from Devil's Corner and crashed it in Shands," said the Guard.

"Hmm," said the man.

"Who are you to say 'hmm'? Huh?" said the Guard.

"I'm Kendal Kornick."

"You the one that's been holding those meetings? Or are you the one that's been schooling people?" said the Guard.

"You're confusing me for someone else," said Kendal.

"If I find out different, I know where to find you," said the Guard.

He stepped away from Kendal and signaled to the other Guard to drag Sander away from the scene. Kendal stepped out of the doorway.

"Excuse me," said Kendal.

The Guards turned to him.

"We ain't having a talk here," said the Guard.

"Fine enough by me, but he's not the boy you're looking for," said Kendal.

"Look at his clothes. And his hair. The Guards on the scene said about his hair," said the Guard. "Even if it weren't for those things, he's got all kinds of cuts and he's limping around. I'd say he's our guy."

"There's more than one way to get cuts," said Kendal. "Things get a little rough around here. Boys fight from time-to-time."

"Looks a little worse than a fight to me," said the Guard.

"Maybe you haven't seen too many boys from around here. These cuts aren't much at all. I'm sure the other boys he fought look much worse. Don't they?" said Kendal.

"Yeah. A lot worse," said Sander.

"I think—"

"When did this airship incident occur?" said Kendal.

"Last night," said the Guard.

"Then he can't be the kid you're looking for. He was with me last night. Attending a service at Utheneece Cathedral. You know it?" said Kendal.

"Yeah. Don't mean it's not him," said the Guard.

"No, I suppose it doesn't, unless my friend here is somehow two people at the same time. He was paying his respects to Wareis and Uryston, which I witnessed, and also taking your ship from Devil's Corner and crashing it. That seems…improbable," said Kendal. "Tell me where you two typically patrol."

"We're both mostly in the fields," said the Guard.

"So if that's true, you wouldn't know what boys around here look like, would you? I can't say much for the kids in Devil's Corner, but my friend here looks exactly like the other boys I work with," said Kendal.

"Work?" said the Guard.

"Teaching them the lessons of our gods. The truth is through Wareis and Uryston, is it not?" said Kendal. He stepped inside the door and called for the boys. The filed out onto the street, one-by-one. They carried themselves with dignity. And luckily for Sander, he didn't look too different than them. "Gentlemen, wasn't our friend with us last night at Utheneece Cathedral?" The boys nodded. "Now if we're lying, all of us are guilty of insulting a Guard, which is worth, I believe, a visit

to the Spiral. None of us want that. We love our great young ruler Killian Grey and we respect the Guard."

The Guard released Sander. He joined the other boys.

"We'll be seeing you again," said the Guard.

The Guards walked away. Kendal sent all the boys but Sander inside.

"What's your name?" said Kendal.

"Sander."

"How old are you?" said Kendal.

"Fifteen," said Sander.

"My sister's fifteen. I know all about fifteen," said Kendal. "You did what they said?"

Sander nodded, feeling no need to hide the truth.

"You had your reasons?" said Kendal.

"To survive," said Sander.

"You have somewhere to go?" said Kendal.

Sander shook his head.

"If you want to learn there's more to life than just surviving, I can help you out. How does that sound to you?" said Kendal.

"I have no other choice," said Sander. "Why didn't you let them take me?"

"I could tell you weren't ready for taking," said Kendal.

"I didn't think people could talk to Guards like that," said Sander.

"You can if you know what they like to hear," said Kendal. "Come on inside. We're preparing ourselves."

Sander hobbled inside the building.

"Preparing for what?" said Sander.

"A revolution. And whether you know it or not, you're already a part of it."

TREVOR CRAFTS is the creator of *Lantern City*, and is no stranger to building worlds. Winner of the LATV Festival and numerous industry awards, including an Emmy˚, Trevor has spent his career creating dynamic stories with striking visuals featuring strong characters. Now CEO of Macrocosm Entertainment, he has acted as producer, writer, and director for projects *Like Experimenter* (2015), *Manson Family Vacation* (2015), *Enemy of Man* (2015), *Deep in the Heart* (2013), and *Smokewood, Nevada* (2013). You can get updates from Trevor and follow Macrocosm at www.macrocosm.tv and through Twitter @trevorcrafts.

BRUCE BOXLEITNER was cast as the lead role in Disney's cult film *TRON*, which garnered him science fiction fans worldwide. In 1994, Boxleitner joined the cast of the popular TV series *Babylon 5* as John Sheridan. Boxleitner again starred with Jeff Bridges in *TRON: Legacy*, and Boxleitner reprised his role in *TRON: Uprising* on Disney's XD TV network. The veteran actor has appeared in numerous recurring roles on TV series, including *Cedar Cove*, *GCB*, and *Heroes*, and has guest-starred on *NCIS* and *Chuck*. In 1999, Boxleitner authored *Frontier Earth* and in 2001, its sequel *Frontier Earth: Searcher*, published by The Berkley Publishing Group. Follow Bruce on Twitter @boxleitnerbruce.

MATTHEW DALEY is a screenwriter who, when asked by his grandparents at age ten what he wanted to be when he grew up, answered confidently, "a writer, historian, or comedian." He wasn't too far off, finding himself in adulthood writing for film and television (winning an Emmy˚ along the way). He has always been attracted to genres, especially horror and sci-fi, and recently wrote the horror movie *Flay* (2015). He wrote the *Lantern City* prequel novel *Rise* and is currently at work on the *Lantern City* comic book series. Follow Matt on Twitter @matthewjdaley.

MAIRGHREAD SCOTT is a comic book and animation writer. She has written for such books as *Marvel Universe: Guardians of the Galaxy*, *Swords Of Sorrow: Chaos*, *Transformers: Windblade*, and her first original series, *Toil And Trouble*. Her television work includes writing for the Emmy Award-winning *Transformers Prime* as well as *Rescue Bots*, *Ultimate Spider-Man: Web-Warriors*, *Transformers: Robots in Disguise*, and the upcoming *Marvel's Guardians of the Galaxy*. She lives in Los Angeles with her husband and their comic book collection. You can follow her work at www.mscottwriter.com

CARLOS MAGNO is the oldest son of Zenite and Paulo Sergio, and he has two young sisters, Thaís and Fernanda. He has a degree in Fine Arts from Escola de Música e Belas Artes do Paraná, Brazil. His comic works include *Zombie Tales* (BOOM! Studios), *Captain Universe* (Marvel Comics), *The Phantom* (Moonstone Books), *Countdown, Green Lantern Corps, Cyborg* (DC Comics), as well as a two-year run on *Transformers* (IDW Publishing). His favorite works include *Planet of the Apes* with Daryl Gregory, *Deathmatch* with Paul Jenkins, *Robocop* with Josh Williamson, and currently, working on *Lantern City*. Carlos lives in Sao Jose dos Pinhais with his wife Ingret and his two children. See more of Carlos's work at his website, http://www.carlos-magno-comics.com/sobre-nos/

CHRIS BLYTHE has been a stalwart presence in the comics scene for nearly twenty years. During that time, he has been a permanent and influential contributor to 2000 AD in the UK, along with working with DC, Marvel, Dark Horse, Nintendo, and Hasbro on hundreds of titles including *Star Wars, Aliens, Action Man, Transformers,* and *Need for Speed*. His critically acclaimed self-published graphic novel, *Angel Fire*, was translated for the mainstream by Casterman and Carlton Books as well as being optioned to become a movie. You can see more of Chris's work by visiting http://ceebee73.deviantart.com/

DERON BENNETT is an Eisner and Harvey Award-nominated letterer, and has been providing lettering services for various comic book companies for over a decade. His body of work includes the critically acclaimed *Jim Henson's Tale of Sand, Jim Henson's The Dark Crystal, Mr. Murder is Dead, The Muppet Show Comic Book, Darkwing Duck,* and *Richie Rich*. He has also ventured into writing with his creator-owned book, *Quixote*. You can learn more about Deron by visiting his website www.andworlddesign.com or following @deronbennett on Twitter.